The Secrets of Montrésor

Book II in the French Orphan Series

by Michael Stolle

Dedication

For Susie (she knows why)

For Christine

CONTENTS

THE STORY SO FAR...

Brought up in a monastery school in Reims, Pierre believes he is a penniless orphan until his best friend, Armand de Saint Paul, decides to root out the truth. When Pierre discovers that he is in fact the heir not only to the aristocratic de Beauvoir family on his father's side, but is in fact also heir to the Duchy of Hertford on his mother's side, his world is turned upside-down.

But life is never that simple. Pierre's cousin, Henri de Beauvoir, so like Pierre in looks, but with a heart of pure evil, wants to be Marquis de Beauvoir more than anything and will stop at nothing to achieve this. Aided by the machinations of the powerful Cardinal Richelieu, who also fancies the de Beauvoir heritage to swell the coffers of the Church, Henri tracks Pierre across England and France in his efforts to remove him and claim the heritage for himself. When we last see Henri he is standing over the corpse of his rich lover, whom he has murdered for his fortune. Unbeknown to him, his actions have been observed...

Pierre manages to escape the best (or should that be worst?) attempts by Henri and Richelieu to make him disappear, and with the help of his English cousin Charles, his friend Armand, and the lovely Marie (a cousin of Armand's, with whom he has fallen desperately in love) he has been accepted by the royal courts in both France and England. His acceptance at court comes with a price-tag though – he and Armand promise to retrieve some long-lost treasures for the secretive Knights Templar in return for the support the society offers them. This quest will take them beyond France.

Discover Pierre's next steps...

The impressive library was hot, very hot.

The elegant visitor sitting on the carved but rather uncomfortable chair reflected that it was certainly no coincidence that the preferred room of a high prince of the French church should be as hot as any given place in hell. His host, the powerful Cardinal, Duc de Richelieu, looked frail and shrunken in his scarlet robes. A golden cross dangled heavily from his neck – in truth, it seemed far too heavy to be carried by this fragile body. But the facade of frailty was not only misleading, it might as well be just another of his carefully staged appearances, as the Cardinal's shrewd eyes were as alert as ever when he glanced at the immaculately dressed Marquis de Saint Paul sitting elegantly before him, seemingly unaware of the intense heat emanating from the huge fireplace.

Richelieu wondered why his visitor had insisted on calling upon him for a private audience, as normally a polite but none the less intense – and at times merciless – war was raging between the noble clan of the Saint Paul family and the offices of the prime minister of France.

Richelieu had important issues on his mind; soon he would have to find a way to remove the King's young favourite, Cinq Mars, from the royal court and – much more difficult – from the King's heart. Therefore he was not too keen to start fighting on a second front, but why else should the Marquis have come to see him?

"I'm delighted to see your Eminence in good health," the Marquis lied shamelessly.

Richelieu's eyes blinked in amusement; he had, of course, detected the irony of the Marquis's statement.

"The same applies for me, my most noble Marquis," Richelieu answered politely. He opened a precious silver box decorated with enamelled ornaments in the Oriental style that contained candied cherries and offered them to his visitor.

The Marquis looked warily at the dark red cherries that glistened temptingly in the light of the candles; politely yet firmly, he refused the offer.

The Cardinal chuckled. "You've always been a very cautious man," he said, and dipped his claw-like fingers into the box. With great gusto he chose the biggest specimen. "You really should have tried one! I get them directly from Italy. Even dear Mazarin is crazy about them but he has not yet been able to find out where I buy them from."

2

The Marquis only smiled and shook his head politely; he vividly remembered several cases of fatal food poisoning that had swept away unsuspecting enemies of the Cardinal soon after they had been entertained by him.

Cardinal Richelieu had closed his eyes as if to concentrate on the intense taste of the delicate cherry but only seconds later his piercing glance was directed at his visitor and he continued the discussion. "Is there anything that I could do for you? Has your youngest son Armand decided to repent and return to the fold of our Holy Mother the Church? Would you like me to find a suitable position for him?"

The Marquis looked amused. "Even if Armand does carry the same Christian name as your Eminence, I'm afraid his services would be no asset at all to the Church – unlike yours. I think my son is a soldier at heart."

The Marquis paused, and looking straight into Richelieu's eyes he decided that it was time to come to the point of his visit. "I wonder if your Eminence could do with some help in your present worries?" he advanced cautiously.

Richelieu was taken by surprise; what did his visitor have in mind – had any of his usually well-guarded secrets leaked out? The Marquis could be a force to be reckoned with. His outward appearance remaining unruffled, however, the Cardinal answered, "Are you preparing your way to heaven, my dear Marquis – you seem to have become charitable?" he asked politely, with just a slight raising of his eyebrows indicating how improbable he judged this option to be.

"I'm afraid that I might feel rather lonely up there, I'd miss the company of *Your Eminence* especially – and I hope it's a bit too early to go there," the Marquis retorted, but then he continued with a forgiving smile. "No, I have to confess that my motives are linked to more profane matters actually. I'd like to offer Your Eminence a donation – something more valuable than money – in the name of Pierre de Beauvoir."

The Marquis paused, but it was impossible to read the mind of the Cardinal. Richelieu's face had become a polite but utterly non-committal mask.

The Marquis continued. "I think that there have been some unlucky… let's call them… misunderstandings in the past that finally should be clarified and resolved. I know that you have important issues on your mind at present and think we should concentrate on those, rather than continuing some old and rather obsolete battles. If I can count on Your Eminence to recognize the present Marquis de Beauvoir – as his Majesty has graciously done already – I shall be able to contribute and I might be willing to help your Eminence with some fairly interesting documents."

While he continued speaking the Marquis took out some letters from his waistcoat and handed them over to the Cardinal. "These letters are just copies, but if your Eminence agrees to an arrangement, the originals will become yours," he stated matter-of-factly.

Richelieu quickly scanned the content of the first letter and although he was a master of disguise he couldn't hide his satisfaction. The letters contained an explicit invitation from Cinq Mars to his friends to join the fight against Cardinal Richelieu – and to support rebellion in the name of King Philippe IV of Spain.

Richelieu was not shocked by the content – what else could have been expected from such a political dabbler – yet he was amazed how stupid some people could be. These letters were nothing but a shortcut to the executioner's block. Quickly he scanned two more letters – one seemed to be more brainless and compromising than the other. A quick smile flashed across the Cardinal's face: these documents would allow him to rip out the entire weed (as he viewed it) that had taken root at the King's court during his last prolonged illnesses – up to him to determine the best time to play his hand. These letters were worth a fortune, a noble gift indeed.

"My most noble Marquis, you always seem to possess the ability to amaze me," the Cardinal said with one of his rare smiles. "I think we have an agreement. I'll be very happy to receive the Marquis de Beauvoir with you during an official audience and recognize him, once the originals of these letters have found their way – let's say, miraculously – to my desk."

The smile flashed across his thin lips once more. "By the way, I shall immediately order a stop to the legal procedure in the church courts that you have been assiduously delaying," and making a sign to the Marquis to stay silent as he tried to insert a protest, added, "of course, it was nothing but an unlucky undertaking by some extremely zealous but basically incompetent minions."

The Marquis returned the smile. Richelieu was eating out of his hand – as he had predicted when he had discussed the idea of this meeting beforehand with his wife. There was one last issue that needed to be settled though and he cleared his throat. "What about Pierre de Beauvoir's possessions, will those be restored to him?"

"My dear Marquis, you and I know from sad experience that honesty and diplomacy do not always go well together, but I must confess, this time I have truly no clue what you're talking about! If anything should be missing, I'm afraid it's his cousin Henri de Beauvoir who should be viewed as the culprit – my reputation might be tarnished in some circles, but I can assure you, my most noble Marquis, I am not a thief."

4

The Cardinal raised his bony hand with the golden ring of his office, stifling any protestations by the Marquis that he had been misunderstood. Yet the Marquis de Saint Paul realized that he had been dismissed and felt that the Cardinal's surprise regarding his last remark had been genuine enough. So, they'd need to search for Pierre's diamond ring elsewhere; Richelieu – for once – didn't seem to be involved. As the ring was one of the keys to finding the hidden treasure, this was not good news.

The Marquis went back to his waiting coach, deep in thought. The only remaining place his possessions could be was with the family bankers, as he knew from Pierre's servants that Henri de Beauvoir had not been able to lay his hands on them. They couldn't wait any longer; they'd need to meet Pierre's bankers as soon as possible to clarify the situation regarding the de Beauvoir treasure. Pierre de Beauvoir had been installed as the new Duke of Hertford and today the last remaining obstacle to Pierre's French heritage had been removed, with the mighty Cardinal Richelieu accepting a truce.

But now Pierre de Beauvoir and his son Armand would need to fulfil their part of the bargain and reunite the three ancient rings that were the key to the ancient treasure they owed to the Brotherhood – and to do so they first must find and get hold of the diamond ring. If the ring had truly been stolen – and the Cardinal Richelieu for once hadn't been involved – all traces pointed to Cardinal Mazarin, an enemy as formidable as Richelieu.

From the frying pan into the fire… The Marquis sighed.

*****

The Marquis inhaled deeply. The smoke-filled winter air had been replaced by a delicious soft wind blowing from the south carrying the scents and promises of sun and flowers. Soon spring would turn into summer. The trees of the royal Louvre gardens were in full bloom and created a fitting frame for the merrily cascading fountains. The Marquis regretted profoundly that he must sit in his stuffy coach, surrounded by a small army of his own liveried footmen. But his high rank commanded that protocol should be respected and furthermore it would have been foolish to take any chances in Paris. There was no opportunity for him to ride his horse and enjoy the sun.

He decided to give orders to drive directly to the Palais de Beauvoir where a curious Pierre would be waiting for him and he'd bet a fortune that his son could be found there as well – those two were inseparable. The Marquis smiled and the warm smile transformed his haughty face; he would never tell Armand, but he had always considered him his favourite son.

His expectations had been correct. Pierre and Armand were waiting in a sunlit salon, evidently bored. Both youngsters jumped out of their chairs to greet the

Marquis de Saint Paul with due decorum while Pierre looked at him with his intense blue eyes, his whole face a question.

"Welcome my dear father, you look like the cat that's got the cream," Armand exclaimed disrespectfully. "I therefore assume that your mission was successful?"

The Marquis gave his son a stern look – he always painstakingly respected protocol and expected his children to do so as well. "Would you mind showing a bit more respect to your father, my dearest son, or I might suddenly remember some important tasks to be executed at our chateau in remote Bretagne which will need your urgent and prolonged attention."

"I'm sorry, dearest Father, I promise to improve and repent," Armand answered, but his laughing eyes betrayed his humble words.

"Yes, I can give you good tidings. The Cardinal is now practically our dearest friend, he could hardly hide his satisfaction when I gave him the letters to read. My personal recommendation is that if ever you should be playing cards or gambling with Cinq Mars, make him pay immediately. I have an inkling that his handsome head may be rolling off his shoulders sooner or later – sooner, rather than later."

The Marquis helped himself to a glass of wine and then he continued. "Our little agreement will settle an important issue for the Marquis de Beauvoir. I'm therefore pleased with the result of my discussion with His Eminence. But what puzzles me greatly is that the Cardinal seemed to be genuinely surprised when I mentioned the valuable property that has disappeared. Pierre, we must urgently meet this Monsieur Piccolin to shed some light on the problem; do you know if he has returned? "

"Let me thank you first from the bottom of my heart, Monsieur le Marquis," Pierre exclaimed and rushed forward to take the Marquis' hand and shake it vigorously. "You have accomplished an amazing task! I really don't understand why you expend so much of your valuable time and energy for me. I have no idea how I can ever reward you! I feel deeply and eternally indebted to you!"

The Marquis looked slightly unsettled; as a head of the Saint Paul clan he never encouraged emotional scenes in his family.

Armand noticed his father's discomfort, and grinning broadly he answered instead: "My father is only too grateful that you put up with me, that's takes a lot of effort from him!"

The Marquis shot his son a stern look. He didn't think that this flippant remark was particularly funny. "You're impossible, Armand," he said curtly.

"Yes, father, I'll shut my mouth now, I don't want to be sent to Bretagne," promised Armand, but was evidently not particularly intimidated.

As much as Pierre was relieved that finally the conflict with Cardinal Richelieu seemed to be coming to an end he was becoming uncomfortably aware that now his priorities needed to change. Armand and he had no more excuses, they would be obliged to fulfil their part of the original bargain and find the accursed rings. Deep in thought he looked at the ruby ring that he had been wearing since he had followed in the footsteps of his grandfather. The dark red stone seemed to be sleeping, and only when Pierre moved the stone close to a candle or into the sun would it awake and flash angrily with the colour of darkest blood. What kind of secret did this ring keep?

"Yes, finding Monsieur Piccolin will be our first priority now, he has to help us to find the diamond ring," Pierre said aloud.

"I'm with you," commented Armand. "Just a pity that the key to the diamond ring should be a wrinkled old man and not a beautiful young lady. My talents will be wasted!"

Two days later a message was delivered by a young groom that the honourable Monsieur Piccolin requested the favour of an urgent appointment. Hence the two friends, accompanied by Armand's father, gathered once again curiously in the living room of the Palais de Beauvoir, a spacious salon freshly redecorated and proudly displaying the portaits of Pierre's parents above the marble fireplace.

The old family banker had arrived exactly on time, not an easy accomplishment in the dense traffic of Paris. He hesitated shortly as to whom he should greet first, as Pierre – being not only a Marquis but a Duke as well – would be of higher rank, but the Marquis de Saint Paul was without doubt of higher seniority and yielded much more influence in France. He decided to bow to the Marquis de Saint Paul first, which proved to be the right decision, as the Marquis would not have appreciated being ranked below Pierre.

Having finished his elaborate greetings Piccolin accepted with a pleasurable sigh the invitation to take a seat. Then he formally addressed the three men looking at him expectantly in his pleasant Italian accent. "My most honourable Marquis, your Grace, your lordship! Let me first of all express my deepest pleasure and satisfaction that the son of the late Marquis de Beauvoir – finally – has been able to ascend to his rightful place, and to see him triumph above his enemies. My family and our bank have done whatever was possible to safeguard the family fortune and treasures that had been entrusted to us by the late marquis. Let me humbly mention that this task proved to be more challenging than we anticipated as we suffered intense pressure from some ill-guided members of the de Beauvoir family. It sometimes crossed my mind that some of those might even have harboured desires to change the natural course of this heritage."

He paused briefly to gauge the effect of his little speech but Pierre managed to keep a straight face, although he understood that the last remark was a clear hint regarding his dangerous cousin Henri. As nobody attempted to interrupt the flow of his conversation the old banker decided to continue. "But having had the honour and privilege of serving Your Grace's family for several generations already, all of our efforts of course had been concentrated on defending the interests of the true heir. Today I'm happy and proud to confirm that as soon as all documents have been signed and verified, Your Grace will have full access to the family fortune that is in our safekeeping."

Beaming at Pierre he added, "And of course it would be our greatest pleasure to have the honour to continue serving Your Grace and the de Beauvoir family if ever this should be Your Grace's desire."

The Marquis de Saint Paul thought it time to stop the flowery flow of words. "Are you sure that you're talking about *all the treasures* that had been deposited with your bank?"

"May I ask your lordship why you ask this question?" Piccolin's eyebrows started to twitch slightly.

"Because, Monsieur Piccolin, we have obtained intelligence that His Eminence, the Cardinal Mazarin, tried to enter this house and confiscate its treasures only some weeks ago."

The voice of the Marquis now took on a decidedly sharp edge. "And – what is admittedly most disturbing – when we met your son a fortnight ago he refused to give us a clear answer about the Cardinal Mazarin's actions. Please confirm clearly that not a single item has been handed over to him – and I am referring especially to the famous diamond ring which has been part of the de Beauvoir heritage for centuries!"

The voice of the Marquis had taken on a steely note; he was no lover of hide-and-seek games.

If he had anticipated reducing Piccolin to a bundle of nerves, the Marquis had erred as the banker suddenly smiled, full of mischief, and answered, "If my most noble Marquis will permit, I do have my own little secrets as well. Secrets that I didn't even dare to entrust to my son. Please promise me that our discussion will be kept strictly confidential – may I even request that your son leave the room, as what I have to tell you must be reserved for the ears of the concerned persons only!"

For the first time Pierre judged it about time to interfere in this conversation that was now taking a strange turn. "There can be no question of Armand leaving this room; his secrets are mine and vice versa. You can have full confidence, if you're open with us, that we shall not betray your confidence."

Piccolin looked sceptically at both young men. The concept of having full confidence did not exactly seem to be part of a banker's view on life, but finally he gave in. "His Eminence, the Cardinal Mazarin, did indeed visit our offices. His ultimatum was clear: either we were to remit the de Beauvoir treasures to his safe-keeping or he would make sure that my bank's license would be revoked – which means that our bank would be closed down."

"That's going in rather heavy," Armand commented. "How did you answer this challenge?"

"He was speaking to my son, who of course was *extremely* worried. It was out of the question to betray the confidence of one of our customers – but we all know that the Cardinal Mazarin will most likely become the next prime minister…"

"In short you had to choose between your honour and the future of your bank. Tell us then, what decision did you take?" asked the Marquis.

"Being of Italian origin means that we have grown up with a particular sense of pride – but also with a keen sense of flexibility. It is known all over France that the Cardinal is a passionate lover of diamonds – I therefore guessed that this story of safe-keeping was a mere pretext and an almost desperate attempt to acquire the famous de Beauvoir ring, a ring that the late Marquis had in fact pledged to our bank when he urgently needed a large amount of money."

"You mean that the ring in fact belonged to the bank and not to me? Pierre interjected, totally taken aback.

The banker fumbled at his waistcoat and carefully extracted a document, stamped with the seal of the Marquis de Beauvoir and a majestic signature. He remitted it to the Marquis who scanned it carefully and passed it to Pierre. It set out a loan for a huge amount of money, and the description of the diamond ring that was pledged in the event that the loan could not be reimbursed fitted perfectly – it even mentioned the mysterious engravings.

The room lay silent.

"What the hell did you decide to do?" Pierre asked in a hoarse voice.

9

Henri de Beauvoir gave a last kick and the half-dead body of the Count de Roquemoulin disappeared in the rapidly flowing waters of the Loire. Jean-Baptiste de Roquemoulin was gone forever.

Now it was time to cherish those, oh, so wonderful sweet feelings of triumph. Here he stood – Henri de Roquemoulin, the new and undisputed Count of Roquemoulin. He was rich. He was free. He had done it – he had rid himself of this elderly, ever complaining and disgusting lover, this silly man who had been stupid enough to adopt him, expecting his constant attentions and who had latched onto Henri like an amorous leech.

Still feeling the warm glow of triumph flooding though his veins, Henri turned back to mount his horse. As he glanced casually uphill, his heart nearly stopped beating. Three riders were waiting on the narrow path above the slope, and must have been there, watching him, for some time already. Feverishly he searched for a weapon and cursed; he had left his pistol and sword with his own horse up there on the path. Now he'd no choice but to encounter the three horsemen unarmed. As there was nothing else that he could do, he decided to climb back up the path and face the inevitable.

One of the riders dismounted and while Henri was still climbing upwards to regain the path, the man had started to run towards him drawing his sword, but strangely enough he started waving at him.

Hell and damnation, what am I going to do now? Henri feverishly went through all the options that seemed available. Suddenly he realized that the person who was approaching fast was in fact not a man but a woman. The person who was rushing toward him was Marina, his gipsy mistress. A wave of relief swept over him; this situation he could surely handle…

Marina rushed into his arms. "Oh Henri, my darling, you finally got rid of this silly man! I knew that it would happen today, I read it in the stars!"

Henri freed himself from her stormy embrace and pointed to the two riders who had remained on their horses like marble statues. "Who are they? Why didn't you come alone?"

Marina smiled at him but Henri wasn't sure if he liked this smile.

"Those are my father and my brother," she remarked.

Henri scrutinized the two men. They had the same proud bearing and he could detect a family resemblance. They all had hair of the darkest and glossiest black

10

he had ever seen. The skin of Marina's brother was slightly darker than hers but he was also spectacularly handsome.

"Should I say now that I'm delighted to meet you?" Henri snarled.

"Yes, you should," retorted Marina, her eyes flashing with triumph. "I suppose that it's a bit of a surprise for you but you're about to meet your future father and brother–in-law!"

Henry didn't know if he should laugh or explode with anger. "Are you crazy? I'm Henri de Beauvoir, Count de Roquemoulin, my ancestors conquered Jerusalem together with the kings of France, my family has royal blood in their veins, I shall never marry a mere gypsy slut!" he shouted.

Before he had time to finish his outburst, Marina slapped him hard, her nails biting into his flesh and leaving deep bloody marks.

Still reeling under the sudden attack he noticed that her brother was suddenly pointing a crossbow at him. Her brother's face conveyed a clear message: he'd be pleased to kill this raging stranger who had just insulted his sister and her tribe.

"You're nothing, a nobody!" she spat at him. "I'm the one who's of royal blood, my father is the king of our tribe. You've taken my virginity and according to our rules either you marry me or you die. My son will not be born out of wedlock. You choose."

Before Henri could speak out in rage or return her slap, he heard the hiss of the first arrow. It hit his horse, which reared in panic and pain before it lost its hold on the slippery path and tumbled down the slope into the Loire, shrieking with panic and pain almost like a human being. The terrible cries returned as an echo, a horrifying sound, as if the suffering of the horse would go on for ever.

Henri's blood froze. Then he heard the surprisingly melodious voice of Marina's brother for the first time. "Better think now before you speak. I don't understand why she wants to marry you, she says that she read her destiny in the stars. But if you insult or distress my sister or our tribe, I vow to kill you, and your death will be a terrible one."

Henri looked at the young man; actually this menace was starting to excite him, and Henri de Beauvoir loved a challenge. *Let's see who's going to win this game. If I can beat Richelieu, I shall survive this adventure as well. I'll make you all bow to my will.*

He looked defiantly at Marina and her brother and answered, "I guess I have no option but to accept. When I have successfully claimed the heritage of

11

Roquemoulin, I shall marry your sister. But if you kill me now, no one wins, I lose my life, and Marina loses her future husband."

"Do you think that we're completely stupid?"

For the first time Marina's father joined in the conversation. "You'll marry her here and now or you join your gullible count in the waters down there."

Henri gulped, his mouth suddenly dry. What could he do but accept? "How?" he managed to say.

"Mount the count's horse and we'll show you!" answered his triumphant bride.

The day I kill you, will be the brightest day of my life. Furiously, Henri pressed his lips together tightly.

They rode across the rolling green fields to the place where the gypsies had erected tents next to some dilapidated wagons and a flock of scruffy goats. Henri was led into one of the smaller tents where he was kept waiting. Marina disappeared together with her father, but her brother kept vigil, his crossbow ever present, his eyes strangely sad but challenging Henri. Only minutes later Henri was marched into a bigger tent where a golden cross had been placed on top of a table that had been covered quickly with a precious silken carpet. An icon of the Holy Virgin and her child was placed next to the cross. The painting appeared to be ancient, the golden frame worn by age and the picture darkened from the grime and smoke of the tallow candles.

Next to the cross a fat priest with a prominent mole on his wobbly chin was already waiting for them and before Henri had fully realized what was going on, his wedding ceremony had already started. *I have landed in a complete nightmare, this is unreal.*

Yet this was real enough, his bride was there, standing at his side with a silver wreath in her luminous black hair, radiating joy and satisfaction. And of course there were his new relatives-to-be, smirking at him. It didn't take much imagination to see that they were congratulating themselves on the fat catch that his new wife had landed.

Listlessly Henri followed the religious service. Never had he imagined finding himself in such a situation with an unwanted wife of the lowest birth at his side. He was as furious as he was disgusted. To keep his sanity Henri repeated in his mind like a mantra: *Let them think that they've got me trapped, I'll find a way out!*

A document was presented for signature and Henri realized that his bride had signed with three crosses – of course she wouldn't know how to write and read.

12

He briefly considered signing with a false name but this was taking a considerable risk if the fat priest could decipher his signature. Quickly Henri decided to sign – did it really matter after all?

The priest beamed at him, satisfied that all had gone well. He closed the ceremony with the last vows and the words "Till death do you part."

Henri suddenly felt uplifted: this was the clue he had been waiting for. *Yes, death will be the answer, Marina darling, you'll regret ever having challenged me!*

As custom demanded he shared the goblet of dark red wine with his bride, even kissed her dutifully. Long before this strange ceremony was finished Henri had returned to his normal confident self: he'd make sure that death would part them rapidly. She had just sealed her fate.

Arrogantly he addressed his new wife. "Now that we're married you must help me to find a good excuse for my absence. I guess that soon the count's grooms will start searching for us if we don't return. I must go back and look as if I have suffered a bad accident, seem bruised and desperate. You'll need to help me. If I play it right, a lot of money can be earned from the count's heritage."

His new family nodded – this was the kind of language they understood.

They rode back to the path close to the river and Henri went once more through the motions of setting up a bogus accident, only this time he didn't need to cut himself – Marina's nails had bruised his face and he had noticed traces of dried blood on his collar. Once again he was to play the part of the bruised victim of an accident; it seemed like the rehearsal of a bad comedy, but sometimes Henri had the sneaking suspicion that the whole world was nothing but a vast stage set either for drama or comedy.

When Henri – now converted into a lone and bruised horseman – entered the Roquemoulin estate riding on the well known, but visibly exhausted , count's horse, the whole place was already in turmoil.

Panic had spread when the two riders hadn't returned at the expected time. Search parties had been organized, but to no avail. Soon the terrible news spread that Henri de Beauvoir had returned alone, a broken man as he had been forced to witness a terrible accident that had happened to the count. Although the sun was already low, the grooms were immediately dispatched to the site of the accident – Henri had told them with a breaking voice that no effort should be spared in searching for their master and that hope should never be given up of recovering him alive.

Late in the evening the grooms returned, their eyes burning from their smoking torches. They could bear witness from the traces of the accident that they had seen with their own eyes – the rearing horses had left deep marks in the muddy path – but no trace of the count himself had been found at the river bank and notice would need to be sent to the authorities to search for his lordship.

But the body of the hapless count was never to be recovered. Weeks later and hundreds of miles away a fisherman discovered the bloated and disfigured remains of what seemed to have been a wealthy man. Thanking the Lord for such a find he cut off the puffy, half-decomposed fingers to recover the precious golden rings and hid the body in the reeds, to the immense satisfaction of the wild animals who disposed of it. Instinctively the fisherman knew that he'd be asking for trouble if he informed the authorities (or his wife). From today on he was a rich man, the value of the rings greatly surpassing anything than he could ever hope to catch in his entire life!

There had never been any doubt that Henri was an excellent actor, but now he played his part to perfection. He displayed the degree of mourning and sadness that was fitting for someone who was known to be the intimate (far too intimate for the taste of most of the servants) and close friend of the late count. Immediately he gave orders to the estate bailiff to inform the authorities and the family notary about the accident. If the count remained missing, the notary would need to inform the close family and identify the heirs. The estate bailiff, who had always eyed Henri with much suspicion, was agreeably surprised. He had been convinced that Henri would try to usurp the count's position and stay as long as possible, as even here in the provinces word had spread that Henri didn't have a *sous* to his name and was living solely on the count's charity.

Somehow it only seemed natural that the count's personal valet should take over the duties of serving Henri, thus acknowledging indirectly that the count's household accepted Henri filling the void during this difficult period of time. Diligently folding Henri's shirt, he had difficulties hiding his emotions. While he kept blowing his nose noisily tears welled up in his reddened eyes. The count had been a good master – too good and too naïve, some would murmur downstairs in the servants' quarters.

Silently Henri endured the unnerving display of the old valet's devotion to the missing count. Henri thought looked at the miserable tearstained face of the valet. *Silly old fool. You'll be dancing to my tune in no time, there'll be no more tearful scenes with me.*

Slowly a feeling of triumph took hold of Henri, a surge of superior confidence that he would be able to master every challenge that might come up, may it be his strange mistress (he simply couldn't name her his wife) or her entire gipsy tribe. As soon as he lay sprawled on his bed a warm glow of deepest satisfaction swept over him. "I'm a genius!" he whispered, savouring the words. "My grand plan

14

has been executed to perfection! Before long the world will know that I am the new Count de Roquemoulin. I shall be a rich man, a man to be reckoned with. Cousin Pierre and Richelieu, beware!" and he broke into a wild fits of laughter.

Henri's mind went back to Marina: she was truly beautiful but she had become a complication, a nuisance. What to do with her? Suddenly a new, delicately devious idea flashed through his mind. Marina and her clan were unknown to anybody else but him – what a great secret weapon they could become! A smile formed on his beautiful arrogant face: becoming the Count de Roquemoulin was an achievement, but he wouldn't stop here. His destiny was to become the Marquis de Beauvoir. Even at his lowest ebb, close to despair, Henri had never harboured any doubt about this.

Fate had smiled upon him and presented him with a new weapon – he'd use his low-born but extremely attractive wife to catch and destroy Pierre de Beauvoir. Only once this task was accomplished would he tackle the question of how to get rid of Marina. Surely there could be no question that Henri de Beauvoir would ever contemplate marriage to a mere commoner. "I'll make you pay dearly for your arrogant pretentions, Marina darling," he whispered to himself.

Soon he was sleeping deeply, with the satisfied sleep that comes after a day of hard but rewarding work. But in his dreams it was neither the hapless Jean Baptiste de Roquemoulin who appeared, nor his new wife – he saw and kissed the face of Marina's aloof, yet so handsome brother.

The old notary who had served the family dutifully – for decades rather than only years – arrived the next day, grieving, excited and flustered. He was led into the stuffy library that Jean Baptiste de Roquemoulin had so rarely used unless he had been dragged there by force by his dutiful bailiff to attend to his odious administrative duties.

Henri once again played his part to perfection. With the respect due to his office and with the correct mix of grief and mourning he received the notary modestly, humbly requesting his help and guidance in this terrible hour of distress. "I know that it had been the last will of my dearest Jean Baptiste to adopt me, but as I'm not aware if this wish has been fulfilled it's my sad duty now to prepare myself for a future without the person who meant so much to me." Henri's voice broke masterfully and he wiped an imaginary tear from his left eye. Maître, may I therefore request you formally to identify the legal heirs and prepare their summons in case my dearest Jean Baptiste should be declared missing by the authorities?"

The notary was visibly shaken, not only by his own genuine grief, but was also agreeably surprised by Henri's humble attitude. The last time he had been at Roquemoulin he had left the chateau convinced that the count must have gone totally mad to envisage the adoption of what he had instinctively judged to be an adventurous, even if high-born, scoundrel with a famous pedigree. The notary had expected to encounter in Henri an attitude of triumph, at least defiance, but not a humble acceptance of fate and grief – he was especially astonished to detect that Henri didn't seem to be aware that he had already been adopted.

The notary cleared his throat. "In fact, his next of kin would be Her Grace, the Duchesse de Limoges," he said in his slow and precise diction.

Henri had to refrain from exclaiming aloud. He was gripped by an almost irrepressible urge to throw himself on the floor and roll around with laughter – this was simply too good to be true! Life could always beat the wildest imaginings. He'd love to witness the scene when the Duchess received the news, the tantrums she'd have as soon as she realized that she had missed out on inheriting one of the fattest fortunes that France had to offer – and all because of her discarded lover. This situation was just perfect.

Hiding his face behind a handkerchief, Henri managed to keep his emotions under control and his visitor interpreted his twitching face as a further sign of extreme emotional distress.

"But in the case of your lordship's situation," the notary continued, "I'm pleased to inform you that the procedure of your lordship's adoption had been completed as requested by the late count," he quickly corrected himself, "I mean by the present Count de Roquemoulin, who sadly has been reported missing. The documents sealed by my authority as notary public had been sent to Roquemoulin already some weeks ago. Actually, I had expected you to be aware of this fact."

He watched Henri intently, but Henri was not to be thrown off balance by such scrutiny. Once more he succeeded in displaying the right mix of emotions: grief, a sudden grasp of the significance of the notary's last words, genuine surprise and finally humble gratitude.

"I don't know what to say," Henri said after a considerable pause. "I know that this was indeed the wish of my dearest Jean-Baptiste and I can only imagine that he wanted to surprise me for my birthday." He turned his face away from his visitor and continued in a broken voice, "But how shall I ever express my gratitude, now that my dearest, paternal friend is missing …" He finished the last sentence in a mere whisper. Quickly he covered his face, trying to hide his tears from the notary.

The visitor was shaken by this emotional statement and, trying to comfort Henri, he made some clucking sounds, not really knowing what to say. He still strongly disapproved of the scandalous motives behind this adoption, but legally Henri had become the undisputed and sole heir to an immense fortune, and the notary had no intention of losing good business over a question of mere morals.

16

Henri succeeded in regaining his composure and shook the notary's hand in order to thank him for his sympathy. He then cleared his throat. "In this case I propose to call the bailiff of the estate. If the count remains missing, I'll need to take over the management of the estate quickly. Jean-Baptiste would expect this of me. Therefore I think it would be better if you inform the bailiff personally that I shall need to be addressed as Henri de Roquemoulin in future."

The notary nodded, the request seemed well-founded enough. The bailiff was called and he arrived quickly, his attitude still defiant. When he heard from the notary that – by law – Henri had become the missing count's son and presumptive heir, he pressed his lips together, yet he bowed courteously towards Henri. "May I congratulate your lordship; do you wish me to address you as of now as our new Lord and Count de Roquemoulin?"

Henri succeeded in keeping his pose of false modesty and declined immediately. "Of course not! We all are longing so much to see his lordship back safe and sound, it's far too early to give up hope. I'm planning to organize further search parties down on the banks of the Loire this afternoon. Let's all pray to the Lord to find his lordship. I cannot even imagine this chateau without my dear Jean-Baptiste. I only wanted you to be informed about the latest news – indeed, I must confess, I only learned today that your master had adopted me before he went missing. I'm still overwhelmed by the magnitude of his trust and kindheartedness."

The bailiff managed to keep his face expressionless. He was far less easily fooled than the notary. He had been running this large household with a considerable staff of servants and managing hundreds of tenants – consequently being lied to was part of his daily routine. He didn't believe a single word about Henri's bewildered surprise nor was he impressed by this show of modesty. But he had a good position – which he wanted to keep – hence he pretended to accept Henri's words at face-value and bowed once more respectfully – if possible, even deeper than before.

Politely but firmly the notary declined Henri's invitation to stay for lunch. He left the estate with mixed feelings. Reluctantly he had to admit that Henri had left a much more favourable impression upon him than the last time – but somehow his sixth sense told him that there was something wrong, and he left the castle still wondering about the sudden disappearance of the count – and worrying. Sinking into the comfort of the velvet-covered feather cushions of his coach he shrugged – there was nothing that he could do but to try to gain as much money from the administration of this heritage as possible.

He vowed to himself that there would be no concessions, he'd make the new count pay as dearly as possible. Having come to this conclusion and a quick calculation of the fees that were waiting for him, his mood brightened considerably. The notary thought about his much younger and stunningly

17

beautiful wife Catherine; soon he'd be able to fulfil her dreams and buy a moated chateau on the Loire.

All Catherine's noble friends had either inherited or recently acquired one and she had barely spoken about anything else lately. If he charged his fees skilfully enough, step by step – never too much at once – the chateau would become her Christmas gift… He sighed pleasurably as he imagined how she would reward him; it had been a long time since he had been allowed to enter Catherine's bedroom. No wonder he was in such good spirits when he reached his home.

Henri was content with the achievements of the morning. He dismissed the bailiff, confident to let him do the work of spreading the news. As could have been expected the castle was humming like a bee hive by lunchtime and the servants bowed even deeper than before. No doubt word had spread that Henri was to become their new master. Henri modestly pretended not to notice any change and dutifully participated in the useless search party that he had organized with much fanfare, pushing the grooms to search until sunset, until they fell from their horses from exhaustion. Of course he had directed their search slightly away from the place of the murder and had insisted on covering all the swampy marshes close to the Loire, astutely avoiding those parts of the river where the body might have landed.

Riding amidst his footmen and grooms Henri noticed from time to time some gypsies who seemed to be hovering on the horizon, carefully keeping their distance. It didn't take long until his men noticed them as well and quickly made the usual disparaging remarks – gypsies never were popular with the rural population. The head groom hotly suggested setting the dogs on them. "Let's chase this filthy scum from the grounds of Roquemoulin, molesting our wives and stealing – that's all they know how to do," he grumbled, to the applause of his fellow grooms.

But Henri managed to dampen his fervour by reminding him that Jean-Baptiste de Roquemoulin would never have accepted such an action and the groom grudgingly accepted the truth of his statement.

But the gypsies' presence reminded Henri painfully that for now he seemed to be under constant supervision. His new family-in-law had no intention of letting their fat prize escape. He'd need to deal with them – but this must wait until later.

Back in the chateau – *his* chateau now – he dropped onto his bed, content with his day's work. Henri felt elated, though totally worn out from the physical exercise of riding and searching, cheering up and encouraging his men, as would have been expected from the beloved adopted son who was searching desperately for his lost father. What bliss it was to doze off and give in to his fatigue, to be able to drop the false mask of the loving son. Before slumber overwhelmed him, Henri remembered Jean-Baptiste's wailing voice and the touch of his sweaty

18

hands. Almost asleep, he shuddered with revulsion. This chapter was closed, and forever. No tears would be shed by him.

Henri must have been deep asleep as he didn't realize that someone was in his room until it was too late. A strong muscular hand covered his mouth with an iron grip and he was pushed deeper into his bed. Finally Henri managed to open to his eyes and get his brain to work in order to realize that the attractive face of his new brother-in-law was hovering only inches above his own.

"I brought you a gift for tonight," the gypsy whispered and loosened his grip ever so slightly, just to close it hard when Henri tried to open his mouth.

What about you, you could be my gift for tonight... flashed through Henri's mind, his excitement only enhanced by the sensation of danger.

"Be a good boy and keep your mouth shut if you want to keep some air in your lungs, look at your gift first," the gypsy commanded with a rough voice.

Henri glanced across the dark room and discovered Marina's silhouette in the moonlight close to his bed. Slowly she turned towards him and started undressing herself, teasing him with every movement and each part of her gown that she slowly removed. She made a sign to her brother to loosen his grip and he heard her hoarse voice close to his ear. "It's time to consummate your marriage and sire your son," she whispered into his ear, brushing his bare chest with the sleeve of her open chemise.

Henri's fatigue had long gone, and the strangeness of the situation quickly made him quiver with longing and excitement. The triumph and elation after his successful murder, the strange set-up, the exotic beauty of Marina and – he had to confess – the knowledge that her attractive brother must be watching their love-making, were having a catalytic effect.

"Didn't you tell me that you were already pregnant?" he whispered back. "But I don't mind giving it another try!"

Marina laughed softly while she ripped his nightshirt open and Henri found himself lying naked on his bed.

Conscious of and actually enjoying being watched, Henri stretched lazily, opening his legs to make sure that Marina and her brother would get a good glimpse of his perfect body and his excited state. Then Henri dragged Marina into his bed and made love to her; never tiring, he drove her close to madness whilst he kept stifling her moans and cries with his fist. Henri was aware that his servants would be waiting in the antechamber on duty, and that their love-making had to take place in absolute silence. But this knowledge only increased the thrill of it all, and the risk of being caught added an additional spice.

When they had finished she lay in his arms, limp and exhausted, her dark hair tickling his chest. Suddenly her brother appeared out of the dark shadows and silently made signs that she should get out of the bed. His abrupt gestures made it clear that he had not appreciated Henri's display of virility. Angrily he made it clear that they had to leave.

"We'll come back," Marina whispered to Henri, "and you can choose if it's going to be more for love – or war." They left the room through the window, as they had entered; God only knew how they had managed to climb up the steep chateau walls unnoticed.

Henri stretched like a contented tomcat in his bed. What a perfect end to a wonderful day, he thought lazily. Maybe Marina thought that she could make him dance to her tune, make him a slave of her wild beauty and radiant sexuality. But like so many of his previous lovers she'd learn the hard way that for Henri de Beauvoir, brain and body were two entirely different matters and never would he allow his brain to be dominated by the whims of his body.

Henri could not remember any lover – male or female – who hadn't bored him after a short period of time. He would make her dance to his tune, Henri vowed before a deep slumber carried him away. But in the meantime he'd enjoy what she had to offer.

"So what did you decide?" thundered the deep voice of the Marquis de Saint Paul through the silent room.

The old banker smiled unperturbed and continued in his melodious voice: "What else could I do but to give him what he wanted?" he answered simply.

Armand jumped up from his chair, furious and ready to assault their visitor, but Piccolin gave him a sign to stay calm. "Wait and listen," he commanded, his voice suddenly full of authority. At once it became clear why this nice, soft-spoken gentleman was in fact the leader of a bank catering for the rich and famous. "Swear to me a solemn oath that you shall never betray the secret that I'm about to share with you this very moment. There may be only one exception to this rule – the Grand Master of the Templars!"

Three pairs of shocked eyes were focusing on the old banker – how could he know that in fact this particular diamond ring had been pledged to the Brotherhood? Reluctantly Armand and Pierre nodded their consent and even the Marquis de Saint Paul, who was still trying to digest this sudden disclosure, gave in and accepted.

"I thought it best to give His Eminence the diamond ring he was craving, but – and I insist that this has to remain between you and me – I had the ring of Your Grace copied before I gave it to him."

And with a large smile and the wave of a conjuror he unwrapped a small velvet parcel and displayed to the great surprise of his three onlookers the original diamond ring that Pierre's ancestors had jealously guarded for generations.

"This is the ring originating from the Kingdom of Jerusalem, worn by generations of your Grace's ancestors – guard it well!"

Pierre took the ring with trembling hands. Suddenly he felt shy. The diamond seemed to radiate power – rays of sunlight had awoken it and, like a living being, it was reflecting powerful, almost angry flashes, content to have escaped the dark folds of its velvet prison. With the greatest care Pierre removed his grandfather's ruby ring from his index finger and placed the two rings side by side. It now became obvious that the strange shape of the golden frames fitted together beautifully and it also became clear that the engravings belonged together – matching perfectly. But the strange engraving remained impossible to decipher. It would take the third ring to complete the set and solve the riddle.

Pierre looked at the ring with awe. "You mean this is truly the original?" he breathed.

"Yes, I swear by the life of my children and by my honour – and," he chuckled, beaming with satisfaction, "I can assure you that it took me several days and the best connections to find a diamond in France with the quality to rival this one. Cardinal Mazarin may be greedy but he's not a fool and he's a reputed diamond expert. I could never have convinced him if the diamond of his copy had been anything than first class." Piccolin tried in vain to appear modest, but it was clear that he was very proud of his conjuror's trick.

Pierre was trying to digest this story but all of a sudden a different aspect dawned upon him. "I'm truly grateful, Monsieur Piccolin, grateful beyond any words that I can express. You've taught us today to believe in decency and not to accept every story at face value. But your noble act signifies that I'm not only very much indebted to you, I must owe you a fortune! I mean, if I understand correctly, my father never had the opportunity to pay you back his loan and now you've bought and advanced on my behalf the money for a second diamond ring of incredible value! Allow me to honour my debts immediately, but to raise such a lot of money will need some time!"

Piccolin had to clear his throat before he could answer. "Your Grace, it's been a genuine pleasure for me to serve the new Marquis de Beauvoir as the head of a family who has honoured us with their trust for generations – and I must confess, it has been a personal satisfaction for me to outsmart a dangerous and impertinent fox like Cardinal Mazarin. I certainly did not appreciate at all his ultimatum to betray the trust of a customer or have my bank closed. This was truly unacceptable and outrageous!"

The banker removed his glasses and started polishing them vigorously before he added in a low voice, "But let's close this issue, the Cardinal is happy and Your Grace is in possession of the ring that rightfully belongs to the de Beauvoir family." He cleared his throat and continued. "In fact I should confess that I happen to be aware why you needed the ring urgently – and why you and your friend shall be obliged to leave France shortly on the quest to find the third ring."

He paused once more and gladly accepted the glass of wine that Armand had offered to him. Pierre looked at Armand and they exchanged bewildered glances. This meeting was indeed full of surprises.

When the banker took the glass of wine he moved his hand and for the first time they realized the significance of the seal of the golden ring that Piccolin had chosen to wear today. Worn by age it showed a peculiar coat of arms, displaying two knights sitting together on one horse – the coat of arms of the Templars.

"There is no need to pay me back right now. I know that your father invested the money we lent him in a venture in the new colonies and I happen to know that this money was well invested."

He chuckled. "Quite unusual actually for a member of the high aristocracy to invest wisely." Becoming serious again he continued, "As for the money I spent having the ring copied, I'd like to propose a deal to Your Grace. Let me go back one year. Before your Grace's uncle Louis Philippe passed away, he must have borrowed a huge amount of money from a Jewish moneylender as our bank decided to decline his request for a loan that seemed highly... let's say... unusual. It's obvious that neither your uncle nor his heir ever paid back the money to the moneylender. Therefore most of his estates are up for auction now. Among them is a chateau that I'd like to acquire. I happen to know the Jew who owns the mortgage quite well, he's a respectable man. He would be willing to give me a very favourable price in compensation for some other business that I can negotiate for him. But of course I'd never acquire this estate against your advice or interest as my agents tell me that the Cardinal de Richelieu is suddenly trying to stop the sales and hand back the estates to your Grace. If you agree that I may buy it all the same as a dowry for my youngest daughter, I'll be happy to offer this ring as my gift to you; please accept it also as a sign of my family's dedication to the de Beauvoir cause."

Pierre looked at the ring: this was a royal gift, a value far beyond his uncle's chateau. He decided that it was time to forget about the stifling rules of protocol or rank and let his heart speak.

And so it was that His Grace, the Duke of Hertford, the most noble Marquis de Beauvoir, a peer of France and the Kingdom of Great Britain, jumped up, rushed to the banker and embraced the old man, as if he were his equal, a member of his own family.

Piccolin was as stunned as the Marquis de Saint Paul was probably scandalized. Even years later it was only with tears in his eyes that the banker could recount this scene to his own family. For him, Pierre's esteem and gratitude were worth far more than two diamond rings.

Trying to regain his composure, he said, "I'm pleased that you appreciate my humble service. I'm truly honoured, Your Grace. I know that soon you must leave for Venice to find the sapphire ring that will complete the set of three rings and I'd like to let you know that it'll be my pleasure to be of assistance in this respect."

Armand, who had been unusually quiet until now, suddenly came back to life. "You've shown a most noble spirit, Sir, and let me, too, thank you from the bottom of my heart. We'll need to do some planning and we'd be honoured if you could join us tomorrow for dinner. You seem to be surprisingly familiar with our mission – and I guess of valuable help to us!" He flashed his famous charming smile at the banker, delighted that the support of a fellow Brother of the Templars would make their mission a lot easier.

"I accept with pleasure," the old banker beamed back at Armand. "I think I can be of assistance in your venture, your lordship. Most people always think that a bank only lends money, but believe me, most of our work is gathering and using intelligence – not unlike our present prime minister, in fact. He'd make an excellent banker – maybe not always trustworthy enough. But this statement would be true for most politicians, I guess."

He chuckled at what he seemed to think was a fabulous private joke and bowing deeply, carefully making sure to bow just a bit deeper to the Marquis de Saint Paul, who noticed this gesture with satisfaction, he took his leave.

The banker had left, yet the room remained in total silence. The three men were stunned, even if Armand's father had succeeded in keeping his usual air of impenetrable dignity.

Of course if was Armand, who broke the silence. "This is unbelievable! We've been searching for this cursed diamond ring, certain of our well-guarded, top secret mission. During all that time this man has had more knowledge about the whole story than the three of us together. I feel like an idiot – but am more than relieved at the same time. I had already pictured myself breaking into Mazarin's palace, trying to find a suitable excuse for the moment he caught me in his bedroom rifling through his huge collection of diamonds. Should I have explained that kleptomania is a family trait?"

Armand's vivid picture broke the ice and Pierre had to laugh; even the Marquis allowed himself a thin smile, although he did not appreciate the idea of linking the august Saint Paul name with kleptomaniacal tendencies.

"Let's get back to your mission then," the Marquis reminded the two youngsters.

"We now know that the third ring should unlock the riddle of the engravings and logically lead you to the hidden treasure. As – to our surprise – even our banker seems to know, the third ring is known to remain in Venice and we must therefore plan your trip to the south. The Templars have kept their part of the deal, you now must keep yours."

"That's evident, no need to remind us, sir," said Armand. "Pierre and I are ready to leave. If you want, I'll saddle my horse tomorrow!"

"I can just picture this, for sure!" retorted the Marquis acidly. "Ever ready for adventure but forgetting that such a venture needs careful planning. You're no longer two boys from the monastery school. Your trip will need to be organized, you need to be accompanied by guards – and I also feel that Pierre should first visit his estates in the Loire. They'll be in a pitiful state after years of neglect. I'm convinced that your uncle and your cousin tried everything imaginable to empty the de Beauvoir treasure chest. You cannot just leave for your next adventure, you'll have to do your duty as the rightful Marquis de Beauvoir first!"

Both young men looked meekly at the Marquis. He was right of course – it was becoming an annoying habit.

"I can only agree with your words, Sir," Pierre answered. "Luckily my estates are located south of Paris. Let's start in the vicinity of the Loire first and then move on to the south. But I'd like to propose that Armand and I should leave France incognito and travel on our own. If we travel to Venice in the style of a Marquis, our mission will become very official and the price of the ring – if it's up for sale – will soar. Worst case – if the ring is not up for sale and we need to find ways to steal it, it will cause a scandal, at worst diplomatic complications. I truly think that we should stay very low-key if our mission is to be accomplished."

The Marquis glanced at Pierre, pondering the arguments Pierre had very convincingly put forward. His face showed that he hated the thought that they might travel once more like adventurers but reluctantly he had to agree to the logic of Pierre's reasoning.

"Looking at Pierre you wouldn't suspect that he can be intellectual!" Armand interjected, "but from time to time he harbours some truly good ideas in this pretty blond head of his – even if one wouldn't actually expect this from someone like him."

Pierre looked at his friend and grimaced; he would keep his more outspoken answer for later.

The Marquis looked as his disrespectful son sternly. "At least Pierre de Beauvoir seems to know respect and shows intelligence and consideration in his thoughts, something which seems to be entirely absent in the conduct of my youngest son!"

Now it was up to Armand to grimace and Pierre grinned at him. Revenge was sweet, he thought with delight.

*****

The next days passed quickly; the old banker joined them for dinner as promised and even offered further funds for the purchase of the sapphire ring, an offer that was politely but firmly rejected by Pierre.

They had been chatting animatedly during dinner about Venice and Pierre learnt a lot about this famous city. Monsieur Piccolin explained that he knew Northern Italy and the city of Venice extremely well, as he still had plenty of relatives in those parts of Italy. "Venice is simply wonderful," he sighed. "When I was young I had the privilege of living and working for several years in this fantastic city. I must confess I envy you!"

Venice, he explained – where his bank operated a branch office – was a proud republic, governed for centuries by the same circle of leading noble families who guarded their dominance jealously. Those families didn't even trust each other and made sure that the position of the elected head of state – the doge – was passed on after the end of each term in order to avoid one of them ever becoming a true king. Over the centuries they had become rich and powerful beyond imagination as they had been amassing fabulous treasures from the Orient for generations.

Armand and Pierre listened spellbound as Piccolin continued. "But then my proud, beautiful Venice started to decline. In endless battles with the Ottoman Empire Venice had continued to bleed and had lost many of her overseas territories, and even worse, trade had started to decline as the new trade routes to the Americas and India took to the west. As if the Lord had decided that this punishment wasn't enough, ten or eleven years ago disaster struck the city. You'll know that all port cities are regular victims to bouts of the plague. But this time the epidemic showed no mercy and killed a third of the population – a terrible punishment inflicted by the Lord."

Piccolin now had tears in his eyes. "I lost many members of my own family, and this time the plague did not stop at the doors of the poor, but like a furious demon it decimated the whole population, disregarding rank or age. My cousin later described to me how my beautiful city had been transformed into an apocalyptic burial site; from morning to evening he could hear the ceaseless chiming of the death knells haunting the living, day and night. Priests and monks were roaming the streets urging the citizens to repent and confess – all citizens were convinced that the day of judgement had come."

Pierre closed his eyes. He could almost hear the sound of the church bells, the chanting of the priests and the desperate cries of the dying – it must have been a living hell.

But Venice had survived and the old banker now painted a vivid picture to his avid listeners of a city that resembled a beautiful lady – conscious of being past her prime, she had started to hide the traces of time by hiding behind veils of refinement and applying extra layers of make-up. Venice by any standards was still a beacon of wealth and elegance, her buildings shimmering in warm colours and constructed from noble stones like marble, painted and decorated in a unique blend of the oriental and the Italian style. Once you entered the buildings, stunning paintings impressed the visitor. All the famous artists of the world had been working for the doges, the rich churches and monasteries, or the great families.

The banker sighed with delight. "A city you'll fall in love with! Its architecture reflects a perfect blend of east and west – and last, but not least, the women of Venice are the most beautiful in the world!"

Built on hundreds of small islands interlinked by canals and bridges, Venice was almost cut into two halves by the famous Canal Grande. Where people would walk or ride in Paris, the Venetian would use a boat or gondola to travel. The lagoon that surrounded the city gave it shelter from the enemy and possible assault. "If I had the choice of living in Paris or Venice, I'm afraid that I would still keep Venice closer to my heart!"

Later during dinner Armand mentioned that he had met the Venetian ambassador and his daughter in London, but couldn't finish his sentence as the banker interrupted him with sparkling eyes. "Oh, you mean that you met darling Julia Contarini!" he exclaimed. "Isn't she a first class beauty? I had the pleasure of having the whole family to stay for dinner in my house before the ambassador went to London and my youngest son was raving about her for weeks afterwards. But as she's from one of the best families Venice has to offer, I told him to forget her – she's certain to marry into the doge's family!"

He hesitated and looked again at Armand who was having difficulty hiding his embarrassment – he had turned a crimson red. Pierre tactfully ignored his friend's agitated state but the old man chuckled and said soothingly, "I can see that my son was not her only victim. It will be interesting for you to know then that she's on her way back to Venice – her father has decided to go back and run for the coming elections for the secret council. I'm sure he has a fair chance of becoming a member of the Ten sooner or later."

"What's the 'Ten'?" asked Pierre curiously.

"It's the secret council of the Ten, which in fact runs the city and its colonies – even if they of course deny such a bold statement. Officially there are the doges and the Great Council and the magistrates who govern the city, but for nearly two centuries the real power has been with the secret council of the Ten. Their reputation is daunting – they have people arrested based on simple slander and those poor souls disappear forever in the infamous 'piombi' chambers, lead-lined prison cells under the roof of the doge's palace – the most terrible prison you could possibly imagine, burning hot as an oven in the sun and freezing cold in winter."

"Venice is truly beautiful," the old man sighed, "but beware of meddling with the Council of the Ten, the Inquisition or the secret police. You can quickly lose

27

your head in Venice if you're not careful – and I'm not only talking about the beautiful girls there. Finding the sapphire ring will be a difficult and dangerous mission. You must plan and act with caution and care."

There was an uneasy silence, interrupted only by a deep sigh from Armand. Pierre wasn't sure if Armand had listened at all to the banker's warnings as all he could discern from Armand's sigh was the name of Julia; apparently Armand was imagining himself already in Venice, holding Julia in his strong arms.

Eagerly Piccolin agreed to Pierre's suggestion to travel incognito. "That's an excellent idea! It will avoid a lot of trouble. If you wish, I can write for you a letter of recommendation. I'll inform our bank in Venice that I've decided to dispatch two young and promising apprentices of good family background to Venice in order to learn our trade. It's quite common and will not raise any suspicion, as Italy is still regarded as the best school for the banking profession. You'll be one of the numerous young and adventurous men who come to the city to spend a year or two until they return."

"That's brilliant!" Armand was very excited now. "It will give us the perfect cover for our mission so we can find out what's going on before we approach the present owners of the ring."

The evening drew to a close far too soon for their liking and they parted on the best of terms.

"What a stroke of luck that we found Piccolin and that he can help us to enter Venice in disguise," said Pierre, stretching his aching back, as he'd been sitting the whole evening in one of his elegant but rather uncomfortable dining chairs.

"Call it providence," Armand suggested, also slumped in his chair. As his father had left, he could drop all pretence of noble manners.

Pierre started to speak. "Now that we have a plan, we should leave soon. Actually I rather like the idea of travelling quickly; staying in Paris and attending the King's boring hunting and drinking parties is not an enticing alternative. I don't understand why some people would give an arm or a leg just to be invited to the royal court. I never could imagine a more depressing bunch of stupid and conceited people – even London was more fun! How Cinq Mars looked down on me the last time…"

Pierre couldn't end his statement as Armand cut in. "He's only scared to death that you'll try to become the King's new favourite. He's been wearing more diamonds, lace and velvet than ever, just to outshine you. But he's too stupid to understand that you'll always look better – regardless how much effort he spends on his wardrobe."

Pierre laughed and shrugged that he didn't care. This was one of Pierre's traits that Armand liked so much; although he must be aware of his good looks, he simply never seemed to bother about it.

Pierre continued, "First I propose to visit my chateau, Montrésor. My valet Jean told me that it's located in beautiful countryside close to the Loire – it must be fabulous and I'm truly looking forward to it." Pierre's eyes dimmed a bit. "…if only Marie could be here, I don't understand why she hasn't invited me to Reims, she just sent some short messages that she's doing fine – do you think that there is something amiss, maybe her parents are being difficult?"

Secretly Armand had harboured the same concerns but immediately he protested loudly, "That's nonsense, Pierre, you're the best match that any diligent mother could possibly imagine for her daughter, rich as a king without the strings that are normally attached to such a marriage. I guess that her father still must be ailing and that she simply hasn't told us the truth in order to spare us any worries."

Pierre furrowed his brow and gave it a long thought but suddenly his face became miserable again.

"What's up?" asked Armand.

"If her father should pass away – God forbid, of course – we shall have to wait for months before we can marry; Marie cannot plan a wedding during her official period of mourning!"

Pierre looked crestfallen and Armand was annoyed with himself; better to have kept his mouth shut.

"It doesn't make sense to worry, Pierre," Armand replied. "In any case, we must travel to Venice first, you cannot drag your bride along. First there's adventure, then it'll be time for love."

"You're a fine one to talk," retorted Pierre, "it's written all over your face that you hope to see Julia as soon as you set foot in Venice. But how's my smart friend going to handle the fact that she's going to recognize you immediately? Great idea, courting Julia if we want to stay incognito!"

"They didn't recognize me in Calais, did they?" answered Armand smugly. "A bit of a suntan and a beard will make all the difference. Everybody will be convinced that I've come straight from Mediterranean shores, a bit of hinting that my father was an infamous corsair will add some welcome spice. But… we'll have to think what we're going to do with you though; at least your beard finally seems to have started growing."

Pierre made faces at Armand; his lack of a manly beard in a period where fashion demanded it was a continuous source of annoyance. But lately he had detected what could optimistically be interpreted as the beginning of a promising male facial adornment.

"I'll stay out of Julia's sight, don't worry," Pierre answered hotly. "I mean, I had better do so – as otherwise she might change her mind and start fancying me!"

"Not so sure," Armand answered, not in the least intimidated. "I'm convinced she can discern quality quite easily. You're a nice guy, but I think there are some things that I can offer…"

He didn't finish his sentence as a cushion landed straight in his face, unfortunately hitting a glass at the same time. The glass broke and spilt the wine all over Armand who just laughed; it took more than a bit of spilt wine to unsettle him.

So once again an exciting journey had to be planned. The well-oiled machinery of the noble household was set in motion to prepare for smooth travelling. Long gone were the days when the two young men could saddle their horses and ride away on a whim. Pierre's majordomo duly informed his equivalent at Montrésor of the imminent visit of their new lord and master, immediately triggering a frenzy of activity there as well.

In Paris carriages were cleaned, their wheels greased, and new footmen were recruited. The mighty Cardinal Richelieu offered a detachment of his own private musketeers to accompany and protect Pierre, a gesture which could only be interpreted as sign of courtesy and appreciation for the Marquis de Beauvoir, which was as surprising as it was exceptional. Pierre declined politely; being surrounded by Richelieu's spies seemed sufficient.

With the greatest pleasure, though, he accepted the same offer from the Marquis de Saint Paul and soon they were ready to leave. This, at least, is what Pierre thought.

"Did Your Grace seek a royal audience to request the King's consent to leave Paris?" his valet, Jean, asked casually. Pierre looked at him as if he were mad. "Why should I need to ask the King? He didn't even want me to come to Paris at all in the beginning. He'll be happy enough that I'll be leaving! And stop calling me Your Grace all the time, 'Sir' is more than enough."

His valet shook his dark head. "Your Grace keeps forgetting your new position. As a peer of France you may not leave the royal court without prior permission of your Sovereign; don't forget that Your Grace is a prominent figure of political importance now." Jean's face remained unmoved but his eyes were laughing – he knew that Pierre hated all this fuss.

Pierre sighed but he knew that Jean was right. He'd need to request an audience and ask the King to accept his departure – a mere formality but protocol had to be respected: it was the essence of life at court, the essence of noble life.

An audience was granted almost immediately, and it was only malicious tongues that whispered that Cinq Mars had rushed through the timing for the audience as soon as he had understood that his greatest potential rivals for the King's affections were intending to embark on a long journey that would remove them far away from court.

Thus only a day later Pierre and Armand were strolling through the endless galleries of the Louvre palace, then further through numerous halls with high painted ceilings to reach one of the rooms where the more private audiences were held regularly.

Bright sunlight was pouring through the large windows of the new wing of the Louvre and it was mirrored by the polished marble of the floors. Pierre and Armand had the impression of wading through golden pools of light, and only the sound of their boots on the hard floors brought them back to reality. Today no trumpets were heralding the arrival of the King and Queen, as the royal couple had already taken their seats in the great salon that served as the background for today's meeting. While he was walking towards the waiting monarch, Pierre observed the group of people that had gathered around the King. As usual the King was sitting on the most impressive golden armchair, his Queen next to him, her chair smaller but matching the King's.

Pierre glanced quickly at the Queen, as it would have been an inexcusable breach of protocol to look at the Queen openly. She was no beauty – but Pierre was impressed all the same. This lady, past her prime and somewhat running to fat, had sharp eyes and a definite regal aura; she was every bit a true Queen of France.

Her fair complexion betrayed her Austrian Habsburg origins, and only her dark eyes showed the heritage of her Spanish roots. The Queen wore a diamond tiara adorned with pearls of the size of pigeon eggs, surrounding her head like a halo and matched by expensive pearl necklaces that weighed on her chest. Her blond wig looked slightly strange on her bloated face, fixed like a painted mask and covered by the heavy white paste of make-up. Pierre was no expert on female jewellery but it took no expert to understand that the tiara alone would send her sister-in-law, the Queen of England, into tantrums of jealousy if ever she came to know about it.

The Queen was sitting next to her husband, bored to death as usual, as her husband rarely addressed a word to her – court protocol ensured she was as if restrained in a golden cage. She was curious, though, to meet the Marquis de Beauvoir and his friend, the youngest son of the Marquis de Saint Paul, who had mysteriously acquired an unpronounceable English title and could call himself a count now.

She was aware of court gossip, and was aware, too, that those good-looking young men had been earmarked already as the next favourites of her husband. But why would they wish to leave court right now if a brilliant career at court was waiting for them? She found this behaviour as unusual as it was enigmatic – what could be so important as to make them leave now if the holy grail of court life, the King's favour, could easily be won?

Secretly the Queen hated every minute that she was expected to spend with her stuttering, awkward and slow-witted husband, just as she was aware that the King must loathe every minute he was supposed to endure her presence – or worse – those rare occasions when Louis XIII was expected to fulfil his conjugal duties. It was an aversion that had lasted almost since the day she had been dragged away from Spain, sacrificed in the name of politics to become queen of this cold and unwelcoming kingdom governed by a cynical cardinal – a mutual aversion, dulled only by the fact that it had become part of their daily routine.

But since she had given birth to the heir of the throne, it was the fact of being separated from her children that would irritate her most. Her children were a priceless gift that God had so unexpectedly bestowed on her after years of waiting, after she had already given up hope. The moment she had realized that she was pregnant with her first son she was stunned – hadn't her court ladies been whispering that she was far too old to aspire to becoming a mother? But once her conviction had grown that – this time – she wouldn't lose her child as she had the others before her time was due, she had experienced the most extreme emotions: a joy she had never even known could exist, and then a sudden onslaught of fright had gripped her heart like a cold hand. *What if this precious child growing in her womb inherited the insanity of her ancestors?* Would her son be born only to be shut away in a dark castle guarded by monks, as had been the fate of her brother?

Her heart had started to race with fear and she had rushed into her bedchamber, shutting out her chambermaids, who had never seen the queen in such a state of nerves. Anne had opened the chest where her jewel-studded bible with the Habsburg family tree was kept. With trembling fingers she had followed the fine drawing with their names written in elegant script, reviewing this impressive line of kings and emperors who were her living or deceased relatives. They had reigned and shaped the destiny of the world for centuries – but for several generations the Spanish branch of the tree had withered and become rotten. She raised her eyes and suddenly the red brocade linings and draperies of her bed and room looked like curdled blood, like the blood in her veins that seemed to be freezing with fear.

Anne, Queen of France, proud daughter of Spain, forced herself to look at the truth, to admit that the curse of insanity must have been running in the Spanish line of the Habsburgs for more than a century, becoming more prominent with every generation. Tormented by fear she had secluded herself in the royal chapel, lying on her knees on the cold marble tiles, praying and crying until she was totally exhausted and her maids urged her to go back to her room and lie down in her huge bed as she was risking losing her precious child – and this the King would never forgive.

But in this hour of despair an idea had formed all of a sudden in her tormented mind, like a ray of light. Kneeling in front of her private altar she appealed to the Holy Virgin: *Let my child become a healthy son, let him grow up to become a great King of France and I shall dedicate myself fully to France, to the future of my son.*

The selfish and spoilt Spanish Princess had vanished forever. Queen Anne of France had been born.

The Holy Virgin seemed to have accepted her bargain as not only her first son, but later a second son, was born strong and healthy. Miraculously they survived the first delicate months that so often killed mother and child. Her eldest son, the dauphin, showed all the promise of becoming a magnificent prince and future king; he was as handsome as his mind was quick and alert. Like a dry sponge Queen Anne from now on tried to soak up any information about France, keen to create and seek potential allies for her sons – her son had to live and to reign and his mother was prepared to sacrifice everything she could in order to make it happen.

Queen Anne's mind came back to reality. Turning her head she took a quick critical look at her husband. He had grown fat; she had noticed that he was eating far too much and drinking heavily lately. He looked unhealthy. The King was speaking now, small amounts of spittle coming out of his mouth as he did so. Secretly the Queen shuddered with disgust. Her glance wandered to the Cardinal Richelieu. As soon as she had started to take an interest in France and its politics she had – reluctantly – started to understand and even admire Richelieu's brilliant strategy. Her son could only aspire to become the king of a powerful country if the frontiers of his realm were safe, and with Spain and Austria occupying vast territories to the north, east, south and west of France there could be no peace. It was Spanish gold that found its way into the pockets of the French nobles, Spanish gold that stirred trouble in France with maddening regularity. Once Queen Anne had made herself aware that her native Spain had to be seen as her son's enemy, her perception of the world had changed.

33

The Queen lifted her eyes and saw the two young gentlemen now standing very close to the royal chairs. The two young men were strikingly handsome – but since she had become a mother and a true Queen she smiled at the Marquis and his friend, the young count, not because they were young and handsome, but because they represented the future of her son's kingdom: youth, money and power – everything she'd need if ever Richelieu or the King should die before her son had turned thirteen and could reign France in his own right.

Pierre saw the smile on the Queen's lips and her appraising eyes and he bowed deeply, looking back and sending a signal that he'd be ready to support her, a message that she understood, as suddenly her smile reached her eyes and she nodded majestically with her head.

Pierre's eyes moved on to the rest of the group; to his surprise he detected Richelieu sitting there like a shrivelled scarlet spider, his burning eyes as alert as ever. The Cardinal's eyes were darting around the room, seemingly not missing the slightest detail. His very presence in bidding good-bye to Pierre was a great favour; the times when he'd shunned or tried to destroy him seemed long gone.

Pierre's eyes moved to the King and Cinq Mars. The latter had taken the liberty of standing far too close to the King, ignoring the requirements of protocol. Cinq Mars was doing the talking – the King listened, just nodding and smiling indulgently from time to time.

Pierre couldn't know that the King wasn't able to say much, in fact His Majesty was deeply upset. Whenever the King was upset, his tongue seemed to be tied into a knot. Only yesterday the King had learnt that the Marquis de Beauvoir and Armand de Saint Paul wished to leave Paris, whereas the King had secretly hoped to have the two handsome gentlemen around him for the coming hunting season. They had seemed such a promising addition to his circle of intimate friends.

Then to make things worse, Richelieu had whispered that he must take care not to shower too many favours on Cinq Mars. The King had greatly disliked this remark. Unluckily he knew from experience that Cardinal Richelieu would never make such a remark without a precise reason – Cinq Mars must have been doing something stupid, and the Cardinal must have some aces hidden up his sleeves.

The King's mind went back to the good-looking boyish Marquis who stood there, so close, but yet so impossible to approach or touch – even for a king. Of course he had to accept Pierre's request to visit his estates and take up his inheritance. Yet the King was deeply unhappy, which meant that his stammer was terrible today. He was content that Cinq Mars chatted animatedly and he had just to nod; at least Cinq Mars seemed to understand that he didn't feel like talking today.

The audience was short, Pierre and Armand presented their request and their leave was accepted in good grace. The two friends bowed deeply, went through the prescribed motions of protocol and left. Watching the two slender and handsome figures moving backwards out of the salon the King had to suppress a sigh.

That evening the King ate and drank even more excessively than usual and when the time for ritual of preparing the King for the night had arrived, his valets and nobles had to undress a totally drunken monarch who was tearfully sobbing incomprehensible names and babbled his prayers in unfitting haste. For the next two days the King was reported as being indisposed.

Bilious attacks were tormenting His Majesty with unknown intensity and his doctors looked at each other with the greatest concern. It was clear to them that the King would not survive too many such attacks – which was a chilling thought, as the heir to the throne was only just learning to walk and to speak.

The Parisian sky was full of grey clouds, and a light drizzle of rain had coated the courtyard and made the cobbled stones slippery. It was a miserable day that mirrored Pierre's mood to perfection.

The day to leave Paris had arrived. "Stop looking so miserable!" Armand cried as his friend entered the courtyard. "We're leaving for Montrésor to have a good time and not to attend a funeral!"

Pierre tried to muster a smile, but it didn't look particularly convincing.

Armand's father had suggested travelling to the Loire region first and staying for some weeks at Pierre's chateau, Montrésor, an important estate that had belonged to the family for three generations. The ancestor who had acquired it, a member of the King's Privy Council, had been a remarkably cunning man. He had served (and survived) a succession of Valois kings during an extremely tumultuous era, and it was to be supposed that it had not been by sheer luck or coincidence that he had been able to vastly increase the family fortune during his long career.

Pierre had hoped right up until the last minute that he might receive news from Marie, and dreamed of changing his plans and leaving to meet Marie in Reims instead, but although she kept sending him letters telling him how much she loved him, no official invitation to join her or to officially propose to her father was forthcoming. Jean hated to see his master so sad, dreading it each time a new letter arrived and having to watch his master tearing open the message eagerly – only to look totally downcast after he had read the contents.

Thus there had been no excuse left for delaying their departure and in the early morning the colourful cavalcade of servants, footmen, musketeers and carriages left the courtyard of the Palais de Beauvoir.

Pierre's mood lightened as soon as they had left the gates of Paris and set off in a southerly direction. By noon the sun had come out and chased away the clouds in the sky – and those in his soul – and Pierre discovered for the first time the lovely countryside that was unfolding between Paris and the Loire River. The valley of the Loire was commonly known as the 'garden of France', but Pierre thought this an understatement; in his mind 'paradise of France' would be more suitable, with its lush pastures, well-kept fields and beautiful villages bordering the roads.

Free from any pressure of time the slow, snaking cavalcade wearing the de Beauvoir colours crept forward at a leisurely pace. Frequently they stopped at one of the numerous inns, or 'auberges' as they were called here in the heart of France.

Portly innkeepers greeted them and bowed submissively, almost touching the ground, as soon as they set eyes on the young Marquis with his impressive entourage. Often the innkeepers confused him with Armand as the latter had dressed most splendidly and looked every inch a genuine prince. Consequently it was Armand who was frequently greeted first and addressed as a Marquis. Pierre loved the small scene that would invariably follow: the innkeeper's reddening face as soon as he became aware of his faux-pas, followed by an endless litany of highly embarrassed excuses.

The two friends were pampered with the most delicious food that Pierre had ever tasted in his life; there seemed to be an unlimited supply of pies, cakes, pork, pasties, poultry, game, or fresh fish from the rivers as soon as Pierre's majordomo allowed the innkeepers a short glimpse of his well-filled wallet with its gleaming golden coins. The excellent food was accompanied by the best wines of the region, crisp whites or warm reds – in essence, every evening meal became a feast.

Armand and Pierre were used to sharing a room from when they had travelled before, and this time Armand hotly accused Pierre of snoring like a pig as soon as he had drunk too much wine. But Pierre was not to be intimidated. "If I snore like a pig, you snore like a boar – better keep your mouth shut."

In this leisurely way they continued for several days until they reached Montrésor in the light of the setting sun. The chateau was of medium size – much smaller than Hertford Castle. Situated on a steep hill above the village it had offered protection for the villagers since the dark periods of war between England and France. Those days were long gone and Montrésor had been enlarged and renovated over the course of the centuries, and new wings had been added. But the chateau still sat proudly and protectively above the village like a mother hen protecting its chicks.

In the mellow light of the approaching evening the chateau appeared as a vision from a fairy tale, its towers and turrets mirrored in the dark green waters that once might have been a moat but now formed an enchanted lake in front of it. The cream-coloured stone was bathed in the rays of the setting sun, transforming its original colour with a rose complexion, a sublime picture of breathtaking beauty. As if an unknown artist had decided to add a final touch to this picture, a group of swans floated majestically on the lake, their white feathering reflecting the colours of the evening sun.

Pierre had insisted on riding the last leg of his journey – he had wanted to be sure to spot Montrésor early enough and not to miss the slightest detail. Now he sat still on his horse, absorbing the first view of his chateau.

He noticed that Armand had moved his horse closer and he heard his friend say, "What a nice little chateau to add to your collection, my dear friend. I only do hope the chambermaids match the beauty of the building."

Pierre had to laugh – obviously not even the most romantic setting could make a deep impression on Armand.

Their arrival must have been heralded early as a whole army of servants was standing to attention when their cavalcade drove up to the entrance. Pierre entered the huge entrance hall with its imposing fireplace and staircase and was greeted reverently by his servants, lined up according to rank, their faces full of curiosity and nervous anticipation. His estate must be bigger than he had thought, as the vast hall was really quite crowded.

He glanced at the bailiff and, keeping in mind the remarks of Armand's father, he studied his face, carefully trying to spot any signs of treachery or nervousness. But his bailiff looked at him with a large open smile as if he were genuinely pleased to welcome his new master.

The bailiff of the chateau was of medium height; Pierre reckoned that he must be well over forty years old. He was of slight build, agile, and he wore his long but sparse locks bound together with a dark ribbon. The bailiff's dress was neat yet unassuming – he looked the perfect incarnation of the old and faithful servant. His brown eyes had a slightly unfocused glance. It was obvious that he was in the habit of wearing glasses.

The Marquis de Saint Paul had warned Pierre several times to make time and check the financial records thoroughly as it was only to be expected that funds may have been diverted by his staff after so many years of neglect. Looking at the smiling face of his bailiff, Pierre felt relieved – probably the Marquis had been too much of a Cassandra after all. He smiled warmly back at the man and said, "I've been looking forward to meeting you very much, indeed. I must confess that I'm totally inexperienced in the art of administration and hope that you'll teach me a lot during the coming weeks!"

His bailiff bowed deeply and answered, "It'll be my pleasure to introduce Monsieur le Marquis to all aspects of this estate as it has been my pleasure to serve the family for decades. Your lordship may be assured that your affairs are in excellent order."

Pierre nodded and turned his head towards Armand as to see if his friend had followed this exchange of words but he noticed that his friend – as usual – had different priorities on his mind. Armand had been scanning the female staff and to his great delight had detected several promising parlour maids eyeing him with interest, smoothing their gowns and moistening their lips to make them look inviting and attractive.

Armand returned their inviting glances with a dashing smile and a challenging wink, which had the effect of knocking the majority of the female staff completely off their feet – no, Pierre had to correct himself, even some of his male servants seemed to be taken in by the charms of his friend. Pierre couldn't help smiling as well – the situation was starting to amuse him greatly.

Pierre wasn't aware though that his smile had exactly the same effect on his female servants. His already handsome face now radiated an even more irresistible charm and there would be hours of animated discussion that evening in the servants' quarters to decide who was more attractive, the dashing young count with the adventurous twinkle in his eyes or the noble and handsome blond Marquis.

"I could imagine having them both," giggled a chambermaid to her best friend, shutting her mouth just in time as the housekeeper had entered the kitchen, a colourless woman with a skinny, almost shrivelled appearance, but who ruled the household with a rod of iron. She had come on the pretext of discussing tomorrow's planning but secretly hoped for a pleasant hour of gossiping with the cook about the newcomers. She waved the chambermaids away like tiresome flies and they fled immediately; the housekeeper was known to be a sharp-tongued woman to be reckoned with.

That night, Armand and Pierre were sitting near the open fire. Although the days had become very warm, almost hot, the castle was as cold as the grave inside and a small fire had been lit. Armand described enthusiastically one of the chambermaids. "She's got truly beautiful eyes, did you notice? And her figure is first class, a bit short maybe, but everything there you could possibly wish for!"

"You're unbelievable! Is this the same man speaking to me who was sitting love-stricken in Paris and kept repeating the word 'Julia' all the time?" answered Pierre, imitating Armand's sighs as he pronounced Julia's name. "Don't you know what you want?"

Armand looked at Pierre as if he came from a different planet. "Of course I know. It's fairly simple: I love and adore Julia, but do I have to like a monk now, so long as I don't even know if or when I'm going to meet her again? Wake up, Pierre, we're not even eighteen years old, why should we live like monks if we're not married? I want to enjoy life – I have spent enough time in a stuffy monastery – and I can only recommend you do the same!"

Pierre spared himself further discussions but Armand had planted the seed of doubt, after all they were really still very young... and he had to admit that the pretty chambermaid had very inviting lips. Pierre decided that it was time to stop these dangerous thoughts and go straight upstairs to his bed – Armand's remarks were becoming highly dangerous! Jean undressed Pierre, but realizing that his usually pleasant master was moody and restless tonight he decided to keep quiet and left the room wondering why Pierre was displaying such a short temper tonight.

The next morning Pierre met Armand for breakfast and it didn't take a lot of intuition to see that his friend must have spent a very pleasant night. He sat on his chair, legs sprawling comfortably and purring like a satisfied tomcat helping himself to a large cup of milk. Some drops of the milk remained like white pearls on his dark moustache, reinforcing the image of a large, contented cat.

"I don't need to ask if you slept well?" Pierre grumbled.

"Not really," answered Armand, his answer coming with a slur as he was munching on a piece of cake at the same time. "But if you desire, I can go into some spicy details," he offered.

Pierre shot him a poisonous glance but preferred to decline this generous offer.

At least the rest of the day offered some diversion. Pierre had decided that he wanted to get to know his estate and thus they found themselves riding through the beautiful landscape of the Loire, vibrant with the vivid colours and flowery scents of early summer. They passed through villages and hamlets, lush meadows, crossed small streams of clear bustling water until they paused to have a picnic in the shadow of an old oak tree that must have been growing there since the beginning of time.

Armand was surprised to notice Pierre secretly scribbling down from time to time some figures on a crumpled sheet of paper. His curiosity aroused, he decided to ask Pierre later what this was about.

The next days passed with almost the same routine, only that Pierre would closet himself away every morning with his bailiff in order to go through the accounts. Luckily he had learnt the secrets of administration from his cousin Charles when he had stayed in Hertford. Quickly he discovered that the system in France was slightly different, but in the end easy to understand and comparable. Keeping Armand's father's warning in mind, Pierre kept feigning inexperience and let his bailiff do the talking – but he had to admit that all records that were presented to him looked immaculate and above reproach.

After a week of this tedious routine Pierre thought that his head was about to explode – he had been inundated by documents, files, bombarded with facts – in truth, he felt as if he had been sent back to the monastery school.

When his bailiff offered to accompany Pierre and his friend to one of his villages in the proximity of Montrésor and to arrange meetings with his tenants, Pierre answered, exhausted, "I feel totally crushed – I think I have seen and learnt enough during these past few days. I'll grant him a day off today. I feel like having a break and will make an excursion to the river with only my friend and the grooms."

The bailiff bowed reverently, secretly relieved to see that his new master had finally seemed to succumb and become bored and tired by the mass of documents he had produced. Gladly he accepted Pierre's proposal and they parted on the best of terms.

Liberated from administrative tasks Pierre, Armand and their grooms left Montrésor and rode down to the Loire valley, eager to enjoy a relaxing day off. They had been riding already for some time when Armand suddenly made a sign for the grooms to stop as they had reached a tranquil bend in the river, ideal for bathing.

The water glistened invitingly in the sun and low-hanging branches of willow trees provided pleasant shade for a picnic. The hot sun had been beating down on them relentlessly since they had left the castle and Armand had long been hankering to plunge into the tempting river as sweat was running down his spine and his wet shirt seemed to be glued to his body.

But nothing in the world could make their grooms join them; secretly they made the sign of the cross to ward off evil – only those who were insane or possessed by the devil would bathe in this cold and clear water! Pierre laughed and asked them to look after the horses but to move on a bit and to rest further away from where they were, just to make sure that Armand and he remained undisturbed.

Pierre and Armand stripped naked and enjoyed their bath, the wonderful sensation of cold water streaming around their bodies. Like happy children they ended up splashing and chasing each other. The grooms looked at each other with knowing glances: those gentlemen were most definitely insane!

Afterwards Pierre lay next to Armand, drying himself in the warm sun.

"That was great!" Armand sighed with satisfaction, "but Pierre, you still look worried all the same. What's on your mind?"

Pierre was fascinated. He always marvelled at how his friend could appear so flippant and yet seem to know exactly all the time what he was thinking. Not answering directly, Pierre fumbled at the pocket of his breeches that lay close to him. He extracted the crumpled sheet of paper and read aloud: "Nine farms compared to 12 farms, 7 to 8 farms….."

Armand looked at his friend as if he had gone mad.

41

Pierre laughed, but Armand could hear that he wasn't really amused. "I can assure you, my friend, I'm not insane. I simply started to count and memorize the number of farms that we visited each day. Later I compared these figures with the revenues and numbers I found in the official records. Nothing matches. Either the number of tenants is too low – or in some cases the number of farms is correct but their yield is only half of what we'd make in Hertford – and yet this region here possesses an even better climate and better soil." He paused and looked soberly at Armand. "My nice smiling bailiff therefore is the biggest rascal you could imagine. He's been shafting me for years. Now, tell me, how do you propose I should deal with him?"

Armand looked at him full of respect. "You're a smart one. Who'd have thought it, what with your baby face and innocent blue eyes!" Then his face became sober and he furrowed his brows. "I'm afraid, Pierre, that you have no choice. If you ignore it or you show clemency they'll all be stealing from you in no time and – even worse – you'll lose all of your authority as their lord and master. You need to be severe, punish him in public and according to the law to make sure that your estate doesn't end in chaos!"

Pierre had become very pale. "I knew that you'd answer like this and I also know that I have no choice. But what does the law foresee in such a case – I really have no experience?"

"For heaven's sake, Pierre, I'm not a lawyer either. Terrible bookworms if you ask me! But from the examples that my father has mentioned in the past, the bailiff will be convicted by the court to death by hanging, I guess. As it's a big thing he won't stand a chance of being deported or sent to the galleys. Even if he bribes the judges, they won't dare to offend you as a Marquis of France and will apply the law without mercy."

Pierre looked decidedly unhappy, and his face had taken on a greenish tint. "Will he be tortured?" he asked with an unsteady voice.

Armand only shrugged his shoulders, but declined to elaborate, yet without any additional words Pierre understood clearly that he had no other option but to persevere – regardless of what might happen to the bailiff.

They rode back in silence and the grooms were astonished that the two young men who had been playing and splashing in the water like happy children all of a sudden seemed so gloomy – but who could ever understand what went on in the minds of noble gentlemen?

Pierre spent a terrible night while nightmarish scenes of past executions he had witnessed as a boy in Reims chased him in his dreams. Gruesome executions had been special events, part of a rare and exciting weekend entertainment. But how different it felt, now that *he* had to take the decision to send someone to the gallows! Pierre decided that he needed to finish this chapter as fast as possible; there was no way that he could go on meeting his bailiff, keep smiling at him as if nothing had ever happened, knowing not only that this man had betrayed him, but that in fact he was now a doomed man.

After a swift and unusually taciturn breakfast, Armand carefully chose four of his father's most loyal musketeers and led them into Pierre's study. Jean saw himself dispatched to search for the bailiff and inform him that Monsieur le Marquis was demanding his immediate presence.

Only minutes later the bailiff bustled breathlessly into the room, holding his usual bulky files under his arm. He must have run hard as soon as he had received the summons.

Today Pierre was already sitting in the carved armchair chair which was usually reserved for the master of the estate, his face extremely pale and serious. Starting to feel uneasy the bailiff suddenly became aware of the unusual presence of armed musketeers in the small room and instinctively he turned his face to the door, maybe hoping to bolt out and escape.

But Jean had anticipated such a reaction and already closed the door blocking the exit with his muscular body. Since yesterday evening Jean had sensed that something serious must be going on. Pierre's moods were rarely a secret to him. Jean was not truly astonished that the bailiff was about to be in trouble. The estate had been left without supervision and a real master for many years. This could only be viewed as an open invitation to steal: an open door may tempt a saint, as the saying went in England.

The bailiff's panicky glance went back to Pierre and his mind went blank. Unconsciously he noticed that Pierre had started to speak; with a detached voice his master kept mentioning numbers, villages, names, produce – it all sounded like dry accountancy but to the bailiff it held a clear message of vital significance: his game was up! This innocent baby-faced youngster had unravelled his intricate schemes of embezzlements in only fourteen days.

It seemed so unreal – the new Marquis had unearthed what neither his uncle nor his cousin, the arrogant Henri de Beauvoir, had ever been able to or had cared to detect. Bored to death by the mass of documents and files the bailiff astutely used to produce for anybody who ever came to query him, and blinded by the position of their own elevated rank, they would listlessly look through the piles of documents, stifling a yawn but unable to hide the greed in their eyes, happy to take home as many golden coins as they could possibly find in his chests.

This callow youth with his innocent blue eyes had not only retained all the important figures but had taken the pains to check them. The new Marquis must therefore be aware that thousands of gold livres had found their way into the bailiff's pockets over the course of the last years. *Should he confess, fall on his knees or – better – plead his innocence and beg mercy of his young lord?* But one look into these blue eyes – eyes that had turned all of a sudden steely cold and full of contempt – told the bailiff that he could spare himself the effort. The judgment had been passed and Pierre de Beauvoir had decided to execute it – the verdict was guilty.

Paralysed by fear, still trying to come to come to grips with the unexpected reversal of his fortunes, the bailiff stood in front of the desk facing his nemesis, in the form of the young Marquis. He had to steady himself as his bowels seemed to have taken on a life of their own, and his heart was pounding like a blacksmith's hammer.

Strong arms were seizing his own, as rough and painful, they bent his own arms backwards and seconds later a string of rope cut into the flesh of his hands and deeply into his wrist. The bailiff winced with pain. A musketeer swiftly bound his hands behind his back, maliciously making sure that the strings not only hurt but would make him move awkwardly as they were too short.

The four musketeers lined up, keeping the bailiff in their centre like a prisoner of state. Then they marched out of the room with noisy boots right through the great hall where the other servants had already gathered (news always spread fast – especially if it related to a juicy scandal). Standing in huddled clusters, the chateau servants were gawking with open mouths at the bailiff. This man had been their superior and the epitome of respectability only minutes ago, and now he had become an outcast. When the bailiff passed one of the grooms he saw how the young man spat on the floor in contempt.

The soldiers and their limping prisoner marched further to one of the towers, home of the chateau's prison. Instinctively the bailiff shied back from its entrance but the heavy oak door with its forged fittings opened with an unpleasant screeching sound and without mercy he was dragged inside, then pushed down the narrow slippery stairs until they had reached the dungeon. A secluded world of its own, the dungeon was a silent universe guarded by centuries-old thick walls and iron bars, devoid of any sound beyond the marching of the boots of the musketeers that haunted the chambers with their eerie echo.

The bailiff's nostrils filled with the smells of this terrifying place, a peculiar mix of dampness, mould, rotten straw and a faint yet much more disturbing notion of dried blood, urine and excrement. His nervous glance roamed the cavernous room where he was standing now, a place that was in fact terribly familiar to him. Yet it must have been months since he had set foot in this place. He tried to remember when was the last time that he had come down into this antechamber of Hades. Like a flash of light the memories suddenly came back – he must have visited this accursed place in order to witness the interrogation of one of the rebellious chateau tenants who had tried to hide a part of his meagre harvest when the time for tax collection had come. All of a sudden, the long forgotten cries of the man seemed to be filling the prison chambers anew. As soon as the bailiff had ordered for the thumbscrews to be put into action, the peasant had proved an easy victim to crack. How well he remembered now the bloodied hands of the howling and sobbing victim.

The bailiff fought a wave of nausea as his thoughts continued to dwell on the victim: the frantic yelling of the convicted man when he had been flogged after this ordeal as his final punishment, until streams of blood had oozed down his back, torn to pieces, and he had lost consciousness. The bailiff's men had only laughed; they relished this kind of diversion.

The bailiff was only too well aware of the torturer's equipment that was kept ready and well maintained in this same room. He tried to avoid looking at the dark shadow of the iron maiden; just the thought of her made his stomach turn and his blood run cold. He was almost relieved not to be tied down on the interrogation chair with the iron spikes or stretched on the rack but was thrown instead into one of the adjacent prison cells – maybe he'd be spared torture but most likely his tormentors had simply decided that he'd be dealt with tomorrow.

The musketeers closed the cold iron clamps that fastened him with heavy chains to the wall, he felt a last painful kicking by someone's boots, then the prison door was closed noisily and he sat alone in the dark prison cell. He heard the familiar sound of the marching boots once more, the hollow echo dying away as the musketeers left the dungeon.

The bailiff started to shiver; inside the prison cell it was cold as the grave. Of course no blankets had been provided – only some rotten straw lay piled on the ground. Disgusted by the smell emanating from the decomposing straw the bailiff decided to stay upright and lean against the wall. But soon fatigue took its toll and his feet gave way – full of despair he sank down like a crumpled old puppet on strings.

As if the leaden silence and the cold were not unsettling enough, the soft sound of scurrying feet all of sudden sent new shivers of fright down his spine. This was the approaching rats, their eyes glowing in the dark. Immediately the bailiff rattled his rusty chains to chase them away and, as expected, they scampered back into the corners. But he knew – as they would know – that sooner or later he would become theirs; it was just a matter of time. Overwhelmed by self-pity the desperate bailiff started to weep. This was hell – and this night was only the beginning.

Back in the chateau Pierre was sifting through piles of documents, records and notes. Armand kept his mouth shut as Pierre's face clearly expressed that it would take very little to make him explode. Pierre was furious and disgusted; he felt hurt and betrayed.

45

In the meantime, village gossip had been spreading the news about the treacherous bailiff with the result that more and more villagers dared to come forward with all kinds of stories and complaints – the dam of silence was breaking. Meanwhile the bailiff's assistants kneeled in front of Pierre, tearfully begging for mercy and offering their full cooperation with the inquiries.

Pierre was disgusted by their hypocritical oaths of allegiance and his first impulse was to have them arrested – he was sure that they must have known what was going on. But after some deliberation and gentle prodding from Armand he decided to give them the opportunity to confess and repent – an act they executed with amazing speed and thoroughness – and which helped the speed of discovery enormously as Armand had rightly predicted.

Both assistants assured Pierre tearfully that they had never seen as much as an extra tankard of ale – all of the embezzled money had found its way directly to the pockets of their boss. By dinner time Pierre had understood that not only a staggering amount of money, but all kinds of produce, such as wheat, wine, and whatever harvest his estates produced, had found their way into the seemingly bottomless pockets of his former servant.

"Armand, this is unbelievable. It actually got worse every year! The past two years this locust even increased the taxes, bleeding my tenants to death. Most families lost at least one of their members during the past harsh winter because there wasn't enough food left to feed themselves!"

Now that people had found the courage to talk, Pierre was to discover that starvation had haunted his tenants during the last winter. Pierre was still seething with anger and frustration, therefore dinner was an unusually taciturn affair. As the lord of this castle it was his right to judge the bailiff and, having heard and seen so much, there could not be the slightest doubt what his judgment would be.

After a second night of difficult sleep and bad dreams Pierre was brutally woken up by his servants yelling outside his bedroom. There was no way of ignoring the shouting voices. Upset, Pierre was just about to yell back that they should shut up and keep quiet when Jean broke into his room, his bronze-coloured face unusually flushed. "Monsieur le Marquis, please excuse the noise, but something dreadful has happened. That scum of a bailiff has escaped from prison!"

"But I ordered him to be kept under supervision day and night!" Pierre shouted hotly – but Jean only shrugged his shoulders. *This must be just another bad dream!* But as soon as his brain had worked out that this must indeed be the truth, he jumped out of bed, splashed some water on his face and dived into his clothes. In the meantime Armand had also been woken up by the faithful Jean and only five minutes later both friends rushed down to the dungeon to see with their own eyes what had happened.

The scene waiting for them was eerie and took them by surprise. In the light of their torches they made out the figure of the lone young guard – now dead – who had been placed on night duty, slumped on his chair, his trunk and arms sprawled on the rough wooden table, an empty cup of spilled ale lying on the floor.

The flames of the torches flickered in the draught and whenever their dancing light shone on the dead body it seemed to come back to life and move. The musketeer holding the torch quickly made a sign behind his back to ward off evil – Armand was tempted to do the same.

Quickly Armand bent down and snatched the empty cup. He sniffed at it and hours later the cup still gave off a strange herbal scent. Having taken a good look round the guard's room they continued the search by inspecting the prison cell where empty chains were dangling idly from the walls as the only reminder that only a night before a prisoner had been chained here.

Pierre studied the chains and the lock of the door. It was obvious what had happened – the bailiff had been freed by a person who had been in possession of the right keys, as no sign of forcing the door or the locks could be detected.

"I don't like this at all," Armand said, his voice unusually serious.

"We have a traitor among us," said Pierre, stating the obvious, hoping that his coarse voice would not betray his shock too much.

"And he didn't hesitate to kill, just look at the poor young lad – he paid with his life for a cup of ale… Which means that he must have known and trusted his murderer." Armand approached the dead guard and covered his distorted face with a scarf.

"I'm quite speechless. Your father did of course mention that I'd be likely to discover plenty of problems, but maybe his feeling of delicacy forbade him from mentioning that murder would be among them," Pierre commented sarcastically.

Armand grimaced. What a terrible start to the day…

Once more Pierre was amazed how fast gossip could spread. When they came back to the hall the servants had already heard about the bailiff's escape and the guard's murder. He saw some of the female servants sobbing quietly, as the young prison guard had lived in the chateau and had generally been well liked.

"An ever so trusting soul," the cook sobbed, "and always so full of jokes and how he loved to eat my apple pancakes, he never could get enough…" The rest of the sentence was drowned in a flood of tears and Pierre retreated hastily into his study to discuss with Armand their next steps. This was a nightmare; until today the chateau's inhabitants had been like a big family. It was even more of a nightmare, as the bailiff had made sure in the course of his many years of service that he had plenty of his own relatives working under his management.

As Pierre and Armand crossed the hall they could already see that allegiances had been forming, and small groups of people were standing together and eyeing the others with suspicion – soon the atmosphere would become unbearable.

"How can I find out who's involved and who's not?" muttered Pierre when they were alone in the study, still cramped with the piles of books and documents of the castle's administration.

"Have the assistants tortured," proposed Armand without a lot of enthusiasm.

"I couldn't." Pierre looked at his friend as if he'd gone mad. "And I doubt that they'd tell the truth. I'm sure I'd confess whatever people wanted to hear from me as soon as a red-hot poker came anywhere near me. I don't think that I'd make a good hero in this respect."

"I guess I wouldn't either, nobody would in fact," Armand consented. "I shouldn't be telling you this openly of course, but, as members of noble families, both of us are expected to withstand small nuisances like torture. But back to your question: you'll need to oust the bailiff's family and relations all the same, you have no choice. If you keep them here, life will be a hell for all of us."

Pierre was just about to agree when Jean rushed unceremoniously into the room. He looked terrible: his bronze skin had taken on a greenish, waxy tint.

"Jean, what's going on?" exclaimed Pierre in surprise, but Armand was already rushing to Jean's rescue, as Jean was choking badly. Armand had concluded that first of all Jean would be in urgent need of a bowl or bucket. All Armand could spot was a large jug of water, which he produced just in time, as Jean started to vomit as soon as the jug was placed close to his face.

"I'm deeply sorry, Your Grace!" Jean stammered, trying to inhale some fresh air and stop choking.

"If you're not going to make a habit of this behaviour, you're excused," said Armand gruffly, but without his usual flippancy. He felt that another disaster must have happened; there could be no other explanation for such behaviour.

Jean succeeded in regaining his composure and after downing the cup of strong wine that Pierre had offered him he spoke. "It's just terrible, Monsieur le Marquis! One of the parlour maids has been missing since yesterday night. They didn't dare tell us because she was known to leave the chateau frequently and meet her fiancé in the village – at least that's what she called him. As she always used to be back on duty on time and was an excellent maid, the housekeeper turned a blind eye to her nightly excursions. We've found her, but I'm not sure that your lordship will want to come and see this."

Pierre braced himself for the worst; wasn't it his duty as the lord of the castle to come and see himself what was going on?

Silently they marched down the stairs, and leaving the castle they crossed the cobbled yard and walked towards the stable doors. The stables were unusually silent. Apart from the faint snorting of the horses they could only discern the sound of frantic sobbing, interrupted by the wailing sound of a woman who kept repeating the girl's name, again and again.

"Her mother," Jean said. "She's been searching everywhere and then finally found her here – I guess she wishes she hadn't."

With a sinking heart Pierre entered the dusty stables, bracing himself for the worst. It took some time for him to adjust his eyes to the dim light, as the shutters that were open let in only a few rays of daylight. A small group of servants had gathered awkwardly around the wailing mother and as their master approached, the servants started to back away and stood respectfully near an empty stall. Pierre was amazed to detect confidence and trust in some of their faces – as if they were convinced that his presence alone could fix the matter.

Pierre and Armand entered the empty stall and Jean started gently to pull the girl's mother away. Although she was completely distraught she seemed to feel instinctively that Jean meant well and allowed him to guide her out of the stall, burying her face, wet from tears, in his protective arm.

Pierre forced himself to look at their find. The murderer must have possessed a peculiar sense of humour, for he had spread the girl's gown as if it was laid out on a bed, only waiting for the girl to step inside – but there was no body. But on top of the gown lay the severed head of the parlour maid, her eyes still wide open in surprise rather than pain. A wide smile had been painted on her face with her own blood, now dried and congealed. Her head was crowned with a fancy bonnet of summer flowers. The murderer had taken such pains to ridicule his victim, it was as if the slaying of the young maid hadn't been horrible enough. The sight and smell of this discovery were truly sickening. No wonder even Jean had gagged.

Pierre heard another choking sound, and this time it was Armand, standing in the corner gagging. He had immediately recognized the girl – she had shared his bed only two days before.

Two days later the sky had veiled itself with a fitting grey of mourning and rain was drizzling from heavy clouds when all the bailiff's relatives obeyed the command to leave the chateau, their belongings strapped to some makeshift carts or on their backs. They had accepted Pierre's decision meekly, understanding that he had no choice – the wheel of fortune had turned. The women had been sobbing quietly, two of them pregnant, one close to giving birth. Pierre had given each of them a goat to provide milk for their babies and the woman whose belly was heavy with child had moved to her knees and kissed his hand to thank him while Pierre had to fight back his tears.

Meanwhile the men tried to keep a straight face. They had no idea where to go to and settle or how to earn a living. In a matter of only three days their lives had been shattered. A nightmare had become reality – for all inhabitants of the chateau.

Pierre withdrew into the chateau and watched from the window of his study the miserable cavalcade that crept slowly out of the gates, now heavily guarded by the de Saint Paul men. Some servants had gathered to witness this modern version of banishment from paradise but they kept silent. To Pierre's surprise nobody seemed to be in the mood for taunting those who had been living with them under the same roof for so many years.

Would this be the end of it? Pierre sighed. Somehow he had an inkling that their trouble was far from over.

The girl sat in the armchair looking listlessly at her embroidery and tapping nervously with her fingers on the armrest.

"How entertaining, my dear," commented Céline dryly, "but if I may make a suggestion, could you please change the rhythm from time to time? It would vastly improve the quality of your performance!"

"Touché, I really am a dreadful bore!" Marie jumped up guiltily and hugged Céline. Sadly it was true, she had become more and more restless and irritated. Although her father's health had improved, her parents were still trying to woo their neighbours, still daydreaming about a marriage that would reunite the vast vineyards of the two families – the chance of a lifetime, as they viewed it.

Marie had intended leaving secretly and accompanying Céline and Charles back to Paris so as to avoid a painful and most likely very tearful confrontation with her parents but Charles had flatly refused any such notion. "You're a lady, not a commoner," he had admonished her. "If you want to come to Paris with us you're warmly welcome – you know this – but you cannot leave your parents and just sneak out of your home like a guilty parlourmaid leaving her job to join her lover. Céline will support you, but please behave properly and ask your parents for their blessing, *comme il faut*."

Meekly Marie had accepted his verdict but since she had spoken with Charles she had suddenly started to refine the art of procrastination. Every day she found something else to do, any excuse was good enough in order to put off the dreaded moment of telling her parents that she must leave. Day after day she said to herself, *I'll tell them tomorrow.*

Pierre's letters didn't help either. Between the lines she could read his frustration that the invitation to join her in Reims and be able to ask for her hand had not been forthcoming, but she simply couldn't summon the strength to write to him with the truth, that her parents had different plans for her future.

This went on for days but finally Marie started running out of excuses to delay any further the dreaded discussion with her parents. One morning she looked critically at her – admittedly very pretty – image in the mirror, inhaled deeply and spoke to herself out loud. "You're a loathsome coward, Marie," she chided herself. "If you want to marry Pierre, stop hiding and speak with your parents!"

Thus it was at dinner that same evening that she decided to take the plunge and speak up. As usual dinner was a sumptuous event but Marie had difficulties savouring any of the delicacies that the cook had skilfully prepared and decorated with the greatest love and care. Mechanically Marie chewed and swallowed whatever her hand had decided to take, spooning down a soup that tasted to her like water. She didn't care and she didn't even notice.

Tonight dinner seemed to stretch endlessly until the servants received the usual sign that they were allowed to withdraw. Taking a deep breath, Marie took her courage in both hands and stood up. Beautiful, though unusually pale, she addressed her bewildered parents.

"My dearest and beloved parents, I have an announcement to make. I must confess that I haven't been able to sleep for many days as I need to make a painful choice – a choice between my love and devotion to you, as a dutiful daughter, and my future: to join the man I love and whom I want to marry."

The dining room suddenly fell silent, but it was a leaden, menacing silence that reigned, the harbinger of a violent storm to come.

Marie's mother gripped her armrest as if she were clinging to a sinking raft. The knuckles of her hands gleamed white as she clung to her chair. Her face turned scarlet and she was fighting to find the right words. Marie's father noticed his wife's turmoil but he gave her a quick sign to keep silent and let Marie speak.

"My dearest father and mother, I'm terribly sorry. I know that I should sit here and wait respectfully until one day our neighbour might consider me suitable enough to become his bride. But if ever Monsieur de Saint Remy does find the willpower to ask for my hand I have decided to turn down his proposal all the same. I cannot and will not marry our neighbour as I'm in love with another man – even if I know that this decision will hurt you…"

Marie's voice broke and tears started rolling down her face. "My dearest parents, I have a confession to make. Although I love you both, greatly, I must follow my heart. I wish to join Pierre de Beauvoir and intend to marry him – for better or worse. Pierre has been waiting patiently to receive your invitation to come and ask for my hand as is customary. But as Mother adamantly refused to meet him, he sent me a message that can't wait any longer, he has pressing things to do. Pierre de Beauvoir will have to leave Paris and visit his estates at Montrésor, he'll no longer be able to come to Reims. Therefore I've asked Céline and Charles if they would be willing to accompany me and chaperon me to visit him there."

Marie paused for a moment and gathered all of her strength. Her eyes had taken on a mutinous expression. "Mother, father, I simply cannot bear the thought of staying here, waiting forever and withering away like an old spinster as I will never give in and marry the son our neighbours. Please let me go and see Pierre de Beauvoir again… and please give me your blessing, I simply cannot imagine a life without the man I love but I cannot imagine a life either without your love and your blessing."

The last words had been uttered in a desperate whisper. Céline sat there, dabbing at her eyes with a handkerchief. She knew that Marie could be an excellent actor, but this speech had been no act, it had come straight from a desperate heart.

Marie's mother still sat frozen to her chair, erect as a statue, but her dark eyes were blazing with rage. All of a sudden she jumped up, lunging forward as if she was going to slap Marie. Marie's fears had been justified; her mother was not willing to tolerate such an act of open rebellion. Girls were supposed to obey, not to think.

But before Marie's mother was actually able to speak up or slap Marie's face, almost choking with anger, Marie's father gave her a sign to return to her chair and stay silent.

With quiet authority he took over. "Marie, you've greatly upset your mother and I expect you to apologize. My house is not a stage for third-class comedians, you're the only child and heiress of a noble family, we're no commoners, you should have learnt how to behave properly."

Meekly Marie whispered, "I apologize, Mother, yet I wish that you could understand me."

The next sentence came unexpectedly and Marie could see how much effort it took her father to continue. "Your mother had a very unhappy experience when she was a young girl like you, and painfully she had to learn to distinguish between real love and devotion as opposed to the stupid blindness caused by the bliss of immature love. She means well, she wants to protect you from the pain and the shame that such feelings can cause. Marie, please believe me, we both want the best for you, even if you may not understand us at this stage."

Marie's eyes started to fill with tears. All he said was true enough, but if her father wouldn't support her case, there was no hope left.

"Of course your mother has already told that you fancy marriage to the young Marquis de Beauvoir – I understand that he recently obtained his title officially. I really don't appreciate your behaviour and obstinacy but... I shall forgive you."

Marie waited breathlessly as her father paused. He then said, "My stance in this matter is this: You may leave with Charles and Céline for Montrésor if Céline promises to guard you well. On no account will you be allowed to remain alone with him, I think this much is obvious. Pierre de Beauvoir will only be welcome as my son-in-law if he proves to me beyond doubt his continuous devotion to you. To test if both of you are serious and the feeling you call love is not only a passing passion of youth, you are to return home to Reims after the summer and wait here until Christmas. If Pierre de Beauvoir's feelings remain unchanged and he visits us after Christmas and proposes to marry you afterwards, then he may have your hand with our blessing. If he doesn't, you've learnt a useful lesson. If you don't return to Reims to wait for him and try instead to precipitate things, you'll no longer be considered my daughter. And this is my final word on this issue."

The room fell absolutely silent. Only the faint noises of clattering dishes and conversation seeping into the room from the servants' quarters could be heard. Marie swallowed hard; all of her senses rebelled against her father's proposal. She had seen herself sinking into Pierre's arms immediately – hadn't they waited long enough already, all these months when they had been staying together in England?

On the other hand Marie had to admit that her father's verdict was borne out of genuine concern for her happiness. It mirrored his deep affection for her, even if she now knew the truth, that she was his daughter in name only. Marie glanced at her mother. She sat there, her cheeks glowing red with dismay. She hated to be reminded of her past and she was only too aware that it would be impossible to keep their neighbours interested in the marriage she had so skilfully arranged for her daughter if any decision was postponed until next year and if Marie remained obstinate.

But her father had made up his mind and her mother would accept his decision – but her mother's furious eyes were blazed at Marie.

Thank goodness looks can't kill, thought Marie.

To their surprise, it was Céline's husband, Charles, who broke the uneasy silence that ensued. "Marie, I didn't realize until today that your father must be a descendant of King Solomon. I don't want to meddle in your family affairs but as Pierre is my cousin I think I'm entitled to speak up as well. I must say that your father's proposal is as wise as it's kind and only fair. Both of you are very young, waiting a couple of months may sound terrible to you tonight, but it's nothing in the long run. I waited years to find the right wife," and he beamed full of affection at Céline who was sitting next to him and had the decency to blush like a young girl when he looked at her.

"And I think I know and can judge my cousin Pierre de Beauvoir's character very well by now. Maybe I should mention that he carries the English title of Duke of Hertford as well – he's a very desirable match indeed. I have grown to love Pierre like a brother. I'm absolutely sure that he'll insist on marrying Marie with the blessing of her family. Maybe the following anecdote will alleviate your fears that he might not be seriously considering a marriage. Knowing that Pierre was head over heels in love with your daughter I took the liberty to negotiate in his name a bargain with the King of England, as Pierre, with his status of the Duke of Hertford needs royal permission to marry a lady of foreign descent. My cousin paid a considerable amount for his Majesty's acceptance as the timing seemed particularly favourable to finding an agreement with King Charles."

Tactfully Charles did not mention the greedy eyes of the cash-strapped King when he had accepted the proposed deal. *He nearly bit my hand off* . Charles recalled the situation and had to suppress a grin.

He now looked at Marie's mother and casually dropped a hint about the heap of gold coins that had passed from the well-filled Hertford treasury into the King's empty pockets. Amused Marie noticed that – against her firmest intentions – her mother was deeply impressed, although she tried hard to remain aloof. The amount was truly staggering; sponsoring a new warship would probably have come cheaper.

"I allowed myself to mention this episode only in order to underline that Pierre de Beauvoir's intentions have always been nothing but honourable towards your daughter. He'll be delighted to come to Reims and propose in the winter."

Marie's father, who had seemed very tense, suddenly started to smile and relax. "If Pierre's only half as pleasant and intelligent as you are, he'll be very welcome in our family."

"That's a great compliment and I accept it with pleasure!" Charles seemed truly delighted by Marie's father's reply. Pierre might only be half as big or heavy as I am, but he'll definitely make a great – better let me say outstanding – son-in-law and I'm happy that he should marry into such a good family."

Marie had still been standing upright, anxiously facing her parents. Now she sensed that the mood was swinging, she relaxed and walked towards her father. Following a sudden impulse she kneeled in front of him, her embroidered silken gown rustling softly as she bent down.

It was customary for members of French noble families to address each other with the distant 'vous'; never would she have dared to use the more familiar 'you' to address one of her parents. The occasions when she had been hugged by her mother had been rare, mostly to console her when something terrible had happened. To everybody's surprise Marie gently took her father's hand, his skin dry as vellum when she touched it.

Slowly and reverently she drew her father's hand to her cheek then she kissed his hand, as a sign of her profound love and respect. She needed to show him that she had realized this evening how much he must love her. She now understood that her father's rejection of her marrying Pierre was borne out of a longing to protect her from a marriage that must look to him like an undesirable, dangerous adventure. Furthermore accepting Pierre's proposal would mean that she'd move far away from Reims and leave her parents – living a life of her own in Paris, or maybe in London. Her father this night had confirmed that he was ready to let her go – what greater proof of love could he ever give to her?

Her father felt hot tears dripping on the back of his hand. He smiled as though he must have understood instinctively her most intimate feelings. Gently he patted his daughter's head. With a low voice, so that nobody but Marie could hear him, he whispered, "There'll always be only one daughter for me, one daughter whom I love dearly. You'll always be close to my heart, wherever you are."

In the meantime Charles had turned all his charms on Marie's mother who started to thaw under this attack and cautiously accepted his overtures. Fighting with herself she finally started to speak. "I may need to apologize for my first reaction. I never met your cousin, the Marquis de Beauvoir, all my concerns were thus concentrated on the well-being of my only daughter. I now may need to change my ideas about his intentions and my daughter's future – as my husband has just mentioned, I wish to repeat our invitation: Once the Marquis has proved the seriousness of his intentions, he'll be welcome in our home as my son."

And as if the full implications of what had been discussed were dawning on her only now, she suddenly whispered, "I still can't fully believe this, my only daughter may not only become a Marchioness, she might even become a Duchess, she'll be invited to the royal court!" Then she jumped up, hugged a surprised husband and a flabbergasted Marie and a totally changed and exuberant mother was suddenly crying for the servants to bring the best wine of the house as they needed to have a toast.

It became a surprisingly cheerful evening after all.

That night, Marie's mother would whisper in the confidentiality of her bedchamber, "A genuine Duke has spent a fortune, enough gold to buy half of Reims, just to marry my beautiful daughter." And with genuine delight she whispered "Who would have thought that life could offer me such a sweet revenge for that handsome scoundrel who seduced me and sired my daughter. The mills of God may grind slowly, but they grind exceedingly fine."

*****

The buzzing sound came closer and closer until he had the impression that it must be heading straight for his ear. Henri cursed and opened his tired eyes. In the half light of dawn he couldn't make out any shapes of the enemy. But he was sure that the enemy was only hiding, as it was silent again.

Henri decided to try to get some more sleep, as it was far too early to get up. Instinctively he buried his ear in the soft pillows of his bed in order to protect it against further attacks. As soon as slumber started to overwhelm him, alas, there it was again, the bloodthirsty mosquito had detected a breach in the ramparts constituted by his pillows and the buzzing sound was coming closer and more dangerous than ever before. Henri jumped out of his bed – he despised mosquitoes!

Flailing wildly around him he danced around the huge bed that had become his own, as he had now officially been installed as the new Count de Roquemoulin. He nearly slipped on the rug that had been placed in front of the bed and grabbed the bedpost to avoid falling flat on his face. He only became aware how ridiculous he must have looked when a deep and melodious laughter came from his bed, a bed he had been sharing with Marina.

"You look like a real hero, fearlessly chasing wild and dangerous animals!" she mocked him.

Henri looked at her grudgingly. With her dark gypsy skin she never seemed to be bothered by mosquitoes, and even the bed bugs seemed to avoid her and preferred his sweet blue blood.

How dare she mock him? But before Henri found a chance to retaliate, Marina seductively dropped the blanket that had been covering her perfect body, lying there naked and inviting.

"Now, my lord, show me if you can sting as well – or if the mosquito has already sucked all the blood out of you!" she challenged him in her throaty voice and Henri blithely forgot about chasing mosquitoes – maybe it was too early to get up but there was never a wrong time to make love!

Afterwards Henri drifted into a satisfied slumber, noticing only in his subconscious that Marina had left his room through the secret door that led down to the tower gate. They had made an agreement that Marina should never appear as his mistress or wife. When Henri had told Marina for the first time that she must remain hidden from public view, even from his servants, his thinly veiled order had led to an outbreak of temper from Marina that had been truly remarkable, as flying at him with rage, she had gripped her dagger and had tried to plunge it into his body.

"Stop behaving like a silly child and listen!" he had ordered her, panting hard while he kept Marina pushed to the ground where she moved in his grip like a poisonous snake, seething with anger. "The only chance you'll ever have to be accepted as my wife will be to follow my plan. Officially we must meet in public for the first time outside France. I shall arrange to have documents made up to prove a noble Italian or Spanish lineage for you, my dearest Marina." Henri's voice was dripping with sarcasm and Marina spat in his face.

"If you keep spitting and behaving like a stupid gypsy girl it'll be hopeless. Now listen seriously: we need to explain your dark skin otherwise you'll never be a credible countess."

Suddenly his voice changed, and became soothing, seductive. "Believe in me, Marina. You dream of becoming a countess, but I can even make you a Marchioness, a Princess – rich beyond your imagination. You'll be my princess. You once told me that you don't believe in love, and neither do I. But we both worship one thing – *power and passion* – and the two of us, together we shall achieve great things, because we both share the same passion!"

Marina relented. Henri's logic and his argument had seemed convincing.

"Yes," Henri had thought. " Marina is definitely a clever girl, but she'll never be a lady."

Of course Henri had no intention of pursuing this plan. Henri de Beauvoir – or count Henri de Roquemoulin as he must be addressed now – would never marry a mere commoner. But Henri needed a truce with Marina and her tribe for the time being. In the meantime Marina had insisted on coming to him at night as often as possible. She was as possessive as she was jealous.

Secretly Henri was amused. Marina didn't seem to realize that at present his only temptation to stray away from her was her good-looking brother – a temptation definitely beyond his reach, for once in his life. Henri might be ruthless, but he was no fool. But each time her devilishly handsome brother accompanied her, Henri had to restrain himself and this feeling of suppressed desire was growing stronger and stronger.

On this morning Henri got up late and the glaring light of the sun was already pouring into his room. His fair skin was blotched with mosquito bites but he was humming all the same. Not only had the night with Marina been extremely pleasant but – what satisfaction – he had hunted down and killed the enemy this morning: a red stain in the bedsheets showed the crushed remains of the insolent attacker.

His valet was surprised to find him in a good humour. It had not taken long for his servants to find out Henri's true character and those who had realized it too late had regretted quickly any insolence under the whip. The new Count de Roquemoulin was a sea change from the previous one. Whereas the previous count had been kind and forgiving, the new count was demanding and the smallest mistakes could carry hefty penalties; the chateau prison – long idle and abandoned – was now back in use and well populated. A tense atmosphere of fear reigned in the household, gone were the merry days of relaxed work, and many mourned not only for the deceased count but also for the good old days, only realizing now how easy life had been for them back then.

Henri covered the blotches of the mosquito bites with whitish face powder. The deceased count had left him heaps of bottles and boxes of make-up – enough to provide for a complete harem. Henri hated imperfections; only his scar had made him proud, and the man who had inflicted it on him had been dead five minutes later anyhow.

Once his valet had dressed and brushed Henri's hair to a gleaming gold, the new count nodded shortly to show his satisfaction and then walked straight to the stables. A cup of chocolate had to do for breakfast. Gone were the days of sumptuous breakfasts (with lots of leftovers for the servants) that often stretched into early lunch.

On his way to the stables a footman hurried behind him. "Monsieur le Comte, pardonnez-moi, a visitor is waiting for you!"

Henri frowned. He did not intend to meet unannounced strangers, he was one of the wealthiest men of France now; how could someone dare to disturb him? "You should know by now that I never receive any visitors without proper appointment." Henri answered evenly, "Or would he like me to have his memory refreshed?"

Henri had not even raised his voice when he had casually added the last remark but his footman started to shake with fear. Yet he managed to reply, "I'm here on the orders of the bailiff, he sent me to you, my lord!"

"The bailiff?" Still the same even but dangerous voice.

"Yes, my lord, I was to inform you that a visitor has arrived who apparently wants to meet you urgently regarding some business with my lord's cousin, the Marquis de Beauvoir!"

"You idiot! Why didn't you explain immediately that the bailiff had sent you?" Henri said, his voice still void of emotion, although hate was spreading in his body like a wave of burning acid that swept through his veins. Only the cracking sound of his horsewhip echoed through the silent stable. Henri looked absent-mindedly at the broken whip and threw it with a dismissive gesture on the floor.

"They say that family matters are the most important matters in life, don't they?" he drawled, and then smiled at the footman who was still shivering with fear. The ghostly smile of his master did nothing to appease his worries. But his lord and master had already dismissed and forgotten him a second later. Henri walked back to the castle, his mind dwelling on one burning question only: Why would an unknown messenger bring news about his bastard cousin?

His bailiff met Henri in the antechamber of the study where his visitor was waiting in order to brief him. Reverently he bowed his head and addressed his new master. "Monsieur le Comte, I apologize for disturbing you, but I thought that this matter could be of importance for your lordship. At least the person who's waiting inside the study kept insisting that this meeting will be of paramount importance for your lordship's personal interest. He informed me that he has been working until recently as the bailiff of your cousin, the Marquis de Beauvoir, managing the estates close to our borders, the chateau at Montrésor. Monsieur le Marquis has dismissed this person for some reason he himself deems unjust..." The bailiff paused, and made it clear that he had his own ideas about this statement. Then he continued, "...and he would like to meet your lordship as he knows and trusts your lordship and desires to appeal to your lordship's sense of justice."

Henri's expression didn't change. He remembered now the bailiff of Montrésor, a slimy toad if ever he had seen one. Only at that time he had needed money badly and had been happy that the bailiff had paid money from the de Beauvoir treasury without asking too many detailed questions as to why money belonging to the heritage of his cousin should be dispensed to him. But now his heart started to rejoice. There was nothing better than a person with intimate knowledge of the whereabouts of his cousin and who apparently now was seeking revenge to help his own case.

He glanced at his own bailiff and replied arrogantly, "Well, I guess you might be right, whenever matters of family are concerned they take priority – of course I will listen with my usual... ah... diligence." And with this vague statement he dismissed his own bailiff. It didn't take a genius to work out that the discussion with his secretive visitor would be better held in private.

He entered the study and found his visitor standing taut and nervous; he hadn't dared take the liberty of sitting down. A quick glance conveyed to Henri that the man had seen better times, as his clothes looked stained and had been mended with hasty stitches. Henri's nose also told him that the man hadn't washed properly for several days either and therefore Henri decided to retreat to his chair behind the old desk that had been waiting for him, loaded with piles of documents and files to be signed or studied. If there was one similarity between the previous count and Henri it was their innate dislike of boring administration and paperwork. Some of the documents gathering dust on this pile had probably been waiting to catch the attention of his predecessor.

Henri sat down and scrutinized his visitor, a man he knew well enough from his previous visits to Montrésor. He found him little changed but was somewhat surprised, as the face of his visitor showed a peculiar mix of emotions – it was as

60

if seeing Henri upset him, but also deeply fascinated him. Henri decided to ignore this and without further hesitation he opened the conversation."You requested to see me urgently." He fixed his eyes on the face of the former bailiff: "I hope you have a good reason for such an insolent intrusion?"

The sharp voice of the Count de Roquemoulin seemed to awaken the visitor from his thoughts, and he bowed once more deeply. "My lord, I'm deeply sorry to have intruded without a proper appointment and I appreciate your lordship's kindness at condescending to receive me nonetheless."

Henri nodded. At least his visitor knew how to address him correctly.

"Don't waste your time on platitudes. Tell me what's been going on at Montrésor – I understand my beloved cousin has taken over the reins?!"

Whereas Henri had expected tearful and lengthy explanations about the terrible injustice that his cousin was supposed to have inflicted on his former bailiff, the latter kept his narrative extremely brief and came straight to the point. "My lord, I have come, because I want my revenge – and my revenge ultimately will be to your lordship's benefit."

Henri raised his eyebrows and motioned his visitor to explain further.

"The Marquis Pierre de Beauvoir has dismissed me from his services – without any compensation – although I have been a loyal servant to the de Beauvoir family for many years. I will not go into the details but I cannot accept such unjust treatment."

Henri could imagine at once plenty of reasons why Pierre might have taken such a decision – none of them particularly flattering for his visitor – and for once he felt a glimmer of sympathy for his cousin. Probably embezzlement, he concluded silently. He'd bet his newly acquired title that his visitor had filled his pockets copiously during the absence of any nominated successor for the estate – the situation must have been simply too inviting.

His visitor continued in honey-like tones. "You, my lord, have also suffered grief and have been treated unfairly. The present Marquis de Beauvoir is an illegitimate child, an imposter who somehow has been able to receive enough support from interested circles to claim a heritage that should never have come to him. You, my lord, should be our rightful Marquis, not this bastard child of doubtful foreign origin."

Although Henri loved and agreed with every single word of the last sentence he kept his face straight and non committal – better to pretend that he had no special interest and play his cards carefully. Absentmindedly he toyed with a large polished magnifying crystal that was lying on the desk. Slowly he answered, "I must admit that I follow and might even share some of your thoughts, but why are we sitting here, discussing issues of the past?"

The mellifluous voice went on, "Because injustice can be healed, the course of events can be changed. I know Montrésor in and out, its secret doors, gates and staircases. Although Pierre de Beauvoir has felt it necessary to dismiss all members of my family I still have enough loyal people working for me and living inside the castle. I can move in and out freely without ever being detected – and so could anybody else whom I would accompany. In the course of such a visit, a – let's call it – unhappy accident might strike Pierre de Beauvoir, and then…" He made a dramatic pause. "You, My lord, shall become our rightful Marquis de Beauvoir!"

"How could I ever trust you?"

His visitor suddenly didn't look so timid and reverential any more. His face had now changed and bore a decidedly sly expression. "You don't need to trust me, you just need to pay me. We'll treat this affair like a straight business agreement. Half of the amount to be paid before I open the doors to Montrésor and half of the amount when your cousin is laid to eternal rest among his ancestors in the chapel crypt at Montrésor."

Henri closed his eyes, cherishing the vision of Pierre's coffin disappearing into the cold underground chambers of the chateau's chapel.

"How much?"

"Twenty thousand gold livres!"

"Are you crazy?" Henri jumped up from his chair, his hand ready to strike the man.

The former bailiff suddenly looked no longer servile, his regard now positively defiant. "It's a small amount of money, your lordship. Don't forget that I know the revenues of your esteemed family in every detail. It will enable me to buy a small estate of my own and I will never work again as a servant. Either your lordship accepts or I'll disappear."

"I could have you whipped and brought straight to the sheriff!" exclaimed Henri, now in a complete rage. Swiftly he approached his insolent visitor, staring into his eyes with a look that could have curdled milk.

"Of course you could," the visitor replied unmoved, "but what benefit would it bring you? In my hands I keep the key to the title of the Marquis de Beauvoir, a heritage that's worth hundreds of thousands of livres and would give your lordship and me the sweet satisfaction of revenge. Your lordship can – with my help only – correct the unjust course of recent events. Why would your lordship

62

throw all of this away just for the satisfaction of seeing me suffer under the whip?"

"You're nothing but a disgusting slimy toad," Henri exclaimed, but he felt all the same that he had been beaten, as his visitor's logic was simply too compelling – and too seductive, "but I must admit you're an intelligent creature. Come back tomorrow evening and I'll have ten thousand livres ready for you. Now, let's talk business: when do you propose to 'visit' my cousin?"

His visitor bowed again reverently while his face remained composed. Henri appreciated that at least he didn't wallow in his triumph openly.

"Your lordship shows great wisdom and will never regret this decision! I shall be back tomorrow. As for the timing, it is advisable we should wait for the right occasion to act. A new moon will give us better cover if we decide to strike at night; at present we have a full moon and it would be rather too dangerous. I have several options in mind, in fact. I am being informed of every single movement of your cousin and I can take action day and night. Your lordship can be sure: starting from today, your cousin will never be safe. You can consider him dead already."

Then Pierre's former bailiff started to reveal some of his ideas, his voice steady and convincing. Henri could not suppress an agreeable shiver of delight. Pierre's fate was sealed indeed – there was not the slightest chance of escaping this trap!

"Ideally we should find two or three persons whom you can trust ready to accompany me the day we strike. I would not recommend your lordship to participate in this venture personally – your lordship should be seen by plenty of witnesses far away in your lordship's own chateau during that day. The sad news of Pierre de Beauvoir's sudden passing will be simply devastating for you – of course."

Henri smiled, an smile that looked evil even to the eyes of his hard-boiled visitor. "I think I know exactly who to send, two professionals and totally devoted to my cause, you'll be delighted!"

A vision of Marina and her brother dispatching his cousin to his cold grave had come to his mind. They'd be efficient and have no qualms at killing his cousin in cold blood. Once they realized that Henri's fortune would increase considerably with the de Beauvoir heritage there would be no stopping them. Although he had started to grow tired of Marina lately, he now recognized that fate had handed him on a golden platter a priceless tool to exact his revenge.

As soon as his visitor had left, Henri walked to the stables, although it was almost noon and the day had become quite hot already. To the surprise of his

63

grooms he insisted not only on riding out during the heat, but he curtly rejected the offer of his senior groom to accompany him as was customary. Henri was in the best of moods – but he needed to be alone now.

He knew exactly where he wanted to ride – and only once Henri had reached his destination, a forlorn place with a deserted plateau high above the vineyards and fields of Roquemoulin, did he allow his emotions to run free, to yell out his triumph: "I, Henri, I shall become Marquis de Beauvoir! Bastard Pierre, you're a dead man! Richelieu, beware, I promise to come back and you're next on my list!"

Below Henri a breathtaking landscape was spread out before him. The blue ribbon of the Loire cut into the emerald vineyards. The fields surrounding the vineyards were still green but soon those fields would turn to a dusty and pale yellow as summer had set in and promised to become as hot as winter had been cold. Behind Henri a group of lonely trees cast their shadow on the meadow while birds were chirping sleepily in the dense leaves – a haven of peace and perfect beauty. But when Henri closed his eyes to cherish his moment of triumph, he didn't see any beauty or perfection. He saw the shadow of death – and he loved it.

*****

At Montrésor a new set of daily routines had set in. Newly hired servants had replaced those who had been dismissed. A new bailiff was expected, recommended and selected by Armand's father to arrive soon and take over the administration in his capable hands. After the disappearance of the bailiff, search warrants had been launched all over the country – but to nobody's surprise the latter had disappeared without leaving any trace.

Pierre wouldn't have worried too much if it hadn't been for the terrible fate of the maid and the prison warden who had been brutally murdered. Impossible to forget the image of the maid's severed head smeared with blood. There seemed no doubt that both incidents must be linked – and that a dangerous murderer was still running free and unpunished. Yet the days passed by peacefully as if the murders had been nothing but an illusion, a nightmare, an episode soon to be forgotten.

Over the coming days the Loire valley was blessed with beautiful weather. The sun shone constantly every day whilst Pierre and Armand continued discovering the beautiful surroundings of Montrésor, the lush landscape bathed in golden sunlight. Riding along the roads and across the vast fields of his estate, Pierre and Armand were greeted like heroes by the estate's farmers and tenants. Word had spread quickly that Pierre had dismissed the corrupt and loathed bailiff and a wave of hope and renewed confidence swept through the villages. Cautiously hope started to grow among the poor peasants that their new lord would not just fill his pockets and steal their meagre harvest but would take care of the estate and fulfil his duties in protecting them as their lord and master.

Days later a small group of armed men was riding for hours across endless roads and open fields. Tired and worn out they were heading back to Montrésor. Armand had given strict orders that all of them were to wear heavy suits of chain-mail, a precaution everybody had understood in view of recent events but now, as the afternoon sun kept burning on their back and was roasting them alive, they all silently cursed Armand, including Pierre, who was riding amongst his men.

Clouds of dust were stirred up by the horses and followed them like a train, wrapping the horsemen in a thick blanket of dust and dirt, clogging their dry throats and forming a dark crust on their sweat-soaked shirts. A musketeer with gleaming blond hair rode in front of Pierre. He was suffering badly; not only was his woollen tunic drenched with sweat and almost worn to pieces by the heavy metal suit, he had also volunteered to ride Pierre's stallion as Pierre had wanted to try out a new horse, a recent and expensive acquisition to his stable.

The young musketeer had been bursting with pride when Pierre had entrusted him with his favourite horse, but in next to no time he had been brought down to earth. The stallion was much more capricious than anticipated and demanded his full skill and attention if he was to be mastered. What had seemed a great opportunity, a unique chance that would make his comrades green with envy, was quickly turning into a nightmarish experience. How happy he was going to be tonight when he got back to the chateau and could escape from his chain-mail and drop into bed. All the same his spirits started to rise as he knew that behind the next curve of the road they would reach a small forest, a patch of woods stretching along a clear stream of water – a welcome change from the open road with the sun beating down.

As soon as the musketeer spotted the silhouette of the forest, he turned back and shouted to the exhausted faces of the other horsemen. "Come on, lads, we'll be in shade soon enough, let's spur on the horses!"

Miraculously the tired group became more lively and, laughing joyfully like children, they dived into the dim light of the forest – what bliss to feel the cool shadows of the trees closing above them. In eager anticipation to reach the cool stream of water running through the forest the group sped forward. The blond musketeer was by now clearly leading the other riders – Pierre's horse was a real gem. He spurred his horse on, eager to be the first to reach the stream of refreshing water. How much they had suffered under the hot sun, roasted alive in these heavy sheaths of metal!

"How strange," the musketeer thought as he sped through the dense foliage, "that there should already be wasps in the forest at this time of the year," when he heard a hissing sound close to his head.

65

Those were his last thoughts.

Two arrows from a crossbow had found their target with deadly precision, iron fitted bolts that cut with ease through the protective chain-mail and dug way deep into the back of the young musketeer – the joyful rider was killed on the spot.

His horse had heard the hissing sounds and felt the grip of his rider slacken. In panic the horse reared, throwing the cavalcade of riders into total disarray, the horses rearing and whinnying, eyes wide open and rolling in fear. Roaring out commands, it took Pierre and Armand a good deal of time to get some discipline back into the group – and to comprehend that one of their members had just been murdered in an ambush.

Armand had to use all of his authority to stop his men from searching the woods. "Stop, you bloody idiots, this is exactly what they want us to do! If each of us starts roaming around we'll make easy targets for their crossbows. They'll pick us off, one by one. Back to the chateau, immediately!" he roared.

The men protested, their blood boiling with hot revenge, but reluctantly they recognized the chilling logic of his command. Taking their dead comrade into their middle they rode back as fast as possible to the safety of the chateau. The group was unusually silent now – everyone scared to hear once more the fatal hissing sound that would herald death. The tension only abated once they were back on the open road and with the greatest relief they greeted the familiar outlines of Montrésor.

The body of the dead musketeer was carried by his comrades into the cold, dimly lit chapel of the castle where he was laid out. His close friends couldn't hold back their tears, as sobbing they lay him to rest in front of the altar. They still couldn't fully comprehend that their friend, lying there as if he were sleeping, would remain silent forever – it seemed only minutes ago that they had heard his joyful command to spur on the horses.

Pierre ordered a watch of honour to be kept for the murdered musketeer until the funeral was to be held. Then he retreated wearily to his room. He was utterly shattered and felt strangely guilty, as he had proposed switching the horses. There could be no doubt that his person had been targeted and that the young musketeer had lost his life only because he possessed the same hair colour and had been riding Pierre's horse.

Jean silently undressed and washed him. The news had spread like wildfire and he had already heard about the deadly ambush. After a first second of shock and revulsion, Jean had secretly praised the Lord that his master's life had been spared. He hated seeing his master so tense and worn out.

I must protect my master, I must help to find this maniac!, Jean vowed silently to himself.

Dinner that evening was an unusually silent affair, as neither Pierre nor Armand were in the mood for talking. The excellent food remained almost untouched – only their cups of wine needed to be replenished more often than usual.

Before Pierre went to bed he decided to visit the chapel once more, as he longed to pray for the soul of the young musketeer who had – unknowingly – sacrificed his life for his own. As soon as Pierre entered the dark chapel with its stinging smell of damp, candles and stale incense – a smell that reminded him so much of his school days in the monastery – he heard a sobbing sound. Once his eyes had grown accustomed to the dim light cast by the flickering candles and torches he realized that one of the kitchen maids was hovering close to the corpse of the dead musketeer – lost in her sorrow she seemed oblivious to the guards of honour who were standing close to the stretcher.

Pierre noticed that they were ill at ease, as if they hated to intrude on the girl's private grief. She was clad in a muddy-brown tunic and a stained apron, looking like a tiny lost sparrow that had strayed from its flock. She was weeping, heartbroken and despaired.

Pierre approached her and when she didn't react he gently touched her wet face. First she shrank back in fear but somehow his face inspired confidence in her and she relaxed a bit.

"Did you love him?" Pierre asked her softly.

"Yes, Monsieur le Marquis," she answered, trying in vain to suppress her tears.

"He promised to marry me and now I'm …" and more tears fell from her eyes, "expecting his child." Her voice rose as she sobbed in hysteria, "My father will kill me when finds out the truth!" the last words nearly drowned in a flood of tears.

Pierre looked at her puffy face. He remembered that she was quite a pretty girl actually, but one wouldn't have thought so seeing her now in her grief.

"Your fiancé sacrificed his life for me," Pierre said with a hoarse voice. "Therefore don't worry, I'll take care of you. I'll ask my new bailiff to pay you a dowry and see that you'll be married to a decent man and can raise your child. This is the least I can do for him."

"You would do this for me?" Her voice faltered with a mix of genuine surprise and excited hope. "But I'm just a simple kitchen maid, why should Monsieur le Marquis bother?"

"Because I like justice to be done," Pierre said simply. "This man has been killed because someone wanted me to be lying here instead, so I owe him my life. Next to paying you a dowry I'll become the godfather of your child to make sure that his father's sacrifice will not have been in vain."

The maid who had stood up when Pierre had approached the stretcher now sank down to her knees and whilst she covered his hand with kisses she said, "God bless Monsieur le Marquis, your lordship saved my life!"

Pierre was fascinated to see her face transformed from total despair to a glow of hope, almost joy. He now realized that this dowry would change her life completely, as even if she was with child she'd suddenly become an attractive proposition, able to choose a husband, lease a small farm and raise a family. Pierre knew as well as she probably did that the young musketeer would never have thought about marrying her. No young man descended from a noble family would ever have bothered about the honour of a kitchen maid. As much as she seemed to have genuinely grieved for him, life had suddenly offered a new chance to her – and eagerly and happily she seized it, the dead musketeer now the past, her child the future.

As for Armand, after he had digested the shock he had come to the conclusion that they needed help – urgently. Immediately he dispatched an urgent message to his father asking for a reinforcement of the small group of musketeers that had accompanied them from Paris. Furthermore he made Pierre swear to stay inside until more soldiers arrived. While they were waiting for the answer, Pierre felt like a lion in a cage. His beautiful chateau suddenly seemed small and stuffy and his mood oscillated between depressed silence and false hilarity.

No wonder that Armand felt a huge burden fall from his shoulders when two days later he looked into the courtyard and saw a troop of musketeers arriving. To his immense joy and relief they were dressed in the familiar uniforms bearing the proud coat of arms of the Marquis de Saint Paul. Not only had his father reacted with amazing speed – he had dispatched at least thirty of his own soldiers – he must have judged the situation dangerous enough to act so swiftly and decisively.

About a quarter of an hour later the butler announced solemnly there was a visitor who desired to meet the two lords.

A tall, young officer with a broad smile on his face entered energetically – a welcome change from the gloomy atmosphere that had lately prevailed in the chateau. He started to bow deeply in front of Armand but then stopped half way – embarrassed he suddenly seemed to remember that Pierre was the owner of the chateau and thus had to be greeted first, furthermore his rank had to be considered as much higher than Armand's.

The officer's face flushed deep red when he realized his faux-pas and he quickly turned and bowed reverently towards Pierre. The latter had to suppress a grin. He knew exactly what the officer must be thinking, that he looked far too young to be considered as being of higher rank compared to Armand who looked every inch a Saint Paul and a gentleman.

Once the formalities of courteous greeting had been fulfilled the officer addressed Pierre to pass on best wishes from Armand's father, the Marquis de Saint Paul. Afterwards he extracted an envelope from his waistcoat and handed it reverently to Armand.

After a short round of small talk and discussion as to where to lodge the newly arrived musketeers, the officer was dismissed and Pierre and Armand were left on their own once again. Armand opened the envelope and quickly read his father's message. Suddenly he whistled and exclaimed, "Oh damn, we're in deep sh-- " But he couldn't finish his sentence as Pierre interrupted him immediately, imitating the tone of the Marquis de Saint Paul. "Monsieur, you are most shockingly rude. I don't think that your august father would appreciate your explicit language!" But then he added in a different tone, "How deep?"

"Extremely deep, to be even more explicit, up to your armpits, Monsieur le Marquis, or should I say, 'Your Grace'," Armand answered with a mocking grin.

"Your father is concerned about the former bailiff and wants his musketeers to protect me?" Pierre stated more than he asked.

"Not only that," Armand replied, making faces.

"What's up then?"

"Rumour is circulating in Paris that your fascinating cousin Henri has used his considerable physical charms to get himself taken in and adopted by the Count de Roquemoulin."

Pierre's face was a question mark.

"The imprudent Count de Roquemoulin regrettably died very soon after your charming cousin's adoption papers had been filed – well, we all know that fatal accidents can strike all of a sudden." Armand's voice had become outright sarcastic.

Pierre's face still resembled a question mark.

Armand sighed. "Oh Pierre, you're still so naïve. Your cousin first sold himself to the count like a cheap whore and when the count – who, by the way, conveniently owned a huge fortune – was foolish enough to adopt him, Henri got rid of him. We all know that Henri has no remorse in this respect. The only surprise for me in this story is that your dear cousin did not even hesitate to sell his body – on top of his other redoubtable qualities."

Pierre flushed deeply and he swallowed hard. "I understand now, thank you so much for broadening my education."

"There's a saying that you can choose your friends, but not your family. We Saint Pauls have a considerable number of crazy specimens among us as well, so don't worry," Armand quickly responded, trying to comfort Pierre who was visibly upset.

"But why is this worrying your father then?" Pierre asked after a short pause and continued, "I would say that now that Henri has inherited a lot of money and the title of a Count he should be less dangerous."

"My father thinks that Henri's totally obsessed by the idea of seeing you lying here in this crypt of the chapel – and do you have any idea where Roquemoulin is located?"

Pierre grinned. "No, it was not part of our lessons, but I can give you the names of all the saints in the calendar of our Holy Church if this can help you."

Armand grinned back. "Well you might be needing them all. Roquemoulin is located only some fifteen to twenty miles from our borders here. My father therefore thinks that your precious bailiff is probably hiding under the protection of your honourable cousin."

Pierre tried to digest the news. "This means…" he said slowly.

"This means, my dear friend, that you're in immediate danger, once again." Armand spoke seriously, he didn't feel like joking any more.

"Let's see the positive side of it then," answered Pierre. "Didn't we say that life had become a bit boring and that we'd love a bit of adventure? Well, here it is."

Armand took a glass of wine and raised it to his friend. "Cheers to adventure then – and to you, my friend."

"Santé!" Pierre replied. "I guess I'll need it."

"I think you'll need something to divert your mind," Armand said suddenly, "and I think I know the best way!"

Pierre looked sceptically at his friend, as Armand was looking suspiciously impish.

That night Armand insisted on accompanying Pierre as bedtime was approaching. This wasn't unusual, as often enough they'd share a last glass of wine and chat until the early hours. But as soon as they had entered his room, Pierre understood that tonight a different programme had been planned by his best friend.

One of the prettiest parlour maids – a girl known to be presently in Armand's favour – was waiting already for them. Timidly she sat on the edge of Pierre's immense bed. Her hair was a dark shade of honey blond, a pretty match to her dark, amber-coloured eyes. She was dressed in some new and expensive nightgown, as nervously she cast coy glances towards the two gentlemen who had entered the room. From time to time she fingered at the thin fabric as if to ascertain that this was reality, as if she could hardly believe that something as expensive and as precious as this gown could ever have been offered to her.

"You cannot be serious!" Pierre hissed towards his friend, who grinned, full of mischief.

Armand ignored his friend's pleas and addressed the young maid instead. "Don't you want to greet Monsieur le Marquis properly?" he commanded sternly.

The young maid blushed and jumped up, then sank into a deep curtsey in Pierre's direction and stammered some incomprehensible words in her local dialect. Whilst she curtsied the top of her gown fell open and Pierre could see inviting pink nipples and beautiful firm breasts. His resistance started to soften; Pierre had to swallow hard and was awkwardly aware that his friend had of course registered his reaction with amused satisfaction.

Armand moved closer to the maid and before she or Pierre could understand what he was up to, he had not only started to kiss her sensuous lips but had loosened the strings of her top with his experienced fingers. As the gown dropped to the floor, Pierre could see the young maid in all of her splendour. He swallowed once again, harder this time.

The girl duly protested – but Pierre had the impression that she objected more because it might be expected from her to do so and less because she disliked Armand's bold action. "Monsieur le Comte, it's a sin, what your lordship is doing, I'm a respectable girl!"

"We've done it already, anyhow," Armand replied lightly. "And you told me that you liked it, although you'll have to go to confess it in church, so isn't it better if you have a bit more to confess? It will make your efforts worthwhile."

The maid did not look convinced, as once more she insisted, "It's truly a sin, my lord!"

Armand smiled at her, knowing that no female had yet been born who could resist his smile. "Listen, chérie, Monsieur le Marquis is your lord, the lord of this castle. If you disobey him, then that would be a true sin? Right?"

The maid nodded, she could follow this line of thought.

"So why should it be a sin then to make love with me and him if he agrees?"

The maid tried to put her concerns into words and finally said, "Because doing it with two gentlemen is a sin."

Armand shook his head. "You're wrong. We just found out that you have to obey Monsieur le Marquis, therefore it can't be a sin. Even the priest will tell you the same."

The maid suddenly giggled with excitement; apparently she found this explanation satisfactory. Instead of continuing to argue she stepped out of her gown that had fallen to her feet and, swaying her hips invitingly, she walked slowly to the bed. There she installed herself comfortably and said naively, "I hope Monsieur le Marquis finds me beautiful enough?"

Pierre was stunned, but aroused at the same time. He cast a furious glance to his friend who had already started to undress himself under the appreciative glance of the maid. Armand answered with a smug grin which said nothing else but: "I knew that you'd give in, you always behave like a saint, but there's a little devil inside you that wants some fun from time to time."

The worst was that Pierre knew that his friend was right, and yes, tonight he was craving some fun!

*****

The general mood was still gloomy in Montrésor but rapidly the arrival of thirty or so young and dashing musketeers had its natural effect on the female staff, not only inside the chateau, but the message spread fast to the surrounding villages. The new and efficient bailiff who had arrived took the administration of the estate in his capable hands, freeing Pierre from the tedious daily work of listening to the sheer endless queue of people who had taken the habit of coming and complaining, mostly about the most trivial of matters.

"If I have to listen to one more complaint today that the chicken won't lay eggs because the neighbour's wife is a witch in disguise, I'll explode," he complained to Armand who sat there laughing at Pierre's despair.

72

"You're far too kind to them," he scolded his friend. "Of course they'll never stop if you let them go on complaining. You should have told this fat cow that either she is to shut up or you'll have her chicken confiscated to check if they're laying eggs before you roast them for your dinner – and have her roasted as well if she's telling lies. In reality she wants to get rid of her pretty neighbour because her husband has been seen shagging her in the fields."

"How do you know?" Pierre asked with big eyes.

"She's the aunt of the pretty maid and she's known in the whole village to be an evil trouble-maker," Armand answered, his pronunciation severely hampered by the strawberries in his mouth while he was already digging his hand once more into a bowl of strawberries that Jean had just brought in. "Delicious!" he mumbled.

"And how do you know that her husband was shagging the neighbour's wife?"

"From the village inn, I heard him boasting that he did it three times in a row!"

Pierre was fascinated, not only that Armand always seemed to know what was going on, but that he had the gift of making friends and getting people to open up to him wherever he went.

Slowly the insidious murders and the attack in the forest seemed to fade into the background of the people's minds. Who could remain gloomy if the sun was shining brightly, the vineyards promised to produce another great harvest and the estate was thriving under the new management? If ever there were any red eyes and tears to be seen, they probably belonged to some young girls from the village who had succumbed to the charms of the newly arrived musketeers and now had to discover that the effects of passion could last nine months and more.

When the next letter from Charles arrived, Pierre was glad of the distraction. He felt that he couldn't leave Montrésor as long as the murders hadn't been avenged. But this feeling of duty had been fighting with his growing longing to leave the confinement of the chateau – and to meet Marie again. Full of curiosity, his heart beating with wild hope, he tore the envelope open.

Armand tried to read his friend's face, crossing his fingers that this message would not contain yet another disappointment. Pierre first looked radiant but then Armand saw his friend's face dropping in total disappointment. *What the hell was it this time?*

"Oh, come on Pierre, don't torture me! What does this English giant of a cousin write? Are they coming to visit us?"

Pierre sighed, an unhappy sigh. Then he cleared his throat. "Well, it's good news and bad news. Both, actually." He sighed again.

"I love a precise answer," grumbled Armand. "It's always a pleasure discussing things with you. Oh, come on, Pierre, spill the beans and don't keep me in suspense!"

Pierre sighed again; Armand could nearly have strangled him.

Finally Pierre started to speak. "Well, it's good news and bad news at once. Charles is writing to me that Marie's father will accept my proposal and that Marie is allowed to come and join us together with Charles and Céline during the summer."

"But that's fantastic!" Armand exclaimed. "You should be dancing with joy or did you lose your unfaithful heart after just one wild night to our pretty maid?"

Pierre shot him a furious glance. "I can always count on you to be discreet and sensitive! Thank you for reminding me of this night right now!"

"My pleasure, Your Grace, my pleasure." Armand was not to be intimidated.

Pierre decided to ignore his friend's comment and continued. "But the condition of Marie's father accepting my proposal is that Marie must return to Reims after the summer and stay there with her parents until Christmas. We're not supposed to meet during this period, and only if we both prove that our love is strong enough, can we officially become betrothed after Christmas! Armand – this means four or five months of additional waiting without any chance of seeing Marie. Just the thought of it is making me crazy!" Pierre's voice wobbled with a treacherous hint of tears and he turned quickly away to gulp down a glass of water that was placed conveniently close.

"That's outrageous!" Armand was dumbfounded. "How can he dare to treat you like a mere schoolboy who's begging to marry his daughter? You're an English Duke and a peer of France and he's nothing but a miserable country squire! "

"He says that we're too young," answered Pierre lamely, "and Charles writes that there's some truth in this and that I should accept the proposal in good grace."

"Bullshit!" Armand said with the deepest of feelings. "Even the King married when he was a mere boy, all noble families marry young. I'm just lucky that I have been able to escape so far the matchmaking instincts of my mother – she's still busy finding a husband for my sister." He chuckled. "And that's not an easy task, by the way. My sister is a beauty but has the character of a dragon."

74

There was a moment of silence when Armand suddenly exclaimed, "Actually, we're total idiots, it's absolutely useless to mope anyhow!"

"What do you mean?"

"Haven't we totally forgotten a very important issue?"

Pierre's face was a question mark.

"We're stuck here because we need to deal with your precious cousin Henri and find our murderous bailiff, but sooner rather than later we'll have to leave for Venice to search for the bloody missing ring! Unless you wanted to drag Marie along with you, we'll be travelling during the coming months anyhow – better she stays with her parents and her father can keep a watchful eye on your little beauty!"

Pierre looked crestfallen. "Oh God, I had totally forgotten about the cursed ring. Searching for a ring, it sounds so medieval, maybe it's guarded by a fierce fire-breathing dragon? How ridiculous! Just throw in a princess and it becomes a fairy tale!"

"So had I," answered Armand. "I agree, if you look at it with a bit of detachment it sounds extremely foolish. We're here, both feet firmly on the ground in enlightened times and are supposed to find a ring that will lead us to a medieval treasure trove from the dark ages. You're right, it does sound like a fairy tale."

"Or a nightmare," said Pierre gloomily. "But…"

"….but as we're gentlemen we have to honour our word." Armand finished the sentence before Pierre could do it.

"Maybe it'll be fun all the same?" Pierre suggested – but not very convincingly

"Probably better than sitting in this chateau and waiting for the next murder to happen." Armand's answer didn't sound very cheerful either.

There was a moment of silence, as both friends sat in their chairs, their long legs stretched out. Pierre absentmindedly stroked a dog he had adopted during the past weeks. The dog's eyes were glued adoringly on his new master – what he was experiencing right now must resemble dog heaven.

"You also forgot something," Pierre exclaimed suddenly.

Now it was Armand's turn to look puzzled.

"What about Julia? Remember that our banker mentioned that she must be on her way back to Venice by now! "

Armand jumped up as if he had been stung by a wasp. He slapped his forehead. "How could I have forgotten her? It must be my advancing age. You're right, Venice is waiting for us! If only we could find this damned bailiff, he's the key to all of our problems! My men have been combing through all the villages and I already paid a fortune to get most of your tenants drunk and talking – but there's no trace. It's so maddening!"

"It is," Pierre admitted, "and that's the understatement of the year. Let's be positive, Marie, Céline and Charles will come soon, it will be a welcome change. If only we could solve the murders before they arrive!"

"Or if something would happen and give us a clue."

Sometimes wishes come true… but not always exactly in the way they have been intended.

Pierre looked dreamily out of the open window. He loved that view: the sun was shining and the sunlight was reflected by the molten silver of the small lake that once upon a time must have been part of the chateau's moat. A lone swan was gliding majestically through the water, leaving behind him picturesque ripples that spread out across the water in the pattern of a gigantic fan. No sound disturbed this picture of peace, beauty and perfection.

Lazily Pierre's glance went further and to his surprise he detected a blurred movement behind the reeds; soon the moving shape became more distinct and Pierre caught sight of a single horseman speeding towards the castle.

It therefore did not come as a surprise when about a quarter of an hour later a messenger arriving from Paris was announced and guided by Jean into the drawing room. Armand arrived as well, certainly driven by curiosity as he must have seen or heard the arrival of the horseman. Pierre was always amazed how fast news travelled inside the community of the chateau.

The messenger came from the household of the Marquis de Saint Paul and he brought long-awaited letters for Armand and for Pierre. Those letters were very much welcome as they contained amusing (and highly interesting) chit-chat of daily life in Paris and at the royal court. Not to mention that Pierre was desperately hoping to receive some news as to when Marie could finally be expected to join them.

Together they ploughed through the pages of meticulous handwriting. Armand's father of course hadn't bothered to write himself, he had dictated page after page to his secretary, which had the added benefit that the deciphering of the letter was fairly easy, at least for Pierre.

"The Marquis de Cinq Mars is still gathering new titles and estates at amazing speed, his sun is shining at the court unobscured," Pierre cited aloud from the letter. "Isn't that pretty daring of your father to mention this openly in his letter, isn't he bothered that Richelieu has probably read a copy of this letter even before we could?"

Armand laughed. "You should know my old man better by now. Of course he does, and if he's writing it so bluntly he wants to kick Richelieu into some action of course!"

"But why would your father want to see Cinq Mars damaged? Finally we have a serious challenge for Richelieu's monopoly of power – isn't this what all the old noble families have been waiting for?"

77

Armand sighed, the indulgent sigh that parents utter when their children are being very naïve or extremely trying.

"My dear friend, politics is truly not your strong point. Although we all hate Richelieu, the idea of seeing our anointed King dance to the tunes of a pretty brainless youngster like a puppet on a string is simply appalling. Especially as Cinq Mars is as stupid as he's handsome. If Cinq Mars ascends to power, France will sink into a nightmare of civil war – and at least the Saint Paul clan doesn't want to see this happen."

"This is the major reason why your father gave the letters to Richelieu? Ending the feud with me was only one aspect then?" Pierre suddenly realized that he had also been used like a chess piece in this game of power.

"Exactly, getting you out of trouble with Richelieu was of course his major goal, but I'm sure that my old man had several ideas in his head when he proposed this deal to Richelieu."

"Nice to know." Pierre was pouting now.

Armand grinned. "You'll need to get used to this. We'll all pawns in some big game and up to us to make the best out of it!"

They had continued reading the letter during their discussion when suddenly Pierre exclaimed, "Marie won't be arriving at Montrésor before July, they have decided to stay in Paris first and replenish their wardrobe, Céline and Marie apparently *desperately* need new clothes – this is at least what they made Charles understand." His voice was oozing with sarcasm.

"You don't look as disappointed as I'd have thought..." Armand asked cautiously.

"To be honest, I don't know what I want. On the one hand I want her to come over immediately and count the seconds, on the other hand I'm scared stiff of having Marie and Céline at Montrésor as long as we still haven't nailed down the murderer. It's giving me nightmares!"

"Yes, we must find him, you're right, it's getting on my nerves as well. It's like sitting on a volcano, you never know what's going to happen," Armand replied.

Reaching the next page it was Armand's turn though to cry out. "Oh my God, this cannot be true!" he looked visibly shaken.

"What's the matter? You sound as if something terrible has happened, but I can only see that your father has announced the arrival of one of your many cousins here – this can't be so bad, it might even be fun!" Pierre looked at his friend, who was clearly upset by the news.

"Have you ever heard of François de Toucy? "Armand asked him in a scathing voice.

"How should I?"

"Well, he's a pain in the arse, and don't tell me again to mind my language. Always dressed like a fag, but somehow ends up dragging all the girls into his bed. Fussy with food, his room and everything that concerns his comfort..." Armand was searching for more words to describe his cousin.

"Could it be that you're a bit jealous because he's such a hit with the girls, my friend?" Pierre threw in. This promised to become highly amusing!

"Are you kidding? François a serious competitor to me? Never!" Armand nearly spat out the words. Calming down, he added, "I don't want to blow my own trumpet, but some have it, and some simply don't. If I want a girl, I'll get her, he's never going to be a match for me!"

Pierre sighed. It would take more than a dashing cousin to unsettle his friend's confidence, that was sure. "What I like about you, my dearest Armand, is that you're not conceited at all." But Pierre's sarcasm was wasted.

"Of course not, I'm just stating the obvious," Armand replied, and only a slight wink of his left eye betrayed that he might have understood Pierre's message.

François de Toucy duly arrived in all his impressive splendour a fortnight later. He had announced his wish to pay a visit to Montrésor via a highly elaborate and formal letter addressed to His Grace, the Duke of Hertford, the most honourable Marquis de Beauvoir. Pierre had sent an equally formal reply to extend his warmest invitation to stay at Montrésor but to Armand's frustration there had been no hint at all in this exchange of polite letters indicating the period of time that his cousin had in mind to spend at Montrésor.

"You'll see this sucker is going to stay on forever. Free meals and pretty parlour maids, that's all he wants." Armand's mood clearly hadn't improved.

"Not if you keep looking like milk that has gone sour. Nobody would like to stay longer with a cousin who looks like a thunderstorm that's brewing."

"Let's hope then that he gets the message!" Armand looked a bit more optimistic now.

Pierre started to feel ill at ease. How on earth would he be able to keep Armand from behaving like an idiot if he disliked his cousin so much?

All of these thoughts were flashing though Pierre's mind when he saw the cavalcade of coaches and horsemen drawing closer into the courtyard. Not only were liveried footmen accompanying the coaches but the Marquis de Saint Paul had even dispatched some more of his own musketeers. Pierre started to worry where to lodge all of these new arrivals to his household.

Three coaches stopped in front of the entrance, all of them loaded to the brim with heavy wooden chests. Pierre's heart sank; this did not look at all like a short stay. Remembering his obligations as a good host he approached the central coach, a large vehicle with a leather roof. The door was opened by a footman so Pierre could set eyes on his visitor for the first time.

As could have been expected, François de Toucy was immaculately dressed. Of above average height, he was surprisingly blond; somehow Pierre had assumed that he would be as dark as Armand. His full blond hair was worn according to fashion, shoulder long, carefully combed and set into curls – the rays of the sun made it gleam with a slightly reddish tint that was reflected in his moustache, crowning a sensuous mouth. François had a pleasant enough face but his most striking feature were his eyes, a translucent grey that Pierre had never seen before. He moved with the elegance of an accomplished sportsman and courtier – a ladies' man and a serious competitor indeed for Armand.

De Toucy refused the help of the footman and jumped lightly out of the carriage. Armand's father must have given a good description of Pierre as François de Toucy walked without hesitation towards him and then bowed deeply in front of Pierre while waving his hat, decorated with extremely long feathers, with an elegant gesture. His greeting of Armand was significantly less elaborate, as apparently he had less esteem for the younger son of the Marquis de Saint Paul, even if Armand could call himself an English Earl now.

Armand's replying bow answered the bare necessities of politeness as well. No warm family feelings were present on either side, Pierre concluded. They walked into the drawing room where refreshments were waiting.

"Did you have a nice journey?" Pierre asked politely.

"Thank you, Your Grace. It was quite agreeable. I had to finish off some bandits on the way, but it was nothing more than a mere nuisance. I just hate to be sitting in a stuffy coach with the blinds down. Not only is it boring, but you feel as if you've been tortured after a short period of time, the roads are simply appalling in the countryside!"

Pierre protested, "Please don't call me 'Your Grace', it makes me feel so old. Pierre will do, Armand's friends are mine as well!"

François de Toucy bowed deeply. "It's a true honour for me, Pierre!"

Armand shot a furious glance at Pierre. There could be no mistake, he didn't feel any friendship for this glittering specimen of a cousin.

"Why didn't you open the blinds of the coach then or ride ?" Armand asked full of contempt.

François looked at him as if Armand were insane. "Ruin my clothes and arrive here like a peasant covered in dust? Are you serious?"

François de Toucy shuddered at the mere thought of committing such a faux-pas and lovingly he looked at the immaculate clothes he was wearing while inhaling some scent from the perfumed ball he wore attached to a long ribbon around his neck.

Pierre was thankful that Armand didn't reply, in fact Armand's eyes said it all.

Thankfully, François now changed the subject and started to deliver greetings from Armand's father and the others, Céline, Marie and Charles.

Soon they found themselves chatting animatedly about the latest gossip from Paris. The Marquis de Cinq Mars especially proved to be a fascinating topic and even though François managed to keep a respectful tone he conveyed the message that the King was completely besotted with his latest favourite and that speculation was ripe at court as to when Richelieu would deem it necessary to interfere.

Even Armand forgot about his initial hostility and soon they were discussing the hottest topics of politics: trouble for the King of England was brewing fast as Parliament was close to open war with its monarch.

Only when François asked if the King of England had already appealed for Pierre's support, did Pierre suddenly become aware that sooner or later he might be drawn into a situation that smelled of civil war in the making. Having spent the past months in France, the politics of England had vanished almost completely from his mind. François de Toucy's question reminded him uncomfortably that he had in fact sworn eternal allegiance to King Charles in England. But was he truly willing to go to war for this strange King, this man with the long bitter face who never seemed to have had a stroke of luck in his entire life?

81

Suddenly the idea of travelling to Venice seemed a much more appealing choice…

Pierre skilfully managed to avoid a clear statement about the situation in England or his own potential involvement. He hastened to explain that he had been out of England now for far too much time as to have any intimate knowledge about the current situation. Owing allegiance in fact to two kings, he added, he'd have to assess carefully in any case what to do.

The grey eyes looked thoughtfully at him – actually Pierre had the impression that they were looking straight through him. Suddenly François smiled, a smile that definitely reflected the famous charms of the Saint Paul family. "My congratulations, you should join the diplomatic service," he answered. "But I can only agree with your words. Joining a war, especially a civil war, is no fun, even if some people might think so. And sadly – often enough – there is nothing to gain, only to lose." Was his glance directed at Armand when he made this statement?

Dinner passed in an animated fashion and Pierre started to relax. It was refreshing to have a visitor come from a civilized city like Paris to take his mind off the insidious attack in the forest and the murders and to feel in touch with the pulse of life at court.

After François had gone upstairs to rest in his room Pierre said to Armand, "After all, he's not at all as bad as you told me. He's got a good brain in his head."

"A head with too many curls for my taste," Armand growled. "He's a clever one, for sure, but you'll see – tomorrow at the latest he'll complain about something. Today it was the coach, tomorrow it'll be the food or whatever, this man might be sometimes amusing but he's a nuisance, read my lips!"

The next days though passed smoothly and without any upsetting disputes. From time to time François dropped a hint that he was having trouble sleeping, but of course, it was *not* his intention to complain! Armand rolled his eyes and Pierre had to suppress a smile as Armand's prophecy seemed to come true. He promised François solemnly to give orders to have his bedstraw refreshed. François thanked him but protested loudly; it had not been his intention to make any fuss or cause any embarrassment! After a short pause though he added that changing the bed sheets would be a great idea as well, he couldn't help it, but he seemed to be so terribly sensitive to bed bugs!

Pierre's housekeeper was nearly out of her mind when Pierre ordered the bed straw and sheets to be changed. Close to tears she swore that the straw was the freshest that could be imagined and that of course the bed sheets had been washed, ironed and changed as well by the maids. Pierre calmed her down with a lot of diplomacy and told her just to go with the job, mindless of the fact that he agreed that it probably didn't make a lot of sense. François de Toucy was a close relative of the Marquis de Saint Paul, an important guest and as such his comfort must have priority. He smiled at his housekeeper but she seemed immune to his boyish charms, her bony face remained frozen with anger. She curtsied stiffly and walked abruptly out of the room.

"What an old witch," Pierre murmured to himself.

In the evening François came down to the library to excuse himself from attending dinner. He explained that he had only recently recognized that one of the officers of the musketeers stationed in Montrésor was an old friend. "We served together while I was stationed with the guards of His Majesty, the King, in the Louvre and he would be terribly upset if I didn't ask him out and have a drink with him while I'm staying here. He told me that there is nowhere around here to have any real fun but there is small inn in the village that serves surprisingly good wine and this will have to do."

Before Pierre could utter a word, Armand interrupted already: "Oh, no problem at all François, have a great time and don't bother!" Armand seemed only too glad to see François leave.

"Are you truly sure, my dearest Armand? Maybe I had better stay, I truly don't want to seem impolite!"

Pierre wasn't sure if he hadn't detected a small malicious gleam in François' eyes; the latter must be certainly very much aware that Armand was only too happy to see the back of him.

Apologizing once more profusely he withdrew and Pierre heard Armand murmur, "Thank God that sponger is gone for tonight!"

Both of them would have been very surprised if they'd had the opportunity of watching François de Toucy that night in the village inn. The polished façade of the spoilt gentleman had vanished, his usually carefully arranged curls were ruffled, his collar open – he looked like any other young musketeer having a night off and looking for some fun. Sitting in a merry circle of young soldiers enlarged by some locals François was playing dice and drinking heavily.

It didn't prove difficult to steer the conversation to the topic of the chateau murders, as speculation of the whereabouts of the bailiff was running wild. "I reckon he's already in the new colonies by now, believe me," stated a fat local farmer, before he belched profusely to underline the importance of his statement.

Eagerly François snapped up all kinds of gossip related to the inhabitants of the chateau or the former bailiff. The next round of cups of wine was paid for and

François discovered that the owner of the inn was becoming more willing to talk – in fact the more silver coins were changing hands, the faster his mouth seemed to move. It was fairly obvious that the innkeeper liked a good cup of wine himself. Yet whilst the wine had the effect of lubricating his tongue, his speech was starting to become blurred. "A real scoundrel and a devil with the ladies he was, this sly bailiff. In and out of their drawers the whole time if they wanted to stay in the chateau, he'd make them accept his favours. The men here simply hated him – with the exception of *one or two*."

François took the hint and with a conspiratorial whisper he said, "How come these guys liked him, you'd think that they all must have hated him. Did they get money from him? I wonder who it was?"

The innkeeper took another large gulp of wine and burped noisily before continuing with a slight but rather drunken giggle. "One of the valets in the castle up there sure liked him, the one with the ugly face who always pretends to be far above us common folks. Shared the young parlour maids, they did!" The voice became conspiratorial now. "But rumour has it that the bailiff even shagged this dreadful housekeeper, the one that has such a sour face that nobody ever wanted to look at her! I wonder if he covered her face when he did it." The innkeeper broke into laughter before he tried to mimic a pious pose and added, "not that I'm one to spread gossip, mind you!"

François joined in the giggling and filled the cups again.

*****

The next morning François looked ghastly.

"Oh, my God, what happened to you?" Pierre exclaimed.

"Oh, please don't bother," François answered with a feeble voice, wiping his forehead with a perfumed handkerchief.

"Maybe I should have been more careful with the wine yesterday but somehow I simply can't sleep in this room of mine, maybe there must be something that's keeping me from closing my eyes during the night. But *please*, don't bother, I'll be absolutely fine!" He hesitated a second before he added. "Maybe it's the fact that my room faces west and heats up like an oven with the afternoon sun right until evening."

François tried to put on a brave smile but failed miserably.

"Why don't you switch rooms with me then?" Pierre proposed in a sudden impulse of sympathy and continued, "My room faces east. I'm not difficult when it comes to lodgings, I mean if you have survived sleeping in the dormitory of a monastery for most of your life, nothing can truly unsettle you any more."

"Oh, *I simply couldn't*, I mean it's *impossible*, I truly couldn't accept that!" François de Toucy seemed to be deeply touched by this proposal.

"Sure, you can! I'll give orders right away and you'll see, tonight you'll sleep like a baby!"

Pierre decided to give orders to Jean to switch the rooms but preferred to keep his instructions secret for a day or two as he still vividly remembered the murderous glance that Armand had sent him when he had ordered to have the straw of his cousin's bed changed and the ensuing scene with the dreadfully offended housekeeper.

Nervously he added, "Just let's keep this between you and me, if you don't mind, until you truly do know if you can sleep much better in my room!"

François answered that he wouldn't mind at all and Pierre went upstairs in search of his personal valet.

Jean had been behaving strangely over the past few days. Normally alert and attentive, he had been acting absent-mindedly, outright moody, to the extent that Pierre had started to worry that Jean might not be feeling well. He found Jean tidying his chamber. Despite Jean's bronze-coloured skin, his valet looked extremely pale and tense.

"Are you all right?" Pierre asked kindly.

Jean swallowed hard. He had to restrain himself in order not to confess to Pierre here and now that he felt dreadful – because he feared for Pierre's life.

"I'm absolutely fine, thank you for asking, my lord," he lied quickly, and turned around so as to avoid that Pierre should see the tears that had started to gather in his eyes. The truth was that Jean felt terrible; he was totally worn out by fatigue as he hadn't been able to get any decent sleep during the recent nights.

It all had started after he had arrived at Montrésor. Soon after their arrival in the chateau a vague sentiment of unease, a strange sense of foreboding had started to grow. This feeling had settled stubbornly in the back of Jean's mind, and lingering on, it refused to vanish – although in the beginning it was still hazy enough to be ignored. But then had come the dreadful day when Pierre had been ambushed, and from this day onwards Jean had been experiencing the same scary dream every night.

Back in his native and beautiful island of Martinique, Jean's parents had been poor farm workers on a huge plantation. Jean's family had been mere slaves, owned by a French noble master who ruled them with a fist of iron and reigned with a frightful temper. Martinique, like most of the Caribbean islands, was raided with horrible regularity. It didn't matter for the slaves if the attacks came

85

from rival colonial powers like the cheeky British or the greedy Dutch or –often enough – by pirates. During one of those raids Jean, by then an adolescent boy, had been captured by pirates, whose turn it was to plunder his island, never to return. His shock and fear had fast been replaced by the pleasure of the freedom of the seas, as soon as the pirates had admitted the boy into their ranks. Jean had never longed to go back, never would he become a slave again in his life, he had vowed.

When Jean had still been a small boy his mother had held him in her arms, swaying gently while she'd tell him stories about her ancestors in her warm Creole dialect. His mother's skin had been dark as chocolate, as her family roots reached far back to Africa. "Your forefathers used to be mighty kings in our country," she'd whisper, "until the evil white men came, killed our warriors, imprisoned our women and children and sold us to this island. But you must never forget, Jean, *we* have royal blood in us, you must always be proud of yourself."

Or she would tell thrilling stories about her grandmother. "A truly wise woman she was. And she had the gift, like I have. We can feel and sometimes even see the future. Trust your own power and the gift may have been handed down to you, my darling. These hypocrites of priests call it witchcraft, and they fear our power. Never ever betray me and tell them that our family has the gift. If you feel that you have it, use it, but use it well and wisely! I've seen in the cards that I'll lose you young but your future will be bright, so I don't mind! But trust me, my son, my spirit will always remain close to you, my dear." And then his mother had kissed Jean and hugged him passionately, her tears belying her own words, that she wouldn't mind losing him.

Back then Jean had been too young to understand her – and even later once he had grown up he hadn't truly believed her stories. How could his mother be of royal blood if they had to sleep in the same room together with their only goat and the few chickens that they could afford to keep and feed? Wouldn't kings or princes be sleeping in golden beds and a palace with servants and plenty of food? Anyhow, as soon as he had left Martinique, those memories were long forgotten, a mere dream of distant echoes from the past.

But now all of a sudden these memories had come back with a violent force. During the past fortnight, each night he had woken up after dreaming about his mother. But those dreams had been frightening – no cosy dreams of a sheltered boyhood. He would wake up with his heart racing, his head pounding and his body covered in cold sweat. In these terrifying dreams his mother would first touch him gently – he could even smell the sweet scent of her skin – but then she would grip him hard, shake him, appeal to him: "Jean, you must save your master, do something, Jean, the danger is imminent!"

86

But how could he save his master? His mind was spinning; the same question kept passing through his head, relentlessly, painfully. His mother was warning, even scolding him, but what could he do? For heaven's sake, what could he, a simple servant, do to protect Pierre de Beauvoir?

Suddenly Jean realized that his master must have been talking to him while he had been lost in his thoughts. Pierre had raised his voice and was addressing him angrily. "Jean, would you mind listening to me when I give you orders? What's going on with you?"

Jean flushed deeply. "I'm sorry, my lord, I was lost there for a moment!"

"Seems to have become a bad habit of yours, you'd better pay attention!" Pierre was visibly upset and he repeated his instructions. "I've asked you to arrange to change my room with Monsieur de Toucy. But I don't want this to be known to anybody, I wish that you arrange this alone and discreetly!"

Jean looked at his master as if he had gone mad. "Change the rooms, my lord?" he asked, as if he couldn't trust his ears.

"Yes, change the rooms! And please don't look at me like this! It's my wish and my order – just do it!"

Now it was Pierre's turn to flush. Once he had left François de Toucy there had been plenty of time to develop doubts and profoundly regret the good sense of his own rushed decision. He was definitely not keen to read in Jean's eyes that he was convinced that Pierre must have gone mad.

"Of course, Your Grace, I'll do this immediately and I do apologize most sincerely! Would Your Grace have any further orders for your humble servant?" Jean answered stiffly with the deepest bow that could be imagined.

Pierre sighed. "All right, I know it's silly. And stop calling me Your Grace, you know that I don't use this title in France. It just tells me that I managed to upset you. But it's my wish and I want you to do it – but do it discreetly – and don't ask me why, I don't even know myself what made me suggest it."

Pierre's angry eyes had changed; they now resembled the pleading eyes of a young puppy and Jean simply couldn't resist this offensive of boyish charm. He smiled back at Pierre and the smile transformed his tired face completely. "I would never forget my position, my lord, and will of course do immediately as you request."

"Armand told me that he'd be a difficult guest, he always seems to be stirring up trouble wherever he goes." Pierre suddenly felt an urgent need to confide in Jean, content to have found a sympathetic listener.

87

Jean listened attentively to Pierre's woes and although he managed to keep the non-committal face of a loyal servant he had to agree deep down, François de Toucy had been nothing but a nuisance since he had arrived at Montrésor. Proudly he would promenade himself like a perfumed peacock in the courtyard but somehow Jean had the suspicion that this polished image of a highly refined young gentleman was nothing else but a disguise for a sinister personality and that his manicured hands would be able to handle a weapon with deadly efficiency if need be.

His thoughts started spinning wildly. Maybe François de Toucy was the real danger – would he be the man his mother had tried to warn him about? It must be more than sheer coincidence that Jean had been waking up every single night since de Toucy had arrived in the castle and that his mother had been insisting that danger was imminent in his dreams since then.

Tonight Jean went to bed, but this time he was impatiently awaiting the next dream in the hope that his mother would finally reveal to him the source of the danger, give him more hints, confirm his suspicion. But when he woke up from just another terrible nightmare, his head still spinning, all he could remember was a single message: "*New moon, beware of the new moon!*"

Jean jumped out of his bed and walked barefoot to the small window of his attic room. It was a rare privilege and a sign of his elevated rank as the personal valet of the Marquis de Beauvoir that he was allowed to have a room for himself. He peeped out of the window and saw a sky of dark velvet studded with stars and a silvery crescent of the moon that reigned in the night sky.

But Jean didn't marvel at the breathtaking beauty of the sparkling stars above him as his heart nearly stopped when he realized how thin the crescent had become. What looked like a beautiful night sky was in reality the harbinger of danger. The new moon would rise soon, far too soon. A night owl shrieked and Jean's hand started to tremble. Immediately he scolded himself, "Don't be such a coward! You want to protect your master but you tremble like a hare as soon as you hear an owl cry? Do something!"

Suddenly a plan of action occurred to him: from tomorrow on he would stay glued to François de Toucy and shadow him – if necessary day and night. The relief Jean felt at having a concrete plan of action was enormous, and he had the impression that a huge burden had been lifted from his shoulders. Yes, from tomorrow on he would follow this dubious gentleman and make sure that he couldn't harm his master. Satisfied with his ingenious plan he dropped back into his bed and was deeply asleep as soon as his head touched the pillow – the first peaceful night's sleep for many days.

Henri de Beauvoir, the proud and freshly appointed Count de Roquemoulin was pacing up and down inside the barn he remembered so well from the past. Vivid memories had been welling up in his mind as soon as he had pushed open the heavy wooden door, while its squeaking hinges protested loudly against the intrusion of the stranger.

Henri glanced at the heaps of hay and the few forlorn rusty tools. Nothing had changed inside since he had waited here the last time, freezing miserably for many hours in the morning of a dark winter's day. His thoughts wandered back to that day. How much he had looked forward to this encounter with Jean Baptiste de Roquemoulin, how much had depended on the success of this first meeting! He could still remember the pricking of his nerves, the sweet feeling of danger mixed with joyful anticipation.

How cold it had been then! Today it seemed almost unreal to dwell on those memories, as it was stiflingly hot inside. As a precaution Henri had preferred to shut the door in order to avoid undue attention from passers-by, therefore no gentle breeze would help to ease the unbearable heat – Henri felt as if he was being slowly roasted in an oversized oven.

Rays of sunlight were streaming into his shelter through the slits in the wooden planks, particles of dust danced and sparkled in the golden beams of light until they reached the floor and painted pools of bright light on the trampled clay that was littered with strands of dirty straw and bundles of hay.

Henri felt his shirt, made from the finest of linen, starting to cling to his body. Soon he would be completely drenched by perspiration – his hair was already stuck wetly to his head. He felt hot, uncomfortable and ready to explode with anger. How dare his visitor keep him waiting here in this unbearable heat? Cursing the heat and his unreliable visitor he stripped naked to his waist. How would he explain later to his valet or his groom that his shirt was totally drenched when he was supposed to be on a lonely, leisurely stroll along the Loire River? They'd never dare to ask, but tongues would wag down in the servants' quarters.

Finally – he had almost decided to leave – he heard the noise of an approaching horseman and quickly pressed his eye against one of the larger gaps to check if the approaching rider was indeed the visitor he had been waiting for. Content to see the former bailiff of Montrésor approaching, Henri stepped back and waited for his visitor, hand on his rapier, boiling with anger.

The squeaking door opened and closed and his visitor stumbled inside, trying to adjust his eyes from the blazing sunlight outside to the shadowy darkness of the barn.

"How dare you keep me waiting!" Henri hissed, his hand ready to strike with his sword at any moment.

Instinctively the bailiff fell to his knees and wailed, "Have mercy on your loyal servant, Monsieur le Marquis, let me explain my delay!"

"You'd better give me a good explanation or I'll show you it's not a good idea to keep Henri de Beauvoir waiting," Henri growled, his rapier still ready to strike.

The bailiff looked at the irate Henri de Beauvoir. With his naked torso glistening in the golden beams of light he looked like the incarnation of a Greek god, but a god of revenge, ready to strike at any moment. The bailiff understood that he had no time to lose and quickly he started his narrative, rushing through the first sentences as if the devil in person were chasing him.

"Monsieur le Marquis, I was about to leave my hiding place when I suddenly heard voices. Let me explain, I'm staying at present with my cousin and his wife as their house has a safe hiding place in the cellar. We had agreed that I should escape to the cellar and hide if any stranger should ever show up. I managed to peep quickly out of the window before I rushed down to the cellar and I could see and hear several young musketeers who were loudly interrogating my cousin's wife in the farm courtyard as to whether she had seen me. Word must have spread that some of my relatives were still living in this small village. I quickly dived into my hiding place, a clever bolthole, located behind big wine barrels, and you need to know that one of the barrels is empty and serves as the entrance."

The bailiff panted and mopped his forehead. The heat and the excitement were taking their toll. "I stayed there, well hidden, for what seemed to me like an eternity, nearly going mad. I was of course aware that your lordship would be waiting for me. Then I heard voices approaching the barrels – I became really scared! They started hitting the barrels with their muskets to check if they were full."

Henri saw that the sweaty stains on the bailiff's shirt starting to spread as he relived his ordeal.

"Luckily I heard my cousin protesting loudly that they were damaging his barrels of wine and would most likely spill his good wine with their hammering. Why not better taste the wine together with him if they needed proof that those were genuine wine barrels? Soon they started discussing the quality of the harvest and abandoned the search completely as my cousin shrewdly offered them more and even better wine that he kept bottled upstairs. As soon as the cellar was safe I managed to sneak out of my hiding place into the stables and I rode straight to this barn. But knowing that the musketeers were on my back, I decided to avoid taking any further risk and did not dare to use the direct way but rode through the shelter in the shrubbery of the embankment."

Henri put his rapier back into its protective scabbard.

"You're excused, but your story only confirms my conviction that we have to act really fast now. Your last plan was a total failure, whereas you told me before that you wouldn't even contemplate the possibility of failure! I paid you a fortune in advance and you'd better deliver soon or you'll find that this earth will no longer be a comfortable place for you to stay on! Do I make myself clear?"

Henri had spoken in a very even voice but the bailiffs felt his bowels contract. The threat was all too palpable.

"Yes, Monsieur le Marquis, I fully understand. But in my defence: the ambush was a success, my men were sure to have killed Pierre de Beauvoir, they saw him going down! That he escaped is beyond any doubt a sign of witchcraft!" and quickly he crossed himself to ward off the forces of evil.

Henri uttered a noise of contempt. Apparently he was no believer in witchcraft. "Witchcraft? You're a bloody fool! Pierre had changed his horse and your men were too stupid to check it out! Do you have any better plans? I tell you, you better had do!"

All of a sudden the bailiff's expression changed and the sly gleam came back to his eyes. Returning to his usual mellow and slimy way of speaking, he answered, "Of course, Monsieur le Marquis. You will be entirely happy with my new plan and our little deal. This time my plans cannot fail. But I needed to wait until the new moon was approaching. Now I'll need two men in your confidence to help me, and they must be trained fighters and agile."

Rapidly the bailiff went into the details of his newest plan – more elaborate and risky than the last attempt to eliminate Pierre de Beauvoir – but waiting for the next chance to stage an ambush would take too much time, as the victim had become too cautious. There was no question for either of them as to the necessity for urgent action. The bailiff was nervous, as secretly he feared he could feel the noose closing around his neck. Only the removal of Pierre de Beauvoir would buy him enough time and money to establish himself comfortably in the new colonies.

Henri de Beauvoir desperately wished to crown his recent streak of luck: Count of Roquemoulin first and now he must become the Marquis de Beauvoir; he could not bear any further delay!

Aloud Henri answered, "We're in agreement then, time is of the essence! Only when my bastard cousin is dead will you find shelter from prosecution. We don't know how long he's going to stay in Montrésor. I've heard that a new bailiff has arrived and it may well be that he'll leave the castle very soon. So you'd better hurry!" He paused and his steely blue eyes looked straight into the eyes of his visitor. "And you'd better succeed this time – if you wish to stay alive!"

Henri moved a step back as his visitor's shirt was drenched with sweat and he stank like a boar. He probably hadn't washed since he had left the castle's dungeons.

"Two men in my confidence will be waiting at the hiding place that you indicated after midnight. I wish you good luck, you may leave now!"

Henri looked at the bailiff arrogantly, every inch the future Marquis he was aspiring to become. To Henri's surprise the bailiff didn't cast down his eyes as might have been expected and in keeping with his inferior position. Haughtily, Henri straightened his back and directed a glacial glance at the bailiff, confident of reducing the bailiff to a heap of wobbling nerves, but the bailiff's eyes looked back at him, by no means afraid. Henri suddenly had the awkward feeling of being himself appraised and judged – he could even read an explicit threat in those beady eyes.

"There is one last detail I must allow myself to mention, Monsieur le Marquis. I have deemed it useful to take the initiative to deposit letters explaining the details of our deal and your involvement with the sudden demise of the late Count de Roquemoulin with a notary public and a priest whom I happen to know well – to be published in the event of my sudden disappearance or death."

"What do you mean, you slimy toad?" The intense blue eyes of the Greek god were now flashing dangerously.

"I would like to explain to Monsieur le Marquis that I'm under the impression that I might need some sort of protection if suddenly you or your men might reach the embarrassing conclusion that my services may no longer be required once your cousin has joined his ancestors."

Henri's hand moved to his rapier but the bailiff shouted out, "Stop, and listen to me, Henri de Beauvoir, or you'll regret it!"

Henri stopped, totally taken aback.

"Let me add, Monsieur le Marquis, that I happened to witness a man dispose of the corpse of the late Count de Roquemoulin into the Loire river, a man whom I could positively identify! That day I was riding along the embankment back to Montrésor. I didn't bother at this stage – it's always awkward getting involved with the authorities – doesn't each of us harbour his own little secrets? But you should know that I'm fully aware who I'm dealing with – and you should also know that if ever I don't survive this adventure, you'll end in the Bastille and on the gallows, Henri de Beauvoir – Marquis or no. I warn you, take care!"

Before Henri found the opportunity to digest the content of this insidious speech and formulate a fitting answer his visitor had executed a low bow fit for the King of France and walked out of the barn. By the time Henri had managed to come back to his senses, his visitor had left already, only the squeaking of the door reminding him that this encounter had been a reality and not a dream.

All of a sudden Henri detected a movement in the left corner of the barn. Eager to rid himself of some of the tension that had built up inside him, he threw his rapier like a javelin in the direction of the rustling sound. How much he would have preferred to ram the rapier right through the heart of this toad of a bailiff!

A screaming sound – almost human in nature – told him that his rapier must have hit the target and Henri moved to corner in order to check out what kind of target he had hit. He saw a cat that was badly wounded, cringing in pain. Henri withdrew his rapier and with a swift movement he decapitated the suffering animal.

Talking to himself, he said, "Don't they say that curiosity killed the cat? How very true."

Slowly and painstakingly he cleaned his blade of the cat's blood before he restored the rapier to its scabbard. Henri came to the conclusion that however gratifying it might be to curse and imagine various ways to finish off the insidious bailiff, this was a totally useless exercise. The first priority had to be to deal with his cousin's demise. But gritting his teeth he vowed that the bailiff would soon enough find out that blackmailing Henri de Beauvoir had been a bad idea and would not contributing to his good health. "You're the next on my list now, you slimy toad – and that's a promise!"

Henri was startled when he realized that he must have been talking to himself. It was about time to leave his shelter, the heat seemed to be having an effect on his brain. He had just opened the door to step out when Marina suddenly appeared in front of him. She certainly had the gift of appearing out of the blue – but then Henri was only half surprised, as he was aware that the gypsies must be following all of his movements closely; he was too much of a valuable prize to be left unattended.

Marina stopped in her tracks when she saw her husband half-naked and her eyes sparkled like the eyes of a cat ready to pounce on its prey. Her glance caressed his body stripped to the waist and silently she took his hand and led him back into the barn.

"Shouldn't we close the door?" he remarked in a coarse voice, as she had lost no time and was pulling at his breeches.

"My people are on guard for us, don't worry!"

Henri heard her voice echoing his own excitement. They dropped into the soft hay and she started to strip off her clothes, tearing at them with brisk movements, in a hurry to get rid of her clothes as fast as possible.

Their love-making was greedy, swift, almost brutal, nothing refined – but when Henri lay next to her, panting in the suffocating heat, he found himself strangely satisfied as rarely before and his tension was gone. He drank greedily form the flask of diluted wine that Marina had miraculously produced.

Suddenly they heard the noise of someone walking through the door and before they could react Marina's brother had come inside. His dark handsome face looked flushed and Henri wondered if he had been secretly watching them. Henri didn't bother to cover himself as Marina did, but stretched like a satisfied tomcat, making sure that Marina's brother was watching him.

"Let's see if I can detect some excitement in this beautiful face," Henri thought, "how I'd love to drag him into the hay now, maybe even together with Marina – now that would be real fun!" The mere thought of it had a visible effect on his loins but to Henri's disappointment Marina's brother only sent him a contemptuous look.

Henri shrugged and started to dress. In a business-like tone he started to speak. "It's good that both of you showed up, I'll need you tomorrow night!"

He had no illusions that both of them had followed him and therefore must know that he had met with a visitor in the barn, which had the added benefit that he could keep his explanations short.

"If I manage to get rid of my cousin, I'll become the next Marquis de Beauvoir and Marina will be married to one of the richest men in the kingdom."

"How rich?" asked Marina, her face still deeply flushed and excited.

"Beyond anything that you could imagine!" Henri answered. "You'd live like a true princess! You would live in a different palace or castle very week of the year, we'd even own a complete island in the new colonies. In my cousin's treasure chests there is more gold than you could ever transport in the wagons of your tribe, the wheels would break under the weight."

Marina's eyes were shining even more like the eyes of a cat. Now *this* was a language she could understand and even her sulking brother looked animated, for once.

Henri explained the part they were supposed to play and they just nodded. For experienced climbers and fighters such as they were, it sounded easy enough.

"What about the bailiff?" Marina asked in a matter of fact way. "Shall we finish him off at the same time, aren't you afraid that he'll talk afterwards?"

"You're not only beautiful, but you're a clever girl as well!" Henri caressed her back and was surprised to receive another murderous glance from her brother – he seemed to be getting jealous. "We'll have to deal with him later, if we finish him off immediately, I'll be in trouble. But you're right, we must get rid of him – but I'll choose the right time!"

When Henri returned to his chateau, his valet found him surprisingly good-humoured – a welcome change, as the new Count de Roquemoulin had become extremely trying and moody lately.

It turned out to be a refreshing night for Henri. The suppressed tension of the past weeks had gone, replaced by eager anticipation that something wonderful was going to happen. Soon his bastard cousin would be dead and he, Henri de Beauvoir, Comte de Roquemoulin, would be appointed Marquis de Beauvoir, to be greeted and kissed by the King of France as his newest and beloved cousin! As soon as he was back in Paris it would be easy enough to find people who could deal with Marina, her brother or the slimy bailiff, all of those people who thought that they could blackmail or manipulate him – he'd teach them a lesson, all of them!

*****

François de Toucy tried to ignore the footsteps behind him. Since yesterday he hadn't been able to move inside the castle without being followed by or bumping 'by coincidence' into Pierre's faithful valet. His intentions were only too clear. He sighed, the valet's behaviour was becoming a bit tedious. He turned his back and indeed, Jean was there – again!

"It seems to me that I have had the pleasure of meeting you quite often today," he greeted the valet. "I am starting to wonder if there's there something amiss with my clothes or my hairstyle that might need your urgent attention? If not, I imagine that your master needs you more than I do!"

Jean flushed and cursed himself. He must learn to become more subtle, this was obvious.

"I apologize, my lord, I didn't mean to be a nuisance, but Monsieur le Marquis has instructed me to make sure that you're feeling comfortable and to be especially attentive to your needs!"

"It would indeed add considerably to my feeling of comfort if you could remove yourself," François de Toucy answered acidly.

Jean bowed and decided secretly that it was time to disappear and figure out a new strategy. François de Toucy was simply too sharp.

That night Jean's dreams were even more vivid than before. The words 'new moon, beware of the new moon' were hammering in his head and nearly made him go mad. An atmosphere of tension lingered in the castle, everybody seemed to be irritated, and shouting and crying could be heard frequently in the servants' quarters, as if a sense of foreboding had wrapped the chateau in a dark cloud.

What a welcome surprise, therefore, for everybody when a surprisingly good-humoured housekeeper suddenly appeared and invited everybody after dinner to some generously distributed freshly brewed ale.

"I made it according to my mother's secret recipe," she boasted proudly. "You won't find anything better!"

Among the pleased cheers of the thirsty inhabitants of the chateau she swung her ladle and filled the cups, making sure that nobody was forgotten or received less than his or her fair share. Everybody was amazed that her normally sour face had turned an animated pink and had brightened for once – word was spreading fast that she must have fallen in love.

"If she really has managed to drag a lover into her bed, he must be fairly shortsighted," grinned one of the musketeers savouring the ale, "but I have give the old goat this, her ale is first class, I think I'll get another cup!"

Once the ale had been consumed the mood inside the chateau improved greatly, and drunken giggles could be heard everywhere. Those who had been abusing the housekeeper's generosity fell asleep rapidly – and there seemed to be a lot of those.

Jean looked at the merry crowd around him and grimaced. Since he had woken up this morning a headache had been lingering and he knew from past experience that drinking ale or wine would only make it much worse. As the housekeeper insisted that he too must toast her health, he took a large gulp in order to please her. But as soon as she turned and walked off, Jean quickly spat it out, no ale for him tonight!

The sun was starting to set and night was falling. Tonight the dreaded new moon would rise in the night sky. Jean's elated feelings had evaporated long ago. Following François de Toucy had revealed no clue to him, and he was totally at a loss as to what he should do. Disgusted, Jean watched François de Toucy not only accept a large cup of ale, but he even insisted at the hilarious laughter of the other servants to plant a kiss on the flabby cheeks of the housekeeper, who blushed like a young maid.

Soon the castle lay in deep slumber and peace – almost.

The four individuals who crossed the dark forest seemed to be at ease, although there was practically no light to guide their way. The bailiff and the handyman who accompanied him knew this part of the forest like the back of their hands and the two gypsies who had joined them before were accustomed to finding their way in the dark.

They dismounted and tied their horses to some shrubbery and then walked the remaining few hundred yards to the chateau of Montrésor, making sure to remain hidden in the dense foliage. They were also careful not to make any suspicious noise. All of them were wearing dark clothes and had rubbed dirt into their faces – a perfect camouflage to blend into the dark night. It had come as a shock to the bailiff when he had recognized that one of the two lean gypsies was a woman, but when the truth had dawned upon him it was already too late to object. They needed to strike tonight in order to profit from the darkness, this calm and moonless night was simply perfect for their daring venture.

The small group of four reached the chateau walls at midnight. A random passer-by would have been astonished that no human noises could be heard; not even a single dog was barking. An eerie and highly unusual silence reigned.

Unperturbed, the bailiff guided the group to a hidden door at the base of the castle's tower. It was overgrown by wild vines – certainly a picturesque view in daylight but tonight none of the group had any romantic inclinations. The bailiff dived into his pocket and produced a large forged key that he inserted carefully into the lock. The key moved easily and silently – as did the hinges of the door. Someone inside the castle must have taken care to grease them fairly recently. The bailiff made signs to his handyman to stay outside to keep guard and entered the silent castle compound with the two gypsies.

Once they had entered the castle the three intruders climbed the steep staircase belonging to one of the castle towers – once again there were no guards to be seen, no noise could be heard. An unsettling veil of silence enshrouded the castle.

The bailiff's nerves were on edge, the silence starting to weigh on his mood – *I'll feel much better when I'm finished with this job.* He greatly disliked Henri's decision to send two gypsies whom he distrusted profoundly. They had barely spoken a word since they had arrived. *It's a good thing that I told the count that I had hidden away a letter to protect myself.* The bailiff tried to calm his apprehensions.

From time to time the shrieking sound of some lonely night owls disturbed the leaden silence. A fairytale atmosphere prevailed, the castle and all its inhabitants seemingly frozen in time.

The bailiff made a nervous sign to follow him and together they crossed the gallery that linked the towers towards the main building with the bedchambers of the lord of the castle and his guests.

Jean had been waiting with trepidation for sleep to arrive, dreading the apparently inevitable torture of another nightmare. The new moon had arrived and he hadn't been able to hunt down the murderer – nor even to keep François de Toucy under control.

"You're a loser, you failed miserably," he scolded himself, self-pity and despair taking over. Although Jean felt the fatigue spreading in his body he couldn't sleep, something was wrong. It took him some time though to realize that it was actually the absence of any noise that was so unusual, almost terrifying. He couldn't simply lie there and wait for disaster to strike, he must do something. Seizing one of Pierre's swords and a flintlock gun as a weapon, he tip-toed out of his attic room down to the floor where his master and the noble guests were sleeping. He heard heavy breathing and snoring and immediately felt relieved – nothing unusual there, the lack of sleep must have made him an easy prey for all kinds of silly nightmares!

He decided to walk downstairs to the servants' quarters where the servants on duty and the guards would be sitting together, playing cards or dice to kill the time. Maybe he could ask for a cup of hot milk and go back to bed.

He opened the door of the servants' room, but the greeting froze on his lips. Maids, grooms and valets lay snoring on the table or limp on the ground, empty cups and abandoned cards still on the table; stray dice had rolled onto the floor.

In panic, Jean bolted down to the guards' room, but once again, only the sound of peaceful snoring greeted him, all of the guards were lying on the table, the tankards of ale still clutched in their hands. To his great surprise even the dogs were sleeping. Jean took the dog's bowl and sniffed at it – the dogs must have been given drugged ale as well!

With trembling hands he placed the bowl back on the ground, afraid of making any noise. His fatigue had gone, the blood was pulsating through his veins and slowly Jean started to panic – the new moon had arrived, and he was here, alone, with no clue what to do!

The bailiff made a sign to use the staircase to descend to the lower floor when Marina's brother suddenly whispered, "Why are we going this way, don't try and trick us, we know that the noble masters always sleep upstairs!"

"Because there is a secret staircase that ends directly in the Marquis's room, but it starts from the first floor! I'm giving the orders here!" the bailiff hissed back, furious at being scolded by a gypsy.

Following his lead, they climbed the staircase downwards, moved silently through seemingly endless dark galleries filled with countless paintings but more guessing than seeing their way until they reached the door that gave way to the secret staircase. Once more the bailiff chose the correct key from his bundle and once again the key turned noiselessly in the well-greased lock.

The intruders climbed upwards until they reached a door that led to the private apartment of the Marquis de Beauvoir. Slowly and cautiously the bailiff opened the door, making sure to avoid any suspicious noise. They had agreed that Marina's brother should enter the room first, ready to strike in case Pierre de Beauvoir or one of his servants should still be awake, but the room lay dark and almost deserted, and only the sound of a peacefully snoring sleeper could be heard through the bed curtains.

"He's snoring like a pig!" whispered Marina, "But why are the bed curtains drawn in summer?"

"These noble folks are often scared stiff of being bitten by mosquitoes, they prefer to suffocate." The voice of the bailiff had taken on a sarcastic note.

"But let's move on and get our job finished!"

*****

Something extremely odd was going on in the castle of Roquemoulin. Not only had the new lord of the castle suddenly been displaying a highly unusual level of good humour and joviality, he had even proposed that festivities should be held on the evening of the new moon to celebrate his recent appointment as Count of Roquemoulin.

Shortly after his usual frugal breakfast Henri had called his flabbergasted bailiff and given orders to organize a gathering for his staff with a lavish dinner – he had even suggested hiring musicians and organizing dances – a true celebration for all of his loyal servants to be topped by the presence of the lord of the castle. His bailiff couldn't believe his ears but managed to keep a straight face. Was the new count going soft?

Tongues were wagging in eager anticipation as Henri had given carte blanche to organize a truly remarkable festivity, and no expense was to be spared. Thus in a great hurry the great barn of the castle had been decorated with fresh green leaves and braided crowns of flowers, the wooden tables had been scrubbed until they were gleaming, before being loaded with rare delicacies like freshly baked bread, meat, poultry, cheese and pastries, and heavy jugs of wine were waiting to be emptied.

Majestically Henri had walked through the crowd, looking every inch the prince with his lace collar and his gleaming curls crowned by a jewel-studded beret. At the beginning the count's presence had an intimidating effect on his servants but it didn't take long for the wine and the merry music to loosen their tongues, the first jokes started to be cracked and the maids let the necklines of their bodices and blouses slip. Henri saw with satisfaction that this celebration was not only in full sway – it would stay in their memory forever.

What a remarkable way to celebrate the demise of my dearest bastard cousin! he thought in amusement, while he tried to ignore the inviting glance of a pretty kitchen maid. *What a disappointment for my enemies that my presence in Roquemoulin will be witnessed by more than a hundred people; whatever happens at Montrésor, I'll be above all suspicion!*

He smiled, revelling that his cousin's come-uppance would be tonight, probably at this very hour. But his smirk tore away the mask of the generous host that he had been wearing until now. The pretty maid who had been sending inviting glances to him noticed this change of expression and, frightened, she dived away into the dancing crowd. Many years later she would tell her grandchildren that she had seen the true face and the cold eyes of a killer.

After midnight huge roast pigs were carried into the candle-lit barn in a truly impressive procession while the count's hunters and grooms were blowing their horns. Liveried servants carried torches in their hands as they preceded wooden stretchers decorated with vine leaves and fruit, not only loaded with the roast pigs but ever more juicy roasts of all kind of venison and delicious pastries. The pastries had been shaped like animals or were adorned with the coat of arms of Roquemoulin, crafted by the hands of pastry makers.

Nobody had ever seen such refinement and such abundance of food. Cries of joy and surprise emanated from the crowd and like a hungry pack of dogs Henri's servants stormed the piles of food that had been placed right in the middle of the crowd and dug with their knives into the juicy meats. Hands, mouths and faces glistened in the light of the torches from gravy and fat while they stuffed themselves until they were about to explode, emptying countless cups of wine until the room started to swirl around them. The feast had turned into an orgy of greed.

As soon as Henri could hear the first moaning sounds as people started to lose the last of their inhibitions and began to couple in the shadows of the corners he decided that it was about time to withdraw. Only a few of his servants were sober enough to notice his departure and most of his people took it as a welcome signal to drop their last pretence of shyness and join the orgy that was in full swing now.

His bailiff had stayed sober and he was still wondering what this was all about – having watched Henri during the evening he was more and more convinced that this celebration was not the result of any sort of impulse of kindness or act of generosity – it must serve a purpose, but what kind of purpose could it be? Disgusted, the bailiff of Roquemoulin looked at the frenzy around him. *Were these people all blind, had they gone mad?*

Céline was sifting through piles of different fabrics. She was astonished that she still loved doing this – would she never get tired of choosing fabrics for new gowns?

Marie sat in the corner, stretching her legs listlessly. "I'll become hysterical if I see another sample of fabric. I mean, we've seen it all: silks, velvet, cotton, black, green, red, brocade – you name it and we've probably seen it. I love choosing new gowns but we did this already three weeks ago – and now you've started it all again, you must be sick!"

Céline laughed and looked slightly guilty. "I admit it's a bit much. But I do have my reasons. And I still love it. You know, for someone who's spent practically the past ten years turning the same gowns again and again backwards and forwards, trying to make them look different, this is not only pure bliss – it's heaven! And don't forget that I was not only poor, I was doomed to be an old spinster as well. Everybody was expecting me to wear black, black or black, maybe some daring drab grey or brown would be tolerable. Out of the question to wear any colours, people in Reims would have thought that I was out fishing for a husband – or worse!"

Now it was Marie's turn to look guilty and quickly she replied, "I do apologize. Actually, I don't mind choosing fabrics. I forget how terrible your life must have been. I suppose you must have nearly gone mad!"

Céline laughed. "Worse, it was much worse, I was *bored* to death. How glad I was when your maid Anne knocked at my door to ask for my help! And what a gift from heaven that I was allowed to accompany you to England. Well, part of my gift seems to be arriving."

The door opened and Charles entered the room with his usual impatient stride. He surveyed the pile of fabrics and exclaimed, "Oh God, don't tell me that you'll be ordering more clothes. We've been through this already! You ordered gowns for hunting parties, balls, evening gowns, gowns for summer, clothes for chilly autumn evenings, sober gowns, colourful gowns, light gowns, I can't even remember any more what kind of gowns. I only remember that I had to sell at least five of my best farms to pay for them!"

Céline was not to be intimated. On the contrary, she burst into laughter and, glancing at her husband full of mischief, she exclaimed, "Oh Charles, my poor darling, I'm so sorry. But didn't you tell me that you'd even buy me a castle for me if ever I fancied one?"

102

Her laughing eyes met his and Charles had to smile. "I admit, I was exaggerating a bit. Maybe it was only one farm after all I had to sell – certainly the one I always wanted to get rid of. But why this latest spending spree?"

Céline looked at him lovingly and said, "Because I'm sure now that there'll be three of us!"

Charles looked at her as if she was simple. "Of course there are three of us! We promised Marie could join us when we travel to Montrésor."

"Charles, you're such a typical man, you don't listen properly and you never seem to understand. I mean that I'm expecting a child, this is why I'll need some more gowns!"

Charles's mouth opened and closed as if he was choking – he looked more like a fish on dry land than a gentleman. "You're expecting a child?" he repeated mechanically.

"What a charming response," Céline answered acidly. "Well, it does happen to all kinds of married people. What did you expect?"

Charles was still trying to digest the news. "I never expected something like this! You know, I saw us sitting in twenty years in one of my castles in the countryside, surrounded by my dogs, comfortable and cosy. Somehow I never expected to become a father, I'm no longer a youngster!"

Céline's eyes were brimming with tears. "You're not happy?"

Charles suddenly jumped up, walked to Céline's chair and fell on his knees. "Céline, I'm happy beyond words – but, I'm … scared!"

Marie had been listening to this conversation and thought it about time to take some action. She was absolutely delighted for Céline; how typical of a man to kill her joy with useless concerns. She got up and found a decanter on the sideboard. Curiously she lifted the crystal cap and sniffed at the contents. Good! This seemed to be powerful enough to swing the mood. Quickly she poured a good portion into one of the Venetian glasses that had been placed next to the decanter and brought the fortifying liquid to Charles. "I guess you need this now!" she said.

Charles nodded and gratefully he took a large gulp of the amber liquid. "That was good!" he exclaimed, his face losing its paleness.

Céline looked at him as he held onto the glass for support, and recovered her smile. "I'd never have imagined that a gentleman who's brave enough to fight against any imaginable enemy on a battlefield should fall to his knees as soon as something as natural as having a child is mentioned. Now listen, Charles, I'm not

103

one of these fragile tiny women who are sick and suffering all the time. I'll be all right! Actually it came as a surprise to me as well, I always tended to regard myself as past my prime. But now it has happened, I'm absolutely delighted and I firmly intend to have even more children. You'll not be able to escape from this, my dearest husband. As for your vision of our old age, just add to the pack of smelly dogs a pack of noisy and dirty children or grandchildren and you'll be fine."

Charles stood up and smiled down at Céline. "Isn't she great, my darling!" he exclaimed, looking proudly at his wife. I knew that you were the right one as soon as I set my eyes on you. If it's a pack of children that you want to raise, well, I'll be happy to oblige!" He drew her in his arms and kissed her tenderly.

"Congratulations! But I have a question..." Marie had something important burning in the back of her mind. "Does this mean that we'll not be able to travel to Montrésor?" she asked nervously. "I mean that Céline probably won't want to travel in her delicate condition – I mean – I'll certainly understand..." Her voice trailed away as she bravely tried to hide her embarrassment.

"Well, I'm afraid we'll have to ask Pierre to come and join us in Paris. You're right, I don't see us travelling under these circumstances!" Charles added.

Céline looked at them as if both had gone mad. "Of course we'll travel to Montrésor! Do you think that I want to stay in this hot and stinking city during summer? I imagine myself sitting in lush gardens, having plenty of fresh air and good food, Charles serving me grapes, wine and cake or whatever I fancy day and night, but I will most definitely not stay in Paris!"

Charles had to grin – although he didn't quite share this vision of becoming her personal valet – but he said, "You can't travel, my love, it's far too dangerous!"

"Hogwash! I discussed it with Anne, who still serves as Marie's maid; she was also her wet nurse, even if she does look more like a musketeer than a woman. She confided in me that Mother Nature has her own rules. According to Anne, I should travel in a coach as long as I feel well and she also thinks that staying in Paris is more dangerous than travelling. She heard from the other servants that the plague still strikes regularly during summer and the city is full of other illnesses we don't even know about. Montrésor will be ideal, but we'll go slowly and make it a leisure trip!"

Charles had already opened his mouth in order to protest but the mention of the plague had the effect of sending a shudder down his spine. Maybe travelling to Montrésor would not be such a bad idea after all.

"Let's finish completing your wardrobe first," he said, resuming the discussion, "and then let's travel to Montrésor at a leisurely pace. I'll make sure that you'll be travelling in the most comfortable coach that Paris has to offer and we'll stop whenever it rains to make sure you can keep the blinds open and get some fresh air. If it takes us two weeks to reach Montrésor, who cares?"

Céline laughed. "That's settled then. But I can see us crawling at a snail's pace. Marie, please send a letter to Pierre announcing our arrival in the coming weeks – but please don't betray our little secret! It'll be difficult enough to endure Charles as a doting husband in the coming weeks…"

*****

The music was playing loud, too loud. The tunes floating into his room from the nearby barn were gaining in speed as did the stamping of the feet. Henri sat in his library, his legs stretched out, sipping from time to time from his glass. He was far too excited in order to go to bed tonight, even if he realized that it would be highly improbable to hear anything from Marina before noon of the next day.

He heard a cautious tapping sound at the door and shouted, "You may enter," wondering who was seeking entrance.

It was his butler who entered the room with a flushed and excited face. He cleared his throat, visibly embarrassed by the audacity of his mission.

"Monsieur le Comte, your servants would like to offer a special toast to your lordship, as your lordship has condescended to display extraordinary kindness in organizing this wonderful festivity for them. Would you mind doing them the favour of coming down once more and granting them the opportunity to cheer you?"

Henri looked at his butler – *what did this canaille dare to suggest?* – then came to the conclusion that this was no joke but a sincere request from his servants, and forced himself to smile and answer, "It will surely be a pleasure for me. Let them know that I'll come down soon!"

His butler looked extremely relieved that his request had been accepted gracefully and left the room.

"That's hilarious," Henri thought. "I'm becoming popular. How ridiculous – but soon they'll know me better!"

After a good quarter of an hour he went downstairs and walked back to the barn. A chair of honour had been decorated like a throne with ivy leaves and the Roquemoulin coat of arms. Cheers erupted from the crowds as soon as he entered the hall, first hesitant, than louder and louder and wherever he looked he saw his servants toasting to his health with their cups – a daring few were no longer bothering to use their cups but had grabbed the wine jars instead.

Henri had to hold his breath – the smells wafting through the barn assaulted his nostrils, the stench was sickening. The mix of roasted meat, ale, spilled wine, garlic, onions and unwashed bodies sweating profusely was nauseating.

How much I loathe them! he thought. Henri forced a smile on his face although he had to suppress a shudder of disgust. As soon as he reached his throne of honour, loud cheers erupted and his servants clapped their hands and stamped with their feet to express their pleasure and gratitude for this wonderful treat. With a smile firmly fixed to his face Henri waved regally and returned the toast with his cup, drawing further cheers and applause from the crowd.

He looked every inch a refined and handsome prince from a fairytale. *How I hate them, how much I despise every single moment I have to spend down here among these stinking commoners.*

As soon as the cheers abated, Henri ordered the musicians to go on and play another dance tune while he disappeared back to the castle, leaving behind the cheering and stamping crowds who were lining up for a new circle dance, faces gleaming with perspiration and pleasure.

Henri went to his bedroom, pretending to be tired. Lying in his bed he could still hear the remote noise of the festivities floating into his room, shrill pulsating echoes of flutes mingled with laughter and stamping feet. He had given permission to go on feasting until sunrise. A true pagan celebration for the final demise of my bastard cousin, he thought, but satisfaction somehow didn't set in. His impatience grew with every minute. How he longed to hear the sound of a messenger confirming that this plan had succeeded – as succeed it must!

106

Carefully, to avoid making any suspicious noise, Marina and the bailiff stepped forward. Marina's brother pulled a pistol from his breeches, ready to shoot. His hand moved to open the velvet curtains that felt smooth and heavy in his fingers.

"Stop it, leave the curtain closed!" hissed the bailiff.

Marina's brother looked at him as if he were mad, his weapon unconsciously pointing now towards the bailiff. "Don't play games with me! We came here to kill the count's cousin, nobody will stop me now!" Marina's brother growled angrily with a low voice.

"This is *not* Pierre de Beauvoir who's doing the snoring. He sleeps in a different room!" the bailiff whispered back. "And stop threatening me with this stupid pistol, you idiot. I know from the housekeeper that the Marquis changed rooms with a guest two days ago – probably he thought to be very cunning! He tried to keep it secret, this coward. But I know where to find him! Your precious Marquis won't escape us, don't worry."

Marina's brother lowered his hand and the snoring continued undisturbed.

Still taking care to remain silent – although the castle seemed to be frozen in a deep and strange slumber – they moved on to the door of what should have been the Marquis's bedroom and opened it cautiously. The dark gallery lay still and deserted while the three intruders tiptoed down towards a room located at the end of the gallery.

Actually they were more guessing than seeing their way as the gallery was wrapped in total darkness. The eerie silence was starting to weigh on their minds. Marina's nerves were strained, every small sound like the creaking of the wooden floor seemed to amplify in her ears. Suddenly she heard something unusual – the sound of a movement – and immediately Marina drew her rapier, ready to fight. Yet she almost screamed when something furry touched her legs – then a gentle mewing sound made her sigh with relief, it was only a cat who had joined them in their search of prey.

The bailiff pretended to remain unaffected by this incident, and sure of himself and without any hesitation he stepped forward in the darkness and opened one of the numerous doors, secretly relieved to find it unbolted – the sleeping occupant must be completely unaware of the threat.

A familiar picture greeted them. The room lay in almost total darkness, and no moonshine would betray the intruders. Only a forlorn flickering oil lamp had been placed close to the bed on the window sill. They could see the contours of the bedstead – but again the curtains had been drawn close and only a slight but regular breathing sound could be heard.

This time it was Marina who took the initiative. With a swift step she approached the curtains, glancing quickly at the bailiff to make sure that this time she'd be hitting at the right target.

The bailiff nodded but he also raised his pistol, targeting the sleeper behind the curtains. *You never know with women, maybe she'll go soft as soon as soon as she sets eyes on him. Pierre de Beauvoir is handsome enough to seduce a woman even when he's sleeping.*

Marina opened the bed curtains energetically, excitement pulsing in her veins.

You'll live like a princess, Henri had promised her, lying together with her in his bed. *We'll be travelling soon together to Italy where I'll buy a new identity for you, you'll become my beautiful princess from the orient, my star, my love. There will be only the two of us and money, chests full of gold and jewels – all for my beautiful Marina. You'll be the Marquise de Beauvoir, the princes of France will have to bow to you, the King will receive us in his castle of gold!*

How soft and seductive his voice had suddenly become and how wonderful his caressing hand – he had known exactly how to please her! Joy and triumph were flooding through her veins, as impatiently she flung the curtains open, almost tearing the precious velvet to pieces, eager to finish off this bastard cousin who was the only obstacle between her dreams and her future.

In the darkness of the room it was impossible to see clearly the identity of the innocent sleeper but she could discern the bulge of a person under the white shimmering linen and without further hesitation or remorse she took her sword into both hands and plunged it swiftly and deeply into the part where his belly must be located.

Before they had entered the castle they had agreed to use dagger or sword and keep the precious pistols only for self- defence, as it was virtually impossible to reload them in the darkness and the deafening noise might awaken the sleeping guards.

Marina was still bending triumphantly over her victim when something strange happened. Her sword was cutting through the bed sheets but where she had expected resistance from a human body, flesh and bone, the blade of her sword glided forward easily – far too easily. She dropped forward as she had not expected the body to yield underneath her.

Marina was still trying to grasp what had happened when a dagger appeared out of the darkness from behind and plunged mercilessly into her own body. The assailant knew exactly what he was doing and where to strike as she only moaned softly before she crumpled onto the bed.

Her brother had been watching Marina, furious that she had taken the lead. When he heard her groan, saw her collapsing on the bed, he was paralysed with horror – this could not be real! And yet it seemed real enough as with his own eyes he saw her falling like a limp puppet. Time seemed frozen. The sound of her last groan as she was dying, the rustling sound of her killer disappearing into the darkness, all of these sounds as subtle as they might have been, seemed to be repeating themselves in his mind, amplifying until they reached a deafening crescendo exploding in his brain.

As soon as Marina's brother had realized that he was not living a nightmare but the horrible truth, his mind became obsessed by a single thought: Revenge! He wanted revenge. Now! He would cut the enemy to pieces!

Seething with rage he rushed forward, tearing down the velvet bed curtains. He cried out in fury and pain.

"Marina, Mon Coeur, my love, my darling!" he shouted in despair and lunged forward. Although his mind still seemed to be shrouded in wrath and sorrow his fighter's instincts were wide awake. Plunging in the direction of the huge bed he detected a shadow of what must be the enemy who had assailed Marina. Instinctively he drew his own dagger and launched it towards the moving shadow with the precision and skill of a well-trained fighter. But the shadow must have sensed the danger as it ducked away, the gypsy could hear the sound of his own dagger digging into the wood of the bedpost, but no crying or sound of a falling body. The gypsy cursed, he had missed his chance and failed the target.

Then unexpectedly a second shadow appeared behind him and lunged at him. Too late for Marina's brother to dodge the approaching handle of the rapier that went down on his head and sent him into the darkest of nights!

The bailiff had witnessed the entire scene, paralysed by fear. All of a sudden his bowels seemed to take on a life of their own. He fought hard not to wet himself in front of the others – their plans must have been known to the enemy, but who had betrayed him? His instinct was to shoot and run – but what target to shoot at? The lethal shadows had vanished in the darkness once more. The was only one chance left: he must run back to the secret staircase, he had to escape, immediately!

The bailiff turned to run back to the exit when he heard the clicking sound of a pistol close to him, followed by the deafening sound of an explosion. The bullet crashed into his left leg and threw him to the floor, his body and mind bursting with an explosion of terrible pain. In panic he tried to open his eyes when the devil in person appeared in front of him, for indeed it must be the devil: dark skin with eyes of the whitest white he could ever have imagined and big flashing teeth that blinked in the darkness, ready to devour him alive.

The bailiff lost control of his mind and his bowels and fainted.

François de Toucy climbed out of the bed congratulating Jean. "Excellent job, my dear Jean, really brilliant! If you ever look for a new position, I have an immediate opening. Pierre should be proud to have such a valet! I hope he pays you well!"

Jean smiled. He was not only flattered by the compliment, but a millstone weighing several tons had fallen from his mind. They had made it! Pierre's enemies lay there, motionless and defeated – his mother's warnings had not been in vain.

"But now, back to business, we have to find out more! I guess we finished one of them off for eternity, but the two other ones should survive after a bit of beauty sleep – look what a stinking mess this one has become! Help me to bind them and I propose that we have an intimate conversation with them down in the cellar with the appropriate equipment."

"The stinking one is the old bailiff of the chateau, my lord!" Jean exclaimed. "If I may make a remark, my master will never allow us to torture them!"

François de Toucy seemed to suppress a yawn. He didn't seem to be particularly bothered or interested in Pierre's concerns.

"This is exactly why I let your master drink ample drugged ale and why we bundled him into the remote safety of my cousin Armand's bed. I need to have a free hand tonight to clean out this pigsty." He paused and continued with a wry smile. "Sorry about that, it must be the smell of our delightful bailiff that made me think of pigs."

Jean understood that François de Toucy had made up his mind and that his decision was final. He hated the bailiff from the bottom of his heart but for a fleeting second he felt a flicker of sympathy for the two captives. François de Toucy was a dangerous enemy to have; no way would he be moved by feelings of compassion or mercy.

They bound the two assailants before they dragged the dead body out of the bed. Close scrutiny had shown that this one didn't need to be bound any more. François' dagger had been efficient enough, the assailant was dead. Suddenly Jean whistled with surprise. "Look here, my lord, look what I found!"

François de Toucy came closer. Although they had lit several additional oil lamps the light was still very poor. Jean had opened the dead assailant's shirt to trace the trail of the dagger and it became apparent that the assailant was not a man – but an extremely well built woman. He whistled. "My dear Lord, that's interesting!" Even François de Toucy couldn't hide his surprise behind his usual mask of refined detachment and sarcasm.

"It'll be *truly* edifying to make them talk tonight, and find out the names of all who are involved in this devious plan to kill Pierre de Beauvoir – and believe me, *nothing* will stop me! I want to solve this riddle and make sure that your master is safe from now on – and all of the culprits will be punished."

"I vow to help you, my lord. Tonight I can confess openly that I nearly went mad over the past weeks. In my dreams I sensed the danger moving closer every minute, but I couldn't do anything, I simply didn't know what to do – it was a nightmare!" Jean's voice was failing now.

"You don't surprise me, Jean. Your face told it all – indeed you're not a very good deceiver. It was definitely hilarious to watch you pursuing me – no secret that you were convinced that I was the villain in this story. "

"I do apologize if I wronged you, your lordship, but I had no other idea whom to suspect beyond Henri de Beauvoir, my previous master. Everybody else in the castle seemed to be well known."

"And yet, the bailiff must have had accomplices right under our nose here in the castle. One of them I could identify before, it's the valet whom we bound and stored in Pierre's bed and who lay there snoring behind the closed curtains, as I had made sure that he got an extra portion of the drug. I would swear that the housekeeper knew what kind of potion she was distributing freely tonight, but we'll have proof soon. I have my methods."

The latter statement was uttered with an even voice, but Jean was suddenly happy that he wouldn't be the one to test the methods of this strange gentleman. Jean was still amazed; this demanding and difficult coxcomb had not only fought in cold blood against dangerous villains, but seemed perfectly at ease in a situation that would have sent most people into sheer panic.

This man must be a very different person from what we all have assumed, Jean mused, burning with curiosity to get to know more about François de Toucy.

Waking up the guards and musketeers proved to be hard work and took several buckets of cold water until they could be made conscious and kicked into action. Their minds were still clouded by the drugged ale and slumber but they started to understand soon enough, once they set eyes on the dead body and the two bound intruders. They hastened to raise an immediate alarm, but François

111

stopped them and instructed them to keep quiet. "Get hold of the housekeeper first!"

The housekeeper lay snoring peacefully in her room, by all accounts drugged as well. Her mouth was open and spittle was dribbling slowly down her chin. The guards shuddered; even sleeping, she was no beauty.

She's been clever enough to drink some drugged ale so as to be able to feign ignorance, thought François de Toucy while he supervised the guards dragging her out of her bed.

As soon as François de Toucy entered the dungeon he saw to his satisfaction that the two surviving intruders and the conspiring valet had been brought down already. Buckets of cold water from the deep well of the castle were being emptied above their heads and one by one they woke up and regained consciousness.

One of the guards hummed whilst lovingly lighting the charcoal fire. The tall gentleman who had taken command had ordered him to heat the iron rods, as a 'painful interrogation' would soon take place.

In no time smoke and the stinging smell of the fire filled the prison cells. Torches had been lit but their flickering light penetrated the dense smoke only with difficulty. An iron mask glowed fearsome and toothless in a corner. Jean shuddered at the mere thought of the agony that its past victims must have endured.

Simultaneously fascinated and repelled, Jean watched the different reactions of the culprits. The housekeeper became outright hysterical. Slowly she had woken from her drugged sleep and only now had started to realize that torture was waiting for her. She sobbed, pleaded innocence and swore at them like a whore, spittle dripping from her mouth.

The dark gypsy didn't move. His handsome face seemed paler than usual; only the deep lines in his face betrayed that he must be suffering from a terrible headache as a huge lump was forming on his head. He pressed his lips tightly together. He wouldn't yield.

The valet was crying and wailing, repeating the same words again and again. "Your *most* noble lordship, have mercy, let me go, this must be a terrible mistake, I swear by all the Saints that I'm innocent, I'll tell you everything I know, but let me go!"

Next to him the bailiff lay half naked, bloodied legs and loins exposed as his stinking breeches had been removed. He was shivering from cold, fear and pain, unable to control and silence his chattering teeth.

112

François de Toucy looked at the bunch of culprits and was satisfied. With the exception of the gypsy he'd make them talk fast and easily, he had dealt with much more difficult characters in his time.

"Bring the bailiff into a cell and bolt it well, I wish to interrogate the other culprits first!"

His command was executed at once and the bailiff was dragged into an empty prison cell. His cries of pain echoed along the prison chambers, every move of his shattered leg no doubt hurting terribly. Suddenly there was an unexpected and welcome silence, as the bailiff must have lost consciousness.

François de Toucy decided that making the valet talk would be the easiest task and immediately he bellowed a short order. "Guard, fetch the thumb screws!"

The guard carried out his command immediately and with an almost loving gesture he took the dreaded instrument from the shelf where it had been stored, almost forgotten, as for many years the dungeon had only served as a welcome cool store for vegetables, apples or other fruit of the summer harvest. Montrésor had been a peaceful paradise.

Years ago the guard's father had shown his curious son how to handle the thumbscrews and if he was lucky tonight those thumbscrews would be coming into use again. Maybe it was the guard's face, glowing with enthusiasm, or the sensation of the cold metal touching his skin. The moment the valet's thumbs were placed under the screw thread he uttered an almost inhumane cry – and started to talk.

François de Toucy had found out to his satisfaction that one of the musketeers sent by the Marquis de Saint Paul was able to write and soon the unfortunate musketeer, now appointed secretary, had a hard job to follow and scribble down the flow of words and revelations that the valet was confessing with amazing speed.

An endless flood of words escaped the mouth of the valet who wouldn't stop once he had started talking. A whole network of spies working for the old bailiff was revealed, as in trying to ingratiate himself he gave away every name and detail. It appeared that even one of the chateau guards was implicated. His friends ground their teeth – luckily he was not on duty today. His arrest was thus made while he was still sleeping.

"Your noble and mighty lordship, it's all the sole responsibility and the doing of the bailiff. He blackmailed me to make me collaborate!" The valet was sobbing now.

"Why would you listen to the bailiff and betray your true master, the Marquis de Beauvoir?" François de Toucy replied sharply.

"The bailiff threatened to dismiss me from the service of the Marquis and oust my family from our small cottage! I was facing shame and poverty, starvation and death for my family!"

François de Toucy was unmoved, he suppressed a yawn. "Maybe you were just afraid that the bailiff might stop providing you with willing young maids. I have ample evidence that you seduced them together with the bailiff..." François de Toucy dropped this comment in, not at all impressed by the dramatic picture of need and despair the valet was trying to paint.

During the valet's interrogation the housekeeper had been sitting in the same room on the floor, silent, motionless and detached after her first tantrums. But as soon as François de Toucy had finished his questioning, she suddenly opened her eyes, burning with rage and fire and spat in the direction of the valet.

"You spit all you like, you skinny old goat!" the valet shouted at her, forgetting his act of a helpless victim. "Yes, your darling lover was tired of your wrinkled bosom and your skinny legs. Whenever he could escape your jealous eyes we had fun with young flesh, nice young maids – and plenty of them!"

The musketeer turned secretary frowned but continued to scribble it all down – trying to keep pace with the interrogation – and the pages kept filling up.

François de Toucy decided that it was about time to interrogate the housekeeper.

"Do you admit that you were scheming with the bailiff to kill your master and that you drugged the ale?"

The housekeeper laughed arrogantly. "Why should I? *My* conscience is clean! Don't listen to this louse of a valet, my lord, I've been doing my duty for the most noble house of de Beauvoir for decades, you couldn't find a more dedicated and honest servant!"

"If you're so sure, you won't mind if we test your commitment to telling us truth?" François de Toucy turned his back on the housekeeper. Jean could see the hate glowing in her red-veined eyes.

"Iron rods," François de Toucy ordered curtly and the guard who had been thoroughly disappointed that the thumb screws hadn't really come into action looked at the glowing rods with eager anticipation in his eyes.

His mouth started to water; he'd never forgotten the stories his father used to tell him: "They screamed like pigs in the slaughterhouse when we put the red-hot

114

rods on them, up the arse, that's especially nasty. And then the smell of their own burnt flesh, makes them vomit – if they're still conscious."

His father's eyes had gleamed when he told those stories and the prison guard was ready – what great stories he'd be able to tell tonight in the village inn, he'd be the hero of this night!

Cautiously he took the glowing iron from the blazing fire and then he faced the housekeeper, considering carefully where to start – he definitely didn't want to spoil a unique opportunity. The new Marquis had forbidden torture, so there'd been no chance of any of that until now.

The housekeeper had watched the guard approaching, holding the heavy glowing rod in his gloved hands. She could smell the strange scent of hot iron mixed with burnt charcoal and when the guard finally decided to start with one of her hands and lowered the iron rod she screamed like mad even before the iron had touched her skin – the intense sensation of the approaching heat was unbearable.

Her scream pierced the ears of the bystanders and echoed in the surrounding cells of the dungeon. Jean felt sick, his skin was covered with goose bumps. Memories of his own castigation came back and assaulted him all of a sudden, fresh as if it had happened only yesterday. He remembered the iron rod with the red glowing sign of the lily moving closer, the same smell and then the pain! A pain that had been so sharp and agonizing as he had never experienced before. The violent pain would linger for hours and days until the wound had finally healed, leaving the mark of the condemned forever on his otherwise flawless skin. The lily of France had been burnt into his shoulder the day he had been caught and convicted with his fellow pirates. Jean had only been spared hanging as he had been judged to be too young and useful to be sent to the gallows.

"Confess!" Jean shouted in desperation, "Confess, you're doomed anyhow – the pain will be unbearable!" François de Toucy gave him a long thoughtful glance but didn't comment on this sudden outburst.

It may have been Jean's sudden exclamation or the sight of the glowing rod coming so dangerously close to her, but all of a sudden the housekeeper's resistance crumbled, and sobbing hysterically, she started to confess: "Yes, I admit, I did conspire with the bailiff, he's my lover, he seduced me – I offered him my virginity!" The last statement was uttered with a strange sense of pride, a pride totally out of place in this dark dungeon.

Now she had started to talk she admitted to having added a sleeping draught to the ale, the bailiff's idea she stressed, as it had been his suggestion that she should drink from the same ale to deflect any suspicion. In a last act of defiance she insisted not to have known that the Marquis was to be murdered.

"If I had guessed that any harm should have been meant for my gracious lord, I wouldn't have done it, I thought that it was all meant as a joke. May God protect my lord and master and grant him a long life!"

The musketeer was trying to catch up with his notes and François de Toucy was pondering about her last statement when suddenly the valet cut in. "You stupid bitch, telling lies won't get you out of this prison! You forget to mention that you killed the prison guard, and if that was not enough, then you killed the parlour maid. I saw you feeding her body to the pigs, you just left the head of the poor girl on the bed as a warning to the others to make sure they kept their hand off your precious bailiff in future!"

His statement dropped like a bombshell. The room lay in total silence. The housekeeper's face briefly showed a flash guilt and defiance, before she shouted arrogantly, "You're lying, *you* did it, you son of a bitch, you killed them!"

The prison guard had heard enough. The valet's accusation made perfect sense and he lost control. Without further hesitation or waiting for a command from François de Toucy, he rammed the glowing rod into the left leg of the house keeper – the murdered guard had been his best friend and all he wanted was revenge, not justice.

It was just as his father had told him, yet no satisfaction set in – on the contrary. The prison chamber filled with the terrible and nauseating smell of burnt human flesh, the housekeeper was screaming, her piercing voice ringing in his ears. The housekeeper was close to madness and writhed frantically in her chains, trying to flee in vain from this place of hell.

"Confess, you witch that you murdered my friend and the maid or I'll tear you to pieces and roast you alive!" Once again he approached her with a fresh glowing iron rod.

De Toucy watched but didn't interfere.

The housekeeper saw the iron approaching and instinctively she tried to flee from the approaching guard although she was chained to the wall. Once she realized that she couldn't escape she started to scream. "I confess. I killed that slut – and she deserved it, she stole my lover. She can rot in hell for this! But I swear, I didn't kill the prison guard, the valet did it, he freed the bailiff from prison!"

Jean rushed into an adjacent prison cell. He simply couldn't watch this any longer. He had just enough time to spot a bucket in the corner where he could relieve himself and vomit. Dampened by the thick walls he still could discern what must now be the screams of the valet, the latest victim of the glowing iron rods.

116

Jean breathed deeply and steadied himself, then he forced himself to go back into the interrogation room. The guards were dragging the sobbing house keeper and the unconscious valet out of the room, their fates sealed.

François de Toucy had sternly forbidden any further torture; justice could now be done by the hangman, they had gathered enough proof. He now turned his attention to the gypsy. Besides the unnatural pallor of his skin, he seemed strangely detached, almost unmoved by the intimidating scenes he had witnessed.

De Toucy looked at him impassively. *He'll prove to be more difficult, and I don't want him to be butchered alive. I have to find a better way to make him talk –and I think I know how.*

Aloud he said, "Will you confess readily so that I can spare you the painful interrogation? You've seen that I won't hesitate to apply torture if necessary in the interests of justice, so better tell me immediately who told you to break into the castle."

The gypsy confidently shook his head. "My people are proud, we don't shit in our breeches for a bit of pain like you do!" and he spat to show his contempt.

If he had meant to provoke François de Toucy, he failed miserably.

Business-like, François de Toucy ordered, "Strip him naked!"

It needed four guards to execute this command, and everybody present was wondering what François de Toucy was up to.

At last the handsome gypsy was tied to the ground, the guards still holding on to him as he struggled madly. Although he was lean, he was as strong as a tiger.

"Now open his legs," he ordered.

Jean felt sick again – he had seen it all before when the pirates wanted to humiliate their victim.

My Lord, spare me this! He prayed, vivid images of his past, of Henri de Beauvoir's face gleaming with lust and excitement kept appearing in his mind, panic and fear spreading in his body as if he were lying there.

Slowly and menacingly François de Toucy approached the helpless naked gypsy who lay with splayed legs on the ground, holding a gleaming dagger in his hand. "If you don't talk, I'll cut off your manhood, that's all. You'll be allowed to return to your tribe, but you'll no longer be a man, you'll have to go begging with the women."

The gypsy pressed his lips together but Jean was sure to have seen for the first time a fleeting shadow of panic in his eyes.

François de Toucy bent down and although the gypsy was struggling like crazy, his dagger cut into the scrotum of the helpless victim and the first beads of blood dripped onto the ground.

The room lay totally silent, the men holding their breath in surprised shock, each of them almost feeling the blade of the dagger cutting into their own private parts. They were fighting hard to keep their composure, and only the frantic panting of the struggling victim could be heard echoing from the naked stone walls.

Jean watched spellbound, torn between total revulsion and a morbid fascination. He had wished hell and damnation for Pierre's assailants – but tonight's reality was surpassing by far any punishment he could ever have imagined.

"Stop, I'll talk - but under one condition only!" the gypsy suddenly yelled out.

"I'm the one to dictate conditions here," François de Toucy replied haughtily but all the same he stayed his dagger. "But speak up, I might consider your request."

"I promise to tell you the truth and I swear to the Holy Virgin that it'll be nothing but the truth. But afterwards you must give me a dagger and leave me alone. According to our rules I must remain silent or die – but if I die, I wish to die by my own hand."

François de Toucy looked thoughtfully at the gypsy. Jean even thought he detected a note of sympathy in his eyes.

"I agree. But I want the whole truth – why are you involved? Who gave the orders to kill Pierre de Beauvoir? Why were you accompanied by a woman?"

The gypsy was allowed to put on his breeches and sit on a chair. His dignity restored, he drank greedily a cup of water while he stared into a dark corner of the prison cell, unsure how to start his narrative. After a considerable pause for reflection he suddenly uttered a cry of despair, his voice breaking under the strain of his emotions.

"What a damned fool I've been! But the truth is that we were *all* tools in the hand of this devil, Henri de Beauvoir!"

François de Toucy remained unmoved. "I agree that you've been a fool, but please explain more if you want me to honour our deal!"

The gypsy seemed to come back to the dreary reality of the dungeon. Torches had been burning for hours, and now they would soon need to be replaced. Their smoke and acrid odour filled the torture chamber, mingling with the smell of burned flesh. The rusty instruments of torture gleamed in the background, close at hand.

The low stone ceiling of the chamber glistened with the damp, and although it was usually cold in there, the presence of so many people and the heat from the furnace were making the guards perspire profusely. Only François de Toucy seemed to be unperturbed, his appearance immaculate as usual. Only a closer look would reveal that his eyes were rimmed red.

The gypsy started to speak again, his voice steady and composed now. "The woman that was killed tonight was a girl of our tribe, Marina, is her name. I have never met a girl so wild and so beautiful. When I set eyes on her for the first time I fell in love, desperately and hopelessly. Marina promised to marry me – but not immediately, later, she kept saying. She had arrived with her father from a foreign land, far away from the Orient. Although she was one of ours she insisted that she didn't want to stay all of her life in a tent and roam the country. She wanted more, she dreamt about money and gold. She made me swear that I would follow her blindly – accept whatever she would do for the sake of our love. Being madly in love, I accepted and swore my eternal devotion."

The gypsy swallowed hard and continued. "I had no idea that one day this devil Henri de Beauvoir was to appear in Roquemoulin. Our people had planned to stay there during the winter as the previous count de Roquemoulin was known to be kind and his people wouldn't starve – there would be plenty of food left for us."

Plenty of food to steal… I know very well how it works, Jean thought to himself. After he had fled from the galleys he had spent some time with gypsies, hiding from the authorities. He still felt grateful. They had never asked stupid questions – he wouldn't have answered anyway – and they had shared their food with him. Their kindness had come naturally and as their skin was as dark as his own, for the first time in years he had felt accepted and welcome.

The gypsy went on with his story, seeming strangely relieved to be able to share it. "Soon I was to discover that Marina had managed to seduce the count's visitor, Henri de Beauvoir. I went mad with rage, I threatened to kill her, but she reminded me that I had sworn to follow her blindly, and somehow she convinced me that – whatever she might do – she'd only love me, forever. Fool that I was, I gave in and agreed to follow her – for better and for worse. I'm sure that in the beginning Marina was just hoping to pluck the golden goose, find a good opportunity to steal jewellery or gold – but soon she sensed that Henri was hiding some dark secrets. She was intrigued, wanted to get closer to him and blackmail him. I was too weak, whenever I objected she told me that she'd love only me,

119

never would she feel anything for Henri – it was purely business. She had told him that I was her brother – and fool that I was, all I did was stay close to her and … watch helplessly." His voice broke and he took another sip of water – but François made a sign to Jean and Jean gave him wine instead. The gypsy didn't notice or didn't care – he drank the wine like water – but his face lost its deathly pallor and reverted to its natural dark colour.

You're telling the truth, Jean thought, *and I'll bet Henri tried everything to drag you into his bed as well.* Knowing well the tastes of Henri de Beauvoir, who had been his previous master, he could easily imagine that Henri would set everything in motion to get such a handsome man into his bed.

"One day we were riding along the embankment of the Loire and witnessed an accident – at least this is what we thought at first. Two horsemen were riding along a narrow path when suddenly one of the horses reared and the first rider was catapulted onto the slope. The second horseman stopped and turned – and then something strange happened, the second horsemen joined the first who lay there – injured and helpless – and then, we didn't believe our eyes, we could clearly see him pushing the helpless man down the embankment until he plunged into the river. We could even hear the desperate cries of the victim. Needless to say, the second horseman was none other than Henri de Beauvoir! We rode closer and identified ourselves. Marina's wildest dreams had come true – she had Henri de Beauvoir in her hand, one word from us and his next appointment would be with the executioner. Marina's father even had the idea of organizing a false wedding ceremony to tie him down, and Henri was trapped – at least that's what we thought."

Another pause followed, the gypsy was clearly exhausted.

"Damned fool that I was, I failed to notice that Marina had started to fall in love with this devil. I now understand that it was not the kind of love normal people feel. She had always been ruthless and I guess she was attracted by his wicked character, a cruel ruthlessness that surpassed even hers. The more he neglected her, the more she craved his attention. These past weeks I guess she was living in a dream, wanting to travel back to her native land in the Orient with Henri at her side. Of course she'd say that she'd travel with me – but tonight I realized the truth, I forced myself to open my eyes – and now I know better. Henri de Beauvoir found out from the bailiff that Pierre de Beauvoir was staying close to Roquemoulin and he convinced Marina that the Marquis had to die – to make way for him – and Marina. Marina still swore to me that as soon as Henri became a Marquis we'd take his gold and jewels and run – it was our future she wanted to build. Now of course I realize that I fooled myself, I wanted to believe her and to show my devotion and love I agreed to join tonight's foray. I also wanted to protect her as I never trusted the bailiff."

The gypsy had stopped talking, maybe the smoke from the torches had been getting into his eyes, and he rubbed them.

"When I saw Marina falling on the bed, when I realized that she was dying right under my eyes, my heart died with her. Though I know now that Marina never loved me, I'll never love another woman, I might as well die tonight as well."

The last sentence had been uttered in a matter of fact way, a simple statement without any pathos, and therefore it was all the more striking. Jean had a lump in his throat, he could understand only too well how Henri must have seduced the bride of the gypsy. If he wanted to, he could be deadly attractive.

François de Toucy gave the gypsy another cup of wine. This time the wine must have been stronger as the gypsy made a face when he drowned the cup. Without resistance he followed the guards into a prison cell.

"Will you give me now a dagger?" he said, but his speech had become a bit slurred – probably too much wine after such an ordeal, Jean thought.

"Yes, don't worry. The guards will drop it into your cell tonight. A promise is a promise. We first have to finish the interrogations, I'm afraid heaven or hell will have to wait for you a bit," François de Toucy answered, and had the door bolted.

As soon as he was back to the interrogation room he said to the guards, "I gave him an overdose of the housekeeper's sleeping draught. He'll die tonight peacefully in his cell, there will be no need for a dagger." Jean felt strangely relieved. This gypsy had come to kill Pierre, but somehow he had been as much Henri's victim as he had been a perpetrator.

Daylight hours would be approaching soon and a grim fatigue had spread across all of those who were present.

"Let's tackle our last jailbird, the brain behind today's masterplan!" François de Toucy exclaimed with false cheerfulness.

The bailiff was thus dragged in, no longer able to walk on his own. Not only were his knees feeling like jelly, but his injured left leg had only been dressed with a makeshift bandage. Blood was seeping through the dirty cloth, forming dark and crusted stains. The pain in his leg where the pistol ball was stuck was unbearable, and he was crying. His shirt was hanging loose as his stinking breeches had been removed. The bailiff was shivering yet sweating simultaneously. The prison cells in Montrésor were always cold and damp – even in summer – but now fever was spreading through his body. The bailiff had reached a state of mind where he was willing to do anything to terminate this suffering – immediate death seemed like a precious gift, a redemption from the hell he was going through.

François de Toucy looked at him gravely and with a stern voice gave a short résumé of the statements and accusations that had been recorded.

The bailiff tried to concentrate on the spate of accusations and almost mechanically he uttered, "I'm innocent!" and with a shadow of his former sly expression he added, "…and you have no proof, my lord!"

François de Toucy walked over to the bailiff. Until now he had handled the interrogations with detachment, even politeness, but suddenly he shouted in a sharp voice that echoed through the prison cells, "I want to know everything, you'd better listen, every detail, you scum! When did you start embezzling the money, how much, where did you hide it? I want to know every tiny detail about the murder plot, your implication and the involvement of Henri de Beauvoir! I swear to you, if you don't confess immediately and if I find the slightest inconsistency in your statements you may live some more time, but every second will be hell for you, every single second, do you hear me?"

As if to underline the chilling sincerity of his statement he kicked his boot against the bailiff's injured leg. Taken unaware, the prisoner howled in pain. Jean closed his eyes, he could almost feel the pain himself.

It took the bailiff some time to be able to speak, the intense pain had taken his breath away.

"I confess, my lord, I confess, but stop it, please!" the last words were barely audible as they were drowned in heavy sobbing.

The prison guard came closer holding the rusty thumb screws like a treasure in his hand. François de Toucy ignored the pleading glance of the guard and slightly shook his head. Disappointed, the prison guard put them back on the shelf. His face displayed deepest frustration, as he felt that a unique opportunity had been wasted. But it soon became apparent that there was no need to apply any torture. The bailiff started to talk and the musketeer-turned-secretary struggled to keep up with the stream of words and facts once the gates of truth had been opened. The scratching sound of the quill on the paper became a constant background noise as the bailiff kept talking.

All of a sudden Jean fell off the low wooden bench where he had been sitting and listening. A night without sleep and the smoke-filled gloomy prison cell had not been very helpful in keeping him awake. Despite the grim atmosphere, François de Toucy had to laugh when he saw Jean sitting on the floor, rubbing his hurting head, trying to understand what had happened to him.

In the meantime the bailiff kept talking and it became evident that all sorts of embezzling had been going on for more than a decade. The uncle of the present Marquis had had no head for business, and had accepted and signed whatever documents or figures had been presented. Henri de Beauvoir would have passed from time to time with the sole intention of leaving Montrésor with pockets full of gold, gold that actually would have belonged to his cousin.

Slowly a clear picture of the amounts that the bailiff had embezzled became obvious – and those amounts were simply staggering. The bailiff had invested a large part of it and he named several estates that he had bought assuming false identities. He only played coy when François de Toucy insisted on knowing where the bailiff had hidden his gold coins. François de Toucy did not insist further, he just stepped forward menacingly.

Immediately the bailiff understood the message. With panic in his eyes he started to reveal that money and gold had been placed in the safekeeping of his relatives, astutely hidden behind big barrels of wine. Every year the amount of funds that had been diverted had grown, nobody had ever seemed to care or to wonder why the stream of money from Montrésor to the de Beauvoir household in Paris had completely dried up.

"Did you contact Henri de Beauvoir – or the count de Roquemoulin as he's called nowadays – after you fled from the chateau or even before?" François de Toucy asked.

"Yes, my lord, I contacted him. After I fled from this dungeon it seemed… " The bailiff's voice failed him, his lips were dry, his vision was blurred and he had problems seeing his nemesis clearly.

"It seemed… so obvious and profitable?" François de Toucy ended the sentence for the bailiff, his voice dripping with contempt.

"Did Henri de Beauvoir order the murder of his cousin Pierre?"

Immediately Jean became alert; he thought that he knew the answer, but yet…

"Yes, my lord, he insisted that I should murder him and gave me a deadline, in case I should fail, and he threatened to kill me." The bailiff was sobbing now, immersed in self-pity.

Jean felt strangely satisfied. They had managed to unearth the truth, there could be no more doubt. But instinctively he also understood that Pierre would never be safe as long as his murderous cousin stayed alive.

Watching François de Toucy he noticed that he seemed most satisfied, like a tomcat that had just detected a delicious saucer full of cream.

And in fact there was plenty of reason why François de Toucy could really be satisfied. Here, in front of him, he certainly had the most despicable example of mankind, but tonight he had received undeniable proof. Now the Crown had a clear case to charge Henri de Beauvoir with plotting the murder of his cousin Pierre.

Combined with the gypsy's statement that Henri had disposed of the body of the late Count de Roquemoulin, Henri would be doomed and the imminent danger for the Marquis de Beauvoir removed.

François de Toucy was certain that his superiors would be content with his work.

Early morning was looming and the last torches were burning low when the formalities of interrogation were finally completed. An exhausted musketeer-cum-secretary sprinkled sand across the last page to soak up the splattered ink and handed the document to François de Toucy, who painstakingly read every single page, correcting some random mistakes.

"I thought you attended a proper school?" he scolded the tired secretary who trembled and blushed like a young maid and started to apologize profusely.

François de Toucy laughed and cut him short. "I was only joking, you did an excellent job, I don't know if I could have covered so many pages until the early morning with barely no light, well done! I'll recommend you warmly to His Eminence!"

The musketeer-cum-secretary blushed even more, but this time from pride.

Then he handed the document to the bailiff who – old habits never die – started to read it carefully. But soon the letters started to become blurred and seemed to be dancing on the paper. Fever and pain were taking hold, and he was incapable of making any sense of the phrases that he should confirm and sign, a signature he sensed that would settle his fate. He hesitated shortly, then shrugged wearily. All he wanted now was some respite and peace, and not without difficulty he signed the last page, his signature shaky and no longer the proud and impressive hallmark it used to be in the past. In truth he didn't care any longer which of his many failings would seal his fate. *Let the end come fast and spare me torture* , he begged, more than prayed, silently.

François de Toucy took the precious document with an air of satisfaction and stored it in his waistcoat. He wouldn't be taking any chances.

"My task has been accomplished," he said turning to the bailiff, "the rest is in the hand of your judges. Better pray that they send you straight to the gallows!"

Before he walked out of the prison François de Toucy ascertained that this time his prisoners would be well guarded – no surprise escape would happen under his command.

He must have been drifting into a light slumber despite his initial intention to stay awake, as it took him several minutes to realize that the gentle tapping at the door that linked his private staircase to the servant's quarters was not part of a dream.

An exhilarating mixture of excitement and triumph spread like fire through his body: *It must be Marina and her brother, their mission is accomplished, the bastard is dead! May he rot in hell forever! I, Henri de Beauvoir, shall be the new Marquis de Beauvoir!*

In his mind he savoured the tantalizing image of King Louis bowing to kiss the cheeks of Henri, his newly appointed beloved cousin, and automatically started to consider the options as to how to use this opportunity to take his revenge on Cardinal Richelieu.

I'm coming back, beware, you poisonous toad!

He jumped out of his gigantic bed and rushed towards the door, his heart beating madly with joy.

I've never truly been in love, but I suppose that must be how it feels.

Making sure to guarantee his privacy, Henri had encouraged his valet to take the evening off with the other servants and to enjoy himself in the barn. Henri congratulated himself that he had taken all precautions to keep the arrival of Marina and her brother secret. No rumours among his servants about gypsies visiting his room should tarnish his hour of triumph!

In gleeful anticipation Henri opened the secret door that had been skilfully fitted into the decorative wooden panels of his imposing bedroom. No expense had been spared by the late count, the room was literally bursting with candelabras, paintings (preferably of half-naked Greek gods in questionable situations), statues, carved wooden chests filled with jewels – whatever seemed to have been in fashion at court and expensive enough had been purchased and brought to Roquemoulin whenever the count had deemed it necessary to redecorate his Parisian palace, by all accounts a quite frequent occurrence. The result was definitely no testimony of refined taste, but resembled rather the overcrowded cavern of Ali Baba than the elegant bedroom of a leading member of the French aristocracy.

Henri held the door in his hand and bent forward to greet Marina with a kiss when he realized that his visitor was much smaller than the person he had expected, for it was a young gypsy boy of about fourteen years who was about to enter. Henri started, but then he remembered that he had seen the boy hanging around the gypsies' camp before. The boy looked at him with strange dark eyes and made a sign asking for permission to enter. Henri obliged mechanically, still trying to work out why Marina had preferred to send a messenger instead of coming herself. Their mission couldn't have failed, the plan had been fool-proof – maybe she'd come later and just wanted him to know that she was fine.

The boy started to speak in a low voice. At first Henri had difficulties understanding his broken French but soon the truth dawned on him.

"I come, sent by Marina, sir. She give me orders to stay, keep watch. Marina tell me she no trust small man. I must hurry and warn you if danger. This is why I here." The boy was more whispering than speaking, but the effect of this message couldn't have been any more dramatic if the very trumpets of Jericho had accompanied it.

"She enter castle and all like plan. All quiet. Much time later I hear lot of noise, I see torches, hear men in courtyard. I very worried. I check what going on. I see José and small man drag by soldier to prison castle. I think José dead. I no see Marina. I run and warn you, I swear to Marina."

Henri was dumbstruck – nothing had prepared him for this, there had been no feeling of foreboding, no nightmare while he had been sleeping. Did the boy really understand what he was telling him? – of course he didn't! This beautiful new world he had built for himself with so much skill and cunning, it all had gone to pieces in a matter of seconds!

Henri's mind was racing. *Should I kill the boy? He knows too much! But what's the use – if they have arrested the bailiff, it's only a matter of hours until he cracks under torture and my name is mentioned. I'm doomed, I must flee, tonight, but where to? I must leave immediately!*

He saw that a single tear was rolling down the messenger boy's cheek, the fatigue and the knowledge that two of his tribe were doomed taking their toll. But the boy looked him straight in the eye, he was too proud to yield.

On a sudden impulse, Henri took a golden coin and gave it to the boy. "You've done the right thing, I'm sure that Marina will be all right. Tomorrow I'll see what I can do for her brother." He was lying.

The boy looked at him, bewildered and opened his mouth as if he wanted to protest but then decided to keep quiet and just bowed. The golden coin had disappeared in seconds, the door closed noiselessly behind him, and no steps could be heard. The boy left as quietly as he had come. It might all have been an illusion – but looking at his empty hand, Henri could see the coin in his hand had gone.

127

Henri looked around. How thoughtful of the late count to have filled his bedroom like a treasure trove, he thought ironically, sarcasm now the only line of defence left to him. He'd need to gather as much gold and valuables as he could possibly transport tonight. Henri, the wealthy Count de Roquemoulin, would become a figment of the past. For several months, maybe years, France would become forbidden territory for him.

"Damn that bastard!" he cursed, but it was useless, urgent action was needed.

Mechanically Henri opened the treasure chests which stood close to his bed, sifting carefully through their contents. He dismissed all items of artistic value: what he needed was gold and jewels, compact and easy to carry and hide – and easy to sell. Soon his bags were filled with golden necklaces studded with jewels, freshly minted gold coins, loose precious stones and rings. Luckily for him, the late count had left a fortune.

Roaming through the room he found some miniature paintings set in golden frames with diamonds: those would also come in handy, he decided. Then he put some fresh shirts on top of the bulging bags and changed his breeches. Suede breeches would be perfect for a prolonged period of travel. Henri looked around one last time, not for the sake of dwelling on useless emotions, but because he wanted to make sure that he had missed no item of value. A pity that the golden candelabras were too cumbersome to carry – he'd bet that they'd fetch a good price.

Henri had just finished stuffing the last shirts on top of the leather bag that was almost bursting under its load of gold and jewellery when his personal valet suddenly entered the room – unexpectedly and without announcing himself properly. Incredulously the valet looked around the room, noticing the open chests and the piles of shirts and breeches that Henri had thrown carelessly on the ground.

"I, I – heard a noise, M– My lord," he stammered, desperately holding on to the bedpost as he tried to steady himself. His stale breath and his unsteady glance were further testimony of tonight's heavy drinking.

Henri looked at him coldly. *This idiot will gossip about my departure. I must silence him, at all cost.*

"You should know better than to barge in like that! You should have announced yourself, but now that you're here, you may as well tidy up. I need a clean shirt and everything has fallen to the floor," he commanded curtly.

The valet reacted instinctively to the order and, swaying slightly, he walked, not without difficulty, towards the heap of clothes that lay on the ground then bent down to pick them up.

His death came swiftly. Just a short moan could be heard as one of the late count's daggers found his heart. Henri drew out the bloodied dagger and looked thoughtfully at the slumped figure that lay sprawled across the heap of clothes, a red stain slowly spreading across the shirt that lay on the top.

"Actually, I should thank you for your appearance, you've given me an excellent idea!" he said to the dead servant with a mock bow.

Energetically he grabbed the dead valet and dragged him towards the bed. While he made sure to limit the noise of his actions Henri started systematically to ravage the room. He tore the bed curtains down, tucked his bloodied dagger into the right hand of the dead valet – not without regret, as the dagger was decorated with precious stones – and draped a part of the bed curtain around the corpse. It now looked as if his servant had found his death during a violent struggle with some villainous intruders – killed in action whilst bravely defending his master. Bloodstains on the sheets added to the dramatic effect.

Henri looked around once more and like an artist he decided that the scene needed a finishing touch. Swiftly he knocked down some candelabras, picture frames and cups, until the room looked as if a horde of vandals had passed through. Satisfied with his work he looked around. His bedroom now looked like the setting of a Shakespearian drama.

Having accomplished his work, Henri grabbed the leather bags and once more thankful that one of the count's predecessors had constructed a private staircase leading down to the back door, he left his room. This time his luck held and he didn't encounter any further servants who might have questioned his untimely departure.

Down in the stables he needed to be careful, or he'd risk waking up the sleeping grooms, but his dagger was ready. Treading carefully and with all his senses tuned to detect the noise of approaching steps he entered the dark stables, with only a single lantern to guide his way. Candles or torches were strictly forbidden in the stables, as the danger of fire was an ever present hazard.

To Henri's relief the feast with its accompanying orgy of heavy drinking seemed to have removed all obstacles. The stables were empty, and the only remaining groom he could detect was snoring loudly, still hugging his empty jar. Henri kicked him to see if he'd wake up and might present any danger, but the groom only protested in his sleep and closed his arms even tighter around the precious jar.

You're lucky, I might have sent you to eternal sleep.

The horses were nervous, they sensed that something unusual was going on, after the lavish party in the castle had interrupted their usual routine. Henri chose a huge stallion, one of the priceless thoroughbreds that had been the pride of Jean Baptiste de Roquemoulin. The stallion would be challenging to ride but could be sold in Paris where he would fetch a fabulous price. Luckily Henri had already ridden him on several occasions and the stallion didn't protest when Henri saddled him and led him out of the stables. Not used to doing a groom's job, Henri fumbled with the straps in the moonlight but finally the saddle was fixed and the precious bags were safely attached. Henri was ready to go.

Only minutes later Henri could be seen flying on his horse across the dark fields and pastures of Roquemoulin heading towards the shelter of the small forest that lay behind the estate and where the pigs were fed each autumn on a diet of rich acorns. Henri then intended to make a detour to the south in order to deceive potential pursuers before he headed back to Paris.

Arriving in the shelter of the forest the tension of the past hours started to abate and for the first time Henri had the opportunity to consider the full impact of his present situation – and try to put some distance between him and the unexpected turn of events that seemed to have engulfed him with all the force of a hurricane. Until this very last minute his mind had been focusing completely on the priority of staging his escape. But now he'd have to tackle the challenging task of planning his future. To his great surprise he realized that his feelings were mixed: on the one hand he felt a burning rage – a rage so intense that it hurt – that his great plan had failed and that his bastard cousin had once more escaped the trap he had so assiduously laid for him. He, Henri, was the only true heir and no matter what had happened, fate in the end would select him, and only him, to become the next Marquis, and never, ever would he accept anything else. His cousin must die!

But on the other hand – and this feeling genuinely surprised him – Henri experienced a strange and unexpected sentiment, a feeling of freedom, almost joy. Riding alone through the forest he realized all of a sudden how much he had felt bored and oppressed by the endless list of daily duties and tasks, of being cast in the mould of lord and master of an army of servants and hundreds of tenants. The knowledge that each of his steps was always followed and commented on had started to annoy him, and his days had become tedious and predictable.

And then there had been Marina, the maddening gypsy woman who had excited him so much in the beginning – but how she had started to annoy him lately. What a challenge it had been in the beginning to tame her, what a wild, dangerous and unpredictable woman she had been, how different from any other woman he had known, seductive, defying all conventions, proud and independent!

But with time their relationship had changed, and gradually he had sensed that she had fallen for him and in the end he had succeeded in making her eat out of his hand. How she had looked at him with trsuting eyes when he had painted for her the rosy and oh-so-naive picture of a future as his beloved oriental princess – how could she ever have swallowed such stupid bait?

Deep in his thoughts Henri hadn't realized that he had already left the small dark forest with its meandering paths. In the treacherous twilight he had been concentrating on finding his way and making sure that his horse didn't stumble on the potholed track. But now that Henri had reached the road to Saumur he raised his eyes as the golden ball of the rising sun appeared, blinding him, and bathing the surrounding vineyards in its golden light, a picture of perfection and beauty.

The road was lined with patches of grass and wild flowers; moist from the morning dew, they glistened like jewels in the sunlight. Henri was no lover of nature but his mood brightened, and the dazzling sun seemed to contain a promise. *Beware, Paris, and you, my bastard cousin, I'm not defeated yet!* he cried in his heart and spurred his horse on.

*****

Pierre felt uncomfortable. A foot kept kicking his left calf – but that was impossible. He was alone in his bed, it must be a dream…

He had just come to the immensely satisfying solution that the kicking had only been an unpleasant dream when the next kick came, but this time he couldn't ignore it any more as the point of a sharp elbow had found its painful way right into his chest.

Angry, he opened his eyes, ready to take revenge against the unknown attacker. This task proved more difficult than foreseen, as someone had draped a red translucent curtain in front of his eyes and when he tried to reflect how this curtain could have arrived there he became aware to his great annoyance of another obstacle: part of his brain must have been substituted by wool during the night; no wonder he couldn't think properly!

All of a sudden a voice cut into his thoughts, a voice that sounded very much familiar and yet he couldn't place it immediately.

"How sweet to watch two friends sleeping peacefully in their bed, one could almost speak of it as an example of brotherly love, how edifying!" the voice drawled on. "A pity that I'm not a skilful enough painter, how much I'd love to preserve this lovely picture for posterity!"

Pierre tried hard to ignore the wool in his head and to sit up, a decision he regretted as soon as he had executed it. Not only was his head spinning but it had started to hurt terribly. Suddenly he felt an overwhelming thirst and he croaked: "Water, I need some water!"

Jean who had been waiting for his master to wake up had already anticipated his needs. He stood ready with a large carafe of water in his hands and a filled cup. He grinned at François de Toucy – they knew exactly how terrible Pierre must be feeling after a large portion of drugged ale.

Pierre emptied the silver cup greedily. The cool water soothed his burning throat and with enormous satisfaction he felt that the pile of dust that had piled up in his throat seemed to be dissolving. Cautiously he tried to open his eyes again and peep through the red curtain. He detected François de Toucy sitting, disgustingly relaxed, in a comfortable armchair close to his bed, looking at him with a sympathetic grin.

Now it dawned on Pierre that this was *not* his own bed at all. He opened his eyes a bit wider and luckily the red curtain receded: he was in Armand's room, in fact he had been sleeping in Armand's bed, and his best friend was lying next to him, naked, sprawled across his bed in a deep and peaceful slumber!

"What am I doing here?" Pierre croaked and extended his hand to reach for another cup of water.

"What do you want to know? That you've been drugged by your charming housekeeper or that we dragged you into Armand's bed to make sure that you'd be protected from the villains who tried to make mincemeat out of you last night?"

François de Toucy's tone was non-committal; he might as well be discussing a social event.

"I'm afraid that's too much for my poor brain. Jean, please give me some of your miracle medicine, my head is bursting. And for goodness sake, let's wake Armand up, as even in my present state I can guess that you're about to tell me something important."

Jean had – of course – already expected this request and a second later Pierre was holding a cup filled with Jean's secret potion. Pierre made a face as he swallowed the bitter fluid but then watched with satisfaction how François de Toucy resolutely woke up his cousin: he didn't waste any words but immediately emptied the remaining carafe of cold water over Armand's head.

Armand jumped up, cursing, and not having noticed that his cousin had been the true culprit he started to kick Pierre, accusing him not only of having invaded his bed but of being the most perfidious of all friends.

"Armand, stop talking nonsense and put on some clothes, it's positively indecent, hopping around naked and cursing at the same time!" François de Toucy interjected laughingly.

132

Only now did Armand notice that he had two visitors watching him, and looking full of contempt at his cousin he answered, "I – contrary to some persons around here – don't have anything to hide!" but he started to pull over a shirt all the same.

"Anyway, why are you sitting here in my room, looking all important like an inflated peacock, you son of a – ?"

"Beware my dearest cousin, please remember that my mother is your mother's youngest sister. Any insult will reflect on our family. Let me explain though. I'm here because, my dearest cousin, Jean and I took the liberty of saving the skin of your precious friend while you, my noble cousin, spent your time sleeping and most probably having lewd dreams!"

"I do admit the dream part," Armand said and grinned broadly, even a bit complacently. "Go on, please explain your strange allusions – and Jean, please give me some water, don't just look after your master! I am completely parched and I have a headache."

François de Toucy started his narrative of the events that had occurred during the previous night in the chateau and soon two pairs of ears were hanging on his every word, and even Jean was eager to hear it all again as he was sure he had missed some parts.

"Why did you let the housekeeper give me the drugged ale, if you already suspected that she had tampered with the ale?" Pierre asked, visibly upset. "She could have killed me! This stuff is horrible, my head hurts like hell!"

"I'm terribly sorry Monsieur le Marquis – " Pierre frowned and quickly François de Toucy corrected himself. "I'm sorry, I meant to say Pierre of course, but frankly speaking it would have been impossible to poison you with the dose she gave you and it would have been outright stupid of me to interfere too early. All of our actions had to seem natural to her and her cronies, as if we had no suspicions at all and that their master plan would proceed smoothly. I had noticed, however, that your valet Jean had not consumed his portion and I was happy to know that I'd have at least one ally. Let me add that your valet has been most useful, indeed outstanding, although he tried very hard to get rid of me at first!"

Jean grinned sheepishly. "I do apologize, Monsieur de Toucy, but I was truly convinced that you were the culprit in this story, the one who had been sent here to kill my master."

François de Toucy smiled back and continued telling his story. Pierre was shocked when he became aware how narrowly he had escaped. He flushed with hot anger when François de Toucy came to the point that he had written proof that his cousin Henri had masterminded the ambush and this last attack.

"There can be no doubt that Henri de Beauvoir was the evil mind behind this foul play!"

Skilfully François de Toucy circumvented the details of how the confessions had been obtained.

Jean closed his eyes – he could still smell the terrible smell of burning flesh in his nostrils. He lost himself briefly in his thoughts: *I'll never forget this night my whole life, but I'm glad we went through with it, my master's life has been saved.*

After François de Toucy had finished his narrative, there was a minute's silence.

Pierre was still trying to digest the story but Armand looked at his cousin and said, "I have to apologize to you, François, frankly speaking I thought that you were nothing but a windbag, all façade and no substance, I was blind and completely wrong! But tell me, it's no coincidence that you came to visit us, now it's your turn to come clean and tell us the truth!"

"I'm amazed to detect – alas – feeble signs of modesty and intelligence in my cousin, I'm truly stunned, my dearest Armand!" and skilfully he avoided a kick from Armand, then roaring with laughter he said, "I've been sent by your father, the august Marquis de Saint Paul and – you will not believe what I say – instructed to protect his lordship, the Marquis de Beauvoir, by His Eminence, the Cardinal Duke de Richelieu who happens to be my superior commander!"

"I can't trust my ears," complained Pierre. "*Cardinal Richelieu* has dispatched you to save me from Henri de Beauvoir? You must be joking!"

"How can you work for the Cardinal, if you're a de Saint Paul, the Cardinal has always been our arch-enemy!" Armand threw in, all indignation.

François de Toucy lifted his arms as if protecting himself from multiple blows. "Have mercy on me, my lords!" he cried, "I'll explain everything!"

Not at all intimidated by their questions, he assumed a comfortable pose in his armchair and explained.

"My story starts several years ago when my father died all of a sudden and left my mother without any income, in fact to be precise, he left his widow saddled with a mountain of debt. My father – God bless his soul – had the bad habit of taking offence too easily. Unluckily he had launched expensive litigation not only with one but with several of our neighbours, and needless to say, he lost all of his lawsuits and consequently he lost all of the family's money. I had

134

therefore only three options left: appeal to Armand's father for help – which my pride forbade, join the clergy (actually no real option for me) or become a soldier. The choice seemed obvious to me. After I joined the musketeers, His Eminence, the Cardinal Richelieu, seemed somehow to have noticed me and offered me a promotion if I accepted a position in his personal guard. I gladly accepted and thus I started to work for the Cardinal, first as an officer in his guard, then later as – well, let's call it a man for special cases. We had a clear agreement though, never would my services be employed against the interests of our family – and I must say that the Cardinal has always respected our agreement to the letter."

François de Toucy now rose from his chair and started pacing around the bedroom while he continued his story.

"Several weeks ago I was summoned by the Cardinal to assume an urgent mission. You can imagine my surprise when I met not only the Cardinal but my uncle as well. Rumour had been spreading in Paris that Henri de Beauvoir had been adopted by the late Count de Roquemoulin. Actually, Henri's last mistress was out of her mind as she would have been the next in line to inherit this fortune and she kept running from salon to salon of her friends lamenting over her perfidious lover. Simultaneously news arrived that Jean Baptiste de Roquemoulin had disappeared under mysterious circumstances and both men, Armand's father and the Cardinal, were extremely worried. This occurrence seemed a bit too fortunate for Henri de Beauvoir to be mere coincidence. Taking into account that Roquemoulin is located only a few miles from Montrésor it didn't need the mind of a genius to figure out who'd be the next victim on the list of Henri de Beauvoir."

Pierre looked at him with huge eyes and cried, "Do you truly mean that His Eminence pretended to be worried about me? That's the biggest joke I've heard in years! Last time I can remember he sent a ship loaded with cannon to send me to the bottom of the sea!"

François de Toucy smiled. "I don't know what the Marquis de Saint Paul did, but the Cardinal seemed to have forgotten all previous feuds. I was sent here with clear orders to protect you and even received a special warrant signed by his Eminence in person allowing me to pursue, interrogate, and even execute any person of harmful intent regarding the most honourable Marquis, Pierre de Beauvoir."

Armand whistled. "A license to kill! Future generations will be talking about that!"

François de Toucy only laughed. "You can imagine that I arrived here somewhat nervous. Knowing that not only the Cardinal but my uncle as well were placing their trust in me to protect the Marquis de Beauvoir… and then when I learnt about the ambush with the crossbow, I realized that their worst premonitions had come true. Like them I was convinced that Henri de Beauvoir must be pulling strings to have Pierre de Beauvoir removed and to acquire his title. The worst was that – after staying here for several days – I had no clue as to who else could be involved – and yet I was convinced that some of the chateau's inhabitants must be part of the plot. I was close to despair – and Jean didn't make my task any easier as he stuck to me like a leech, entirely convinced that I was the villain of the piece."

Jean made a face but didn't dare to interrupt the flow of the story.

Thus François de Toucy continued unperturbed. "One night, when I went out with my friend, the officer of the musketeers whom my uncle had dispatched here for further protection, I suddenly had a stroke of luck. I gained the confidence of the innkeeper who, having drunken heavily of his best wine (paid for by me), started to complain about the bailiff, said that he was seducing the maids and girls of the village together with one of the valets. He's this ugly guy with the bad breath who was gagged last night by Jean and me and put into the bed where I should have been sleeping. When the innkeeper was joking about the bailiff having had a fling with the scrawny housekeeper, all of a sudden I had a hot lead to follow – I felt like finding Ariadne's thread in the dark labyrinth. You can't imagine how relieved I felt this evening. I spun some story to make you change rooms but in fact I had no doubt that the housekeeper would be aware of any such move and it was just for show, she and the valet should have no idea that I suspected them."

Pierre groaned. "How stupid I must have looked, offering to change beds with you…" He smacked his forehead in mock despair.

François de Toucy laughed out loud, his personality totally transformed. The polished, over refined and slightly bored gentleman had been replaced by a fun-loving young man full of mischief.

"Well, the rest of the story I told you before. Let me add one more remark: I envy you Jean's loyalty, never have I met such a dedicated servant before. I don't think that I could have overpowered these villains without his help. If ever he should be looking for a new position…"

Jean's dark skin became a shade darker, such was the effect of the praise.

François de Toucy continued as if he hadn't noticed the change. "If you will allow me now to take my leave, I must ride to Paris in order to brief the Cardinal and the Marquis de Saint Paul of the situation and request a warrant to have Henri de Beauvoir arrested. I don't exclude though the possibility that His Eminence might not want to risk a public trial and I can imagine him preferring to keep this story under wraps, as indicting a personage of the high aristocracy is always delicate…"

"And Henri might talk a bit too much about the Cardinal's previous implications in his attempts to get rid of Pierre," Armand interrupted his cousin. "I have a feeling that this warrant will never be issued!"

Pierre had been looking from one to other and felt that it was about time to add his own comments, after all, he was the person at the centre of all this. "Maybe the two gentlemen will allow me some humble remarks?" he said, and only the irrepressible Armand answered, "Maybe, Your Grace, yes, I think I feel disposed to grant you a word now!"

Pierre shot him a scathing glance and continued, turning to François de Toucy. "François, you saved my life, I'd be honoured to call you my friend too from today on – like your terrible cousin Armand!"

François de Toucy blushed like a young maiden. "It's I who should be honoured, it's my pleasure, Monsieur le Marquis – I mean Pierre – of course."

Pierre smiled and not for the first time François reflected that Pierre de Beauvoir had received a very precious and rare gift from a good fairy when he had been born: he had the gift of winning the hearts of people. No wonder his valet had been ready to sacrifice his life for his master.

"Second," Pierre continued unperturbed, "I do not agree to your leaving us today. We will have a decent meal and open a bottle of my best wine to celebrate. Then both of you will go to bed. You and Jean look like ghosts from the underworld – and no wonder, after such an eventful night! Armand is right, Richelieu will not hasten to have Henri arrested, Henri knows far too much and this shadow could fall back on the Cardinal. There is no need to leave today in a hurry."

Dutifully François de Toucy protested but secretly he was more than happy to oblige, and the vision of a soft pillow and a comfortable bed were just too seductive!

"Third, if I calculated correctly, the arrest and the confessions of the bailiff will help me to recover hundreds of thousands of livres, money that this slimy crook has embezzled over more than a decade, as you just explained to me: estates sold to cronies below their true value, money and gold hidden away. It's only fair that you shall receive a third of this amount. I also want Jean to receive five thousand livres. Jean, you're a rich man now, and a free one – you may leave me whenever you want."

Pierre smiled but to his great surprise both men had tears in their eyes.

"I shall never leave your service, Monsieur le Marquis!" Jean exclaimed, "Unless your lordship should wish to dismiss me, of course," he added, sinking to his knees in order to kiss Pierre's hand and to thank him for this reward – *How proud my parents would be today*, Jean thought.

"Jean, that's nonsense, of course I want you to stay! But if you will stay as my trusted servant, it's by your own free will from now on." Jean couldn't speak, as silently he nodded and kissed Pierre's hand again.

Now François de Toucy started to speak, not without difficulty, as he had to clear his throat first. "Pierre... Let me tell you that I'm deeply moved by your proposal but I can't accept it. I can't allow you to pay me. I have accepted this mission and will be paid handsomely by the Cardinal and Armand's father; I would not be worthy of belonging to the Saint Paul family if I accepted your generous offer, but Pierre, please let me say that I shall never forget this day and I'm deeply moved."

"Oh, dear Lord, tra-la! Here comes the noble knight, François de Toucy!" interjected Armand, disrupting the emotional scene.

"Dearest cousin, let me advise you to shut up and think first. You *must* accept Pierre's offer and forget about your knightly inhibitions. First of all, Pierre is right, you deserve it. That's a fact! Second, I happen to know that at home you have four – actually I lost count, maybe even five, hopeful sisters waiting to get married and who desperately need a dowry to have a realistic chance of picking a suitable and not too horrible husband. Don't pretend to be noble if acting nobly means being selfish in truth. Pierre is offering you a unique opportunity to make up for – sorry to be so blunt – the stupidity of your late father. This opportunity must not be thrown away! Accept it, please, if not for your own sake, then think about your family!"

As François de Toucy looked at Armand, it was impossible to detect what thoughts were passing through his mind. All of a sudden he smiled radiantly and said, "Armand, I misjudged you as well. I always thought your mind was simply focused on the pleasures of hunting, fighting, drinking or seducing the never ending army of chamber maids that must have marched through your bed already, but, my Lord, you've got a sound brain as well – and I confess that you're right. I shall thus accept Pierre's proposal. By the way, I have six sisters... but two of them are married already. But dearest Armand, you've given me an idea. Maybe you might take a fancy to one of them, now that I can offer a dowry, perhaps you could choose between a brunette and a redhead?" François proposed jokingly.

"Oh, Lord, you sound just like my mother, always scheming to arrange favourable marriages for the family. Forget it, I like my independence!" retorted Armand immediately. "I mean, thank you, I feel very honoured, but I'm far too young," he added lamely.

138

The ensuing lunch was very much a private affair. To their great disappointment, the nosy butler and all the footmen were dismissed from serving the lunch party and Pierre insisted that Jean alone should serve them. This news was not well received, as rumours were running rife in the chateau and the servants had been looking forward to some eavesdropping during lunch and becoming the undisputed stars later during dinner in the servants' quarters. Grudgingly the butler left and closed the doors, not before having polished every last glass to perfection. But when he started to polish the wine decanter as well, Armand's patience was worn out and he threw him out of the room.

"How come butlers are always so nosy?" he complained.

"Part of their professional code of conduct, I presume," François answered, attacking a roast chicken.

The new friends kept eating and discussing as Pierre and Armand besieged François relentlessly with thousands of questions until he gave up.

"I must apologize, but I'm dead on my feet now. This excellent wine has simply finished me off. I'll be a good boy now and go to bed, let me thank you once more for your friendship and the generous offer that you made me."

No protests could keep him, and not ten minutes later he was sound asleep.

*****

Bad memories were stirred up once again when the bailiff and his accomplices were judged and executed, and no one was to be spared. The bodies of the two dead gypsies had been handed over to their tribe and only one day later not a single gypsy was seen anywhere in the region. They had disappeared as silently and secretly as they had arrived.

A huge crowd had gathered and watched excitedly when the convicts were paraded into the courtyard. Pierre knew from his schooldays in Reims that executions were seen as a welcome change from daily routine. Therefore he was not at all surprised to find that the crowd had gathered in an outright festive mood. Some of the younger girls had used the rare opportunity of abandoning their drab daily routine and had added daring bright scarves to their gowns to make sure that they'd not remain unnoticed and would draw the desired attention from the opposite sex.

The sentences were known to everybody; the bailiff and the valet were to be hanged. But the housekeeper was less lucky. Her trial had been brought forward, not only based on the charge of poisoning: almost immediately the prosecution had extended her charge with the serious crime of witchcraft. Witches were known to brew secret potions and looking at her bony and shrivelled figure the judges came to the conclusion that witchcraft could be the only possible explanation for her relationship with the bailiff.

As a witch she was sentenced to be burned at the stake. This news had spread quickly and added considerable spice to the event, drawing visitors from far away. To see a witch burned at the stake was a rare occurrence, something definitely not to be missed. Furthermore it was common knowledge that the ashes of burned witches retained some of their magical powers and the executioner would make a good income from secretly selling the charred bones of the witch. Luckily nobody would ever notice that he stretched what was a limited supply by adding charred bones produced with foresight in his own kitchen fire...

Hence a noisy and good-humoured crowd filled the courtyard where a gruesome-looking scaffold had been erected for the gallows. Next to it a terrifying stake had already been prepared with thick logs of firewood surrounded by loose bundles of brushwood. The festive atmosphere was enhanced by flasks of wine that were being freely exchanged. Fruit, bread and cold delicacies were consumed in abundance to fortify body and soul for the forthcoming strenuous events.

The densely packed crowd was being jostled by ever more people arriving until the first onlookers collapsed in the intense heat and the constable decided that he had no option but to close the chateau gates. This decision drew furious comments from those unfortunates who had arrived too late to gain entrance, but there was simply no more space available.

Suddenly the noisy crowd went silent as the beating of the drums commenced. With their dull and menacing rhythm they caused goose bumps to appear on the skin of the spectators – the show was starting, justice would be done in the name of the king.

The valet was the first to arrive. He screamed and sobbed, pleaded for mercy and asserted his innocence – but to no avail. He was led to the gallows by four musketeers who looked suitably grim, their polished mail shirts glistening and dazzling in the sun. The girls sighed secretly; how dashing those musketeers looked, compared to the boring young men from the village farms.

At the gallows the priest was already waiting for the valet. The latter was given a last opportunity to repent and kiss the cross before the hooded hangman took over and soon – far too soon as far as the spectators were concerned – the valet could be seen dangling on the rope. All the same, a pleasurable shiver of excitement ran though the crowd. This had been a nice opening for a memorable event indeed.

The injured bailiff was the next to follow. He was no longer able to walk – his naked leg showed that his wound had started to fester – thus he needed to be

140

transported in a wheelbarrow to the scaffold and was then carried up by the musketeers.

To most of the public the valet had not been well known, and his arrival on the scene had only provoked a few isolated jeers and shouts of disdain. Only once he started to plead for mercy had the crowd answered in unison, and booed and ridiculed him.

The stage was set now for the arrival of the bailiff, and his appearance set off a storm of emotions. Feared and despised by almost all of the spectators, for the crowd the bailiff was the incarnation of evil, corruption and greed. Eagerly they looked forward to seeing justice being done. The crowd wanted revenge, they wanted his blood.

The distance between prison and scaffold measured a scarce hundred yards. As soon as the bailiff's face was spotted, rotten fruit and all possible forms of rubbish were hurled at him. Every spectator seemed to have brought along something unsavoury in order to humiliate his last minutes on earth. But the shrivelled man in the wheelbarrow came as somewhat of a disappointment – he did not live up at all to the fearful villain of their memories. Here they saw an old and unkempt man, hunched, cringing in pain, frightened and lost, no longer the merciless and imposing figure they remembered, feared and hated over so many years – a man who had mercilessly exerted power as proxy for the absent Marquis. Flushed with high fever, the bailiff was dragged unceremoniously out of the wheelbarrow. The guards showed no sympathy as they pulled him by his arms, ignoring his cries of pain.

Pierre could only imagine how much his leg with its smashed bones must be hurting, as the bailiff was pulled up the steps to the waiting executioner and the priest – but it was unclear if the sick man was even fully aware of what was going on. Only when he caught sight of the hooded executioner could the spectators in the front hear him crying out in despair, "No, no, no, please spare me!" as he was dragged further forwards.

The fat priest approached him, his forehead glistening and his skull cap dark with sweat as the hot summer sun beat down mercilessly on the inner courtyard and the scaffold. He urged the bailiff to repent in the name of the Lord Jesus and his Church and kiss the cross. The priest had a melodious firm voice that carried well across the courtyard and reached even the last row of the spectators. It made a pleasant difference from the whining protestations of the bailiff.

Receiving no response, the priest solemnly took his golden cross in his hands. The cross dazzled in the sunlight, drawing admiring exclamations from the crowd. But the bright shining cross seemed to scare the bailiff as he shied away anxiously and refused to kiss it. First a whisper then an outcry went through the

141

crowd – *this* was the final proof – if a man refused to kiss the cross, he must be possessed by evil spirits, worse, he must be in league with the devil!

The executioner didn't waste any time, and in a the blink of an eye the noose was put around the bailiff's neck and before anybody had time to realize what was going on, the bailiff's end had come and, like the valet before him, he could be seen dangling like a puppet on the hangman's rope.

The formerly awe-inspiring bailiff, the powerful representative of the Marquis de Beauvoir, hung there – reduced to a miserable corpse, swaying on the rope in his soiled breeches. The crowd felt slightly disappointed, this miserable sight somehow did not seem to be a fitting end for the odious villain they had known him to be.

Full of expectation the crowd now watched out for the housekeeper – and indeed her appearance more than made up for the shortcomings of the first two entrances, which had been disappointingly uneventful.

Erect, she walked to the scaffold, refusing to climb into the wheelbarrow which had carried the bailiff. The musketeers started to poke her with their long rifles, which made her turn round in hot anger, cursing first the soldiers and then the spectators around her, swearing and spitting into the crowd. When she was made to mount the scaffold, all of a sudden she tried to tear open her chemise, laughing madly.

As was customary, the priest approached her now, urging her to repent, but the housekeeper only laughed at him and spat viciously first into his face, then at the cross, uttering the most obscene of curses. The priest was visibly shocked and made a sign to the executioner to bind her to the stake and silence her as quickly as possible.

Pierre watched the scene from his gilded armchair, placed on a podium opposite the scaffold to ensure that he would have an excellent view – and could be seen by the crowd as well. Justice was being done today not only in the name of the King but in his name too, as lord of the castle. He was surrounded by Armand and several local dignitaries; only François de Toucy had already left for Paris as he needed to report to the Cardinal.

Pierre hated every minute he was forced to sit in the public glare, but he was aware how important the public execution of the judgments was, to ascertain that justice would prevail and to deter future crimes.

Armand had insisted on wearing their best mail shirts and a metal helmet to look suitably impressive for the crowd. Although a canopy with the Marquis de Beauvoir's coat of arms was held above them by two servants, Pierre felt he was being roasted alive in the hot summer sun, as the canopy afforded them only meagre shade.

Fascinated, Pierre watched how the crowd reacted to the housekeeper's performance. The pitiful figure of the bailiff had not inspired any fear any more. But this tiny, bony, obscene and spitting person made them shiver and he could see how people made the sign behind their backs to ward off evil. Some cautious mothers quickly hid their children, not willing to take any chance.

It was normal practice that the relatives or friends of persons sentenced to be burned at the stake would come forward to bribe the executioner and ask him to strangle the poor victim shortly after the fire was lit, thus sparing the victim the worst of the suffering and pain. But nobody had come forward on behalf of the housekeeper and thus the terrible sentence was carried out to the letter. The brushwood was set alight and greedily the thin flames started devouring the dry wood, licking and caressing the bundles of firewood below until all of a sudden the fire seemed to explode in an orgy of flames, enshrouding the housekeeper in a blazing halo of red light. Her frantic cries and the sickening smell would haunt Pierre for weeks to come.

The musketeers started to beat the drums again to drown the cries of the dying housekeeper but it took an agonizing eternity before her cries became more subdued, swallowed by the sound of the crackling flames and the thick curtain of smoke. Then, all of a sudden, the voice was silenced, the drums stopped and only the sound of the burning wood echoed in the spellbound courtyard. The crowd, the angry animal that had lusted for the blood of the housekeeper was strangely subdued; it had been a slow and painful death.

Now that the ordeal was finished Pierre decided that it was time to flee from the lethal combination of unbearable heat and stench lest he should faint under the watchful eyes of the spectators. He was just about to stand up when a commotion went through the assembled spectators like ripples across a pond. Cries emanated from the crowd and people started to point upwards to the sky. A large crow was circling above the courtyard, its lustrous feathers of darkest black glittering in the sun.

"A sign, this is a sign that she was a witch after all!" The words ran through the crowd and Pierre saw people crossing themselves hastily, some women quickly covered their faces with their veils, as if the thin material could shield them from evil. The fat priest reacted quickly and fell on his knees. "The Lord has sent us a miracle!" he shouted and on the spot he started a litany of religious prayers and chants, forcing Pierre and Armand to cross themselves and wait piously until he finished. To Pierre's immense relief, however, the priest kept his intervention short and with a last stern warning to obey at all times the Lord Jesus and their lawful master, the Marquis de Beauvoir, the crowd was dismissed. The mood was already changing back to a festive one. Everyone had the impression that they had attended the biggest event of their lifetime, and this needed to be celebrated.

Pierre and Armand had seen and experienced enough. Back in the castle they went straight to Pierre's room where Jean helped them to take off the heavy mail shirts, and sighing with satisfaction they also ripped off their sweat-soaked shirts.

"I hated every second of this," Pierre sighed. "But I understand that carrying out the executions in public was an absolute necessity. I can't tell you how relieved I feel that this nightmare has ended, thanks to François and Jean. They were magnificent." He sighed again. "And finally we can resume a normal life now, how I have hated to be stuck in Montrésor like a bird in a cage!"

"And ready to be served roasted at any minute... but there's only one tiny flaw in Your Grace's brilliant analysis," quipped Armand. "Your Grace tends to forget your loving and caring relative, your dearest cousin Henri!"

"I agree with the wise words of your lordship," answered Pierre, mocking the formal words of his friend. "We have only won a battle, not the war!"

They were interrupted as a young parlourmaid entered, bringing fresh shirts. She blushed attractively when she noticed the two handsome young gentlemen standing there, dressed only in breeches, bare-chested. Giggling nervously she handed Jean the shirts and left the room, not without having sent another long and very inviting glance to Armand.

Armand noticed Pierre's envious look and he grinned. "I agree that we haven't won the war yet, but I have the feeling that I just changed my priorities, and tonight I'll be fighting yet another battle – but a very pleasant one!"

*****

Henri's journey to Paris was uneventful. He avoided the major roads and approached Paris from the east. From time to time, when he stopped at small inns to sleep and refresh himself, Henri drew curious glances as soon as the grooms or innkeepers set eyes on his splendid stallion. The impressive horse didn't quite seem to match the simple attire of the handsome blond horseman. But closer scrutiny of his long, flowing locks betrayed his noble ancestry, as did his proud demeanour. One look into Henri's ice-blue eyes and even the most curious of men got the message that questions were not welcome, it would be dangerous simply to ask. Henri thus arrived in Paris unperturbed, and having bribed his way through the gates he entered the city undetected.

It hadn't taken Henri very long to figure out that there was only one place where he could hide safely in Paris. As soon as he entered the sprawling city he directed his horse straight into one of the less fashionable – at times highly dangerous – neighbourhoods. He had to watch attentively as the winding narrow streets were potholed like a Swiss cheese, dirt and excrement making the few patches that had been paved randomly with cobblestones treacherous and slippery.

As usual the noise level in Paris was deafening; people were shouting and talking at the top of their voices, food stalls offered their products, compensating for the questionable quality and freshness with vociferous and boastful advertisements. A talentless street musician was playing a popular tune on his flute, making up for a lack of skills by playing as loud as he could. Plenty of idle young men seemed to be hanging around, most of them rascals by their appearance, clothes worn and torn, waiting for the rare opportunity to steal or make some money. Henri continued at his ease. He had taken this way often enough when he had visited the sleazy taverns of Paris at night with his friends; riding along these run-down streets in daylight presented no particular challenge to him.

Suddenly a brawl broke out right in front of him; two young lads had started to argue and were shouting at the top of their voices – Henri guessed that they were quarrelling about a girl. Kicking and fighting, they blocked his way and Henri had to slow his horse down as otherwise he would have tripped right over them. He was still watching the two fighting lads when all of a sudden he noticed a dark shadow lunging at his horse from behind with a dagger gleaming in his hand. Within seconds Henri drew his own sword and lashed out. A grim smile played on his lips as he heard a young voice howling with pain as the razor sharp blade cut into his flesh.

The two lads stopped their fight immediately. Shocked, they watched their friend writhing in pain, blood gushing out of his hand. A single finger of the young man's hand lay in the dust as if it had been plucked at random from a puppet. Their scam had failed, the strange gentleman defying them with a single stroke of his sword. Before they could make up their minds and avenge their friend, the strange horseman had already spurred on his huge stallion and disappeared, only the trail of blood and their mutilated friend bearing witness to what had happened only seconds before.

Unperturbed, Henri continued his way to a shabby inn that was conveniently located close to the Seine. Convenient, in a sense that all kind of garbage, including the bodies of unwelcome visitors, could easily be disposed of. If possible the street he had selected was even dirtier and narrower than those before, and the roofs of the thatched houses now seemed to be touching each other, plunging the whole street into an everlasting shadowy gloom, despite the blazing summer sun above Paris.

Henri stopped his horse in front of a rundown inn with a stained wooden board swaying wearily in the hot summer breeze. Miraculously a groom appeared as soon as Henri dismounted from his stallion. Henri handed him the reins without hesitation and entered the shabby house without even casting a glance behind him, visibly indifferent to the fate of his precious horse, let alone the precious saddlebags loaded with the treasures of Roquemoulin.

Inside the inn, two cheap whores were slumped at a table, staring absent-mindedly into their empty cups of wine. Both – women and furniture – had seen better days in their youth. But as soon as the ladies of easy virtue became aware that a potential customer had entered their establishment, the instincts of their trade prevailed. Resolutely they pushed their bosoms up into what they supposed to be a more appealing position and displayed an inviting smile – a shame that so many of their teeth had been lost long ago, along with their virginity.

Henri glanced at them with disdain. "The day I should ever envisage joining the list of your unlucky customers, I'd rather commit suicide. Don't just sit there, staring at me, call Nicolas, come on, move your fat backsides!"

The two women exchanged a quick glance but seemed to come to the conclusion that they'd better respond to the command of this haughty stranger. The younger whore got up, and giving it a last try, she approached Henri, as smiling coyly she stroked his crotch and purred, "Maybe I'll remember where Nicolas can be found if we have a bit of fun together upstairs first, sweetie. I'm offering you a deal, I'll not charge you the full price today, you can have it twice if you want to."

"If you don't want me to slit you open from head to toe like a butchered pig, you'd better call Nicolas here and now, do you understand?" Henri had not raised his voice but the tone and the way he looked at her made the blood freeze in her veins. Hastily she turned and waved him to follow her. They disappeared behind the counter where a filthy curtain separated the public room from a small, sparsely lit back room. She tapped angrily against the wood-panelled wall in a certain rhythm, a procedure that she repeated three times.

There was no answer and it took a good five minutes until all of a sudden a part of the panelled wall gave way and a secret entrance appeared. Henri didn't seem surprised – blithely he entered and the panel closed almost noiselessly behind him.

A servant was already waiting for him; dressed in a clean livery of shining silk, he looked as if he had materialized from a different planet. Henri followed him through the dark corridor until they reached a magnificent salon. Although Henri knew exactly what to expect – and he would never have admitted it – he was stunned anew each time he arrived here. The rundown inn was nothing but a cleverly devised camouflage for what could only be described as Paris' most exclusive and luxurious gambling den. The well-appointed salon was filled with sunlight but the big gambling tables lay idle, protected by linen covers.

146

The sunlight streaming into the room from the unusually large leaded windows that dominated one side of the room was reflected by plenty of gleaming silver mirrors, which served in the evening to reflect the light of the attached candelabras. Polished to perfection, they would immerse the salon in a sea of mellow light. The walls of the salon were panelled with the most exotic kinds of wood imported from Africa; no expense had been spared. Exquisite paintings and Gobelin tapestries depicted classical myths in colourful detail, showing half-naked bodies of pagan gods and goddesses, shamelessly and alluringly exposed. Naked breasts and voluptuous bodies would welcome an illustrious circle of guests – a radical and enticing change from the sombre religious or heroic paintings that adorned most noble salons. Thick oriental carpets of the finest workmanship dampened the noise of Henri's boots. The salon was a haven of luxury and refinement, combined with the best entertainment Paris had to offer.

His host was waiting already for Henri at the end of the salon, standing close to a window that had been opened to let in fresh air and unfiltered sunlight. Henri could hear voices from the river floating through the window, he could even smell the river – in summer there was always a slight and fairly unpleasant aroma of sewage. The Seine was within easy reach, and the house even had its own jetty, ideal for noble visitors who preferred to remain incognito and wanted to avoid the dangerous streets at night.

Nicolas, Henri's host, stood there, a lean figure of medium height, impeccably dressed in the height of fashion, as usual. Henri could not remember having seen him otherwise. His gleaming auburn hair was cut a bit shorter than the fashion might prescribe for gentlemen of noble birth but his bearing was as proud as that of any man of noble pedigree. Henri had never been able to find out where Nicolas originated from – his roots could be Italian, or just as likely Spanish or any other part of the Mediterranean, maybe he had even come from as far as from the Ottoman Empire – he would never tell. His eyes were of the darkest onyx that could be imagined, capable of melting any heart if they wanted to. But behind this façade of beauty and refinement there was a core of steel. In fact Nicolas was the undisputed king and dictator of the gambling world – and ready to defend his kingdom at any price.

"Welcome, Monsieur le Comte de Roquemoulin!" He greeted Henri in his warm and dark voice. "What has led your lordship to my humble dwellings?"

"Becoming more humble every day!" Henri exclaimed and looked around, appraising the expensive new furniture. "Your wealth would appear to have grown somewhat!"

"I do manage from time to time to generate some modest income, your lordship," Nicolas answered, his laughing eyes belying his own words and teasing Henri.

147

"I can't say that I'm surprised, but I understand from your welcome that you've already been fully informed that I inherited the title of Comte de Roquemoulin," Henri stated, and looked at Nicolas to test his reaction.

His host only nodded and looked at him with an expression that was difficult to read. As he didn't reply, Henri was forced to continue.

"Knowing you well, you'll already have some idea as to why I've come here, part of my motivation of course coming from my desire to enjoy the unrivalled pleasure of your company?" he suggested cautiously.

Nicolas avoided a direct answer but replied all the same. "As your lordship can imagine, Paris was brimming with rumours when the news of your lordship's adoption started to circulate. The Duchesse de Limoges nearly had a fit, as despite her advanced age she had been expecting to add the considerable fortune of our *cher* Jean Baptiste sooner or later to hers – somehow she had never expected him to grow old. She was lamenting everywhere that your lordship has not only been perfidious enough to break her feeble heart but that your lordship betrayed her, she claimed to have nourished a – what was it? Oh yes, a vicious viper at her bosom! It all sounded fairly melodramatic, but we do all know our esteemed duchess." Nicolas' eyes were laughing again.

He must be mocking us most of the time. How stupid the majority of us must look in his eyes. Henri mused anew at his host.

"Suddenly the news arrived that your *beloved* new father had suffered a fatal accident. The general opinion was that this accident happened a bit too fast after the adoption papers must have been signed and proved to be rather too beneficial for your lordship!" Again Nicolas' eyes seemed to be mocking Henri. "Therefore my impression is, if your lordship would allow me to express my humble opinion, your lordship might feel more comfortable hiding for some time from the ever so critical, albeit perhaps prejudiced, eyes of the public – and might therefore have envisaged condescending to do so right here?"

"I'm of the conviction that in this kingdom, Cardinal Richelieu has only one serious competitor – and that's you, Nicolas. A pity that you squander your talents hidden here in this building!"

"My lord, believe me, sometimes I think I made the better choice. At least I have more fun than the Cardinal," Nicolas answered, bowing towards Henri to express his appreciation of a rare compliment from a man who was known to be very critical.

"What else do you presume?" Henri asked curiously.

"That your lordship soon might be at risk of losing your title, and might need to leave this kingdom as soon as possible as to preserve your freedom of movement?"

Henri bowed his head in admiration: "You make me curious now, how did you reach this conclusion? "

"In the saddlebags of this splendid stallion of yours, your lordship carried gold and jewellery enough to pay a king's ransom. All of the treasure comes from the Roquemoulin heritage and is worth a fortune – well, most of it is… this doesn't look to me like a random and leisurely ride to Paris, it more looks like a hasty decision to leave Roquemoulin…"

"Why do you say most of the items? And how do you happen to know this?" Henri asked angrily, coming to the conclusion that his host knew a bit too much about his plans for his liking.

"Jean Baptiste de Roquemoulin – may God bless his soul – was a man of many qualities, but certainly not a very sharp man," Nicolas answered. "One adoring glance and a loosening of the breeches from any good-looking man or boy and he'd open his wallet. Some of the jewellery that your lordship brought along was actually sold to him indirectly by me, therefore I must confess that I happen to know that among them are some worthless copies – but copies of excellent quality, of course. I do apologize, had I ever known that your lordship would become the ultimate owner, I'd have refrained of course from such dealings!"

Henri didn't know if he should be scandalized or amused, but decided on the latter. Jean Baptiste would have swallowed any bait, of course Nicolas would have profited from the occasion – it must have been too tempting! Yet he was deeply annoyed, he needed the money badly.

"I'm afraid your analysis is brilliant – as usual. By the way, I will personally kill you if one single coin or ring goes missing, I know exactly what I brought with me. And you'll have to substitute the faked ones against the real stuff Jean Baptiste paid you for. I want you to accommodate me here for some time until I have made up my mind where to go. I'll pay you handsomely for this. In the meantime, please sell the jewellery and the horse for me, I need the cash, as indeed I do feel an inclination to change climate and leave France."

Now it was up to Nicolas to look scandalized. "You'll be here as my guest, of course, and I'd never steel a single *sous* from you, indeed, you should know me well enough for that. I'll make enough money when I sell your jewellery and your horse and take my usual commission, but you know this as well – and," he sighed, "I'll substitute the fake jewellery for genuine."

149

Henri just nodded in agreement. Naturally Nicolas would be making money out of him, but who wouldn't?

Nicolas had approached him while he was speaking and suddenly he embraced Henri and kissed his cheeks murmuring, "You are truly welcome in my house, be my guest, Henri de Beauvoir!"

"No more 'your lordship' here and there?"

"No more, Henri, you and I know that your precious title is lost. I don't know yet why and how. I guess you'll let me know later – but from today on you're one of us, and you knew it the moment you entered my house." Nicolas replied and kissed Henri once more, but this time Henri sensed a passion that Nicolas had managed to hide until now.

"My stay here won't be so boring after all," Henri thought, and pretended not to notice that Nicolas had embraced him much longer than was necessary for a mere polite welcome.

A light snoring sound heralded the fact that Pierre was deeply asleep. He was breathing evenly, his mouth slightly open, happy and unperturbed until a strong hand appeared out of the shadow, covered his mouth with a quick grasp and pushed him backwards. Pierre tried to scream and regain his balance but the hand was too strong. Without mercy, he was pushed from behind until he fell out of his comfortable hammock right onto the lawn. Awoken from a beautiful dream Pierre opened his eyes, and trying to gather his wits, he scrambled to his feet, ready to fight for his life.

After a second's shock, he managed to focus his still sleepy eyes on the attacker, a giant man he couldn't recognizes, as his face was obscured by shadow. Pierre grabbed his dagger when he heard a familiar voice.

"You'd better not do that! You wouldn't kill your own kin, would you?"

Pierre felt utterly stupid. This was no evil villain attacking him; he was looking into the laughing eyes of his cousin, Charles.

"Charles, you rascal! *You* nearly killed *me!*" Pierre cried out with genuine pleasure. "When did you arrive? Where's Marie?" and guiltily remembering that he should have mentioned Céline before, he added, "and Céline, of course!"

"Oh Céline, she's absolutely fine," Charles retorted, pretending not to have noted Pierre's lapse of manners.

"And Marie?" Pierre asked, unconvincingly trying to sound casual.

Charles slapped his forehead. "Oh, I'm so sorry, I completely forgot to give you her best regards!"

Pierre looked totally crestfallen. "Are you telling me that she hasn't come?"

Charles felt a stirring of mercy; he couldn't hold out against this look of Pierre's, and his puppy-dog eyes.

"Oh my Lord, Pierre, you really do need to learn to hide your true feelings! Of course we've brought her along, we wouldn't have dared set foot in your beautiful chateau without her. The ladies are in their rooms already, they didn't have the courage to face you before they'd finished what they call 'freshening up' – I call it major renovation work. But I guessed you wouldn't mind if I came over as soon as we arrived."

151

"To kick me out of my hammock and tease me?" Pierre grumbled. "Of course I don't mind, maybe you don't realize, but I quite love it. Feel free to continue!"

Charles just laughed. He knew Pierre well enough to know that he'd soon be forgiven. He embraced Pierre and, looking down at his slim cousin, he said, "You can't believe how happy I am to see you here, it's a miracle that you escaped this adventure unscathed. You must have been born under a lucky star. When the ladies join us, there will be plenty to discuss, I'm sure."

"Oh, yes, there will be – I feel like I haven't spoken to you for ages!" Pierre answered. "Let's walk back to the chateau and have a glass of wine while we wait for the ladies. I bet Armand will be there as well, he has a sixth sense for that kind of thing."

Not waiting for his cousin's consent, he had already retrieved his dagger from the ground and was hastening straight back to the chateau gate, Charles following behind good-humouredly with his big stride. He didn't need to be a wizard to know that there could be no stopping Pierre once Marie was involved.

Pierre's assumption had been right. Miraculously Armand had already heard that their friends had arrived from Paris (the miracle being linked to his intimate connections with the servants' quarters) and, sitting comfortably on a sofa, his legs sprawled out in front of him, he was waiting in a sun-filled salon that faced the moat and the river.

As soon as he saw Charles he jumped up, but his left foot got trapped in one of the rugs that lay in front of the sofa and he lurched forward, right into Charles' arms.

"Dear Lord, that's a smashing welcome!" Charles exclaimed. "I know, of course, that I'm hugely popular, but this greeting is simply overwhelming. By the way, have you become rather heavy of late?"

Armand recovered quickly from his fall and retorted, "This question cannot really come from *you*, Charles! You, of all people, calling me heavy, that has to be a joke!"

Charles looked down with a hint of guilt. "There is a possibility that I may have gained some weight lately, but you do look somewhat broader as well!"

"It's all muscle," Pierre answered instead with a broad grin. "Armand is so much engaged in coaching my female staff that he doesn't have any time left to eat properly."

"All lies and sheer jealousy from Pierre!" Armand cried, but his laughing eyes betrayed him.

152

"Whatever, the lazy times are over," Charles continued. "I have brought with me one of the best fencing masters from Paris, I thought it time to take up our lessons once more!"

This statement was met with a general expression of joy as, even if they hadn't admitted it openly, the friends had started to become somewhat bored during the past weeks and were craving some decent diversion.

However, in reality Pierre had different issues on his mind: he felt extremely nervous of meeting Marie – it seemed an eternity since he had held her in his arms. What if her feelings had changed? But when it came to it, it didn't take more than one look into her beautiful amber eyes and all his doubts and trepidation were forgotten.

Needless to say, the ensuing meal was much more than just a normal dinner – it became a great party. Charles – it probably should have been expected – made a slip of the tongue when he mentioned Céline's delicate condition. Although Céline kicked his foot to make him shut up, it was too late and the two friends insisted on being enlightened as to what he had meant. With a mix of pride and embarrassment, Charles confessed that they were expecting offspring by end of the year.

A storm of congratulations broke out and there was no more stopping the celebrations, the best wine was brought up from the cellar and as soon as the nosy butler had overheard enough to pass on the news the whole chateau was buzzing with the good news.

"Are you absolutely sure, my friend, that you're the real father?" Armand teased Charles. "You know, there are plenty of nasty stories around about naïve, aging men marrying young and attractive women!"

Before Charles could reply, Céline intervened. Putting on a tragic face she said, "Oh yes, absolutely sure, he's the father. Armand, the terrible truth is, nobody else ever wanted me!"

Marie and Pierre nearly fell over with laughter and the mood remained hilarious until it was Pierre's and Armand's turn to start telling their adventures of the past months.

As it happened, Armand told most of the story. He chose to put a humorous gloss on the account of their adventures by mimicking brilliantly all the characters, from the sex-starved valet and the aging spinster of a housekeeper to the whining bailiff – Armand had always been a born comedian.

All the same, Marie and Céline were gripped by fear when they started to realize how narrow Pierre's escape had been. It also turned out that no news of the crossbow ambush in the forest had ever reached them in Paris and when Pierre confessed that the musketeer riding his horse had been struck down, tears started rolling down the cheeks of the ladies and Marie hid her face in shock.

The candles had already burned low when they finally left for their bedrooms, and with some regret, as it had been a remarkable evening. Marie was convinced that she wouldn't be able to close an eye – who could, after having listened to such an ordeal?

The next morning Marie was woken up by an amazingly fresh-looking Céline. Marie was fully convinced that she must have been asleep for a short while only, after all, she still felt terribly sleepy! But blazing sunlight was filling her room, as Céline had opened the curtains, vigorously ignoring Marie's feeble protest, denying her this option.

"How late is it?" groaned Marie.

"Nearly noon," Céline answered in a voice that seemed far too cheerful and energetic for Marie's taste.

"Have a nice hot cup of chocolate!" Céline suggested.

Marie gratefully seized the cup and cautiously tried to open her eyes fully now, despite the bright light in her room.

"How you can be so disgustingly cheerful and even talk about chocolate?" Marie protested. "All pregnant women I have ever known pretended to hate the idea of smelling or eating any food!"

Céline looked rather guilty and replied, "I must admit it sounds weird, but I seem to feel hungry all the time – and besides that I simply feel gorgeous. I know that I'm supposed to be lying on my bed moaning and suffering, but I feel wonderful, so why should I pretend otherwise?"

Marie only sighed and sniffed the steaming liquid. After two delicious sips she started to feel almost human. Stretching like a lazy cat, she said, "I had a wonderful night. Just imagine, no more travelling on bumpy roads and a real bed on my own – isn't this simply lovely?"

Céline smiled. "I'm sure we'll have a truly wonderful time now. But I promised your parents to guard you well, I'm afraid therefore that I can't leave you alone with Pierre, I hope that you won't mind too much."

Marie sighed. "I know, this was part of our agreement and I understand of course that this is the way it has to be. Don't worry, I'll be a good and upright girl in Montrésor."

Céline was relieved and Marie was content as well, she hadn't really promised anything beyond the borders of Montrésor … *always good to leave some options open.*

The next few weeks reminded them of the enchanted and restful time they had spent the previous year in Hertfordshire. Far away from the obligations and restrictions of life at court, they explored their surroundings, organized picnics or spent their afternoons lazily in the shadow of the large oaks in the park, watching the swans glide on the lake or the river.

One beautiful summer day Pierre surprised them with a boat trip on the Loire River. Comfortably they sailed down the gleaming river at their leisure until they reached a shallow bank where a picnic was waiting for them. Musicians were playing and Pierre glowed with satisfaction when he noticed how enchanted the ladies were.

"The perfect garden of Eden," Céline sighed as she nibbled some grapes. "Just what I had in mind when I told you I wouldn't stay in Paris for any gold in the world!"

Marie agreed dreamily. The white wine had made her sleepy and she closed her eyes, basking happily in the sun, although her mother had warned her again and again that a true lady who cared for her looks shouldn't ruin her complexion by exposing it to harmful sunlight.

Messages continued streaming in from London and Paris, decisions needed to taken and requests to be answered, but nothing really disturbed the leisurely pace of the late summer months.

"If I could only stop time," Pierre remarked one evening when the gentlemen had retired to their preferred sanctum, the library.

"I know, we've had a wonderful time, but in the autumn Marie has to go back and we'll need to decide where to travel next," Armand answered.

Charles hadn't really been listening. He was reading a letter from London that had arrived that morning. Apparently the news was not very good, as he frowned and uttered angry exclamations from time to time.

"Pierre, look, your giant cousin is trying to read a letter. It seems to be hard work for him, maybe we should leave the room, cousin Charles looks really worn out by his efforts!" Armand joked.

Charles simply grinned. He was used to Armand's remarks and had usually given up commenting on them but tonight apparently he felt talkative.

155

"Not only am I able to read my letters, contrary to some people in this room whom I don't want to mention, I can even understand the content!"

"Content that doesn't seem to be especially edifying, judging by your reactions," Pierre ventured cautiously. "What's the matter?"

"Poor King Charles seems to be sinking fast! He's appealing to his noble lords to come to his help – well, not really, he's telling us to share in his victorious cause…" While Charles was speaking, he kept shaking his head in disbelief. "Our enlightened sovereign has just officially declared war on Parliament in London…"

"This means that civil war is unavoidable !" Pierre answered. "It was to be expected, you were already predicting this last year!"

Armand took a sip from the excellent whisky that Pierre had smuggled from England and shook his head. "Are the English going mad, how can those people in Parliament – low-born commoners – dare to go to war against their anointed king! My father would know how to deal with those *canaille!*"

"However," Pierre answered trying to calm his friend, "The King has to fight and I'm afraid we'll have to return to England sooner than I'd like. I took the oath of allegiance when the King made me my grandfather's successor. But Charles did the same, which means both of us might have to leave almost immediately!" He tried to put on a brave face but failed miserably. It was obvious that he hated the idea of leaving Marie so soon.

Charles and Armand exchanged a long glance; there was no need to speak.

Armand cleared his voice. "Pierre, have you forgotten all I explained to you about the rules and games of politics? Of course, all nobles take this oath, it's part of the centuries-old ceremony. But if you assemble all the aristocrats of France and England together who would be truly willing to fulfil their oath and die for their king, you probably couldn't even fill this room. Supporting the king is a matter of personal strategy and general politics and not about your personal honour."

"I must look totally naïve to both of you, but don't I risk losing my title if I don't go to support my King – now that he's officially asking for the support of his nobles?"

Again Armand and Charles exchanged a long and knowing glance.

"Both of us need to be cautious and play the game, of course," Charles answered. "Our King must never have anything in hand to justify calling us disloyal or dishonest. I can't tell you how happy I am that Céline is expecting a baby. I informed his Majesty already that this had come as a total surprise, an unexpected gift from heaven. But in view of the fragile health of my wife – who happens to be French and of fairly advanced age – we dare not go back to England at the moment."

Armand giggled. "You're aware that Céline will kill you the moment she hears about this?"

Charles grinned back at him. "Believe it or not, she suggested that I should write this. She has a very sound head on her shoulders and she thinks that we should better disappear from view until the winner is known – although I'm afraid I know already that the winner will not be our King. Céline wants her baby to grow up with a father and not with a painting of a hero hanging in our gallery of ancestral portraits."

Armand couldn't help bursting into laughter. "At least your portrait would be the biggest! No way could your child ever miss that one! But really, Charles, nobody will ever believe this excuse, wives always seem to be pregnant, no true nobleman would ever stay at home for such a silly excuse!"

Charles laughed. "Point taken, I do sound a bit feeble, don't I? I did add, though, that I have to look after her estates that are in total disorder after the death of her father."

Armand nodded, satisfied. "That's more credible, nobody would care about a pregnant woman, but if estates are at stake, it changes the picture!"

Pierre grinned. His enormous cousin Charles didn't fit his idea of a weakling. Then he looked at both of them. "What do you suggest I should answer?"

"Oh, that's fairly simple. You keep him in a good mood, but waiting. As you happen to be a Marquis and peer of France as well, King Louis will have to allow you to leave France first of all and you must write to King Charles that you have submitted your request to join him. Armand's father already made it clear with Richelieu that this permission will never be granted. King Louis will deliberate a while but then will request your services and you'll be sent on a mission to…"

"I have a premonition that this mission will guide us to… Venice, right?" Armand interjected.

"You're so smart," Charles quipped. "It's such a pleasure to be surrounded by intelligent listeners. Yes, Venice, it'll be – I don't quite remember why, but I remember vaguely there is a mission that's still waiting to be accomplished."

Pierre looked at his ruby ring and sighed. "Yes, there is something that needs to be found, that bloody third ring. Well, that's settled then. We'll leave for Venice in the autumn instead of London, probably a better choice anyhow, as I really hated the weather in London in November!"

"You'd better warn Marie that we won't be back in Reims by Christmas, I'm afraid that will be impossible," Armand added, having calculated in his mind the distances and travelling time.

Pierre made a face but answered bravely. "Whatever. We must find this damned ring, we swore an oath…" and winking at Charles he added, "and this time it was a genuine one!"

*****

Life continued at a leisurely pace until the day a messenger arrived from King Louis. Convinced of his own importance, the messenger refused categorically to be received by anybody other than the Marquis himself. Armand was foaming with rage as the messenger had made it clear that he did not deem the youngest son of the Marquis de Saint Paul important enough to receive a royal message first hand.

Pierre was found by his angry friend in the chateau grounds where he was spending a delightful time accompanied by the ladies. Armand kept voicing his opinion loudly about stupid and inflated royal messengers – his pride was suffering terribly. Reluctantly Pierre followed Armand and returned to the castle, wracking his brains as to what this fuss could be all about. *What could be important enough to justify a royal summons and request his personal and immediate presence?*

All the options that came to his mind were not precisely contributing to improving his humour and by the time he met the messenger he felt outright nervous. Plenty of thoughts flashed through his mind. Would he need to join King Charles after all? Had his cousin Henri been found? Or had King Louis decided that they should return and attend one his infamously boring hunting parties?

The messenger bowed deeply and greeted him with all the decorum that would have been appropriate in a royal palace, but seemed slightly out of place here in the more informal atmosphere of Montrésor. Pierre gave him sign that he saw no need to continue the litany of courteous greetings and endless enumeration of his titles.

"You may hand me his message now," said Pierre, interrupting the ceremonious greeting.

The royal messenger looked slightly offended, after all, he was here in lieu of His most catholic Majesty Louis XIII, by the Grace of God, King of France.

Stiffly he handed a document to Pierre, who opened it slowly. Certainly he didn't want to show any undue haste or apprehension although he was burning with curiosity – even slight trepidation – to learn the reason for the presence of a royal messenger.

Quickly he scanned the letter and a weight lifted from his shoulders, the stilted formal document containing nothing but a summons disguised as a polite invitation for himself and his party to join the King, who had decided to visit his brother, known simply as 'Monsieur'.

'Monsieur' was the nickname of Gaston, Duke of Orléans, who was residing in royal splendour in the nearby castle of Blois. Of course everybody knew that he had been exiled there by his brother, as generally Monsieur was known as the 'rebellious' brother – didn't every family have a black sheep?

"Please inform His Majesty that I'll accept his invitation with the greatest pleasure!"

Pierre rang the bell and the butler appeared immediately – his habit of eavesdropping was becoming somewhat annoying.

"Please lead the royal messenger downstairs to the kitchen and make sure he's looked after properly," Pierre ordered, and the messenger had no option but to go through the appropriate protocol for his leave, managing to convey only the slightest hint of disapproval and discontent at this sudden dismissal.

But the messenger's disappointment vanished as soon as he arrived in the servants' quarters. Down here in the comfortable kitchen he was treated with all the awe and respect due to a royal messenger. While the cook and the butler heaped delicacy after delicacy on his plate of delicate Chinese porcelain and served the best of wines the adoring glances of the kitchen maids were like balm for his wounded ego. These people at least knew how to pay respect to an important person.

Upstairs, a very content Armand grabbed the royal invitation and read through it. "I'm glad you put this inflated windbag back into his royal boots."

He whistled as he read the letter. "This looks like a state visit in disguise. It must have been ages since the King set foot in Blois! I guess you know that the King hates his brother, especially as his stupid mother always preferred Gaston, who doesn't stutter. I wonder though, why Cardinal Richelieu has arranged this strange reconciliation; if you ask me, there can never exist any true peace between the brothers, especially ever since King Louis miraculously managed to sire a son. My father told me that the Duke of Orléans was foaming with rage when he received the news – he had been so sure of becoming the next King of France."

Pierre waited until dinner before he dropped the news about the invitation. As expected, the ladies were enchanted – what a great opportunity to wear the new gowns that they had recently acquired in Paris!

"If the Queen is attending as well, there will be a grand ball, I can wear my new silver silk gown!" Marie exclaimed excitedly.

"You'll look stunning, I'm sure about that, and there'll be an endless queue of young and handsome gentlemen asking for my permission to dance with you. But I'll behave like a true dragon, *nobody* but the King will be allowed to dance with you!" Céline answered, with a small wink towards Charles.

Marie didn't seem to be particularly impressed. "Nobody would ever risk mistaking you for a dragon – you look more like my sister and I recommend that Charles should better keep an eye on *you!*"

As the invitation had been sent not only in the name of the King and his brother, but explicitly mentioned the Queen as well, there could be no doubt that not only a ball but also a series of other exciting festivities would be waiting for them. Marie's eyes were shining with delight; she could already see herself dressed in her new splendid gown of purest shimmering Chinese silk, dancing through the night with Pierre under the light of hundreds of candles.

Time flew by and only a fortnight later a small cavalcade of coaches, musketeers and horsemen left from Montrésor in the direction of the royal castle of Blois. As Blois was located only some forty miles north of Montrésor they anticipated a quick and agreeable journey, although they'd need to cross the Loire river. The sun was shining generously when they left the courtyard, the roads were dry and the horses would be able to stride freely. Only a few clouds had gathered in the sky; quite harmless, Pierre concluded.

Yet they discovered that many people were following the summons of the King. Several coaches with impressive coats of arms painted on their doors were already waiting on the banks of the Loire for a lone and frail ferry to make the crossing. Thus the friends were forced to rein in their horses and stop right here, mentally prepared to wait patiently until it was their turn to be ferried over to the northern shores of the Loire.

Meanwhile the sun was roasting them on their horses, and turning the inside of the coaches into a furnace although all blinds and doors had been opened. The ladies sat outside in the shade, nobody could stand the heat. Armand was at the end of his tether and he cursed wildly, ready to run his rapier through the ferryman as soon he realized that the coach of a local squire who had arrived much later was to be given priority.

But Charles intervened on time. A subtle hint to the ferryman that not only a Duke, indeed a Marquis, was being kept waiting, but also that a member of one of France's greatest families was becoming extremely upset to the point of taking action – accompanied with two extra gold coins – did the trick and the irate owners of the other coaches found themselves suddenly watching Pierre and his party boarding the ferry.

But their ordeal was not yet over: the only decent road leading towards Blois turned out to be completely clogged with horsemen and coaches arriving from all corners of France. The King had sent an invitation to all his nobles and whoever had been able to respond seemed to have chosen to join them right now on the road to Blois. Charles was cursing as they tried not to breathe in the clouds of dust that were raised by the hordes of people, horses and coaches heading at a snail's pace towards the chateau. He was mostly concerned about Céline, but she only laughed and told him not to behave like a mother hen.

Noon had long passed but still they kept creeping forward at the slowest pace imaginable. Pierre looked nervously to the sky as the harmless white fluffy clouds started gathering, and far too quickly transformed themselves into threatening monsters of menacing grey.The hot summer air felt ever more heavy and humid than before. Damp shirts were sticking to the suffering horsemen's chests and sweat was trickling down their necks and cheeks. As if their ordeal was not enough, a swarm of bloodsucking horseflies had discovered the horses and riders – a welcome and exciting gourmet addition to their usual diet of cow and peasant blood!

It almost came as a relief when the first crashing bolt of lightning appeared in the leaden sky. Accompanied by the frightening noise of thunder close by, the heavens opened and torrents of rain poured down on the hapless voyagers, drenching the horsemen and slowing even more the progress of the coaches.

"I did expect fireworks and trumpets, but not of this magnitude," Armand commented sarcastically, trying to empty a pool of rainwater from his hat. "I guess I'm supposed to be thankful and greatly impressed."

"It is generally known that the French like overdoing things when it comes to matters of pomp, especially their kings," Charles jested, while trying to fasten his coat – had his damned coat shrunk in the rain!?

The relief they felt when the imposing outline of Blois came into sight was beyond description – dry shelter and the lovely vision of clean clothes and comfortable rooms appeared in their minds. But as if the forces of nature had decided to mock them, the fierce thunderstorm died down as quickly as it had appeared, the clouds parted and the rain stopped as abruptly as it had started.

Still continuing their journey at the sluggish pace dictated by the numerous coaches on the now slippery and muddy road, they finally approached Blois and entered the courtyard. Right in front of them a magnificent building appeared, like a castle from a fairy tale, basking in the golden light of the late afternoon sun.

Blois chateau was an imposing yet strangely puzzling sight, as it looked as if a playful giant had taken a fancy to gluing three different castles together – different in style, size and even in the colour of stone that had been used for their construction. Three imposing wings constructed by different owners over the centuries had been grouped around a central courtyard dominated by its famous spiral staircase – some boasted that the great Michelangelo himself had designed it, and it was so large that a horse could walk up it. The latest addition to the castle had been constructed only very recently, as scaffolding could still be seen erected at the new wing.

"It should have been finished several years ago," explained Armand in a low voice, the wet feathers of his hat drooping pitifully from the rain as they entered the courtyard.

"So why did Monsieur stop the construction works?" asked Marie, as she studied curiously the imposing façade.

"Richelieu hates the Duke of Orléans but he kept supplying him with money as long as he was considered heir to the throne. But the minute the Dauphin was born three years ago, Richelieu stopped the payments and the Duke has been searching frantically for fresh money ever since."

"Will the Cardinal join the festivities?" asked Céline. "I'd love to see him after having heard so much about him. I must confess, I'm as curious as a cat."

"I imagine so," answered Armand, then carefully looking around him as not to be overheard, he whispered, "If the King has decided to come to Blois, I would bet a fortune that the Cardinal must be the true initiator. Apparently Richelieu feels that it is about time to show Monsieur some royal presence and splendour, there's too much rumour around that Monsieur is accepting money and gold from the Spaniards. Anybody else but the King's brother would already have been sent to the executioner for treason."

Owing to the high rank of the Marquis de Beauvoir the majordomo greeted them personally – he wouldn't have wasted his precious time on a mere count or baron – and led them to the rooms that had been reserved for Pierre and his entourage.

Luckily their rooms were not located in the attics – those rooms were kept at the disposal of visitors of lesser rank. The building was agreeably cool inside yet

Pierre was happy when he was finally alone with Jean and could tear off his clothes that were clogged with dust and drenched from rain and sweat.

Jean fetched fresh water and Pierre sighed with delight when his valet had washed him and laid out clean clothes.

"I'm becoming spoilt – and I'm loving it!" Pierre remarked happily as he slipped into his fresh clothes. "When I lived in the monastery school, I owned two robes. One for the week, one for Sunday, there could be no thought of changing the robe during the week – I remember one day there was thunderstorm and I was so wet that I left a puddle of water wherever I went."

Jean grinned and continued to carefully stow the big piles of clothes into the oaken chests – he had brought several chests as he was aware that this invitation to a 'hunting party' was to be regarded in all respects as an appearance at court, and Jean wanted his master to look his best. Proudly he looked at Pierre. There could be no doubt, it would be difficult to find a more handsome man at court – although Armand would have protested wildly at this statement, as he viewed himself as the most handsome man on the planet.

The hopes of the ladies were fulfilled. Soon it was ascertained that a series of balls, picnics and all kind of festivities was waiting for them. It was generally known that King Louis hated all kinds of official events – the Cardinal therefore must have had excellent arguments to hand to convince him to leave Paris and make an official visit to the brother he loathed.

The festivities started that evening and blaring trumpets heralded the ceremonial entrance of the King and the Queen of France into the vast hall where dinner would be served later. Their Majesties were greeted by a smiling host, regally dressed in silk and velvet, decorated from head to toe with shimmering jewels. Gaston bowed low and kissed his brother and sovereign reverently before greeting the Queen of France, his sister-in-law. Not even the most critical observer could detect the smallest hint of the hostility that must have been stirring in the minds of the royal family; brought up within the rules of strict protocol, they played their parts to perfection. Gaston had made sure that the decorations of the impressive hall were not only fit for a king, but their splendour could have satisfied an emperor. With satisfaction he noted that his brother stuttered more than usual, probably upset by such a public show of extravagance.

I should be the true king; Louis has got the pettiness and the soul of a grocer, thought Gaston, full of contempt.

Some weeks before, Gaston, Prince of France, Duke of Orléans, had been paralysed with shock when he had received out of the blue a letter from the Prime Minister, Cardinal de Richelieu, announcing the impending favour of a visit by his royal brother.

163

In a first bout of bad temper he had cursed the loathed Cardinal in all the words and languages that came to mind, of which Gaston had quite a repertoire at his disposal. It helped that he could still remember some hefty and very vulgar Italian curses from his mother, Maria de Medici, who had acquired the annoying habit of quarrelling noisily with his father about almost anything, from his detached attitude to the catholic religion to his affairs with an endless row of mistresses.

The Duke's first instinct had been to pretend to be ill, but he knew the Cardinal well enough – Richelieu couldn't be fooled easily. Through his extensive network of spies and agents Richelieu would probably know more about the Duke's health than Gaston himself ever would. *Somehow this poisonous toad must have found out that I have just pocketed a large amount of gold from the Spanish king*, Gaston thought, boiling with anger.

Monsieur, the Duke of Orléans, needed this money desperately to pay off some of his most pressing debts and to finish the new wing that he had added to Blois. He was less concerned about his creditors – who would dare to pursue the brother of the King of France? – but he felt extremely passionate about his own addition to Blois, a design so elegant and beautiful that all of Europe talked about him and – if rumours were correct – some of his peers had even started copying him.

But a royal visit would ruin him! Immediately Gaston had rung for his majordomo who was thrilled to enumerate the bare necessities for such a visit: the majordomo reckoned that several hundred pigs, about a hundred oxen, thousands of chickens, several peacocks, swans, at least a hundred lambs would need to be bought and slaughtered. Barrels of fish would need to be brought in from seaside – a pity that it was far too hot to think about oysters! Then there would be thousands of loaves of the finest bread and hundreds of cakes to be baked. Thousands of jars of ale together with hundreds of casks of the best wine had to be considered.

There could be no royal visit without fireworks, only the best quality from China would do. As the king loved hunting, huge numbers of live deer would have to be bought to make sure that the woods were well stocked and the king would find enough easy targets for his rifle – which would have the advantage that the kill would help to feed the guests and add venison to the menu. The majordomo reckoned that there would be hundreds of noble guests to be housed, more than a thousand if their servants were counted as well.

Close to joyful delirium the majordomo had breathed deeply and continued: skilled musicians must be hired, a poem had to be written to glorify his Majesty and – of course – a piece of music had to be composed for this special occasion. Regrettably it would be too late to have a new painting commissioned to glorify the stay of King and the Queen of France in Blois.

The duke had asked in a weak voice if the majordomo could give him an idea of the budget and his worst nightmares came true when the majordomo – after long deliberation – had mentioned an amount that seemed just about adequate.

Beaming with delight, the majordomo congratulated the Duke of Orléans. "Isn't it wonderful that Blois is back in royal favour after the king has been absent for so many years?"

The Duke had only closed his eyes in pain: his brother's visit would not only cost him all the gold that the Spanish had paid to organize a revolt with the help of Cinq Mars against this very brother – depending on the time the king would stay for – it might leave him even poorer than before. This devious Cardinal had found the most elegant way in the world first to paralyse and then to ruin him: the royal favour of a prolonged stay!

The majordomo saw himself dismissed and as soon as the door had closed Monsieur had slumped into his chair, lost in deep thought. The meeting with his majordomo had taken place in the panelled cabinet room that had been one his mother's favourite rooms when she had lived in this chateau. Only she and Gaston knew behind which panels, carved adornments and pillars a secret cupboard was concealed, where the indispensable tools of power were stored: poison and coins of gold, Spanish gold in this case.

Suddenly an idea flashed through his mind – bold and daring, seductive – but why not? History hadn't been shaped by the fearful, Gaston thought, his mood wonderfully restored. Maybe this visit after all was a sign that his destiny was set to change.

Not the slightest hint of these reflections could be seen in the face of Monsieur as he respectfully greeted his royal brother. Gaston de France had been widowed young, but his second marriage to a princess of a neighbouring country, a country regrettably judged hostile and thus undesirable for a prince of royal blood, had never been endorsed by the King.

To Monsieur's greatest aggravation his brother – under the influence of Richelieu of course – had even forced him to annul the marriage. Thus his new wife had been banished from court and there would be no official hostess tonight, unless his young daughter from his first marriage would be regarded as such. The story of Monsieur's failed marriage provided a never-ending source of delicious gossip as the Duke in truth had never relented, but defying the royal ban, he continued to meet his banished wife and still considered himself married.

The Duke of Orléans was not only all charm as a host; once he had swallowed the bitter pill he had vowed that he'd show the world how a *true king* would receive guests, and consequently the chateau of Blois had been dressed in regal splendour. The already impressive reception hall had been decorated in a luxury and refinement never seen before – even in decadent Paris. As the King was known to be thrifty to the point of being stingy, this display of luxurious extravagance made a remarkable change from the usual invitations to attend the intimate hunting parties of Versailles – gatherings where women were not tolerated and which usually ended in an orgy of heavy drinking.

Tonight gold and silver plates and centrepieces decorating the huge tables at Blois could have served as a king's ransom. Queen Maria de Medici – Monsieur's mother and former inhabitant of Blois – had amassed a gigantic treasure trove. The small detail that most of it had been stolen from her husband and should now rightfully belong to King Louis didn't seem to perturb her, nor did it cause Gaston any sleepless nights.

Stunned by such extravagance, Marie and Céline looked at dinner tables that were almost breaking under the weight of gold, silver and the finest porcelain imported from the Chinese Empire. There were crystal sculptures as well as sculptures carved from jade and onyx, engraved ostrich eggs which shimmered like porcelain, and delicate Murano glassware from Venice gleamed in the light of a thousand candles.

But most stunning was the display of food – mounds of it had been skilfully arranged on the tables. Pastries and stuffed animals had been covered with layers of gold, stuffed birds and peacocks were decorated with their colourful feathers. An extensive variety of food was presented tonight in the most wonderful and artistic ways that could be imagined, and to crown this display of wealth, a fountain of wine gurgled from golden cornucopias.

Céline tried to digest all of these impressions. Like a curious bird, her head moved from left to right, eager to absorb every tiny detail. The mellow light of the candles made the guests' jewellery, tiaras and medals shine and glitter in all colours of the rainbow, like small fireworks of sparkling colours.

"This is so beautiful, it's like a fairy tale," Marie whispered to Céline while they were waiting for the ceremony to start.

"It is," agreed Armand. "I only wonder who paid for this?" he added in a low tone.

The sight and smell of the food was almost unbearable, they felt so hungry! The journey from Montrésor had taken much longer than anticipated and they had found no time or opportunity to have a decent meal since they had set off in the early morning. But there could be no question of touching any of those delicacies displayed seductively directly under their noses until the King officially opened the banquet.

"If I have to wait much more time without eating, I'm going to faint. I'm so hungry that I could turn into a cannibal," Marie whispered to Céline.

"Find me a juicy morsel then, I'll join you!" Céline added drily. Looking critically at the people around her she added, "But most of the people around us don't really look very appetizing, I'm afraid."

Marie looked around her and could only agree. Even under the forgiving light of the candles the thick layers of chalky make-up could not hide the withering beauty of most of the ladies around them.

"It seems that we're the only juicy ones close by," stated Marie.

"The advantage is that you'll be able to pick and choose your dancing partners later today," replied Céline, a remark that had the effect of cheering Marie considerably.

Sitting among hundreds of nobles, swallowing hard and trying to ignore the alluring smell of the food, they had to endure the welcome speech and endless praise for the King and the Queen presented by Monsieur, a eulogy as long as it was hypocritical, to be followed by a poem recited by Monsieur's daughter from his first marriage, fittingly called 'Mademoiselle'.

The pretty princess was approaching the age where marriage could be seriously contemplated and was generally considered the best match on the market. Not only of royal blood, she was blessed on her mother's side with a fortune, and thus the richest heiress on the market. Her gown was studded with pearls and diamonds, matched by expensive jewellery dripping from her ears and neck. Mademoiselle's poem was recited in a loud and well-schooled voice and compared King Louis to a handsome and fearless God from the Greek myths. Despite being so hungry, Marie had to suppress the urgent need to laugh out loud – comparing this ageing and overweight King, with his sagging features, to a Greek god seemed simply preposterous!

Cardinal Richelieu sat close to the King dressed as usual in his scarlet cassock. His heavy golden cross dangled from a neck that seemed far too frail to carry such a weight. Richelieu listened attentively to the poem while he sat motionless, only his ring of office seeming to have acquired a life of its own, glowing and blinking dangerously in the candlelight.

Finally, when Céline was close to despair, the King graciously accepted the first dish tasted ceremoniously by Monsieur himself – this was the sign that dinner was officially begun. Like a pack of hungry wolves the crème de la crème of the French aristocracy attacked the food, tearing off bones and festive decorations, greedy teeth sinking into pastries and meat, poultry and fish.

167

Full of joyful anticipation Céline bit into a piece of swan – wasn't this bird considered so rare and precious that in England all swans were considered the sole property of the King of England? But what a disappointment, she nearly spat out the food! The meat was tough, it had a strange, rancid taste that was only partially disguised by the liberal use of spices. Céline tasted several pieces of venison, but once more, the meat was cold and tough, exotic spices fighting against unsavoury notes of meat that had spoiled in the intense summer heat.

Pierre and Armand knew the pitfalls of official banquets and had picked those dishes that were less likely to have been created by the chef in an attempt to enhance his master's importance by using the most expensive and exotic meats and ingredients. Laughing at Céline's disgusted face, Charles gave an order to the servants to put some freshwater fish and roasted piglet on her plate, which she thankfully accepted. After the first bite she closed her eyes with delight: *Finally something edible – heaven*!

As soon as the ladies had discovered that the chef patissier was an unrivalled master of his profession and the cakes and pastries not only decorative works of art but delicacies loaded with honey, nuts and all kinds of delicious fillings, the dinner was declared a success and everybody felt ready to face the dances.

The dinner was concluded and Monsieur invited the King and Queen to open the ball. As was customary, a minuet followed, a dance held in high regard as it was judged to be the epitome of courtly sophistication. Marie was suitably impressed by the stylish perfection of the dance but secretly she preferred the joyful dance tunes played at the royal court in England.

Soon the ball was in full swing and Marie cherished every single minute she spent on the dance floor. She noted with delight that an impressive queue of elegant men had formed to request the honour of a dance with her from Céline, who was acting as her chaperone – and the fact that Pierre didn't appreciate her undeniable success, as shown by his stormy expression, made it even better!

"You're a total idiot when it comes to women," hissed Armand, when he noticed that his friend was grumpily watching Marie dancing.

"And you're a master of this game, I presume," retorted Pierre.

"I am, indeed!" answered Armand smugly. "First rule, make her jealous. See the pretty girl sitting there next to that fat old dragon? Ask her for a dance and you'll see that Marie suddenly has more time for you, don't be an idiot and stand here suffering!"

Reluctantly Pierre accepted the superior wisdom of his friend and approached the dragon. Courteously he requested the favour of a dance with the pretty girl – a wish that was granted instantly. The old dragon might be short-sighted but she knew when a good catch was near!

"But mother, you promised the dance already to somebody else!" the girl tried to object, but the old dragon put on a determined smile and sighed.

"These young girls are all the same, they mix everything up! Go and dance with Monsieur le Marquis, my dear, don't worry! Rely on maman, she always knows best."

The girl looked doubtful but soon her reserve melted under Pierre's charm and Marie suddenly discovered a smiling and joking Pierre having a great time with his young and pretty dance partner. Delightedly, Armand saw Marie's murderous glance and grinned – the old tricks always worked best!

After midnight the festivities were to continue outside. The elegant guests walked through galleries lit by liveried footmen holding torches. Built by the King's father, these galleries led from the castle to the famous garden plateau, adjacent to the older wings. Here in the gardens a massive firework display had been planned to conclude the ball as testimony to the glory of the monarchy.

Accompanied by triumphant music, the blazing initials of the King and the Queen were outlined in fireworks and a gasp of surprise went through the crowd as miraculously the lilies of France appeared in the sky. His Majesty was visibly pleased, and in rare harmony the royal brothers returned to the chateau.

The night was balmy and the air caressed Marie's skin like velvet. The friends had cherished every single minute they spent under the star-studded sky in the gardens watching the fireworks and almost regretted it when the last lights in the sky had vanished and the party returned to the ballroom. But the ball continued – and would last until the early hours of the morning. Worn out, but content, they dropped into their beds – banquet and ball had been worthy of a king, there could be no doubt.

Two days later a grand hunt, the official highlight of Monsieur's festivities, was scheduled in order to entertain the King and Monsieur's noble guests. It was late summer and some muttered that it was still far too hot for a successful hunting party, but as the King loved to hunt, hunting it had to be!

All the men were expected to take part unless they had a credible excuse. In the early morning the pastures were still glistening with fresh morning dew when a formidable pack of horsemen started to gather outside the castle. The noise was deafening. Countless dogs were barking hysterically with excitement, horses were pounding impatiently with their hooves while the gathering gentlemen were jesting, shouting loudly to welcome newcomers or trying to calm down their nervous horses.

Then – luckily before horses and dogs became uncontrollable – the King arrived. He was accompanied by his brother and the Marquis de Cinq Mars, his true favourite. The King was riding a priceless thoroughbred and, surrounded by his own pack of dogs, he greeted his noblemen jovially before he took the lead.

Now the hunt could start.

Usually Pierre loved a good hunt. The atmosphere of suspense, the sheer physical pleasure of riding a good horse, the companionship – all of this was certainly as important as the fact that he had become a master of the musket and the bow and could easily outdo most of his companions. Only Armand and Charles still managed from time to time to beat him.

But Pierre had come to despise royal hunting parties. Several times he had experienced the disputable pleasure of participating in such events in England, and then later in France, and he had come to hate the intrinsic choreography and protocol that formed the essence of a royal hunt. Every participant had to pretend to give his best and theoretically the king would be treated as an equal among hunting companions. Pierre was amazed that the king seemed to swallow this bait and even seemed convinced of the superior quality of his hunting and riding skills.

In truth, of course, King Louis always had to get the easiest, biggest and best kill. This meant that hunting with the King was extremely nerve wracking as Pierre had to watch out not only for the game, but keep an eye on the King's progress and his intentions, making sure on the other hand that he'd beat the rest of his noble companions turned competitors in this sport. Competition was tough and there was no expectation of fair play between gentlemen; the King's favour was the highest prize and gaining his attention and winning his approval during a hunt was paramount.

The King had surprised his nobles, proposing that only bows and arrows should be used, as the hunt was to be organized in honour of his royal ancestors. Modern weapons such as muskets would be banned. Some secretly cursed the King – who hunted nowadays with bows – how medieval!

But the younger circle of his intimate courtiers had immediately applauded the creative spirit of their King; enthusiastically they voiced their opinion that using such ancient equipment would be a unique challenge and make the hunt so much more exciting. The King was genuinely pleased that his idea had been so well received, and only Richelieu had needed to suppress his sardonic smile.

Pierre was supposed to stay close to the King due to his high rank. This meant making sure that he kept track at all times of the King and the core of the pack that was riding fast through the dense forest. Armand would be riding behind, out of the limelight, as he was only a younger son of a Marquis.

170

The hunt was in full swing and although everyone knew that the never ending supply of fresh game had been arranged by a well-oiled machinery of beaters hidden in the forest, soon the hunting fever took over and everybody tried to surpass his neighbour. Pierre excelled in the use of his bow and the King applauded several times when Pierre had managed to hit his target.

I have to slow down, Pierre thought. *If I'm not careful I'll surpass the King and he'll never forgive me!* Then he grinned and suppressed a shudder. *Or worse, I might become his new favourite.*

All of a sudden Pierre caught a glimpse of the fleeting shadow of a stag or hind and forgetting his best intentions and all caution he stormed forward, his bow and arrow raised and aimed, ready to deliver the deadly blow. Only when Pierre had almost released his arrow did he guiltily remember that the King might be targeting the same prey. Quickly he turned back as he reckoned that the King must still be riding close to him, on his left side if he remembered correctly. He didn't dare loose his arrow if the King had spotted the hind as well.

As Pierre turned his head backwards he suddenly noticed a flash of light, like the reflection of sunlight on metal. But this reflection came from the undergrowth, where there should be none. Without hesitation, driven by instinct rather than deliberation, Pierre aimed his bow in the direction of the flash of light, and without giving it a further thought he instantly released his arrow. As Pierre's arrow was launched towards its hidden target, a split second later – almost simultaneously – a deadly arrow originating from a hidden crossbow zoomed out of the undergrowth. But Pierre's arrow must have hit its target a split second earlier and deflected the insidious arrow from the crossbow.

King Louis was unscathed, and the crossbow touched the left rear leg of Pierre's horse instead, and landed right in front of the King's horse. While Pierre's horse reared with pain, catching Pierre unawares, a cry emanated from the undergrowth. Pierre's arrow must have found and hit its target.

It took everybody several seconds to understand what had happened but as soon as it dawned on the participants that an ambush on the King had just failed under their very eyes, chaos broke out. Orders were bellowed and the shocked and frightened noblemen, including the Duke of Orléans and Cinq Mars, quickly formed a defensive ring around their king, shielding Louis with their bodies.

Pierre saw none of this as his rearing horse had catapulted him right into a clearing where he landed, flat on his face, and lay there with sprawled limbs, like a shattered doll. Armand reached his friend first. Shaking Pierre and crying his name in despair, he tried to bring him round – but to no avail.

A trail had been laid – not for the first time. Huge, mouth-watering breadcrumbs gave off an enticing smell of freshly baked, delicious food. *Come and savour me!* was the beguiling message, strong and irresistible.

Carefully, he picked up the scent of the bread but simultaneously he registered a confusing diversity of smells that floated in the room: dust, vellum, soap, the faint but dangerous scent of a cat, the obtrusive smell of lady's perfume (almost covering the fresh scent of the young lady), milk – and despair. He took in the scents again, inhaling deeply – yes, there it was: he could clearly detect the smell of despair in the air, but this wouldn't stop him, the smell of the fresh bread was simply too alluring. He sniffed again and came to the conclusion that the terrifying scent of the cat was too old and too stale as to pose any immediate danger… As for the strong scent of the girl in the room, he had grown used to it. Still looking around nervously, the little mouse left its hiding place.

Julia watched the mouse tripping out of its hole and she had to smile. "Here you are again, my friend!" She spoke softly. It felt so good to greet a friend and finally to be able to speak with someone.

"Today I prepared some extra big, fresh crumbs for you, but there will be no cheese on the menu," she added guiltily. "I was so hungry, I ate it all myself!"

The mouse didn't seem to mind. It had taken the first crumb in its paws, and sitting on its rear – tail carefully curled – it started to nibble at the delicious treat. The rays of the sun were streaming into the room and made the mouse's ears glow dark pink while the dust in the air sparkled like tiny stars around it. Having finished its meal of breadcrumbs the mouse detected the saucer of milk that Julia had placed close to her and after a short moment of hesitation scurried towards it. It lapped at the delicious liquid with its pink tongue while its beady eyes kept surveying its environment attentively, ready to bolt back to safety at any second.

Julia wanted to caress the mouse but didn't dare move; it had taken her weeks of patience to make the mouse come out of its hole and accept her presence. These moments had become precious to her – surely she didn't want to spoil the only company and entertainment she could enjoy. Julia's thoughts trailed back to her journey to Venice – so different from what she had anticipated…

On their way back from London they had crossed the Channel and then travelled overland through France. Their party had reached a secluded village near Avignon where her mother had unexpectedly fallen ill. Mysteriously she had perished under the eyes of her helpless and terrified daughter in a matter of only a few days.

Julia had been in shock – even now she still sometimes dreamt that her mother would walk into her room at any moment, that her death must have been just a bad dream, a nightmare – not reality.

Wrapped up in her bereavement, Julia had noticed all the same with some consternation that her father's eyes had remained suspiciously dry. Her mother had been hastily buried in a small provincial monastery in France, and it had taken Julia's insistent pleas to make her father open his wallet and donate enough money to make the monks read regular masses for her mother's eternal soul – to make sure that her beloved mother would be rescued from purgatory.

Back in Venice her father had given an outward show of mourning as was to be expected from a leading member of the Venetian aristocracy but soon – far too soon – it had become obvious that a beautiful and much younger successor for her mother had already been in hiding until the period of mourning was over and she could take her place.

Julia also discovered that her father had speculated with the family money and she realized that by now he had lost most of his own fortune. Ships he had judged to be sure investments had been shipwrecked or fallen prey to the Ottoman pirates. Thus the considerable family fortune had dwindled to a miserable pittance and the only heritage that could restore the family's previous splendour could come from Julia's aunt. But apparently her aunt had no confidence in her father, and to her father's great surprise – and to Julia's – it was Julia who was named the sole heiress of her godmother's fortune in her will when her aunt was carried away by a bilious attack. In the weeks that followed, her father raged on and on about Julia's deceitful character, how she had deprived him – the loving and caring head of the family – of a heritage that by any just means should have fallen into his hands.

Finally he decided that the best way to keep Julia's money under his influence would be to marry Julia to one of his cronies, a marriage of convenience to a rich and influential member of the new Venetian aristocracy – how could it be otherwise – a man so rich himself that he would pay her father handsomely to arrange a marriage into the most exclusive circle of Venetian society.

The first meeting with her aspiring bridegroom would remain seared in her memory forever. Her father had arranged a lunch to take place in their beautiful palace – a palace located on the Canal Grande that had belonged to her family for generations, decorated in the sophisticated blend of Western and Oriental styles that had made Venice famous, and in the style her mother had preferred.

Venice was facing hard times – the continuous wars with the Turks, the plague and the opening of new trade routes to the Americas had depleted the treasury and decimated the population. Nobody had been spared, not even the old families who had governed Venice as their fief for hundreds of years. The old

173

aristocracy had been compelled to do the unthinkable and – for hard cash – reluctantly started to admit new members into their elitist club. The golden book of the city – closed for centuries – had suddenly been opened to new entries. A class of new nobles was being created.

And so her father had betrothed Julia – without asking her consent – to one of those newcomers, an elderly nouveau riche who would pay any price to marry into the highest circles of society, and Julia was one of the highest prices Venice could offer: young, beautiful, educated, rich and of the most noble blood in Venice. In Julia's ancestry the number of former princely doges of the city was legendary.

Julia's fiancé entered the room and she nearly fainted. Swarthy, running to fat, pockmarked and – as she quickly found out – uneducated, he was the very opposite to the picture of the young and dashing Frenchman who had been haunting her dreams since she had left London. Julia had been raised like the princess of a royal house and consequently she knew that romance would never play a part in her future marriage, but never ever could she have imagined being used by her father as mere merchandise, her only purpose to replenish his empty treasure chests and to be handed over to a man who would always remain a commoner behind the façade of his new noble title. Julia had thus done the unthinkable: alone with her father, she had told him flatly that she refused the proposed marriage of convenience. For the first time in her family's history, a girl had mustered enough courage to openly oppose the will of the head of the family – a scandal was created.

Shocked and not knowing how to react, her father had tried to argue with Julia; he had her close relatives try to influence her then asked her confessor to bring her back to her senses. When Julia refused to cede to the pressure, her father had reverted to the ultimate threat: he imprisoned Julia in a small room in the family palace, not allowed to see anybody, her meals cut down to water and the simplest of staples.

Her father – knowing that Julia had been a spoiled child – had been confident of breaking her will very quickly. But this happened several weeks ago and Julia still remained adamant: she would *not* consent to this marriage.

The thought of her father made her blood boil. "How I hate him," she hissed, and immediately the mouse darted back to the safety of its hole.

"Oh, stupid me, scaring the poor mouse," Julia chided herself, but then she realized that the mouse must have detected some other noise, as now she could clearly discern the steps of a heavy person approaching her room. She heard the noise of bolts being pulled back and the turning of a heavy key in the lock. A prison couldn't be any worse, she thought. But the visitor was not her father, whom she had started to loathe. Today he had sent her confessor instead.

174

The Father confessor entered the room, perspiring profusely and panting from the strenuous exercise of mounting the stairs. Her father had ordered Julia's confinement in a room close to the attic in the expectation that the summer heat would break her willpower. The confessor was ill at ease; although he had argued repeatedly that it was her filial duty to respect her father's orders, Julia had the slight suspicion that he did not entirely agree with her father's decisions.

"Please be seated, Reverend Father!" she greeted the clergyman respectfully, and thankfully he dropped into the only chair in the tiny room that looked solid enough to support him.

"Thank you, my daughter," he panted, pausing for a long time, as it seemed almost impossible for him to breathe in this stuffy room.

Finally he managed to talk but in a furtive way, making sure to avoid Julia's intense glance. "My Daughter, did you say your prayers and are you ready to show the respect that can be expected from an obedient child? "

Julia gritted her teeth but managed to answer placidly. "Yes, my Reverend Father, I did say my prayers but it seems that the Lord failed to enlighten me, I still do not agree to this marriage and I'm afraid I never shall!"

The confessor looked at her, startled. Apparently he had not expected such a clear answer. "You're truculent, my Daughter, whereas the bible commands daughters to be obedient to their fathers."

Julia could detect signs of a new strain in his face; apparently her confessor was ill at ease. Sweat started to form in little beads at his throbbing temples and she could see it running down his face. Not without effort, he continued the conversation. "Your father, who only has the best of intentions for your future, has asked me to deliver a message to you!"

Julia looked at him attentively, every fibre of her body expecting a new blow. "What did my father, who I imagine is still in the deepest bereavement over the sudden loss of my mother, instruct you, Reverend Father, to tell me?"

Julia had managed to keep her voice even but the priest's face twitched all the same. She had touched on a sensitive point, as all the tongues in Venice were wagging about the impending and all too hasty new marriage of Julia's father.

Her confessor preferred not to comment on Julia's remark, but casting his eyes upwards he said, "The holy Scripture says: 'Repent and therefore be converted'. If you do not repent, my daughter, you are committing a serious sin!"

"I cannot repent, dearest Reverend Father, as I have not committed any sin. I just don't want to marry a man whom I find disgusting! I have been studying the bible during the past months as you recommended me to do – but there is no

175

mention that it should be regarded as a sin to refuse marrying a man one hardly knows."

The confessor mopped his bald head. The discussion was not taking the right direction, for his taste. "My Daughter, your father has asked me to inform you that he'll lose patience soon – and I can only implore you to come to your senses!"

Julia looked at the priest with her big brown eyes and he quickly turned away to avoid this intense gaze. "What does my father propose?" Julia asked him in her soft voice.

The confessor cleared his throat before answering, not without difficulty, "Your father has decided that he will send you to a convent if you do not obey!"

Descending to hell must be like this: to be plunged into a black hole of despair. Tentacles of fear gripped him, choking him and holding him tightly – this was a living a nightmare, it couldn't be reality. Yet when Armand looked at his friend lying there, pale and paralysed, there was no doubt that this was indeed reality.

Pierre was dying before his very eyes and all these silly idiots around him were doing was rushing to be close to their King. There was keen competition to assure the king at the top of their voices of their ever-lasting loyalty and that every single noble of his kingdom was ready to die for him.

Armand looked down at the motionless Pierre, fighting hard to suppress his tears. Pierre's face was deadly pale, like a waxen death mask. Quickly Armand pressed his ear to Pierre's chest – his heart still seemed to be beating and he could detect the sound of breathing, although only very lightly. Terrified, Armand looked around him, hoping to find someone in this chaos who would come and help, but all the assembled nobles of the kingdom seemed to care about was crowding around their King. Nobody seemed to be bothered that the man who had probably saved their King was apparently expiring helplessly before them.

Suddenly a deep voice behind Armand said, "Let me assist you, I have some experience with hunting accidents!"

Armand looked up to identify the owner of the voice and realized that the master of the hounds had knelt down. With experienced hands and not really waiting for Armand's answer he had started to touch Pierre's body, with careful movements trying to find out if Pierre had broken any vital parts.

"I'm not a physician but there is hope. We must get him back to the chateau on a stretcher but avoid any jerky movements." He bellowed some orders and miraculously things started to happen.

All of a sudden the King seemed to have recovered from his shock and surprise. He turned his horse in Pierre's direction and like a colony of bees the rest of the hunters swarmed around their king towards the forlorn body lying in the clearing. Yet the King's arrival didn't make it any easier for the servants who had started to assemble a makeshift stretcher and now had to stop their actions as they were obliged to bow reverently to the King, who not only approached Pierre on his splendid horse but even paid him the most unusual respect by dismounting. Armand felt an urgent impulse to shout at the King to get out of the way but he restrained his emotions and managed to greet King Louis XIII as reverently as protocol prescribed.

177

The helpful servant who was looking after Pierre had quickly gone through the motions of court protocol, but once he had been performed the prescribed gestures, unperturbed he continued giving orders to his own men. The King doted on his dogs and the master of hounds had a unique position in the royal household. Now, under royal supervision, Pierre was prepared to be transported back to Blois.

In the meantime the King's musketeers had been searching the thicket and with much clamour dragged out a middle-aged man who was desperately clutching his crossbow. The man was dressed in the simple garb of a peasant, but a quick glance sufficed to make it apparent that it was too late to question him. The suspect was dying quickly under their hands as Pierre's arrow had inflicted a deadly wound. He was covered in thick, scarlet blood that glistened in the light, and yet more fresh blood kept gushing out of the wound.

Suspicious glances were being cast cautiously in the direction of the King's brother who – for once – had been idling at the back of the pack. But no fault could be found in Gaston Orléans' behaviour. Shock, awe, consternation, soon Monsieur was the loudest to lament about this most perfidious ambush imaginable and to demand that the men behind this ambush must at any cost be identified and punished in the most severe way imaginable.

As soon as Armand reached Blois he rushed into his room and changed his soiled clothes, and only minutes later he hastened back to Pierre's room. His heart was pounding with fear, never had he felt so terrified; Pierre's pale face kept haunting him – he was still in the grip of a terrible nightmare. But, to his total surprise, Armand was stopped at the entrance to Pierre's room. Two impressive helmeted guards equipped with halberds had been positioned at Pierre's door and it took Armand several minutes of excited and noisy arguing to gain entrance. He noticed with satisfaction that the soldiers bore the King's coat of arms – this was unusual, as it would have been the task of their host, the Duke of Orléans, to send his men for Pierre's protection. The King – or Richelieu – had clearly decided not to take any risks...

Finally the doors opened and Armand had to swallow hard. Pierre was lying on a huge bed under a golden canopy, laid out like a corpse. The curtains at the windows had been closed and the light of the candles and the smell of expensive incense created a strange atmosphere, as in a chapel – and as if prepared for a funeral. Two of the King's personal physicians were hovering over Pierre. Sure of their own importance, they were conversing solemnly in Latin, loftily ignoring all bystanders.

All of a sudden some commotion in the gallery leading to the room could be heard, along with cries and the clatter of heavy boots and finally the rattling of arms that were presented by the guards at the entrance. "Yield for His Eminence, the most noble Cardinal, Duke de Richelieu, Prime Minister of His Majesty, the King of France," a voice was echoing through the gallery.

A minute later Richelieu entered, accompanied by a swarm of his personal secretaries and servants.

"What diagnosis can you confirm, reverend magisters?" The Cardinal addressed the physicians curtly in Latin, cutting short their elaborate greetings.

For the first time ever, Armand was happy that he had learnt enough Latin in Reims to be able to follow a conversation.

The physicians bowed deeply and the eldest one started to answer. "Your Eminence, this is a very serious and complicated case but – I may say in view of our experience – not entirely without hope. We shall need considerable time and effort though, probably we shall have to bleed the patient first, and as a last resort we envisage trepanation, if he fails to wake up."

Richelieu sent a sceptical glance to his personal valet who stood close to the bed and who shook his head ever so slightly.

"I thank you, my honourable and esteemed masters of the art of medicine and science. I grant you leave now so as to report to His Majesty and his royal brother the condition of the patient and your diagnosis. In the meantime I shall look after the patient with the assistance of my staff."

This was clearly a dismissal, but as it was impossible to object to an order of having to report to the King, the two physicians withdrew in dignity but with a visible air of offence.

"Your Eminence dismissed them?" Armand couldn't help exclaiming.

Richelieu looked at Armand with a wry smile. "If your lordship wishes your friend to survive, it's probably the best solution. I have brought my valet, he worked as a physician during the years when he was still a soldier in the field and I must say he has probably saved my life already several times when the King's physicians had decided to bleed me to death – bleeding seems to be the only treatment they ever employ."

Armand was alarmed. It seemed very strange that the same man who had sent out an armada of soldiers and scoundrels to have Pierre removed from this earth and from his inheritance should suddenly become his saviour.

Saulus turning into Paulus. Being raised in a monastery school I should believe in miracles, but it's hard to believe in miracles when the Cardinal is involved.

179

And yet, he could see that Richelieu's valet was examining Pierre with experienced hands, taking care to keep him as undisturbed as possible under the circumstances.

"What's your conclusion then?" asked the Cardinal.

"Your Eminence, it's a concussion and hopefully he should wake up soon, but it's surely a miracle, not only is his skull without fracture, I can't detect a single limb that has been broken – there are only terrible bruises. How is this possible – I heard he fell head-first from his horse? In any case, he must not be bled, all he needs is a bit of peace and quiet now."

Armand sent a small prayer of gratitude for the Italian fencing master whom Charles had dragged along from Paris, who made them practise falling down and getting up from the most impossible of situations. The friends had been arguing with him to stop this kind of boring and tedious exercises but he had insisted, speaking coarsely in his hard Italian accent: "Either you learn 'ow to fall correctly and avoid accidents or – Signori - my mission is finished," and they had obliged – luckily.

*****

A flute was playing, he could hear it clearly enough. The tune seemed familiar, first playing softly, then it became louder, the rhythm increased its speed, urging him to get up and dance. But how could he dance? He felt so tired and his head was throbbing. With a deep moan Pierre opened his eyes.

"He moved, praise the Lord, look he's opened his eyes!" Marie was crying, tears of relief streaming down her face.

"Who had the idea of letting someone play the flute?"

"In all modesty, that was I," said Céline, "but there is no need to tell me that I'm a genius, I know it already!"

Jean quickly started helping Pierre to imbibe some of his secret draughts he had concocted in a rare collaboration with the Cardinal's valet. Shortly after having swallowed the liquid Pierre's eyelids drooped and he fell back into a deep slumber, but the terrible pallor of his skin had been replaced by a livelier tinge.

"He'll be much better soon," exclaimed the Cardinal's valet with a note of satisfaction in his voice. "He seems to be a tough customer."

"Yes, he looks like an asparagus – all slim and white – but he's quite tough," Armand added.

180

"Not all people can boast your flourishing looks," Céline added, with more than a hint of irony.

But irony was lost on Armand. "Yes, I'm quite satisfied with the way the Lord made me, I can't really complain."

Marie kicked him, forgetting for an instant that she was supposed to behave like a lady. "You're so terribly conceited, how can Pierre possibly bear to be with you?"

Armand just grinned and looked complacently at his reflection in the polished silver mirror that was hanging in the room. Today he had chosen a daring shade of purple for his waistcoat, with open sleeves showing his white silk shirt. A Flemish lace collar added a last note of perfection and the admiring glances of the ladies in the castle had confirmed that he had chosen well. His contented look went down to his high-heeled leather boots which had been polished to perfection by his valet, the latter bursting with pride as soon as he had noticed with satisfaction the envious glances of his colleagues.

Once woken up, Pierre's recovery made rapid progress, and soon most of his friends' energy was spent trying to keep him in his bed and make him get some sleep. A restless patient, Pierre insisted on standing up and moving, although once he had done so, he had to admit reluctantly that he was still feeling feeble and dizzy.

To Armand's great relief the King's physicians never showed up again, the reason being that the King and his court had abruptly decided to travel back to Paris. The notoriously fragile relationship between the King and his brother was damaged beyond repair by the attempted assassination. Only the Cardinal Richelieu seemed strangely content behind his usual mask of statesmanlike reserve – it was as if the result of the royal visit to Blois had somehow met his expectations exactly.

Back in Paris the King had held a private council. Seething with anger, he hotly demanded that the masterminds behind the attack should be found and punished. The Cardinal was only too happy to oblige – secretly he had already assembled sufficient proof that Cinq Mars was implicated in this conspiracy, together with the Spanish enemy. The fact that the Duke of Orléans had also played a hand in this dirty business would of course never be revealed to the public – the Duke was a Prince of France, and any indictment of high treason was therefore an extremely delicate matter, a state secret.

Consequently the King's favourite and only threat to the Cardinal, Cinq Mars, would have to serve as a pawn, especially as nobody seriously envisaged declaring war on the Spanish right now. No wonder the Cardinal was purring like a cat. Once again he had made the right moves in the game he liked best, the

181

game of power and intrigue. If Richelieu had been astonished, it was not about the attack as such – it was more about its boldness and the crudeness of the timing. Were the Spanish or the Duke of Orléans becoming desperate?

As an immediate consequence the furious King had ordered the eternal exile of the Duke of Orléans from court and – even better – Richelieu received carte blanche to prosecute the King's current favourite, Cinq Mars. The young, handsome Marquis de Cinq Mars was to become a simple anecdotal mention, an irrelevant footnote of history.

Such an elegant solution, pure genius. Nobody in France can present a serious challenge to me now. Maybe Mazarin, but he's clever enough to wait until the Lord calls me, thought Cardinal Richelieu.

*****

Tonight Pierre had taken his leave and gone to bed quite early. His first excursion on horseback had been much more of a strain than he would ever acknowledge openly to his friends. The bruises had started to heal but during the night Pierre would still wake up from time to time, trying to find a comfortable position for his aching limbs.

Around midnight it happened once again that Pierre's sleep was interrupted, but tonight his slumber was not to be disturbed by a sudden pain in his arm or back. It was a strange noise that must have woken him up.

First Pierre thought that the noise might have been part of a dream, but still drowsy and fighting against sleepiness, Pierre heard the ever so slight squeaking of the door hinges as the door of his room was pushed open, very slowly and cautiously, followed by the rustle of a garment and the light tapping of bare feet on the marble floor.

The curtains around his bed had been drawn shut as usual and Pierre lay in complete darkness – although he strained his eyes, not even a moving silhouette or a fleeting shadow could be seen through the narrow slits that had been left open. The blood was pulsing through his veins, and now Pierre lay wide awake, ready to parry the assault that he expected to come at any minute.

His hand moved underneath his pillow to the spot where he kept his dagger, but tonight his hand failed to touch the reassuring cool shaft – the dagger was gone. Cursing himself silently and trying to suppress a wave of panic Pierre suddenly remembered that he had worn the dagger that afternoon and when he had dropped into his bed, exhausted from their riding excursion, he had forgotten to put it back in place.

The sound of the approaching feet moved uncomfortably close, the attack must come at any moment now. Trapped like an animal, Pierre lay in his bed, tense as a coiled spring. Once again it seemed that fate had decided to challenge him…

*****

A full, silvery moon was shining through the leaded window panes and its pale rays caressed Armand who lay motionless in his bed. Armand, stark naked, as it was still warm at night, had been pleasantly sent to sleep after an amorous encounter with a charming lady – a married lady, but in urgent need of his special attention. The linen bed sheets were still in turmoil, a silent reminder of the battle they had witnessed.

The silver rays started to dance before his eyes. Armand reluctantly woke up, not at all amused to find his sleep interrupted. Still drowsy, he turned around and buried his face in the pillow, hoping to fall back into a deep and peaceful slumber. And yet this was not to be. He tossed and turned sleeplessly, the irksome rays of the full moon making sleep impossible.

Trying hard to go back to sleep Armand counted and recounted numerous sheep, but again this didn't seem to be helping at all. Although he felt worn out and dead tired he was unable to fall back into his slumber. Still tossing and turning in his bed, Armand tried to recall some pleasant memories, but whatever positive line of thought he started, his mind managed to play evil tricks on him. Relentlessly his imagination conjured up terrifying images that made his blood run cold .

Suddenly his concern centred on his friend. For sure, Pierre had miraculously survived the almost fatal fall from his horse – he was tough! But what could be done to bring him to safety? Would Pierre's enemies ever stop threatening and pursuing his friend? Vividly Armand suddenly remembered the numerous occasions when Pierre had escaped a fatal encounter only by a whisker. Armand's mind wandered further to Pierre's cousin, Henri, an unscrupulous killer on the run. It was known that Henri had vowed to destroy Pierre, so there could never be any peace for Pierre as long as Henri was still at large.

Cold sweat was now trickling down Armand's spine. Where might Henri be hiding right now? Maybe Henri had been the mastermind behind the attack on the King and… had the crossbow been meant in truth for Pierre?

A chilling idea flashed through his tortured mind: maybe Cardinal Richelieu had cunningly laid the trap and focused all attention on a potential assassination attempt directed at the King, whereas in reality it was Pierre who was the intended victim?

Armand's mind was racing now under the strain, he felt wide awake. An overwhelming sense of foreboding had overcome him, and he grew more and more convinced that Pierre was in immediate danger!

I must check if Pierre is all right! I simply can't lie here and wait until the next morning. Doing nothing and waiting for the morning to come will drive me crazy!

Pleased to have reached a conclusion he decided to take action. Armand jumped out of his bed and grabbed his nightshirt, swearing profusely as he got caught up in one of the sleeves and almost tore the fine linen to pieces in his haste.

His room was only sparsely lit by the moonlight that filtered through the window panes. In his haste Armand bumped his head against a bedstead and cursed like a trooper until he managed to light a candle and find his boots and his rapier. It was a strange feeling to dive into his boots without breeches and stockings but Armand couldn't risk losing any more time. By now he was convinced that every second counted!

Panting hard, Armand reached the antechamber of Pierre's bedroom. He tore the door open and rushed inside. All seemed quiet but suddenly a hand appeared out of the darkness, strong and firm as iron, and seized Armand. Armand had no time to cry out or draw his rapier, and before he could even think, the hand was followed by an iron fist and he fell to the floor unconscious.

*****

Pierre listened attentively, trying to concentrate all of his attention on the sound of the approaching feet – a sound dampened, made almost inaudible by the thick brocade bed curtains.

He sent a quick prayer to his patron saint and breathed deeply. Convincing himself that surprise was probably the best form of defence, he lunged towards the sound of his approaching night visitor, tearing the curtains of his bedstead wide open.

His surprise strategy turned out to be a complete success, and the attacker shrieked in surprise. As the unknown attacker stepped back, he failed to spot a low table that was in his way and fell head over heels right on the floor, but the fall was dampened by a soft bearskin that lay in front of the marble fireplace.

All of a sudden Pierre's skin turned to goose-bumps, but not from fear. The shrieking voice did not belong to a villain lusting for his blood; it had sounded uncomfortably familiar and, full of anguish, Pierre now rushed out of bed and bent down over the body that lay slumped on the bearskin.

184

"Marie, ah, mon Dieu, what are you doing here? Are you hurt, my darling, my love?"

When no answer was forthcoming, Pierre took her face gently in his hands, then his hands slid down and he tenderly embraced her slender body. He suddenly felt extremely shy and excited at the same time. Never before had he experienced such an intense feeling of desire. Marie's eyes were closed and her limp body felt wonderfully soft in his arms. Yet she seemed to be breathing normally and, yielding to temptation, Pierre kissed her passionately.

Suddenly Marie's arms closed around him and he found his kiss returned with the same passion.

"What are you doing here? You should be in your room!" he whispered hoarsely, smelling the flowery scent of Marie's perfume that he had come to know so well. She was dressed only in a thin nightgown, and holding her so tight in his arms and feeling her body almost made him lose his sanity.

"Do you want me to go back?" she teased him.

"No!" he exclaimed, adding sheepishly, "I mean yes, of course. Your parents or Céline will kill us when they find out what we're doing here... I guess they'll grant me the honour of torturing me before they kill me!" he added reflectively.

Marie didn't seem to take this reply very seriously as she snuggled even more comfortably into his arms.

"Pierre, I know of course, that it's against all rules and conventions, but I came because I love you!" she answered in her soft voice. "When I saw you being carried back, not knowing if you were dead or alive, I was nearly out of my mind and thought how can life be so cruel? Now that you've miraculously recovered, we both know that it's time to say good-bye far too soon – and we don't know if it's adieu or au-revoir."

She felt Pierre's grip suddenly became tense and knew that he wanted to protest, but she put her finger on his lips and continued. "Don't tell me any white lies, Armand told me the truth. To be honest, I *made* him tell me the truth. There is some secret vow that both of you made back in London, something linked to your heritage. You'll have to leave soon and there is practically no chance that you'll come back to Reims before next year."

Marie inhaled deeply, and deciding to take the plunge, she continued, "I therefore decided to come and spend this night with you. Married or not, I don't care. But I don't want to sit in Reims, being lonely and miserable and thinking every day that something dreadful might happen to you, without having this memory to help me through the next months and give me strength and comfort."

She paused a moment and added quietly, almost in a little girl's voice, "I mean, only if you want me, of course!"

Pierre was stunned. But a true gentleman had no choice, his code of conduct was clear – to save her honour, he could only react in one decent way. There could be *no* question of accepting Marie's invitation. He'd stand up now and very gently but firmly he would send Marie away. Anything else was impossible, unthinkable! If ever Marie's parents or Céline came to know about this night, she'd become an outcast! And all of this would be his fault, because he'd have given in to the sweet temptation of a moment and seduced an innocent virgin who had trusted him.

Taking a deep breath, he started to explain his decision, the only right and decent one, he was sure. "Marie, we must be responsible and sensible…" he started to say softly into her ear, but he was never meant to reach the end of his sentence. Marie turned her head and kissed him passionately, stifling his weak protest. Her pink tongue started tickling his mouth, sending shivers of excitement through his body, suffocating any attempt to deliver the elaborate and noble speech that he had prepared in his head.

The gentleman Pierre suddenly vanished and answering her kiss hungrily he carried Marie to his bed.

Paradise – so unlike its biblical description – must be like this: total bliss, a unison of bodies and spirits, as intense as Marie had never even dared to imagine. Of course she had noticed that Pierre was no longer the innocent young man that he was supposed to be, but she had harboured this suspicion for some time, and she didn't mourn the loss of the innocent boy. This night was simply perfect.

Pierre lay next to Marie, panting, feeling her lovely body so close. Still trying to figure out how he had merited this stroke of luck, he turned his head and could see Marie's slender silhouette in the silvery light of the moon filtering through the window panes. Her glossy dark hair was spread like a halo around her head on the pillows, the perfect crown for her perfect body.

Pierre stopped wondering and decided just to savour every second. Tenderly he took her hand and slowly kissed every single finger.

"I'll always remember this night", he whispered, more to himself than out loud. "Even if the day comes when I might have forgotten everything else."

"I'll take this as a compliment," Marie answered, and he could almost hear the smile in her voice. "But I will as well. Whatever happens in the future, I had my bridal night with the man I love – and it was perfect!"

She kissed Pierre once more but her kiss had the taste of a good-bye and she refused to be drawn back into his embrace.

"You must be tired now," she chided him gently. "I think making love three times might be a bit too much!" Gently she withdrew her hand and started to leave the bed.

"Why are you leaving, can't you stay the whole night?" Pierre was begging now, his eyes as soulful as a puppy's.

"I can't, and you know exactly why it's impossible!" Marie answered, in what she hoped was a stern voice.

Pierre sighed and gave in, but on the condition that Marie grant him a last long and passionate kiss.

What seemed like only a second later, Marie disappeared as silently as she had come – Pierre could only hear the soft tapping of her feet as she crossed the room, the squeaking of the door, its soft closing, and then the room lay in total silence. But the scent of Marie's perfume still lingered on his body and on the pillows, a subtle scent that held the promise and pleasures of summer, reassuring Pierre that all of this had not just been a wonderful dream.

Meanwhile Jean had been waiting for Marie in the antechamber, prepared to assist her with a dressing gown. She thanked him and gave him a conspiratorial smile.

Jean smiled back, allowing himself to comment, "I understand that my master is fully recovered?"

"He is, Jean, don't worry," Marie answered with a smile.

Jean walked to the door and was checking if the gallery was empty when he heard Marie gasp in surprise.

"Jean, is this Armand lying here?" she whispered. "Is he all right?"

"I sent him to sleep." Jean tried to keep his voice even as he continued, "He tried to save my master, but I guessed that Monsieur le Marquis would never have forgiven me or Monsieur Armand if he had succeeded with his intervention. I therefore saw no other option but to send him to sleep, but I'm afraid tomorrow morning Monsieur Armand might be very upset with me."

Marie had to giggle. "You definitely did the right thing!" She gave it a short thought and then added, full of mischief, "Why don't we drag him together back into his own bed? When he wakes up tomorrow morning, we'll all pretend that we haven't seen him – he must have had a bad dream!"

187

"A very realistic dream, he'll even feel the bump on his head," added Jean dryly but he didn't hesitate in following her suggestion. Thus the two conspirators started dragging Armand back into his bedroom.

"I never imagined he could be so heavy," Marie whispered, dabbing her forehead, as they finally managed to pull Armand back into his bed.

Armand only sighed and continued sleeping.

*****

The sound of angry voices floated up to his room – probably servants having a dispute underneath his window. Reluctantly Armand woke up. He must have had a terrible dream, memories of it were so intense that even his body was hurting.

Cautiously he opened his eyes, a decision Armand regretted immediately. The blinding sun pierced his eyeballs like a dagger and viciously stimulated the headache that had lain dormant yet malicious, not unlike a wild and dangerous animal that by all means must be kept in its cage.

He rang for his valet and minutes later he found himself listlessly sipping a bitter-tasting dubious liquid that his valet had served him. "A potion to ease my lord's headache, with the compliments of Monsieur Jean, the personal valet of the Marquis de Beauvoir."

Armand looked doubtfully at the thick liquid but as Jean's potions were legendary, he decided to give it a try. Yet it took a good hour until he felt ready to face the world, and even longer until he was dressed to his satisfaction and felt himself fit enough to visit Pierre in his room.

His best friend was still lying in his bed, radiating a carefree cheerfulness that Armand simply found disgusting, especially as he still felt miserable.

"You look decidedly happy and cheerful," Armand remarked sourly to his friend who was sipping a cup of chocolate with great delight.

"Why shouldn't I?" asked Pierre innocently. Not enough that he radiated happiness, he even had the impertinence to start whistling a merry tune!

"I had a terrible night," Armand replied, avoiding a straight answer, hoping to receive from his friend the sympathy that he thought he merited.

"Oh… I understand now. It's of course unfair of your best friend to feel happy if you, my friend, the noble Armand de Saint Paul, are feeling a bit indisposed. I do apologize!"

188

"No need to make fun of me! I had a truly terrible dream only because of you! I was convinced that you were in terrible danger and I dreamt that rushed to your room in order to save you!"

"That's very noble of you! I mean, obviously I didn't really need to be saved, but I do appreciate your good intentions and most noble spirit!"

Armand looked doubtfully at his friend. "You're not taking me for a ride here, are you?"

"I wouldn't dare! I would have done the same for you!" Pierre assured him. "But continue your story, please, you make me curious!"

Mollified by Pierre's insistence, Armand continued. "Well, then my dream suddenly stops. What I don't understand is why I woke up this morning with a headache, dressed in a nightgown although I went to bed naked, my boots on, but no breeches and why I have a huge lump on my head?"

Pierre looked at him. "Are you joking?"

He suddenly realized that Jean, who was standing hidden from Armand's view, was fighting an inner battle not to laugh, and a notion of the truth started to dawn upon him. Quickly he diverted his friend. "Don't worry, Armand, there is only one explanation. This is a clear case of somnambulism, I'm sure that Jean can give you one of his miraculous potions to avoid this ever happening again!"

Armand turned round with eager eyes towards Jean, who had suddenly noticed that a buckle on his shoe needed his urgent attendance.

"I've never heard about this somnam…whatever… I mean this strange illness, but if Jean could help, that would be great. I feel simply terrible!"

Jean didn't dare speak, but just managed a nod and left the room abruptly.

"Strange, how impolite he seems today," Armand commented, offended. "Pierre, you really must insist on more discipline with your servants, or you'll regret it. They really should look after you more diligently and treat you and your friends with the greatest of respect!"

Pierre was smiling at Armand with the beguiling smile that was so typical of him. "Believe me, Armand, Jean has already done far more for me than you could ever imagine!"

*****

As the days became shorter, time suddenly started to race by. They had left Blois about a month later than planned due to Pierre's hunting accident and long convalescence. The luxurious chateau had practically been at their sole disposal, their host never to be seen again after his royal brother had left Blois in a fit of rage which had caused Monsieur to disappear from view and keep a low profile until the storm passed. But rumour had it that Gaston d'Orléans was seeking consolation in the arms of his wife-in-waiting, defying once again the orders of his brother to stay away from this unsuitable princess.

Autumn had set in and back at Montrésor, urgent messages were already piling up for all of them. Marie's parents were anxiously asking – if not demanding – when she would come back to Reims as she had promised, Armand's father insisted on receiving more details about the perfidious attack on the King and, as if this hadn't been enough to remind the friends that the secluded and happy days of Montrésor were over, a day later the same pompous royal messenger who had delivered the invitation to Blois was knocking at their door once again.

The messenger produced an envelope containing a letter with the seal of His Majesty, the King of France, whilst taking care to display all the necessary pomp and ceremony. Armand rolled his eyes with exasperation but as Pierre gestured to him to keep his mouth shut, he swallowed his acerbic comments.

Curious, Pierre opened the letter and found an invitation, some might call it an urgent summons, to join His Majesty for an audience in the Louvre palace. Meeting the King in the Louvre and not in Versailles meant that a formal court audience had been planned. Knowing that he had no other option but to be delighted by the King's favour, Pierre accepted the invitation gracefully.

Their eventful summer at Montrésor was over; a new chapter in their lives was to begin.

Pierre was prey to a mix of conflicting emotions, both sad and exhilarated at the same time. He felt sad because this wonderful time he had spent with Marie and his friends had abruptly come to an end. At the same time – if he was honest – he felt relieved. Now that Marie and he had spent a night together, both of them desperately wanted more, but what had been a secret and wonderful adventure in Blois, something precious and unique, would turn into a scandal if it were ever repeated and detected here in the confines of Montrésor. Instinctively Pierre and Marie knew that they must avoid this at all cost, but the glances they exchanged were full of secret longing and knowledge.

Pierre came to the conclusion that he had no choice, he must either leave quickly or become insane. How painful to see Marie daily, smell the scent that had lingered on his body, look into her eyes, those luminous eyes that seemed to invite his soul to drown in them. Marie was so close, and yet never to be touched, and Pierre was close to despair.

Céline noticed that something had changed but she was convinced that Marie's and Pierre's change of mood was caused by their knowledge that separation was looming, and tactfully she refrained from any comment.

In his more upbeat moments Pierre's imagination took him already to southern Europe, eager to discover regions he had never seen before. What great adventures must be waiting for him out there! So be it... Even if every fibre of his body longed to be close to Marie, a part of him was looking forward to experiencing new adventures with Armand at his side. Pierre decided that it was useless to try to understand this paradox: maybe human nature was simply like this, always yearning for something different, always striving for new goals.

The sky itself seemed full of tears the day the three friends left for Reims. Autumn weather had set in and a grey and heavy sky bore no resemblance at all to the sunlit skies that had been their constant companion during the summer.

Armand and Pierre stood waving until the last silhouette of the coaches had disappeared; Pierre's face was wet from the rain, although his friend suspected that more than a single tear might have mixed with the raindrops. Anyhow, it was time to embrace the future and plan their journey to Venice.

"I have no idea what to do and where to go!" Pierre looked unhappily at an old and dusty map he had found in the library, showing France and its neighbouring countries. He looked doubtfully at the map. Although adorned with elaborate paintings it didn't look particularly up to date or trustworthy.

"Is it true that close to Lyon there are mountains full of fierce dragons?" Pierre asked sceptically, looking at the blood-thirsty illustrations.

"You should know better! Don't be stupid, dragons might have lived there in earlier times, but the only one I have ever seen is jealously guarding the kitchen downstairs," Armand retorted, and was just about to start explaining their journey in detail when they heard booted footsteps fast approaching the door of the library. Simultaneously they could hear the excited voice of the butler echoing through the door, seemingly quite upset, as his offended voice was almost breaking and they could hear, "My lord, you *may not* enter," and "It's *my* duty first to announce Monsieur to Monsieur le Marquis!"

The door burst open and to their great surprise, François de Toucy strode into the room, his boots still wet and spattered with the mud of the roads.

"Can you please stop this wrinkled toad of a butler from harassing me!" he greeted them with a big smile. "I told him that you wouldn't mind if I entered your inner sanctum, but he seems to disagree!"

Pierre laughed and jumped up to embrace his friend. "How wonderful to see you again, what made you come back to see us all of a sudden?"

Armand had also jumped up and embraced his cousin, old resentments long forgotten.

"I've informed his Eminence that I quit my position, as Monsieur le Marquis had been foolishly generous with his reward, and I won't need to earn my living as a humble musketeer anymore." He winked at Pierre, giving his speech a slightly ironic twist. "His Eminence accepted my decision in good grace, but he insisted all the same that I ride down to Montrésor once more to get you back to Paris on time and in safety."

"Does Richelieu think that we're inexperienced little boys, incapable of looking after ourselves?" Armand was steaming with indignation and fury.

François de Toucy didn't seem to be particularly impressed. "Yes, probably you're right – but obviously I had no interest in correcting his opinion. I was quite keen to come back and see both of you. I thought that travelling together might be fun – unless you decide to continue pouting. But let's become serious now, is this butler of yours just good for decoration or can he do something for me other than just staring at me? I'm dying from hunger and thirst!"

Armand was still digesting the fact that his cousin didn't seem to care at all about his hurt feelings but Pierre roared with laughter. Quickly he clapped his hands and kicked his servants into motion. "Bring food and wine for this gentleman and don't stand around staring at us like biblical pillars of salt!"

A frenzy of action was the immediate response to Pierre's orders and in no time trays loaded with all sort of mouth- watering delicacies appeared. François de Toucy didn't show any restraint, and made short work of the meats and cheeses brought for him, using his dagger to cut into the food with amazing dexterity and speed. While he was eating he kept on talking, which made it somewhat difficult to follow his speech.

Watching his cousin devour the food, Armand became hungry as well and soon the three friends were having an early dinner together, chatting about the latest news from Paris.

Pierre was delighted at this change of events – how he had been dreading that evening! All had been set for a depressing night, both of them moping in the big dining room, missing Marie's chatty conversation, Céline's ironic remarks and Charles' dry sense of humour.

François de Toucy's arrival was a gift sent from heaven, well, not directly from heaven – he had been sent by heaven's representative in France, the Cardinal de Richelieu.

"I'm still surprised that the Cardinal should be concerned about my well-being," Pierre said, once he had washed his greasy hands in a basin and the servants had finally left the room.

François de Toucy chuckled. "You certainly should be! But the King has taken a great fancy to you – you're now being called 'his saviour' – and His Majesty has instructed the Cardinal to make sure that you arrive safely in Paris. As your lunatic cousin Henri has vanished without a trace, Richelieu and my uncle are worried that he might give it another try to become the next marquis!"

"Oh yes, Henri!" Pierre exclaimed. "I must confess, I had completely forgotten about him!"

"You shouldn't," Armand suddenly interrupted him with a sober note. "Henri will never leave you in peace as long as he's alive!"

"Your lordship doesn't seem to be particularly amused," the voice drawled from across the bed. "Nothing out there to cater for your lordship's exquisite taste?"

Henri de Beauvoir threw a last glance through the viewing hole that had been skilfully fitted into the panelled wall and allowed an excellent vision of the orgy that was in full swing in the salon of the establishment that had become his home during the past weeks.

Tasteful furniture and expensive tapestries from the Orient and gold-framed mirrors gleaming in the light of candles that had been lavishly placed in the huge room were the luxurious setting for of one of those decadent parties that high society of Paris was whispering about and craving for – and which had made the fortune and unrivalled reputation of his attractive host.

Henri let his eyes wander across the room. He saw stunning young ladies of doubtful virtue, some stripping , some already naked, numerous members of the aristocracy he knew well from his previous stays at court in a telling state of excitement and young toyboys playing with far too old men who had – in vain - tried to freshen up their sagging looks with the help of ample chalk-paint and rouge. The girls were screaming in high-pitched voices as they faked amusement and delight. Henri could make out the newest attraction: a naked dwarf, who was trying to mount a totally drunken young slut to the animated cheers of the bystanders.

He turned towards the bed where Nicolas was lying. Nicolas held a slim girl in his arms, at least Henri had at first thought that this nymph-like being was a girl until she had fully undressed and Henri had registered a sign of manhood – albeit somewhat shrivelled. Nicolas had decided to amuse himself tonight with a rarity, a beautiful young castrato from the choir of the cathedral of Notre Dame.

Henri knew that he should feel thankful and excited. Nicolas had tried to find a new diversion, but he felt more and more irritated, wasting his time here in this golden cage.

"Send him away, we must talk," he said curtly.

The boy looked at him, his blue eyes filling slowly with big tears. "My lord doesn't like me?" he sobbed.

Nicolas caressed him quickly but gave him a sign to leave. "Don't worry, the gentleman is not feeling well today, wait for me outside, we'll spend some time together later tonight and I swear that you'll receive later the nice gift that I had promised you."

The boy looked comforted, wiped the tears away and left the room.

Nicolas watched him leaving the room and commented, "Nice boy, I was convinced you'd love to try him – he pretends that he's still a virgin, but I wouldn't like to place a wager on that."

Henri looked at Nicolas who lay naked in the bed. Dark and handsome, he knew his worth. But Henri didn't feel inclined to marvel at the physical beauty of his host, and simply felt irritated and frustrated.

"Nicolas, I need to leave urgently or I'm going to explode." With an impatient gesture he tore at the tangled bed sheets. "I shall surely kill somebody, if nothing is going to change!" Henri exclaimed, striding up and down the room. "I feel like I'm trapped in a golden cage!"

"I'm happy that at least you admitted that it's a golden one!" Nicolas smiled and looked at his guest with the same fascination with which he'd observe a wild and intriguing animal. Henri's fair classic beauty had always fascinated him, but even more he felt attracted by the aura of danger and dark sensuality that Henri radiated. He had never met someone like Henri before, a man who would drag his victims without remorse into an abyss of desire, a hell only a chosen few would escape. This man must be in league with the devil, Nicolas had concluded long ago – and had desired Henri even more for it.

The day Henri had turned up at his door – in urgent need of a hiding place – Nicolas had been only too happy to accommodate him. What a unique opportunity to combine business with pleasure, and what a triumph to bed the man who had made all of Paris crazy with desire – men and women alike. But Nicolas had always known that the day would arrive when Henri would want to leave, indeed he had expected this to happen far earlier.

"Tell me then, precisely what do you want?" Nicolas opened the conversation.

"That's easy enough, I want to kill this bastard who has taken my place!"

"I couldn't really criticise you for not being precise enough," Nicolas smiled cruelly. "Any idea how you're going to achieve this, though?"

"I have to leave France first, Richelieu's agents will be searching for me everywhere and you'll have to organize this for me, Nicolas. By the way, did you sell the jewellery I brought along from Roquemoulin?"

195

"Maybe… but maybe I preferred to keep it for me, do you have any witnesses to say that you brought any?" Nicolas answered evenly.

Henri rushed to the bed and without prior warning his strong hands closed around Nicolas's neck. But Nicolas had anticipated his reactions and soon they were on the bed, wrestling hard.

"You wanted me to come into your bed," hissed Henri, suddenly realizing the ridiculous aspect of his behaviour. "You've been manipulating me all the time!"

"So true, my lord!" murmured Nicolas, his voice hoarse with excitement.

Later, as they lay panting on the bed, Henri's thoughts reverted to his plans to leave Paris. "The worst thing is, I have no idea where to go to," he confessed. "I've only been to England once, after I left France last time, but I can't go back to London, it's too risky. Where do you recommend that I should hide until things have calmed down here? Do you have any friends I could go and visit? And, by the way, how much money did you get for my stuff?"

Nicolas was sitting with crossed legs in the bed. Imitating a fortune-teller with a crystal ball, he frowned and said in a hollow voice, "I can see that you'll be leaving shortly for Venice where a family reunion will be waiting for you!"

"Venice? Why should I go to Venice?"

Nicolas jumped up and walked to the spyhole where he beckoned Henri to come and join him. "Do you see the fat bald man whose eyeballs are nearly popping out of his head while he's watching the naughty dwarf?"

"Indeed I do, he's simply disgusting!"

"Well, you'll see him in a different light soon. He works in the office of our esteemed Eminence, the Cardinal de Richelieu. He told me that your beloved bastard cousin will soon be leaving for Venice, the Cardinal is preparing a letter of protection for him."

Henri whistled softly. "I have never underestimated you, but sometimes you still surprise me – how on earth did you make him talk? I guess part of Roquemoulin's jewellery went into his pockets?"

"Only a small part, actually. When my contact person dropped a hint that he might be invited to one of my famous parties he nearly bit his arm off and started to sing like a canary. It's a hush-hush, top secret mission, something linked to a ring that your cousin needs to acquire, I haven't found out the reason for this yet."

"No need really, I'll make sure that he never reaches Venice anyhow!"

Henri peeped through the spyhole once again and watched with a mixture of morbid curiosity and disgust.

The fat clergyman had started to grope a young woman, almost a girl. She played coy and managed to escape from his grasp – but Henri could see all the same that she made sure that the priest in a telling state of excitement could still follow her. But suddenly he swayed as he tripped over the sprawled legs of a couple making love on the floor and fell down close to them. The young woman followed him and assiduously started to work on his private parts until he started moaning with delight.

"That fat priest is simply disgusting! I'd like to ram my rapier up his fat backside. But who's the beautiful girl?"

"She's one of my best," Nicolas said, barely hiding the proud satisfaction in his voice. "I promised her a nice reward if she gets him addicted to our little parties. Once they have tasted this, they're hooked and ready to give me any information I need. That's how I make most of my money. She's a very clever girl, and beautiful too. And the best, she's ready to kill without false remorse if any money is in it for her!"

Henri turned his head away from the scene in the salon, he had seen enough. "And how shall I travel to Venice? Any other brilliant ideas?"

Nicolas smiled and rang a bell. Almost immediately a panelled door opened and a discreet valet entered.

"Bring the clothes for the Reverend Henri, please," he ordered.

Before Henri was able to make sense of this order, the servant reappeared, holding in his hand the travelling clothes and hat of an Abbot.

"This will be your disguise while you're travelling to Italy. The choir boy whom you just sent out of this room will accompany you, both of you will be visiting the Archbishop of Venice, the boy is a gift for his choir."

Henri whistled softly. "What a perfect disguise, nobody will dare to disturb a travelling Abbot. I can even see that you have thought about the correct ring and the rosary!"

"Try them on," said Nicolas.

Henri put on the clothes and it wasn't difficult to see that they had been tailor made for him. The bell was rung again and the servant ordered to bring a polished silver mirror. Henri looked at himself, marvelling at his transformation into a distinguished man of the church.

"Perfect!" he said and evidently having had a complete moodswing, "Now let's test together my new ward, the choir boy!"

"Surely nothing can ever surpass pure Christian brotherly love," murmured Nicolas and rang for the boy.

Pierre was greeted at Montrésor by his servants as if the resurrected Saviour himself had walked into the house. The majordomo couldn't hide the tears in his eyes, his maids curtsied deeply and covered his hands with kisses– not even the King himself could have hoped for a more cordial and triumphant welcome.

Pierre was enthralled, even embarrassed by this display of emotional attachment to his person. He looked at his friend and could see that even the normally cynical Armand was impressed by the nature of their welcome.

Before dinner was served Armand had already discovered the reason for the strange behaviour of Pierre's servants. As was customary for him, Armand had been chatting with the servants – from chambermaids to the butler – and had soon found out that the Palais de Beauvoir was teeming with rumours about Pierre's accident in Blois. It was thus the established wisdom of Pierre's household that several villains had tried to assassinate the Marquis de Beauvoir and only the bold and brave action of the King of France in person had prevented the worst from happening.

Pierre looked in fascination at his friend. "Are they really saying this? Who's behind these rumours?"

"Aren't we lucky to live under the reign of such a glorious and brave King?" Armand quipped, then changing to a more serious tone, "Who else but our revered Cardinal Richelieu could be behind such rumours?"

"But why?" asked Pierre, "Why would he want those rumours to circulate?"

"Dear Lord, sometimes I don't understand why Thou madest Pierre the best scholar in our class but Thou hast rendered him incapable of understanding the most simple moves in the game of politics," groaned Armand, casting his eyes in despair to the ceiling.

"Then tell me, clever Monsieur Armand, how does politics come into play this time?" Pierre retorted, visibly offended.

Armand sighed, but started to explain. "We all know that Cardinal Richelieu is a sly old fox. He changed the story first of all to ingratiate himself with the King. Sooner or later the King will be convinced that he has indeed been very brave and that he almost saved you – or contributed a major part to your rescue at least. By depicting you as the target of the attack and the true victim, the Cardinal spares the King the embarrassment of having his own brother's name linked to something that smells rather like high treason. Yet Richelieu will keep enough proof up his sleeve so as to hit out at Gaston d'Orléans or Cinq Mars at any minute, but he'll choose the timing that works best for him. Once again, we have to admit, the Cardinal is the true master and we all are merely dancing like puppets on his strings!"

Pierre digested the explanation and reluctantly he had to admit that his friend's analysis not only sounded convincing, it was brilliant. Obviously they had again been used as mere pawns in Richelieu's game of political chess.

Swallowing his pride he grumbled, "I guess you're right, I missed the point with the King's brother."

"Of course I'm right," answered his friend. "When it comes to women and politics, nobody can beat me!" and complacently he caressed the proud moustache he had been growing lately as fashion dictated.

"Did you ever hear that conceited people die young?" Pierre asked sweetly.

"That's impossible," Armand answered, not at all shaken by his friend's comment, "otherwise my father should have been dead and buried a long time already!"

*****

The Louvre Palace bore no resemblance to the more rustic dwellings of the King's hunting lodge at Versailles. But the Louvre bore dark memories, as for many years it had been a prison for the King when he was a boy under the iron rule of his infamous mother. The King had never forgotten, nor forgiven, and even today he cherished every day he could spend far away from this imposing building and the unhappy memories it awoke in him.

Over the centuries the Louvre had been enlarged, redecorated and rebuilt by generations of kings of France. Sprawling along the River Seine it had become a huge testimony to the power and glory of the kingdom of France.

On this sunny day in autumn Pierre and Armand entered the cobbled driveway leading into the courtyard in their gilded coach that now proudly displayed the coat of arms of the Marquis de Beauvoir and – Pierre had insisted – the stags of the Duchy of Hertford.

King Louis XIII, eager to show his special concern and favour, had sent a guard of honour to accompany them and thus progress of the coach through the roads and alleys of Paris had been unusually fast and smooth as the proud friends could hear the shouts of the officer riding in front of their coach, clearing the way for them in the name of the almighty King of France.

The two friends were dressed in their finest, their polished boots and gleaming rapiers sparkling like mirrors in the sunshine. Their shirts and waistcoats were made from the finest embroidered silk their tailor had been able to find, at a horrendous price that Pierre preferred to forget.

Armand had laughed at Pierre's expression when the tailor, bowing reverently to the ground, had mentioned the price.

"You'll never become a true Marquis if you harbour in your chest the soul of a merchant. We're meeting the King, forget the money, we must look our best!"

As a last finishing touch their elegant appearance was crowned by fashionable hats adorned with long and colourful feathers. Armand had been so happy with his appearance that he had paraded in front of the mirror like a proud peacock admiring himself until Pierre had had to drag him away, as their coach was waiting.

The galleries leading to the great audience hall echoed with the sound of their footsteps, accompanied by the noisy boots of the musketeers in their guard of honour accompanying them until the doors of the hall were opened by the King's lackeys and Pierre heard the voice of the lord chamberlain solemnly announcing their arrival and reeling off a seemingly endless litany of his titles. *I somehow still can't believe that this is really me, Pierre, a mere orphan from Reims, he's announcing, it still seems so strange.*

Most members of the court were already waiting, only the Royal family had not yet arrived and Pierre could almost feel the glances directed at him like daggers by the nobles who were present. The animosity behind the polished facades was palpable.

This surprised him greatly, but giving it some thought he suddenly realized how naïve he still was. In his mind he had prevented an attack on the king, if not his assassination – and today he should be rewarded. Maybe he'd receive another golden chain – not that he really cared, he possessed so many already. For Pierre, this episode thus should come to an end. He had done his duty, nothing spectacular in his eyes.

But in the eyes of the courtiers he had committed the ultimate crime: he had stolen the limelight of the royal court.

One bold action had catapulted him into the focus of royal attention, the ultimate goal every courtier craved. Soberly, Pierre looked around and detected – with only a few and notable exceptions – hate and hostility, albeit camouflaged by the politest of smiles that had been pasted into their faces.

"Cinq Mars is absent, that's strange," whispered Armand, nudging his friend with his elbow, "as even the Cardinal de Richelieu is here already."

Armand's last words were drowned by the sound of trumpets announcing the arrival of the King. Today he had chosen not only to be accompanied by the Queen but had decided to present the Dauphin, his heir, to the waiting court as well.

The Dauphin was clinging to the hands of his nurse. Scared by the deafening noise of the trumpets he had started to cry as soon as their sound blasted through the great hall. Unperturbed, the royal family walked ceremoniously towards the waiting golden chairs that were crowned by velvet canopies displaying the royal coats of arms.

First the King took his seat, then there was a short commotion while the ladies-in-waiting made sure that the Queen was seated properly and her dress, made from the stiffest of brocades and woven with threads of gold and silver, was arranged and displayed correctly. The Queen didn't alter her expression; born a Princess of Spain, she had grown up with strict court protocol.

Now the ceremony could commence. The King started by greeting Pierre – a tedious task, as his stammer grew worse as soon as he had to speak in public, and tedious not only for the King but for his audience as well. The assembled courtiers had to pretend to listen with rapt attention and not to notice the imperfections of his speech.

Pierre managed to look sufficiently attentive whereas Armand not only had a smile on his lips, he looked positively enthralled. Armand had noticed a singularly attractive lady-in-waiting in the Queen's retinue and although he looked in the direction of the King, all of his attention was focused on the young lady, who was skilful enough to pretend not to have noticed his attention but sent a casual glance from time to time in Armand's direction all the same.

The King had now reached the passage in his long-winded speech where he was about to thank his beloved cousin, the Marquis de Beauvoir for his services to the Crown. It took him ages to pronounce the letter 'b', let alone the rest of his name. Pierre's smile started to freeze on his lips and he pitied the King, who was perspiring profusely, such was the sovereign's anguish in delivering his simple speech. Even the Dauphin must have captured the tense atmosphere as he had stopped crying and fell silent. No one dared talk, a painful and oppressive silence reigned during each pause of the King's speech.

All of a sudden the loud noise of clicking heels could be heard outside the hall accompanied by an angry voice shouting loudly, "Open up, you idiots, you know me well enough. I'm the Marquis de Cinq Mars, His Majesty's master of the horses!"

The King had stopped in the middle of the word that he had been trying painfully to articulate. Quickly his eyes darted to the closed doors, then towards

202

Richelieu, seeking guidance on how to deal with this unusual and inexcusable breach of etiquette.

Pierre noticed that the Cardinal shook his head ever so slightly and for a second the mask dropped and the King's face showed an expression of pain, almost fear. The impressive doors with their carved coats of arms swung open and Cinq Mars stumbled into the hall. His usually handsome face looked puffed and swollen and those standing close enough to him could tell he reeked of wine. Cinq Mars had been drinking heavily.

"Your Majesty," he cried, his speech thick and blurred, "I would give my life for you, I'm your only and most loyal servant, tell them!" He staggered forward and was now whining. "Tell them, I'm the only one who loves Your Majesty dearly!"

Remembering protocol he tried to bow deeply before his sovereign, but putting too much zest into his movement he lost his balance and fell to the marble floor. It was not immediately clear if it was the impact of his fall or the drunkenness, but Cinq Mars lay helpless on his back, like a stranded beetle. The audience was in shock, yet utterly thrilled – what a delicious scandal was unfolding right before their eyes! They were witnessing nothing less than the end of the King's favourite. The King never could or would forgive such behaviour.

The courtiers' brains quickly calculated potential alternatives. Would the young and handsome Marquis de Beauvoir become the new favourite, or his dashing friend? Neither of them was married, how to woo the new rising stars? Which member of their numerous young and attractive relatives – male or female – could be thrown into the arms of the new favourites to profit from the potential royal favours likely to be showered on them?

Meanwhile King Louis XIII sat frozen on his throne. Long practice helped him to keep a straight face but he was at a loss as to what to do. He knew of course that he should call in the guards but he still loved Cinq Mars dearly – a silly and hopeless love – at this moment maybe even more than ever before as he saw him lying here so vulnerable, depending on him. But Cinq Mars had committed the ultimate crime; he had ridiculed the King, and this could never be pardoned.

But before the King had made his mind up, the educated voice of the Cardinal de Richelieu cut through the embarrassing silence, a voice that was surprisingly strong for his frail body. "I'm afraid that our dear friend, the most noble Marquis de Cinq Mars, is feeling unwell. Guards, please accompany him to my apartments, I shall take good care of him."

The guards bustled into action and a whining and protesting Cinq Mars found himself dragged rather than escorted out of the great hall. He was never to see the King again.

Seeing his favourite leaving the hall, the King suddenly lost his composure. Like a fish on dry land he opened and closed his mouth, trying to continue his speech, but no words would come. The great hall lay in absolute silence, only the ticking of the clocks could be heard.

Pierre decided that it was time to take the initiative and stop this agony. Slightly bending the rules of royal protocol he moved forward and kneeled reverently in front of the King. "It has been my pleasure entirely to render a small service to Your Majesty," Pierre said in his pleasant voice, "but I'm sure that every single gentleman here in this hall would have done the same. Long live Your Majesty!"

The last words were shouted loudly, and full of enthusiasm the other members of the court repeated them, hailing their King. Armand later commented with a grin that their enthusiasm in shouting and praising the King had been predominantly motivated by their urgent desire to end the agony of his stammering.

King Louis was moved by this display of loyalty from his nobles and with moist eyes he motioned Pierre to stand up and he embraced him.

"We shall grant you the favour of a private audience, wait in the antechamber." The King spoke softly into Pierre's ear. Still in the grip of the emotional scene he had suddenly forgotten his stammer.

Pierre was wondering about such an unusual turn of events. Furthermore, Armand's jokes that this private audience might be nothing else but the royal version of a private lesson by Brother Hieronymus didn't help to alleviate his nervousness. He looked at his friend quizzically and replied, "Friends are meant to share, aren't they? You'll come with me, my friend, for better and for worse!"

Armand laughed and answered, "Touché! For better or for worse, I'll join you!"

*****

Impatiently Pierre looked at the golden clock that was ticking away the seconds. A work of art in itself, it was standing on a richly carved table. The top of the table was lavishly decorated with ivory inserts depicting the King's favourite pastime: hunting. Armand looked closer at the table and suddenly he grinned. "Have a closer look, Pierre, these ancient Greeks had a strange turn of mind. See that goddess there being seduced by a stag? Isn't that deliciously scandalous – she really doesn't seem to mind!"

Curious to see for himself, Pierre approached the dubiously decorated table when the door of the adjacent room suddenly opened and a lackey appeared to guide Pierre into the room where the private audience was to take place. Pierre insisted that his friend should join him and the servant – after a moment's hesitation – announced both friends in the most elaborate manner of court etiquette. When the lackey pronounced Pierre's and Armand's English titles Pierre had to suppress a smile: the Duke of Hertford had been transformed into the "duc d'Ehrfor'" – nobody in France ever seemed to be able to pronounce his English title correctly.

The private audience chamber was much more intimate than the grand hall. It looked more like a study than a salon. The King was sitting on a simple armchair and as if he had wanted to stress the informality of the occasion, one of his beloved dogs was snuggled at his feet. The dog slowly moved his head when the two friends entered but decided not to bother, and yawning profusely remained at the King's feet. Next to the King, the Cardinal de Richelieu was seated. The small group was completed by a secretary who was hovering in the corner, ready to take notes as soon as requested.

Probably for the first time ever Pierre was relieved to see the Cardinal. Clearly no Brother Hieronymus-style private lessons were on the agenda.

The Cardinal opened the audience speaking with a brisk tone. "His Majesty graciously wishes to express his gratitude to the Marquis de Beauvoir. The brave and bold action of the most noble Marquis has impressed His Majesty greatly and shielded this kingdom from potential disarray. Officially we have not yet taken any action to indict or prosecute the persons who master-minded this ambush but His Majesty has expressed his desire that those persons are to be identified and punished and no efforts will be spared in fulfilling His Majesty's request."

The Cardinal paused and looked at his sovereign, who sat in his chair listening and nodding at the Cardinal's words.

"We have therefore decided to show you our special favour and we have instructed His Eminence to make sure that you shall be rewarded for your noble deed!" the King added, looking into Pierre's eyes. Sitting here comfortably in a small group, his stammer had almost disappeared.

Pierre nervously tried to remember if protocol demanded that he should look into the King's eyes or cast his eyes down but luckily the Cardinal now took over and addressed him. Clearing his throat, he said, "I have the great pleasure to inform you that His Majesty in his generosity will appoint you a member of the

Ordre du Saint Esprit, the most prestigious order of our kingdom. As a member of this order your place will be among the most revered peers of France!"

The Cardinal made a sign and the secretary rushed forward with a leather box which he opened cautiously. Inside Pierre could see a rolled vellum document and a medal, studded with diamonds and adorned with the lilies of France. Pierre tried to remember what royal protocol demanded for such an occasion and he came to the conclusion that falling on his knees and kissing the hands of the King might be the appropriate move, in any case, at least it didn't seem to be desperately wrong.

But the King's voice cut short his reflections. "My dearest Richelieu, are you joking? The Marquis de Beauvoir has saved our life and you offer him a piece of fancy jewellery as a reward? You can't be serious!" The King was visibly upset.

Fascinated, Armand watched this scene. He had never witnessed the King criticize the Cardinal in public; apparently the King wasn't just the Cardinal's brainless puppet on a string as most people presumed.

"Your Majesty!" Richelieu interjected, defending himself. "This is not only a very exclusive order, it's a special favour, the Marquis de Beauvoir will rank among the highest peers of France!"

The King shook his head. "He's ranked among the highest peers already because the house of Beauvoir is one of the oldest noble houses of our kingdom and you seem to forget that de Beauvoir carries the title of a Duke in England!"

The Cardinal pressed his lips tightly together and bowed stiffly to the King. He didn't like to be contradicted.

"Is there any special favour that we could grant you?" the King asked Pierre. "His Eminence is our excellent servant, but he tends to be thrifty when it comes to dispensing rewards. As such we do appreciate this attitude, of course, we prefer diligent guardians of our treasures!"

Richelieu looked a bit mollified by this speech and its indirect compliment and now all eyes were fixed on Pierre, expecting his answer.

Pierre's thoughts were racing. What favour could he request from the King, how could he strike the right balance between using this unique opportunity and not seeming to appear too greedy? Suddenly an idea flashed through his mind, and unconsciously employing his most charming smile, he replied, "If Your Majesty insists, I do indeed have a request. I would like to have reinstated the estates that my late uncle lost to greedy moneylenders."

"We do remember your uncle, of course, may the Lord bless his soul. But tell us what happened, why did he lose his estates?"

Pierre now looked at the Cardinal, who suddenly looked very tense, his lips a thin line in his waxen face.

"My uncle was a very unlucky, I'm afraid, even a rather silly man. He made a strange bargain, a sort of wager and he lost – he lost his estates and later his life."

The King looked scandalized: "Do you have any idea who this evil person was who entered into such a bargain with your uncle?"

Pierre frowned and looked in the direction of the Cardinal de Richelieu. "I do have some idea, Sire." He paused at length, contemplating the Cardinal, who looked more than usual like a bloodless figure in his armchair. "… I couldn't tell you precisely, but I imagine that it's a man of the highest intelligence and one never to be underrated as an enemy."

The King shook his head. "You mentioned a moneylender, surely this must have been a Jewish moneylender! Richelieu, how often have we asked you to be more strict and evict this vermin from our kingdom!" The King was very upset, his stutter had returned and it took him some time to pronounce the last word.

The Cardinal bowed slightly in his chair and murmured soothingly, "I have already purged your most catholic Majesty's kingdom from numerous enemies of the True Faith, but even our Lord," solemnly he made the sign of the cross which the King hastened to repeat, "… did not create the world in a single day! Didn't we triumph over the heretics in La Rochelle, your Majesty's victorious army succeeded in destroying a stronghold of protestant rebels, fierce enemies of our kingdom who had resisted your Majesty's ancestors for decades!"

Richelieu had apparently hit the right note, as the King nodded with satisfaction and his flushed face came back to its normal – albeit still very red – colour and he reverted to Pierre's request.

"Your request is granted. We shall ask our diligent prime minister to confiscate the estates and hand them back to you!" he beamed at Pierre and Richelieu, obviously happy to be able to fulfil Pierre's request so quickly.

Armand had to suppress a fit of laughter as the Cardinal de Richelieu looked as if he had swallowed a toad, his waxen complexion having taken on a decidedly greenish tint. Stiffly he bowed in the direction of his sovereign and murmured, "Your Majesty's wish is my command, it shall be done!"

All of a sudden the King seemed to realize that Armand was standing behind Pierre and he addressed him now. "Welcome, Armand de Saint Paul, I know your father very well. When he was as young, he was also a very handsome man – and he used to seduce all of the Queen's chamber maids." He chuckled now.

"Her Majesty used to complain about him regularly. You seem to be taking after your father?"

Armand smiled broadly. "I'm doing my best, Sire, I'm of the opinion that one should use the gifts that the good Lord graciously has bestowed upon us!"

The King laughed but the next moment he suddenly looked sad as he continued. "His Eminence has informed me that both of you have requested immediate leave from our court to travel to Italy. We had intended to invite you to our next hunting party in Versailles but it seems that your plans do not allow any delay. Your request is hereby granted and we wish you a safe journey, may the Lord bless you!"

The audience thus had been terminated and Pierre fell to knees to kiss the hand of the King. Armand noticed that the King closed his eyes briefly, as if cherishing this gesture. *He's a poor devil after all*, Armand mused. *It must be extremely rare that someone kisses his hand and actually means it.*

The Cardinal left together with the two friends and guided them into a small poorly lit room in the proximity of the King's study. The monk who had been waiting outside the audience room accompanied them. He seemed to be the Cardinal's private secretary. The Cardinal settled in a comfortable armchair, flinching briefly as the movement seemed to cause him some pain. As he didn't make any sign for the friends to sit down they concluded that this meeting would be kept rather short.

The Cardinal gave an order to his secretary who opened a worn leather bag. An envelope and a small leather box appeared. The Cardinal came straight to the point. "I understand that you wish to leave for Venice as soon as possible!" he stated, rather than asked.

Pierre looked bewildered at Armand, although he should have expected – of course – that the Cardinal would know all of their secrets.

"We do indeed, Your Eminence," replied Armand, not adding any more explanation.

"As His Majesty has just informed you, your request to leave France has been accepted and furthermore we have established a letter of protection in the name of the King to make sure that you enjoy a safe journey. The small box contains a medal that you are to hand over in the name of the King to the Doge of Venice. He will be invited to join the Ordre du Saint Esprit in reward for his recent support in our negotiations with the Holy See."

Pierre tried to look suitably impressed. He didn't really know how to reply.

208

The Cardinal paused and then continued. "I will also make sure that the estates of the Marquis' late uncle are reinstated. His Majesty's wish will be respected of course. I must add though, that His Majesty, from his august position, sometimes tends to neglect some small details. The Crown will have to buy them back first, the rule of law and order must not be bypassed."

Pierre looked at the Cardinal sitting in the armchair, frail and with a sick complexion, but once more he had outwitted them. If the estates had to be given back, the Cardinal definitely wouldn't pay for them!

"We'd like to thank your Eminence for your support and the concern that you have shown during the past weeks," Pierre finally managed to say, but even to his own ears this sounded false and hollow.

"Did I?" replied the Cardinal and suddenly he uttered some asthmatic sounds that Pierre interpreted, fascinated, as the Cardinal's version of laughing. "May the Lord grant you a safe journey, remember that some evil persons are out there, and don't be as unwise as your uncle!"

Pierre was not sure if he had just received a blessing, a recommendation or a straightforward warning…

"We still have some days left in Paris until we leave for Venice, let's do something exciting!" said Armand while they were having dinner in Pierre's stately dining room. Paris was basking in one of the last spells of glorious sunshine, almost too warm to be comfortable. They had enjoyed the kind of beautiful days that seem to promise an everlasting summer, until the arrival of real autumn weather would show the ugly side of Paris and transform it into a dark and damp city.

Today the dining room window was wide open, the curtains fluttered in the warm breeze and the flames of the candles guttered on the dining table.

Pierre watched a mosquito dancing into the light. Unconsciously he started to scratch himself. He hated mosquitoes.

"You're not listening!" chided his friend, who had been watching him. "You seem more interested in a stupid mosquito than your best friend!"

"At least the mosquito doesn't complain all the time and doesn't tell me that my company is boring," replied Pierre with a grin. "What kind of exciting things do you have in mind, a royal hunting party or dinner with your parents?"

"Oh Pierre, you're truly hopeless," Armand sighed. "You're behaving as if you were forty years old – not almost eighteen!"

Armand's eyes were now sparkling, and in a low voice so as not to be overhead by a servant, he continued, "I ran into one of my old friends yesterday and he told me that there is private gambling parlour, everyone in Paris is dying to get an invitation. It's the hottest place in town and he promised... to get one for both of us!"

Pierre looked at his friend with big eyes. "What do you mean? I have no idea what you're talking about!"

Armand sighed. Sometimes his friend was as trying and naïve as a new-born baby.

"It's a place where you can eat, drink, play cards with high wagers and the maids who serve the meals are not only the most beautiful or exotic ones you could imagine, apparently they're very open to..."

"I can imagine," answered Pierre drily. "Well, that settles it then. I won't go!"

But Armand wouldn't accept any refusal. Pierre didn't know how his friend always managed to convince him to change his mind. Yet before they parted and Pierre went to bed he had given in and agreed to accompany Armand, although a feeble voice of caution in his head kept telling him he would be better not to go.

The invitation arrived as promised and an exuberant Armand, accompanied by an extremely nervous friend, knocked at the door of an inconspicuous building in a small and dark lane. They entered the inn matching the description Armand's friend had provided and found themselves in a run-down tavern, crammed with people, most of them in a state of drunkenness and clearly the kind of company Pierre would have preferred to avoid.

Armand still thought that this was a great adventure, and full of curiosity he approached a buxom barmaid. Her ravaged face told him that she was past her prime but next to being her best customer she seemed to be the one in charge in the tap room.

"What do you want, sweetheart, for a young and handsome man like you I can make a deal, and if your friend wants to join us, I won't mind." Speaking in a coarse voice, she pushed up her breasts and adjusted her neckline to make sure that a potential customer would have a good view.

"Maybe later, sweetheart," Armand answered with his dashing smile. "In the meantime I want to meet with some friends here," and quickly he mentioned the password that – according to his friend – would open the door to the Promised Land.

The password seemed to sober her. Instantly she gave them a sign to follow and they disappeared from the tap room into an adjacent panelled room where she tapped against a section of the panelling in a certain rhythm.

A secret door opened only seconds later and Armand had to repeat the password. They entered a dark passage and were greeted by a manservant with a lantern who asked them to take off their rapiers and daggers. The friends obliged but Pierre's uneasy feeling grew with every second – he felt almost naked and unprotected. A winding and narrow staircase led them upstairs while Pierre fought the impression that he was having a bad dream.

"I hope at least that you're enjoying this," he hissed at his friend, "because I'm not!"

"Don't wet your breeches, it'll be fun!" answered his ever optimistic friend.

But before Pierre found any opportunity to share further trepidations with Armand, a door opened and they found themselves entering a different world, a vast and beautifully appointed salon, more refined and luxurious than anything else Pierre had ever seen before, the Louvre included.

Everywhere gold gleamed in the candlelight, and musicians were playing, although hidden from their view. Pierre could hear the soft tunes but he was unable to identify where the sound was emanating from. They walked on the finest and softest carpets imported from the Orient that Pierre had ever seen in his life; made from pure silk, they glowed in the mellow light of the candles. The room was dominated by several huge gaming tables where small clusters of gentlemen were already immersed in card play, and smoke hung in the air, as apparently some guests were addicted to the new fashion of smoking tobacco.

Impressive piles of golden livres were lying close to them. Pierre marvelled at the young female servants who were carrying trays loaded with wine and food. They all had the lowest necklines and most shameless dresses imaginable. He hated to admit it, but just watching those girls made the visit worthwhile. Armand's eyes glazed over when one of the beauties bent over close to him in order to serve a customer. Pierre was fascinated and scandalized at the same time, the damnation of Sodom and Gomorrah must be close, but he couldn't keep his eyes from the stunningly beautiful girl who offered him a glass of cooled white wine.

At the end of the room they spotted the table where Armand's friend was already sitting with a bunch of his own acquaintances. They had already been drinking heavily, a pile of empty jars and bottles bearing silent witness to their consumption. Pierre was not surprised that the mood at the table was fittingly frivolous. The gambling part apparently wasn't taken very seriously, and most of the men's attention was directed towards the attractive waitresses who kept provoking the group of young men by staying as close as possible and making sure that they were within easy reach of touching and groping.

"They're the best you could find in all Paris," uttered Armand's friend with staring eyes as he viewed the breasts of a waitress who was bent over him, his voice thick from too much wine. "Try the chambre séparée though, paradise has nothing better to offer!"

Armand laughed and they joined the merry party. Soon their friends and the suspense of the gambling drew them into an irresistible whirl of partying, fun and heavy drinking.

A good two hours later Armand whispered to Pierre, "I've lost enough money here, and I have a slight suspicion that the dice are loaded. Let's now have some fun in the chambre séparée!" Armand's eyes were sparkling with anticipation "The dark girl over there told me that she'd have a special treat for both of us!"

Before Pierre could utter a protest, Armand dragged him from the table and they followed one of the waitresses who walked in front of them, her body swaying invitingly.

Feeling agreeably tipsy and excited they followed her down a corridor that was only sparsely lit by some flickering candles and entered a cosy room, pleasantly decorated with the same kind of wonderful carpets, richly carved panels and furniture, and a piece of furniture that Pierre had never seen before, a combination of a very comfortable upholstered armchair that stretched into a sofa. Armand explained to him that this was known as an ottoman sofa, probably imported directly from Constantinople. "This must be ludicrously expensive!" he whispered. "I know because my mother almost fell out with my father when he refused to pay for such a folly."

The large painting hanging above the fireplace showed a naked satyr chasing beautiful bathing nymphs. How fitting, thought Pierre with a tinge of irony.

Two beautiful girls had joined them, one dark, almost certainly of oriental roots with eyes as black as coal and long eyelashes, the other surprisingly fair – her hair almost white – with blue eyes like pools of icy water. She must have originated from the cold countries in the far North. She spoke softly with a lovely accent which betrayed her foreign roots.

Like a conjuror, the dark girl, whose name was Fatma, produced some playing cards and held them in the air. Then she announced the rules of the game: the loser of each round was to take off a piece of his or her clothing! No wonder the room was soon echoing with all sorts of comments and giggles.

Armand grabbed the bottle of wine, but it was already empty, as was the stoneware tankard that had been brought in together with the bottle. He made a face but the dark girl, although already stripped down to her almost transparent underwear, proposed immediately to go and fetch a new bottle.

"This time I promise to bring you something really special, a wine you'll never forget!" she said in her musical voice ,followed by an alluring smile.

Pierre was painfully aware that this unforgettable wine would leave big gaps in his wallet, but why spoil such a wonderful evening? Armand would just chide him again, saying he had the soul of a merchant.

"Go and get the best you can find," he roared, sending her a kiss with his hand and drowning the last of the wine in his cup.

The fair girl had been drinking – if possible – even more wine than they had. Most of the time she had spent giggling and caressing Armand but suddenly she started to speak, with some difficulty, as her speech was slightly slurred.

213

Looking thoughtfully at Pierre whilst trying to fix him with her curious glance, she remarked, "It's absolutely st... strange how one person can resemble another person, I mean... " she burped and her eyes tried once more to focus with difficulty on Pierre. "Your face is so much... like the other one." There was a long pause and the two friends looked at the girl, trying to figure out what she was talking about.

"I don't quite understand you," said Pierre gently, encouraging her to talk.

The girl frowned, apparently she wasn't pleased that he was so stupid. "The one called Henri, of course, but... you seem so much kinder... I mean the other man, he really hurt me." Apparently she was remembering some past incident as a single tear rolled down her face. Then she quickly covered her mouth with her hand, as if the words had escaped against her will.

Pierre and Armand had consumed a good amount of wine but her remark had a chilling – and a very sobering – effect and they exchanged alarmed glances. Armand's thoughts were racing but he decided that it would be smart to pretend not to have noticed the significance of her remark and to keep her talking. Deftly he changed the subject. "Tell, me sweetie, where do you come from?" The girl immediately became more cheerful and told them that she had come from as far as Denmark.

While Armand kept chatting amiably with the Danish girl he walked around the room admiring at the top of his voice the quality of the furniture and the painting while he kept praising the establishment. The girl was happy to oblige and continued to chit chat, tears quickly forgotten while Armand listened and praised the painting above the fireplace. The chilly feeling intensified as closer scrutiny soon revealed why the satyr in the painting had had such a diabolic effect upon him: the grinning satyr had no eyes, they were gaping spyholes instead!

Loudly Armand continued to praise the taste and the quality of the décor until the second waitress came back to join them. She carried a tray with a carafe of expensive Murano glassware filled with a liquid gleaming ruby-red – and four silver cups that had been filled already.

Seeing her busily arranging the tray, Armand whispered quickly to Pierre, "We're in deep shit, we've walked right into a trap, the blonde girl knows your cousin. I bet that the wine will be drugged, look there are even peep holes in the painting, probably your cousin is having the time of his life watching us idiots hopping around here like half-naked idiots!'

"Have a cup of this wine, it's the best that we can offer!" The dark girl smiled alluringly while she held out the cup in his direction. Armand grasped the cup without hesitation but dragged Fatma with his free arm into an embrace, and breathing heavily he exclaimed in a coarse voice, "Fatma, darling, who cares about wine, you're the best that this house has to offer!" and he gave her a long kiss.

Pierre watched Armand's performance with awe. He tried to pretend he was having a great time as well but he felt as if he had been struck a lethal blow. Some friends that Armand had, friends who had lured them right into a trap – and he had no idea how to get out of this room alive!

Cautiously Pierre lifted his eyes and while he studied the painting, he discovered the empty eyes in the face of the satyr. All of a sudden a wild idea popped up in his mind – he had to smile as it seemed so unreal. But they had nothing to lose! Assuming a slightly drunken pose he cried, "We haven't finished our game of cards! I think I lost the last round!" and slowly and seductively he took off his shirt and swung it above his head – making sure that the girls had a good look.

Both girls liked what they saw and when Pierre suddenly threw his shirt high up to the ceiling they screamed with laughter and delight – and found it hilarious when the shirt was caught by an empty candelabrum. Hanging in the air, Pierre's shirt dangled in front of the painting, right in front of the naked satyr.

Armand gave a satisfied wink to his friend. For the time being the curious satyr had been blindfolded.

While the girls had been watching and applauding Pierre's performance, Armand had not remained idle. Quickly he had swapped the cups.

"I'm thirsty as hell!" he crowed. "Where's the fantastic wine my darling Fatma promised me?"

Fatma hastened to oblige and she offered Armand a silver cup filled to the brim accompanied by her most seductive smile.

"Share it with me!" Armand pleaded but she shook her head while she gave the second cup to Pierre, and flirtatiously she took her own full cup and cried, "Santé – let's see who's the first to empty their glass! Show us that you're real men!"

Pierre and Armand pretended to join the fun and all of them drained their cups, Pierre and Armand playing drunk and spilling a good part of it, red wine running down Pierre's naked chest. "Lick it up," Armand commanded in a drunken voice. "Both of you, I want both girls to indulge my friend!"

Proudly the men displayed their empty cups, insisting that the girls now should finish theirs.

Fatma's smile had somehow changed, and looking at them almost condescendingly she said, "If this your *last* wish, let's empty them then," and both girls emptied their cups.

"Let's sit down and continue our game," Armand suggested – ignoring her last comment – and while the girls settled down comfortably on the ottoman, the friends chose two armchairs on the opposite side.

A fresh set of cards was distributed when Armand all of a sudden started to yawn profusely and said in a drowsy voice, "I don't know… what's happening to me… but I suddenly feel soooo tired, strange somehow!"

Pierre joined in and yawned as well. Both of them started to stretch their legs as if they were ready to settle down for a comfortable nap. Fatma watched them with great satisfaction, her eyes shining unnaturally brightly, as if she were extremely excited. They continued playing but both girls seemed to have problems concentrating on their cards. Meanwhile huge dark pools had formed in the ice-blue eyes of the Danish girl, she gave a moan and all of a sudden the cards slipped out of her hand.

Only minutes later the girls' behaviour became distinctly bizarre. They kicked out at thin air, then they seemed to be haunted by invisible ghosts until finally their skin was burning up with heat.

"They've gone quite mad," whispered Armand, "and I think I have a suspicion as to what's going on."

Pierre watched the girls, torn between feelings of horror and morbid fascination: here right in front of his eyes was the evidence that their cups of wine had not only been dosed with some sleeping drug, but this must be the effect of a very potent poison.

The Oriental girl suddenly slumped and fell down on the ottoman whilst her fair companion kept kicking until she collapsed as well, falling almost noiselessly onto the precious Persian rug.

Pierre was still in shock but Armand had jumped up from his chair and quickly he knelt next to the girls, feeling for a heartbeat and examining those strange-looking eyes that were still wide open and seemed curiously awake.

"It's belladonna," he stated matter-of-factly in a low voice. "I know this stuff from my mother, she used to warn my sisters that beauty and death are close relatives when it comes to such drugs."

Aloud he cried in the direction of peep hole, "Fatma, give me some more of this wonderful wine. I feel so strange, but I think I need more wine."

"They'll be listening," he whispered, "but now we must get out of here, fast!"

"Excellent remark, my friend." Pierre whispered back. "Any idea how?"

"I've done my part already!" protested Armand. "Without me, it'd be you lying there!"

"Without *you*," hissed Pierre, "I'd be at home, sitting comfortably in my living room. May I remind your lordship that this folly was your idea?"

Armand waved nonchalantly and whispered back, "Don't waste your breath on silly arguments, you were always the best in our class, now use your brain to get us out of here!"

Pierre looked around, his heart hammering and his brain racing, but there was only one door, and probably the guards would stop them as soon as they tried to leave the room.

He tiptoed to the door – maybe he could peek into the corridor? Pierre reached the door and pressed his ear against the thick wood when he heard the echo of approaching steps in the corridor, steps from booted feet, coming closer very fast.

"Did you say your prayers this morning?" he asked Armand.

"Of course, I did, why do you ask?"

"Because we need help from the Lord now!" Pierre said in a low voice.

The trap had closed.

There had been days in her life when time had raced by for her, lovely days when her greatest concern had been what kind of dress to wear or to choose what kind of ball or dinner to attend. Those days were gone, long gone, it seemed. Julia was sitting in her armchair, not even lost in thoughts but immersed in a sad emptiness that surrounded her like a black shroud. Seconds, minutes and hours ticked away, painfully slowly, as if time itself had almost stopped. Could time simply evaporate?

Once she had heard that some modern scientists were claiming that the Earth was round and kept spinning – well, it couldn't be true! The truth was, nothing moved any more since she had been confined to this tiny room which had become her prison.

Julia remembered the precious hourglass filled with sand that her father had kept in his library. As a child she had loved to play with it, handling the fragile glass with care so as not to risk the wrath of her father. How she had marvelled at the speed of the sand racing through the narrow neck! Once she was older it had even scared her to realize how fast time could melt away.

Approaching steps woke Julia from her day-dreaming. *I wonder who this visitor could be, it seems so early?* Nobody was there to answer, she was talking to herself. She had started this habit of breaking the wall of silence that her prison guards had erected around her.

The sun was still shining outside, hence it was far too early for dinner to be served, whatever terrible food might be called dinner. The sound of the approaching steps seemed far too light for her confessor – she could usually hear him puffing and breathing long before he reached her door and lifted the latch. These steps were light and fast, the steps of a woman, most probably.

Before Julia had been able to finish going through her mental list of potential visitors (a servant, probably, but who and why at this time of the day?) she heard the now so familiar noise of the door being unbolted and with a shock she realized that her oh-so-young and oh-so-beautiful stepmother had taken the pains to grant her the favour of one of her extremely rare visits. Julia would have preferred to be alone; she hated her stepmother with every fibre of her body, and for various reasons.

First of all she was still mourning her own mother, a true gentlewoman with the kindest heart that could be imagined. Julia had never forgiven her father that he had never properly grieved for her mother – and one glance at her far-too-young and far-too-beautiful stepmother had been sufficient to convince Julia that her father had been caught by an ice-cold social climber. A young lady with a beautiful face but with no heart, with a smile that never reached her eyes, a woman of resolve who had started to bully her husband already.

Julia's stepmother had been all sweetness and light during their first encounters, even more so, once she had realized that Julia had inherited her godmother's fortune. But as soon as she had understood that Julia couldn't be manipulated she had dropped her mask of soft-spoken friendliness. Julia was sure that it was mainly her stepmother's machinations that lay at the origin of her present confinement.

Today though, her young stepmother had opted for a new approach: the trust-me-I'm-your-true-friend strategy. All smiles, old conflicts long forgiven and forgotten, she asked Julia with motherly concern if she was feeling well.

"I'm absolutely fine, my dearest Claudia," answered Julia, as if she was replying to a casual social caller. "I hope you're fine as well and find that marriage to a much older man is no burden for you? "

Claudia was all smiles; it would take more than a subtle hint to unsettle her. She was wearing a silk gown of the latest fashion, adorned with Turkish embroidery. It must have cost a fortune. *My money*, thought Julia, clenching her fists, *while I'm sitting here in a gown that is falling to pieces.*

Claudia's long braided hair was dark blonde, the colour of molten honey, even if it was partially covered by a bonnet befitting a married woman. It framed a face of almost perfect proportions. *What a pity*, thought Julia, *that the Lord forgot to give her a heart and a soul.*

"Oh my dearest Julia," twittered her over-friendly stepmother. "Always so concerned about the well-being of your family!" Claudia looked suspiciously at the shabby chairs that had been left in Julia's room and chose to sit down in the one that looked most solid. "I've come to speak to you as a true *friend*, I understand of course that I can never be like a mother to you!"

Tears welled up in Julia's eyes and she hated herself for this weakness, but to hear this heartless person speak about her mother unleashed a storm of emotions inside her: sadness, hate and fury overwhelmed her and it took Julia an enormous amount of self-control not to jump up and strangle this hateful woman.

"Claudia, don't waste your time!" Julia managed to say. "Tell me straight, what do you want from me? Money? My blessing for having married my father, a man you neither appreciate nor love?"

Claudia's eyes flashed. *The woman does have some emotions after all*, thought Julia, satisfied.

219

"Julia, you're still behaving like an obstinate child," her stepmother retorted sharply.

"I'm afraid that your father was right to – finally – show you that he's still master in this house. I've come to speak to you as a friend and to warn you. Today the Abbess of the Convent of Our Lady of the Seas was here and your father has discussed his worries concerning your spiritual well-being with her. He's very much worried about your eternal soul, you should appreciate your father's concerns."

Satisfied with the effect of her speech Claudia paused, and with great delight she noticed that Julia's eyes had widened with fear.

"The Abbess is *absolutely* convinced that your entrance – and your dowry – will be a great asset to her convent. She's willing to assist you to find the way to the True Faith through penitence – it seems that it's absolutely wonderful what a combination of fasting, prayer and isolation in peace can do to purify a soul in search of spiritual guidance."

Claudia let this phrase sink in before continuing, her voice as smooth as honey. "Your father was very much impressed and was eager to make you join the convent immediately but I have been able to convince him that he should have a bit more time to question your heart and your soul. We shall wait, therefore, until we return."

Julia was aware that she should answer and speak up but she didn't know if she could trust her voice. *A convent on an isolated, damp island, her only neighbourhood the largest cemetery in Venice! Even a prison would have been a more attractive prospect!*

Delighted that she had rendered Julia speechless, Claudia stood up and walked towards the door, radiating confidence from head to toes and purring like a cat. "Oh, I was *so* caught up in our conversation that I completely forgot to mention that I'll be leaving next month, in fact travelling with your father for several weeks, my *dearest* Julia. Your cousin in Rome is going to be married and has invited us to join him for the celebrations. We'll be on our way soon – just imagine, we'll have parties, masked balls and absolutely wonderful dinners. Maybe you remember the fabulous food they serve in Rome?"

Claudia's voice suddenly lowered as she turned back and approached Julia who sat frozen in her armchair. In a quiet voice she added, "Either you change your mind and marry the husband your father has chosen for you, or you'll enter the Convent once we're back. That's final. I leave you the coming weeks to decide. But as soon as we're back your fate will be sealed, marriage or convent, I'll not accept any further childish pouting on your part."

She turned to the door and before she left the room she turned once more to Julia and whispered, "By the way, we'll be accompanied by our new young and fantastic-looking groom. All curly hair and the most adorable eyes." She paused a moment before she launched her last remark, knowing how much it would hurt Julia's pride. "I'm sure it's not only his arm that feels like a rod of steel. I have the strange feeling that I'll be presenting your father with his long expected heir soon enough."

Her triumphant laughter lingered and seemed to fill the room, together with a sickening smell of perfume, even long after the door had been closed and carefully bolted.

Julia had to fight the rising nausea as she sat in her chair, breathing heavily, fighting for air. She hadn't dreaded isolation and the stale food – she had been expecting all of that. But being imprisoned in a remote convent as an unwilling bride of Christ would mean being buried alive, her stepmother had found the ultimate weapon to destroy her.

Automatically she calculated how much time was left for her to take a decision. If her father was going to leave with Julia he should be back about two months later, maybe three, if Claudia decided to have some fun and spend the year end in Rome. Julia gritted her teeth; the next bearer of the proud name of Contarini would be a bastard, sired by a groom and born of a soul-less monster.

It had been some time since Julia had prayed for help, but now she sank to her knees, praying fervently not only for her own salvation, but for heaven to bring justice to the house of Contarini.

Pierre was at a loss as to what he should do, and what was worse, he could see in the eyes of his friend that even the astute Armand – the same Armand who used to boast that he could handle any situation – had no clue either. Quickly Pierre grabbed a heavy stoneware jug so as to have a weapon to hand; now he understood why their rapiers and daggers had been collected by the servants before they had been allowed to enter the building! Meanwhile the booted steps came closer and closer – Pierre felt panic rising inside, his body as tense as a coiled spring.

As he held his breath, the steps continued further down the corridor and a deep sigh of relief escaped Pierre – the same sound coming from Armand proved that his friend was as much a nervous wreck as he was.

"We must pretend that the girls are still alive," whispered Armand, and in a loud voice he yelled, "Give me some more wine, where are you, Fatma, light some more candles, it's suddenly so dark…"

Pierre was impressed – Armand's voice was a masterful imitation of slurred whining, the voice of a helpless and drunken man in the grips of a potent drug.

While Armand acted like he was drunk and drugged, making sure that he stood close enough to the painting of the satyr so as to be easily overheard, Pierre meanwhile scrutinized every detail of the room in the desperate hope of finding a way out of their trap.

But there was no window, no hidden door – there weren't even any panelled walls that might hide a secret door. Pierre was close to despair. Escaping through the corridor seemed to remain their only option, but an option that gave him the creeps as the corridor and the staircase were narrow and it didn't take much imagination to realize they must be heavily guarded.

He tried to remember the details of his conversation earlier on with Armand's friends (some friends they were, he thought angrily) who had mentioned that they had arrived by boat directly from the Isle Saint Louis. This meant that the river must be close by.

Mechanically he had lifted the large, square Gobelin tapestry on the wall. The expensive tapestry depicted a bucolic scene of the paradisiacal Garden of Eden with a strikingly buxom Eve biting into a tempting red apple. The unknown artist had succeeded in creating a remarkably realistic scene showing the devious snake turning its charms on its gullible victim. But Pierre had no eyes for artistic accomplishments, time was of the essence. Peeping behind the tapestry, Pierre disturbed a thriving colony of spiders. Spiders of all things! He hated spiders. Ah, but didn't this look like a window frame?

Hope started to grow, but Pierre had no choice but to push bravely through the dusty cobwebs with his bare hands in order to inspect the frame behind the Gobelin. To his immense relief he discovered a smallish window – just about big enough to allow a man of his size to escape.

Pierre had lost the exact notion of time but he knew that it must be around midnight, maybe later. The window must have been forgotten and closed for ages and Pierre had no option but to tackle the disgusting task of tearing off the dusty layers of cobwebs in order to try to open it and to peep outside. Scuttling spiders rushed in all directions, falling on his breeches and touching his skin. Pierre almost screamed.

As might have been expected, the window was stuck. Long forgotten about, it had probably not been opened for many years or decades. Pierre rattled at the latch and frame with all his force, despair giving him hitherto unknown strength. At the same time, he listened intently for any word of warning from Armand as he tried to force the window open.

Suddenly there seemed to be a ray of hope, Pierre thought that the wooden frame moved a little bit! With all his strength he dragged and rattled again but the window remained stuck – and worse, the latch broke. Utterly frustrated and close to tears, Pierre threw the latch to the floor and punched the window pane in anger. Immediately the pane gave way, as the leaded fixings were tired and worn. Frantically Pierre ripped out the panes and the lead fittings, cursing his own stupidity at having wasted so much time.

Balmy night air streamed into the room through the open window – what a relief after the clouds of dust that had gathered behind the tapestry! Pierre tried to hold it back, but he had to sneeze; the sound seemed to echo like an explosion through the small room. The air was full of the smells of the near-by river. Pierre peeked outside, but his feeling of triumph was short-lived – there was nothing to be seen.

Outside the blackest of darkness swallowed all light and form. All Pierre could detect was the shadow of an anaemic moon shrouded by dense clouds high above him and he could hear the close but dangerous gurgling sound of rapidly flowing water. The Seine must be flowing right below their room. Pierre swallowed hard, fighting back panic. How convenient, he contemplated, to dispose of the bodies of unwanted visitors directly into the river. Crestfallen he decided to show his discovery to Armand, although he was at a loss to see how this window could be of any help.

223

Still puzzling over his dilemma, Pierre all of a sudden heard Armand whistle softly. Cautiously, Pierre peeked from behind the Gobelin into the room and his blood froze in his veins. Armand had sought cover behind one of the ottomans. Pierre watched two men with rapiers in their hands striding almost casually into the room: his cousin Henri was accompanied by a good-looking man of Mediterranean complexion.

Both of them had a smirk on their face, obviously having come with the intention of finishing the evening with a bit of what they considered to be fun. Henri was the first to enter the room – a man very sure of himself – but suddenly he stopped and frowned as he spotted Fatma lying motionless on the first ottoman close to the entrance.

"Look, Nicolas!" he exclaimed. The man called Nicolas bent over Fatma and now Henri noticed the second body of the fair waitress lying on the carpet.

"I'm afraid you'll need to write off some of your precious assets," Henri commented acidly.

Nicolas pressed his face against Fatma's breast, looked up, and Pierre could see that he was fuming with rage.

"I don't think that she's dead – yet. But if ever she survives it will be nothing less than a miracle. I wonder how it could have happened, I gave her very clear instructions and she's – she was – a very clever girl."

"I wonder where our pigeons are hiding, it's time they were culled," answered Henri.

"Indeed!" cried Nicolas. "I shall have my revenge! Anyhow, they must be in this room. I had the corridor watched all the time and we saw them with our own eyes playing their silly games with the girls! Let's finish them off."

Pierre shivered. They obviously knew that their conversation was being overheard by their victims – and they seemed to love their little game.

Pierre could see Armand glancing at him in despair. It could only be a matter of minutes, if not seconds, until Henri found him. The back of the second ottoman was by no means an ideal hiding place.

"Look, what have we here," said Henri in a cheerful voice. "I think I found one of the pigeons, it's got rather muscular legs though," and he pointed to the ottoman with his sword.

Armand lay rigid. He had quickly decided that his only defence could be to fake being poisoned and to pretend that he had shared the wine with the girls and not to move.

224

Henri walked closer and looked down at Armand as Pierre's heart started to race. He was still hiding behind the Gobelin tapestry and he had rarely seen his cousin so close. Henri's eyes were sparkling, sparkling in joyful anticipation of murder.

Nicolas joined Henri and stared down at Armand who dared not breathe. Lifting his rapier, he said, "His skin looks too light, he should be glowing red if he swallowed enough of the stuff, let me finish him off to make sure that this chapter is closed, you go and look behind the chairs and the chest there to see if pigeon number two is hiding there. Let's make you a Marquis tonight!"

Henri grinned and nodded as he walked to the other side of the room.

Pierre had no time to think properly or devise a clever plan – he had to act fast or Armand would be dead. A wave of rage swept over Pierre. He would not have his best friend murdered in cold blood in front of his eyes. Using the benefit of surprise he rushed from his hiding-place, grabbed a silver candelabrum with several burning candles and struck Nicolas hard on the head with all his might.

Nicolas had heard a noise but although he raised his sword immediately in defence, the heavy blow from behind struck him down like a felled tree. Furious, Henri turned around, his sword ready for a fight. His face was distorted, transformed into a frightening mask of hate and scorn as he jumped forward, ready to plunge his rapier into Pierre who faced him, bare-chested and defenceless.

But now Armand had sprung into action. The poisoned corpse came to life, and quick as lightning he jumped up and rammed his knee hard into Henri's groin. Henri howled. Stumbling and blinded by the sudden pain he tripped over Nicolas who still lay motionless on the floor. Pierre didn't miss this opportunity and swinging his heavy candelabrum like an axe he hit out with all of his force at Henri's head. Once again, the unusual weapon proved to be highly efficient, Henri's head sank down and he dropped on top of Nicolas with blood gushing out of a large wound.

"Good job, congratulations!" panted Armand, "but the question remains – how do we get out of here? In a matter of minutes all hell will break loose here, they must have heard us fighting!"

As if Armand's words were a self-fulfilling prophecy, they could indeed hear the unmistakable sound of approaching booted footsteps. But something else suddenly came to their attention – the acrid scent of smoke had started to fill the room and was tickling their nostrils. The fallen candles from the candelabrum had set fire to the room, and greedy flames were already licking at the ottoman – in a matter of minutes the whole room would be ablaze.

Pierre swallowed hard. There was only one solution left – and he didn't like it, he didn't like it at all. "Fancy taking a bath tonight?" he asked his friend.

Armand looked at his friend as if Pierre were insane. "Take a bath?" he echoed Pierre's question.

Pierre couldn't answer as the door burst open and two armed servants stormed into the room. In the corridor the noise of more approaching footsteps could already be heard. Without offering any further explanation Pierre dragged his friend behind the Gobelin tapestry, pointed to the open window and cried, "This is the only way out, follow me, Armand – and pray!"

His last words were barely audible, as Pierre had started to climb out of the room. But Pierre's hope of climbing onto the roof and finding support for his feet was immediately shattered as the slate roof proved to be steep and slippery with moss. Yet there was no time left to think properly or even to be scared. Armand didn't hesitate either, as their pursuers were hot on their heels. Following right behind, he pushed Pierre's leg over the sill of the tiny window. Taken by surprise and losing his balance Pierre found himself shooting down the slippery slate roof, until he reached – only seconds later – the thatched roof of a neighbouring building. Desperately Pierre tried to grab something, to hold on to the thatch, but to no avail, as gaining ever more speed he slid helplessly into the blackest of darkness. Falling into the river suddenly seemed the best alternative open to them.

All of a sudden, however, his descent was brutally stopped; his belt must have caught on a peg in the roof. Panting heavily and trying to fight his panic, Pierre was dangling on the roof while he tried desperately to find something to hold on to. His bare chest was scratched and bleeding and it hurt like hell. Although the roof was covered by a layer of soft and damp moss, his descent had been a most painful ride. Pierre succeeded in digging his hands and feet into the reeds of the thatched roof and finally managed to hold on. Pierre breathed deeply. What now?

Regrettably his respite proved to be short-lived, as only seconds later Armand arrived and crashed with his full weight against Pierre's body. The peg snapped, Pierre cried out in surprise, opened his hands – and once more both friends found themselves sliding in unison further down the roof, plunging into the black abyss.

For Pierre had time had stopped. Did he fall for seconds, minutes or an eternity?

When he hit the surface of the river it felt like hitting a brick wall. Nothing had prepared him for such an experience. But the brick wall must have yielded as he dived deeply into the surprisingly cold water that flowed with a strong current, wild and very different to the tame rivers he had experienced before.

Pierre was paralysed by the shock, yet a tiny part of his brain must still have been working as some inner voice seemed to scream at him, "Move, *swim!*" Instinctively he understood that fighting against the strong current of the river would be sheer madness, so Pierre concentrated all of his efforts on one single task: to rise up to the surface, as he needed to breathe – desperately.

How lucky that Armand had taught him to swim – and how awkward he had felt the first time Armand had made him undress and enter a river! Pierre's breeches were heavy with water, as unfolding and floating like heavy sails they hampered him greatly. His boots had been the first things to go when they had been playing their silly game with the girls. This now proved to be a stroke of luck, as they would have weighed him down, perhaps with fatal consequences. Struggling hard against the current, Pierre succeeded in coming up to the surface, then stuck his head out of the water – and *breathed.*

Swimming alone at night in a vast river is an eerie experience at the best of times and not to be recommended for the faint-hearted – to the exhausted Pierre it seemed his ultimate nightmare had come true. Having regained some breath his brain started to function again, but in Pierre's despair all his mind could do was conjure up terrifying images of what might happen to him. The Seine has often been dubbed the lifeblood of Paris, but Pierre was only too aware that it provided not only water and transport for all kinds of people and traders, it also carried dead bodies, served as Paris's sewer and had the unpleasant reputation of being infested with all kinds of vermin, among them enormous rats. Pierre hated rats.

And then, just to remind Pierre that he was not alone in those dark waters, something touched his skin. A fleeting sensation only – it felt thin and slippery – like the tail of a huge rat. Terrified, Pierre forgot to move his arms and legs. This proved to be a fatal mistake, which he regretted immediately, as for a second time he plunged involuntarily below the water's surface and it took much frantic paddling to get his head out of the water he detested so much. To make things worse he was now aware of the fatigue spreading quickly through his body like a chilling paralysis.

Unconsciously Pierre had followed the current of the river, more floating than actively swimming. Total darkness had reigned until now, but all of a sudden some clouds cleared and the first feeble rays of moonlight danced tentatively on the river. Slowly the surface of the river became visible, then blurred shapes of houses and buildings appeared out of the darkness. Pierre's flame of hope – almost extinct – was rekindled, and as the moonlight became stronger and revealed details of the nearby riverbanks, his hope started to grow. Maybe he wasn't quite doomed after all.

Pierre guessed that he must be drifting in the direction of the Ile Saint Louis, right in the heart of Paris. Gathering all his strength, he started to swim in the direction of the silhouettes of houses that promised salvation, dry clothes... and sleep. Someone in heaven must have answered his prayers, or maybe fate had decided that it was time to grant Pierre some respite. The dark clouds parted and the blurred dark shadows suddenly transformed into shapes of houses, a bridge, and then a bit further on, the belfries of churches seemed to detach themselves from the darkness and became visible. Pierre could even identify the imposing silhouette of the cathedral of Notre Dame looming on the horizon. To his immense joy he also realized that the bank of the river was now fairly close.

Was this real or was he imagining things? Pierre listened intently, but he couldn't suppress the feeling of joy and relief that streamed through his body like a wave of invigorating warmth! The familiar voice of his friend Armand was echoing across the river. Familiar enough, but certainly less cocksure than usual. Pierre tried to focus his glance, looking hard in the direction of the voice he knew so well, a voice that sounded all the sweeter at this moment. Pierre could even discern Armand's muscular figure standing on a near-by jetty.

"Pierre, is that you? Answer me!"

Beyond any doubt, this certainly was the anxious voice of his best friend – his ordeal would soon be over.

There is one undeniable advantage of swimming in a river at night: it allows one to shed tears without inhibition. Pierre had never felt so relieved in his entire life. With all of his strength he cried back and waved, new confidence and vigour flooding through his tired and numb body as he paddled as fast as he could in the direction of the voice that kept encouraging him.

Armand was waiting impatiently as he saw his friend's head bobbing up and down in the swirling currents of the river. Sometimes the sparse moonlight seemed to swallow the tiny figure completely and in those seconds Armand's heart almost stopped with fear. By no means an accomplished swimmer, Pierre paddled like a new-born puppy. Normally Armand would have mocked him but tonight he had only one wish: to get Pierre back to safety as quickly as possible. Rarely had Armand felt as worried as when he completely lost sight of Pierre, or so relieved when the clouds cleared and his friend miraculously appeared.

The Church had always taught him that hell was a place of purgatory and the hottest of fires, but Armand wasn't so sure any more. Tonight it seemed to him that hell was an abandoned and very cold, silent place of utter darkness, just as he had experienced right now. He rushed forward and helped his friend out of the water, a manoeuvre that was complicated by the fact that the old and rarely used jetty was made of rotten wood covered by slippery moss.

Pierre was feeling exuberant, yet utterly exhausted. Heavily he leaned on Armand as he hugged his friend.

Armand embraced his wet friend and put on a brave face but secretly he was extremely worried. Miraculously they had escaped a deadly trap, but the next challenge was already ahead of them.

It was an almost balmy, late summer night but they would need to get into dry clothes quickly if they didn't want to catch a serious cold. Whereas Armand still felt capable of walking several miles, Pierre had only recently recovered from his accident in Blois; beyond any doubt he was the weak link now.

Trying to sound cheerful, Armand said, "I feel like a short stroll into town, it's a bit dark and quiet here, what do you think?"

Pierre laughed and answered, still breathing heavily. "You're absolutely right, I can think of far more inviting places to spend our time!" The last words were drowned in a loud sneeze.

Quickly Armand prompted him, "Come on, let's get moving and warm up!" wrapping his right arm around Pierre to keep him warm and steady.

By sheer good fortune they must have landed right inside the city walls. As soon as they had climbed over the wall surrounding the yard of the house which owned the jetty they immediately hit a cobbled street that was lined with the typical houses of downtown Paris. Armand had no clue where the narrow street might be leading them, but he hoped to find an inn or guesthouse – they badly needed some shelter and dry clothes. The two friends limped rather than walked down the street while Armand kept chatting with false gaiety to keep Pierre's spirits up – and to divert himself from worrying too much about his friend and the dangers of Paris at midnight.

Armand was still chatting with Pierre when he heard the alarming noise of screeching metal above him. Instinctively he drew Pierre into the shelter of the next entrance. Not a second too late, as the contents of a well-filled chamber pot were emptied from a window above them directly onto the street – a second later and they'd have been covered!

"A near miss – I told you Paris by night can be very dangerous," quipped Armand, and cursed the owner of the house, who gave a filthy reply, withdrew and closed his blinds.

"I appreciate your wisdom, my friend. It's just a pity that we forgot such wise words when we entered the gambling den," answered Pierre with chattering teeth.

They had reached the middle of a winding and narrow street when the sound of several horsemen suddenly echoed through the street, first only faintly, but much too rapidly for Armand's liking, it turned into a crescendo of deafening thunder as iron horseshoes pounded the surface of the cobbled street. A cavalcade of horsemen was approaching at full speed, and a cacophony of loud voices echoed from the façades of the houses while their torches shed a ghostly light, projecting huge distorted shadows onto the street and the houses.

Feverishly Armand tried to figure out what to do and where to hide. But there was nowhere to go, no hiding place in sight and in any case, Pierre was far too exhausted to run. Whatever plan of action Armand might have come up with, it was too late anyhow – they had been spotted.

A loud, imperious voice bellowed across the street, "Stop, in the name of the King, and identify yourself!"

To his amazed relief, Armand knew this voice very well. He had never thought that he'd ever welcome its sound so much.

"With the greatest of pleasure!" he cried back. "Here's your loving and devoted cousin, forever at your service, my dearest François de Toucy!"

François reached the two friends and dismounted from his horse. Incredulously he looked Armand and Pierre up and down until one his typically sardonic smiles slowly appeared on his face.

"Gentlemen," and he made a mocking bow towards the group of musketeers, clad in the uniform of the King, who had gathered around them, swords drawn and ready to pick a fight, "May I take this opportunity to present to you His Grace, the Duke of Hertford, or should I say the most noble Marquis de Beauvoir and my little cousin, the most noble Armand de Saint Paul."

His voice was dripping with sarcasm and the musketeers viewed with total disbelief the two youngsters standing in front of them. Pierre looked like an escaped convict with his bare chest and soaked breeches. Armand, not inspiring any more confidence, wore a loose wet shirt and sagging breeches. Both of them wore only dirty stockings, and were bootless.

The musketeers were convinced that their officer must be joking, after all, wasn't he well known for his strange sense of humour?

Pierre was so worn out that he completely missed the irony of this presentation and automatically he bowed elegantly, as if meeting a group of musketeers half naked at night were nothing unusual. As he bowed, he sneezed loudly and this seemed to spur François de Toucy into action.

"Stop smirking or I'll teach you good behaviour with my whip," he ordered his men, who responded immediately to his command by putting on suitably impassive faces. François looked at them, obviously content with their reaction and continued, "Being true and noble Christians and living according to the principles of charity, it will be our pleasure – undoubtedly – to share our shirts

230

with you," he drawled, looking at his men who suddenly looked so much less sure of themselves. "Ah, well, what I actually mean is *your* shirts – and breeches, of course." A faint sound of muttered protest went through the group but François de Toucy only glared at his soldiers in disbelief and the protest died down immediately.

"If anyone is of a different opinion, he's welcome to come forward but in this case I suggest that he should walk back to the Louvre on his own. Shirtless, of course."

Giving short and precise orders, two of his men lost their shirts and another two their breeches – the latter having to endure all kinds of filthy jokes from their companions as soon as their captain was out of earshot. Pierre couldn't care less about their reactions. What bliss it was to pull on a dry shirt and get rid of the dripping breeches! Grateful and dead tired he settled on the back of a horse and holding himself tight to François de Toucy they sped back to the Louvre Palace.

Inside de Toucy's cramped tiny office Pierre slumped into an armchair and only seconds later a fascinated Armand saw his friend snoring, his long legs sprawled out, head lolling to one side.

"Now tell me what really happened," François asked his cousin. "And tell me the truth straight away, don't worry about what I might tell your father later – this is a different story!"

Armand sighed. His motivation to come forward and confess the details of their nightly adventure to his father had indeed been rather low. He grinned broadly and accepted with pleasure the tankard of ale that his cousin thrust in his direction. Comfortably, he settled into an armchair close to the snoring Pierre and started his detailed account of the events of this night.

Strangely enough François de Toucy seemed to be quite well acquainted with the gambling den, of course – as he pointed out with a twinkle in his eye – for professional reasons only. "Cardinal de Richelieu always suspected that the owner of this gambling den was the mastermind of a criminal network, but we never managed to get enough proof to start official proceedings. As even a close relative of His Majesty is known to be a regular guest, nobody dared get his fingers burned…"

Gaston d'Orléans, of course, what a charming relative…

A short nod from Armand showed François that he had understood, no need to pronounce the name of the King's brother aloud inside the Louvre palace, brimming with spies of all factions.

231

Armand reached the part of his narrative where they had realized that Henri de Beauvoir must be staying there and his discovery that the wine had been poisoned when François jumped up and cried, "You mean that scoundrel Henri is still in Paris?!"

Excitedly he shouted orders and seconds later his small office was crammed with fellow musketeers. François gave short and precise orders and while he was reaching for his sword he turned to Armand and explained. "We'll ride immediately to the suspect inn. I have never located the true entrance, the few times I have been there I arrived by boat and they made sure that I wouldn't recognize where exactly we had landed. If we're lucky, Henri might still be there; from what you're telling me, Pierre must have taught him a good lesson."

He started to laugh. "Henri de Beauvoir felled by an escaped schoolboy armed with a candelabrum – what an infamous defeat for this proud devil!"

Armand leapt to his feet too. "Get me a pair of boots and my coat and I'll accompany you, I wouldn't miss this for anything in the world!"

François looked sceptically at him, but Armand would not accept any refusal. He finally got his way when he pointed out that he'd be the only one capable of guiding them once they'd entered the labyrinth-like building.

François quickly gathered an impressive number of musketeers on duty although they were already approaching the wee hours of the morning. Everyone was keen for a good fight and in the best of spirits. François had made it clear that they'd be facing an accomplished fighter – what a great occasion to earn a promotion! Minutes later the group of armed musketeers was speeding down the dark streets to the east of Paris. The horsemen were unusually silent, only the echo of the pounding hooves and the whinnying of the horses could be heard in the silent streets of Paris.

Armand gasped as he detected a strange orange glow on the horizon. Soon his worst fears were realized, and the closer they approached their final destination, the more it became apparent that a huge fire was raging right here in the poor suburbs of Paris. Soon their progress was hampered by worried citizens in their night attire, crowding the streets, brutally ripped from their peaceful sleep by the sound of church bells ringing insistently.

People had formed chains to pass buckets of water, men were swearing wildly as women and children were trying their best to help, some crying in fear, and some, bizarrely, seeming to be relishing the atmosphere of danger and adventure.

Mercilessly using their whips to make a path through the crowds, the musketeers reached the street that Armand had indicated, only to find a row of houses burning like torches and crumbling in the light of red hot flames. Plenty of houses were already burnt down, nothing left but black timber beams pointing into the smoke-filled air like half-cremated bones.

There would be no fight tonight. The most famous gambling den of Paris had been turned into a smoking pile of ash and charred wooden logs.

François de Toucy looked at the ruined house, shrugged, and in his typical drawl he commented, "Gentlemen, there's no work left for us, let's return to the Louvre, it seems the Lord has decided to dispense justice before us!"

Three lonely horsemen were riding at their leisure along the endlessly winding road, leaving small clouds of dust behind them.

Pierre rubbed his eyes. The dust irritated him greatly and a growing thirst had been tormenting him for a considerable time. Somehow he had expected to travel south straight to Marseille and then sail comfortably on a boat to Venice – wouldn't it be logical to travel by sea to the most important city port of Europe?

Armand had looked at his friend as if he were somewhat retarded when Pierre had blithely suggested choosing this route. After hectic searching and digging through piles of musty maps of questionable origin in the vast library of the Palais de Beauvoir, they finally discovered a map of Europe that looked reasonably trustworthy.

Pierre had been forced to concede with his own eyes that the shortest way to Venice would lead them over land, right across the dreaded Alps. Suddenly he understood why Armand had vigorously opposed any suggestion of delaying their departure or making a detour via Reims. Crossing the mountains in winter was no joke, he told Pierre sternly, and they'd risk remaining stuck for several weeks – if not months – if they attempted to cross the Alps too late in the year.

Their journey had led them from Paris straight toward the Swiss cantons. During this time the travellers had been blessed with good weather as most of the time a generous late autumn sunshine had accompanied their journey. Today once again golden sunlight was pouring down on the three horsemen, with a glow of such intensity that it seemed to wrap the landscape and the mountains in a halo of golden light.

I bet the light shines like this in Paradise, but I hope there's more water than this to quench my thirst.

"You're daydreaming again," Armand teased his friend.

"It's so wonderful here," Pierre sighed. "Just imagine London with its pouring rain at this time of year, but I admit that a bit of shade and cool wine would be just perfect. Let's have a break," he pleaded, pointing at a group of trees casting inviting shadows.

The lack of rain had turned the dry grass into hard, straw-like yellow tufts, but the vineyards around them were glowing in vivid colours of red and gold and it was a huge relief to sit down and enjoy the beautiful scenery. Jean was already bustling around them and quickly produced a flask of wine, some bread and slices of sausage and hard yellow cheese while they settled down.

Jean had been begging to accompany his master but Pierre and Armand had decided in unison that they'd prefer to enter Venice alone and incognito. Reluctantly they had come to the conclusion that they would be far less conspicuous travelling alone. Travelling in the company of a servant – especially a servant with dark skin – would risk drawing too much attention.

Thus the final plan was to enter Venice, familiarize themselves with the city and then carefully start socializing with the local gentry. According to Armand's experience, affable young gentlemen ready to spend a lot of money were always welcome in the best circles. Of course, they'd try to meet Julia, as they were optimistic that she could be a valuable asset when it came to find the missing sapphire ring. The last information that the friends had received about the famous ring came from their banker, Monsieur Piccolin. He had been certain that the sapphire ring must be in the possession of a Venetian noble family related to the present doge. Julia, being a member of one of the most prominent families of this proud city, must surely move in the highest circles of society. Typically, Armand did not harbour the slightest doubt that Julia might once more fall under his spell and agree to help them.

Jean had been scandalized when he heard about their plan to travel without him. He couldn't believe that they were serious. He begged them, painted vivid scenes of all kinds of horrible disasters that would befall his master if he had to travel on his own. Finally Jean employed his deadliest weapon: he had put on the face of a dutiful martyr, addressed Pierre incessantly as 'Your Grace' – and Pierre had given in. Armand had shut his mouth and only rolled his eyes in despair. So typical of Pierre to relent – he was far too kind to his servants.

As a compromise Pierre had allowed Jean to accompany them as far as Lausanne where they would leave Jean behind, take a ferry across Lake Geneva and travel on to the city of Geneva where they planned to visit some of Armand's distant relatives. Pierre had stopped wondering long ago how many relatives the Saint Paul clan possessed, not only in France but scattered all over Europe. After Geneva they would have to tackle the Alps and then travel straight on to Venice, just stopping briefly in Milan.

"I have heard that Milan is a great city, I think we'll have fun there," Armand had declared, eyes bright with gleeful anticipation.

"Same kind of fun as we had in Paris maybe," retorted Pierre. "You won't get me into trouble this time!" he warned his friend.

"How can you be so negative?" protested Armand hotly. "I thought we had a great adventure – and you have to admit, the girls were first class!"

"And you're hopeless," sighed Pierre.

Jean had accepted their proposal to accompany them until Lausanne with surprisingly good grace. Secretly Pierre expected some further tantrums when the time to say good-bye was upon them. Since Pierre's last adventure, Jean had behaved more like a dog defending his master than a dutiful servant.

Pierre's thoughts returned to reality, and taking a last sip of the delicious wine he saw that Armand was already preparing his horse for departure. Pierre watched his friend lazily. "I guess there are no excuses left. We'll have to continue our journey."

"So true, your Grace, so true! Better move your backside then, I want to see Lausanne in daylight!"

Pierre made a face and got going.

In the end it was Pierre who first made out a blurred shadow on the horizon.

"I think we're approaching Lausanne!" he cried.

Eager to discover more they pushed their horses faster and soon they could indeed see more and more clearly the silhouette of the imposing Cathedral of Lausanne against the breathtaking scenic panorama of the blue lake surrounded by towering mountains already crowned with white caps of snow.

"It's certainly beautiful, but you'd better be on your best behaviour, for once," Pierre warned his friend. "Your cousin François told me that Lausanne is a city which is as famous for its rich merchants as it is infamous for the dreaded Calvinist zealots. They seem to be a dreary lot. The slightest straying from the path of what they consider religious enlightenment will be severely punished."

Armand made a face. "Why are you telling me this only now – who wants to visit a city full of hypocrites with sour faces? I had enough of this during our monastery days in Reims!"

"It was *your* decision to choose this route, my noble lord!" answered Pierre sweetly.

They passed the city gates without any hold-ups, in any case, the soldiers posted at the gate didn't seem to match François de Toucy's story of a city of zealous ascetics. Fat bellies protruded over their breeches and nobody seemed particularly bothered about the visitors arriving from France. Close to the imposing gothic Cathedral – now converted into a protestant church – they found a pleasant guesthouse. Delighted to make a break they stopped and found invitingly clean rooms. Pierre was beginning to like this city.

An excellent lunch was served by a young waitress. To Armand's disappointment she was dressed entirely in a dark and rather shapeless garment, her hair hidden by a chaste bonnet. Although her attire was designed to deter any undue male attention, the effect was strangely the reverse: her dowdy dress seemed to direct all of the attention to her beautiful face, highlighted by blue eyes the colour of cornflowers in full bloom.

Armand was immediately spellbound by her beauty and Pierre had to kick his foot hard under the table as the innkeeper – probably the maid's father – gave a furious look when he saw that Armand touched her arm.

"You're in Calvin's country!" hissed Pierre. "They'll be more than delighted to burn any catholic at the stake if he's behaving immorally!"

"Maybe it would be worthwhile?" Armand sighed, watching the girl disappear.

The furious-looking father was now approaching their table.

"Anything else I can get you?" he asked in a menacing tone, glaring at Armand.

"I was just discussing with my friend if we could attend the church service tomorrow morning, we have heard so much about the famous pastors who teach the true faith!" Pierre answered quickly, in what he hoped to be a suitably pious tone.

The innkeeper still looked suspicious yet he did seem a little mollified. To Pierre's growing amazement he loudly started to praise the Lord, who had surely enlightened his guests. Then he looked straight into Pierre's eyes and added, "I had suspected – the Lord forbid – that I might have given shelter to heathens – or worse: French papists!" He breathed the last word with a mix of awe and contempt as if the very devil himself had dared to visit his humble tavern. Taken in by Pierre's request to attend the service, he not only indicated the time of church service tonight, he even offered to guide them personally to the Cathedral. "It's a special sermon, it'll last at least three hours! The good Lord has blessed us with a visit from enlightened preachers from Geneva," he added proudly.

Pierre saw panic light up in Armand's eyes; Armand had never been a lover of church services, an aversion dating back to their monastery days. Pierre had the greatest difficulty not to burst into loud laughter. Three hours of sheer martyrdom were awaiting his friend!

"We'll be delighted to join you!" he answered quickly, before Armand could intervene and the innkeeper smiled, although he tried to suppress his smile immediately. Yet it seemed obvious that saving two souls must have made his day.

If the friends had hoped that the innkeeper might forget or be distracted from his mission, they had misjudged him. Dressed in sombre black and a clean shirt he knocked at their door on time and dutifully, rather than enthusiastically, they followed their host to the Great Cathedral. The huge church nave was already packed with people, and not a single seat seemed to have been left empty.

Cautiously, Pierre looked around and was astonished to see that apart from a big cross that dominated the nave, there was almost no decoration, no vivid or edifying pictures of the saints, no statues adorning the columns, and the only paintings left on the walls or ceilings seemed centuries old, almost fading into oblivion. Pierre had never seen such a plain church before, it came as quite a shock to him.

The waiting congregation of churchgoers seemed strangely quiet and subdued and Pierre found the strange atmosphere unnerving. He looked around. All of the churchgoers were dressed in simple and unbecoming dresses of dark colours, a sea of black and brown clothes.

They look as if they're already prepared to sacrifice themselves for the purification of their souls. This really doesn't look like it's going to be fun.

Three seemingly endless hours or more later – Pierre had long lost count of time – he had gained intimate knowledge about the terrifying but ever so persuasive powers of evil, could precisely describe hell and damnation waiting for those who dared to stray from the path of righteousness, but could no longer sit or kneel. To his surprise the service was held entirely in French.

Pierre's bottom seemed to be on fire from sitting on the hard and narrow bench, but the famous pastor from Geneva was still preaching, almost screaming at the spellbound congregation. Carried away by his own sermon, it seemed Pierre's suffering would never come to an end. Cautiously Pierre looked to his side, expecting Armand either to be asleep or desperate to flee the church, but to his great surprise his friend was looking with rapt admiration in the direction of the preaching pastor.

Experience told Pierre that it was highly unlikely that a sudden conversion had occurred and, scrutinizing him more closely, he found that Armand's eyes were indeed turned in the direction of the pulpit, but in fact Armand was enjoying an excellent view to the side where the women and children were sitting in pious rapture. The beautiful daughter of the innkeeper was not only sitting in the first row, she had somehow managed to loosen her bonnet and a lock of her blonde hair fell across her black dress, glowing like spun gold in the twilight of the church.

After a last thundering appeal from the pastor to avoid the temptations of evil or risk eternal damnation they were finally released and Pierre swayed out of the

Cathedral amongst a rapt crowd. Not only did his spirit refuse to feel elated, his body felt tortured, and he couldn't decide if his knees or back were hurting most.

The next day the two friends roamed around the small city of Lausanne, home to approximately twenty thousand citizens, as the innkeeper had proudly informed them. Tired of riding along endless roads Armand had suggested hiring a boat and ferrying over to Geneva.

Pierre was immediately enthusiastic "That's a great idea – you're a genius! It'll save us a lot of time and will be a nice change."

"Of course I'm a genius," answered Armand. "Finally you seem to have realized the truth!"

Pierre was still grinning when the innkeeper suddenly appeared. He must have overheard their conversation. "I can recommend a pious boatman who will look after you at a very reasonable price and can bring you to Geneva quickly and in safety."

"That sounds like an excellent proposal," answered Armand. "Let's meet your friend this afternoon and see if he can offer us his services!"

They arrived at the agreed time in the small lakeside port of Lausanne where several modest barges and smelly fishing boats were moored. Asking their way around, they finally found a tall man of indeterminate age with a weather-beaten square face, bushy eyebrows and a mop of unruly black hair speckled with the first strands of grey. His dark eyes were assessing the friends with a most irritating intensity.

Pierre had to suppress a small shiver. *He may be very pious, but I certainly don't like the way he's looking at us…*

Armand had secretly hoped for a hard but entertaining round of bargaining but he found himself quickly disappointed. The gigantic boatman named a very reasonable price, but wouldn't budge by not even a *sous*, until Armand gave in and meekly accepted the proposed deal. The boatman agreed to sail to Geneva tomorrow.

"That leaves us a full day to explore the city," exclaimed Armand, full of optimism. "Let's go and have a look!"

Sadly enough they quickly came to the conclusion that there was nothing to explore. The city was as small as it was neat and orderly. The few women and girls attending the shops or walking around the streets were hideously unattractive. Pierre started to suspect that the nicer members of the female sex had been banned from their sight – it simply couldn't be possible that a city of this size could be inhabited entirely by women that were either too old or too ugly.

They faced a boring afternoon spent hanging around in the inn. Armand had innocently proposed a game of cards in the tavern but a young waiter had rushed to their table and urged them to stop immediately if they didn't want to end up in the pillory being flogged. The friends had therefore gone up to their room to play cards but had been looking forward to dinner to break the monotony.

In the evening dinner was served again by the beautiful daughter of the house, but she seemed very shy and didn't respond at all to Armand's overtures. Armand was annoyed; he wasn't used to being rejected and the less she seemed to react to his words and glances, the more he seemed to be on fire. Pierre registered his friend's frustration with amusement – being rejected for once would teach him a lesson!

"I'm sure she'll join us later in our room," Armand whispered as they went upstairs. "I think that she truly likes me, but she's scared to admit her feelings because her father guards her like a jealous dragon!"

But the minutes and hours ticked away without a knock on the door, in fact not only was their guesthouse unusually quiet, the whole city seemed to be sleeping; only the chiming of the church bells broke the silence at regular intervals.

Visibly annoyed, Armand finally extinguished the candle, and turning over in bed he added defiantly, "Stop smirking, after all, she wasn't *that* beautiful – even a bit dull if you looked closer. I was just kind of bored, otherwise I wouldn't even have noticed her!"

Pierre was wise enough to keep his thoughts to himself.

"I have never felt so relieved to leave a city," Armand confessed, once they had reached the small port in Lausanne. "I'm afraid, too much rectitude has a completely depressing effect on me," he added with a deep sigh. "I prefer a bit of fun and excitement!"

"But our teachers said: you'll never pass the gates of Heaven if you don't repent!" Pierre retorted, imitating the tone of their former teachers.

"Would you honestly want to join this dowdy crowd in Heaven? They'd bore me to death!" answered Armand with a shudder.

"They couldn't!" Pierre answered, meeting his friend's uncomprehending look. "We'd be dead already!"

"Even worse, just imagine: eternal boredom! I really hope that paradise has more to offer than singing praise all day long. It would be a shame if hell were a more attractive alternative. Hmm… just imagine, all those devilishly attractive women we could meet there…"

Pierre quickly crossed himself and protested. "Armand, be serious for once!"

Then he paused a while before adding in a reflective voice, "Strange that Jean took his leave without shedding a single tear. I was more emotional than he was." Pierre frowned. "It seemed so unlike his usual self. I thought he was more attached to me…"

Armand grinned. "Is someone's ego injured here, perchance? Just be happy that he didn't make a scene, I hate that. Why do servants always treat us like newborn babies?"

"I think you're right," Pierre admitted, "but yet, it seems strange, so unlike him."

His last words were drowned in a loud sneeze and with gusto he added, "You can't believe how happy I am to be able to leave this terrible city. Not only is it boring me to death, it's made me sick as well. I feel terrible," and as if to give more credibility to his words he huddled himself deeply into his fur-lined coat.

Armand laughed. "Poor Monsieur le Marquis is feeling unwell and there's no servant in sight to indulge his lordship's whims, how terrible! Come on, stop complaining, it's a just simple cold, nothing else."

Pierre looked back at his friend and answered darkly, "You've got no idea, I'm sure it's something serious!"

Armand sniffed and rolled his eyes, sparing himself the effort of further comment.

The friends had been waiting and chatting at the pier when their boatman appeared. He nodded a short greeting, as apparently he was not in a talking mood and silently he gave them a sign to enter the boat. Pierre shuddered – he wasn't sure if it was only the effect of his cold, but the strange behaviour of their captain somehow made him nervous. But there was no time for forebodings. Their horses didn't appreciate at all the idea of having to cross a swaying gangway. The ferry seemed fairly solid, yet quite cramped and there was not a lot of space left to fit two horses. Armand started to guide his horse over the swaying plank and only narrowly avoided disaster. Pierre swallowed hard. He didn't like swaying planks, nor did his horse, he was sure about that. Yet somehow they managed to manoeuvre the horses securely onto the ferry and set sail, quickly leaving the

241

small port of Lausanne. Pierre watched the shore receding and the huge towers of the Cathedral shrinking to the size of mere toys.

"I won't pretend that I'm unhappy to see the Cathedral disappear," Armand sighed happily as he tried to find a comfortable seat for the journey.

The boatman had not deemed it necessary to engage in any further conversation, if one could indeed describe a grunted 'good morning' as conversation. Suddenly he looked at them in an almost friendly way, and seeing Pierre hunched in the cold wind, he suggested, "Why don't you go inside the cabin? It'll take several hours until we reach Geneva, better get some sleep, you look unwell!"

Pierre was astonished and surprised, not only by the fact that the giant had thought about his well-being, but that he could even talk in complete sentences. Somehow he was reluctant to leave Armand alone, but the temptation to move out of the cold wind was too strong. Happy to oblige he swayed more than walked to the small cabin, careful to hold himself steady as a fresh wind was blowing from the mountains and the lake was surprisingly choppy.

Armand stood close to the boatman who had started to point out features of the coastline. Pierre could see his finger pointing to various tall mountains, their tops and slopes already glistening with fresh snow. Then Pierre entered the cabin shaped like an oversized nutshell; it was just big enough to give shelter to one person.

"If you look in this direction, you'll soon be able to see the first spires of Geneva!"

Armand turned as the boatman kept pointing his finger following the shoreline. The scenery was indeed breathtaking. Majestic mountains soaring above the lake seemed to change colour all the time and with their peaks already covered in fresh snow they looked as if they had been wrapped in a blanket of crisp white velvet. The morning sun still held a hint of pink, just enough to add a warm glow of perfection to this picture. Armand had started to whistle a merry tune.

Armand never felt the blow coming. Like a bag of sand, he crumpled noiselessly to the floor.

Pierre tried to make himself comfortable in the small cabin but a stench of rotten fish assailed his nostrils and made his stomach turn. After five minutes he decided that death in the cold but fresh air was preferable to suffocation in a stinking cabin. He spotted an old fur, admittedly somewhat smelly, and wrapped it around his coat. Thus armed against the chilly wind he made up his mind to leave the cabin and return to the boatman and his friend.

When he left his cabin he was amazed to find the boatman standing alone at the helm. Pierre felt slightly uneasy – *why wasn't there was any sign of Armand?*

Wondering if his friend had decided to go to sleep somewhere he moved forward towards the boatman who stared at him with his strange, fanatical eyes. Pierre had almost reached the boatman, and asked curiously, "Where is my friend? Did the lazy gudgeon go to sleep?"

But Pierre's words seemed to freeze in his mouth as he saw his motionless friend at the feet of the boatman, sprawled unconscious on the ground. Pierre felt paralysed, the situation seemed clear enough and yet his mind refused to believe what he saw. Suddenly the boatman was holding a flintlock pistol in his huge hands and shouted at him, "Don't you dare move or your friend is a dead man. I know that you two are catholic spies in disguise, in cahoots with the devil! My friend the innkeeper told me that you tried to seduce his daughter and even gambled in his house, a house blessed by the Lord! But now, the day of reckoning has come, the punishment of the Lord is upon you! The Holy Scripture commands: *'Whoever does not obey the Son shall not see life, but the wrath of God remains on him!'*"

He paused, and Pierre saw that the boatman's face had suddenly become distorted with a terrifying leer.

"But the Lord's punishment will be terrible. I'll bring you to people who pay well for pretty young men, heathens from the Orient." He laughed roughly. "I'm not sure if you'll keep your balls, this will be a good lesson to keep your sticky papist fingers away from decent maids who respect the true faith! Better start praying – mind you, you might as well not bother, your papist saints won't help you!"

Pierre felt sick, really sick, not just cold and miserable. This simply couldn't be true. It must be a nightmare, the man had gone completely mad!

APPEARANCES CAN BE DECEPTIVE

Pain, all kinds of pain! Pain seemed to be everywhere.

His eyes were closed. Would the throbbing pain in his head ever end? When would those hot needles stitching relentlessly into his cheeks stop their gruesome work of torture? Where the hell was he?

Henri turned restlessly in his bed, his nightshirt soaked with blood and sweat.

"Will he survive?" asked the adolescent boy anxiously. He spoke in a peculiarly high voice.

"He's as strong as an ox," chuckled the old witch who had been called to attend the injured traveller. With delight her experienced fingers travelled along his strong shoulders. "Don't stand there like an idiot staring at me," she spat at the frightened boy. "Help me to take this shirt off, his wounds needs to be cleaned, can't you see he's in a right mess?"

Energetically she tore the nightshirt from Henri's body, ignoring his wild feverish protest. With zest and visible delight she wiped his body clean, while little by little a scent of strong herbs started to penetrate the room. Again and again she dipped the cloth into the pot with the greenish potion she had brought along. The boy watched, fascinated, while he handed her fresh linen. Amazed, he realized that the treatment was bringing immediate relief to the suffering patient. When she had finished she made Henri drink a thick liquid of indeterminate colour.

"The poppy seed will make him sleep, don't worry, love," she said to the boy. With dextrous fingers she fixed a bandage on Henri's cheek. "I wonder what kind of bandits ambushed you here in the middle of Paris," she mused aloud, "but it's none of my concern, so long as you pay me."

With a last appreciative glance she looked at Henri's naked body. "A pity that I'm an old hag nowadays. You won't believe it, but I was a beauty in my days and I'd have devoured him alive. Such a beauty. He'll keep a small scar from this wound, although I did my best." She chuckled again. "Anyhow, one more won't really matter."

The boy had tears in his eyes. He had been convinced that the gentleman left in his care had been doomed. Quickly he opened the heavy purse that Nicolas had thrown at him before he had left them in a hurry and selected a golden coin. The old hag scrutinized the coin with pleasure and care before it disappeared in the depths of her sagging bosom.

"Not a lot of those around nowadays," she remarked appreciatively.

"There's a lot of scum outside there, for sure. Anyhow, keep some of my potion, you'll need it later. But don't give him too much or he'll start to fantasize. You might even kill him!" she warned the boy, and with a last glance at Henri's body she left the tiny room.

The boy started to cry. He felt dreadful. Memories of a raging fire, whinnying horses and a hasty flight through the dark streets of Paris were flashing through his brain.

"You'll be safe here, I know the innkeeper," Nicolas had told him before he had disappeared into the dark night.

Tonight he was here, alone, with this strange man who had seemed like a distant and beautiful god only hours before. Now he lay there like a corpse glistening with sweat.

Henri moaned from time to time but the potion seemed to have taken effect, and he fell into an uneasy slumber.

The boy came to the conclusion that the witch had done everything that seemed possible. Fatigue took over as he huddled in a corner of the bed. Minutes later his head drooped and sleep overwhelmed him.

They spent a good fortnight in the small attic room until Henri felt strong enough to leave the confines of his hiding place. The innkeeper kept his promise and organized a coach, he even insisted on accompanying them to the city gates as he knew exactly how to pass through and whom to bribe.

Hence they had left Paris smoothly: a surprisingly young but ailing Abbott, accompanied by a young monk on their way to the Holy See in order to fulfil a vow.

Henri was in a peculiar mood. He was burning with rage. He felt humiliated like never before in his life. Two schoolboys had outwitted him and the secret king of Paris! He had no idea where Nicolas had gone to – but did it really matter? All he knew was that he had to reach Venice as quickly as possible, as his cousin would be travelling to Venice, sooner or later. In Venice revenge would be done, sweet revenge!

On the other hand Henri experienced the sweet feeling of freedom he had been missing so much during the past months. No obligations, no duties, he was free to do whatever he fancied. Free as a bird!

The boy heard Henri laughing in the coach, but the sound made him shiver. No normal human being laughed like this.

Some hours later they stopped at a post station. The boy looked at Henri with a shy glance but Henri seemed to be back to his normal cool self. They were received by an obsequious landlord who was only too happy to rent a room to such an august visitor. Bowing so low that he almost touched the ground, he asked the abbot if he would condescend to bless him and his family. Solemnly Henri made the sign of the cross. Later at dinner he prayed in Latin for the family and the servants who had assembled in deepest awe – what a story they would have to tell, to have had such a high ranking cleric among them!

Reverently the abbot and his choirboy were led into the best of the rooms that was available. Before they could enter the room the innkeeper cleared his throat and timidly proposed donating a charitable contribution for the long way that lay ahead.

Henri's spirits had already risen considerably throughout this comedy but all of a sudden it dawned on him how he could easily earn enough money to finance his journey to Venice. He accepted the donation graciously and blessed the donor, who flushed with pride.

After dinner, before the dignified abbot strode back to his room, he turned briefly, blessed the family and the servants once again, then bade them goodnight. "Join with me, we have to say our evening prayers!" he ordered the young monk and the door closed behind them.

Inside the room Henri bolted the door carefully. Then he dived out of his abbot's habit and ordered the boy to share the bed with him – this triumph had to be celebrated! Henri wasn't particularly surprised to find the boy obliged without any hesitation. Nicolas had promised that the boy was special – and indeed his angelic appearance was a stunning contrast to his worldly experience. Prayers long forgotten, Henri went to sleep deeply satisfied. Today had been a thoroughly satisfying day.

"We need to explain why we aren't visiting any monasteries during our journey. I cannot risk my supposed colleagues there unmasking me as soon as I open my mouth." Henri was lying on the bed, his head resting on his crossed arms.

"You made a vow?" answered the boy, while he continued caressing Henri's skin.

"What kind of vow?" asked Henri, his voice thick with excitement.

"Something charitable, people like this!" said the boy, continuing his action seemingly unperturbed.

"I'm never charitable," answered Henri, "charitable people make me vomit. So what would you suggest?"

"You need a nice story, my lord. Something like a fellow monk of your monastery fell seriously sick, you prayed to the Holy Virgin to rescue him and offered a pilgrimage to the Holy Father – alone and renouncing the luxury of your position – if the monk recovered. The Virgin granted your wish and I offered to accompany you and to sing for the Holy Father. That's very credible, you know I have a beautiful voice." Suddenly the boy's voice was sad. "I paid a high price for it," and a single tear rolled down the boy's cheek.

"That's why they cut your balls," Henri answered brutally. "Stop crying, other boys lost their lives. I'm never charitable, and don't count on me for any compassion. Life means fighting, nothing else."

The boy swallowed but stopped crying.

"Your idea is excellent," said Henri after a pause, "but from which monastery do I come? We're still running a big risk that someone might find out."

He was now speaking to himself, the boy wouldn't be able to help.

"We once had a guest with a peculiar accent, he came from a city called Mons in the Spanish Netherlands," the boy suddenly said. "Why don't we tell them that you come from a monastery far away in the North, nobody will ever have heard of such a city."

Henri examined the boy with sudden respect. "Seems we've got a smart boy here after all. The North it is!"

Thus a pious abbot from a city in the far North was travelling to the South, accompanied only by a chaste young monk, who looked more like a choir boy than a monk. To be on the safe side, they avoided the major roads, although this slowed down their speed of travel.

In order to add a touch of perfection to his disguise Henri had decided to ride on a mule – had the Lord Jesus not ridden on a humble donkey? In any case, it was better to ride than to sit in a coach on those bumpy roads that had seemingly never been repaired since the last Romans had left France. By definition their mule had obstinately set its own pace and wouldn't be rushed – but Henri was in an exuberant mood and he didn't really mind.

Wherever they decided to stay for a night, shelter and food was granted with reverence and pleasure and quickly their already fat purse swelled beyond Henri's imagination. I always suspected that these fat parsons make a fortune on our back, he mused, but I had no idea how much!

247

Henri had calculated that they'd reach Italy during wintertime. Crossing the Alps was therefore far too risky. No person with a sane mind would cross the Alps in winter. Thus they were heading along the River Rhone in the direction of Aix, travelling further to Marseille where Henri intended to find a ship and sail along the coast to Genoa. By early spring he'd be in Venice, maybe he could be there in time for the famous carnival.

While his mule was trotting along at its steady pace, Henri's eyes strayed to the boy riding in front of him. His shoulders were sagging, he looked tired. *What shall I do with him? For the time being he's immensely practical, replacing my valet and when it comes to sharing my bed, he's really skilled. Nicolas was right, as always, in such matters. But the boy knows too much – and this could become dangerous if ever his tongue slips.*

Weighing the pros and cons he decided not to make any decision until they reached Italy. Henri had just come to this conclusion when he felt the boy's eyes on him. "You're a lucky boy!" Henri shouted

"Why, my lord?"

"It's 'Why, reverend Father'!" Henri corrected him.

"Why, reverend Father, am I supposed to be lucky?"

"Because you have me to provide, food, shelter and protection! I shouldn't need to tell you this!"

"I'm sorry, reverend Father, of course I'm grateful for this! Yes, I suppose I am very lucky!"

Even more than you can imagine, I might have decided that your services were no longer required, Henri added to himself.

The boy turned his head and looked back to the road ahead. What a strange gentleman! Never would he forget his devilish laughter. He shuddered slightly. But did he have any other option but to keep following this fake abbot? Castrati were rare and highly prized, but they were kept like slaves and were easy prey if they had no protection. Sure, he had thought about running away – but he had no idea where to run or to hide. It didn't take much imagination to know that the revenge of this strange gentleman would be merciless and brutal. He shrugged his shoulders. There was no point pondering on any escape. All that would happen was that he'd exchange this strange, but at least young and attractive master, for the next one. Worse, he might fall into the hands of a new lord like the fat, bald priest in Paris who had abused him and sold him on to Nicolas.

The boy shuddered again. No, he'd be better off if he stayed with Henri de Beauvoir.

A SURPRISE

Pierre stood motionless, frozen.

The situation was utterly unreal. Here he was, standing on a forlorn sailing boat surrounded by scenery of stunning beauty and perfection. Pristine mountains in the background touched a sky of the most intense blue imaginable, a blue so vibrant and ethereal that it almost hurt his eyes. But was this the end? Had his luck finally run out? For a mad second he imagined that the lake's surface would open up, that huge tentacles of some fierce monster would soar out of the silvery depths to seize the raging boatman and drag him to the bottom.

In the meantime the boatman continued his litany of insults, in his religious fervour painting gruesome pictures of Pierre's and Armand's future. Slowly Pierre awoke from his state of paralysis – but it was not fear or despair that took over. He felt a wave of hot anger washing over him. He would not yield to this madman. He might well lose his life, but he would not lose his honour!

Keep him talking, as long as he keeps talking I can still try to figure out what on earth I'm going to do.

"My friend is innocent," he protested vehemently, "If you want to take revenge, take me!"

As Pierre had expected, the giant laughed with derision, but Pierre's comment did the trick and the boatman launched a new and lengthy sermon about their rotten, putrid characters. Yet the sermon ended far too soon. Pierre still had no clue what to do. He was prepared to fight but realistically his chances were almost zero, as long as the madman had a pistol in his hand.

Let's finish this now.

He shouted at the boatman, "You're nothing but hypocrite scum. You talk about the Lord and yet *you* serve the devil. The Holy Scripture commands: Thou shalt not kill!"

"You two are possessed by the devil!" The boatman was now screaming with rage. Pierre had hoped that his anger would make him imprudent and rush forward. His adversary was certainly a giant of a man, but Pierre knew that he'd be able to win a fight as he was more agile. But to Pierre's dismay the boatman didn't take the bait.

"You'll be able to see soon enough that the devil is waiting for you!" the giant growled, and pointed his pistol at Pierre.

Sometimes time flies past, and sometimes it creeps like a snail. What could only have taken seconds, would stay burnt into Pierre's memory, replayed over and over again.

Pierre saw the pistol rising, saw the eyes of the giant boatman changing to slits as he focused on his target. Strangely Pierre's senses suddenly seemed sharper than ever before. He could smell the lake, the rancid odour of the old crumpled nets, he felt the rays of the late autumn sun warming his skin. He was convinced that he could even smell the mountains, white and crisp. Pierre heard the piercing shrieks of the seagulls that were patrolling their ship, the creaking noise of the sails, the moaning and whispering of the boat as it rolled on the waves. Yet he never heard the hissing sound that heralded the end.

*****

"Do you think that Pierre is all right?" Marie asked anxiously. "And Armand, of course," she added lamely.

Céline was finishing some embroidery, and happy to interrupt her boring work she looked up and answered, "Of course my sweetheart, why shouldn't he be?"

"I had a peculiar dream this night," said Marie, "and I've been worrying the whole day!"

"What did you dream?"

"That Pierre called out for me to help him, but whenever I wanted to touch him, he suddenly disappeared. It was simply awful!" she shuddered.

"Oh, I understand now!" Céline had been looking at her, frowning, yet suddenly she slapped her forehead.

"You know, my love, it must have been the almond pastry. It was loaded with egg yolk. I also had a nightmare last night, I think I shall have to ask cook to skip the pastry for tonight!"

She stood up and lightly caressed Marie's lovely hair. "I'll go downstairs and do it immediately. Please don't worry. I'm sure that they're all right. Charles told me that they must be close to Geneva now. It's known as the country of Calvin. All I have ever heard from this part of the world is that the Swiss are virtuous and industrious to the point of being total bores. What could ever happen to them there? "

Marie had to laugh. Céline always had the gift of making things seem straightforward.

"Poor Armand, he hates virtue. I expect he's in danger of dying of boredom!" she laughed.

Céline smiled at her. "That's much better already, you'll see, the next time we receive a letter from them, Armand will be complaining bitterly about the awful Calvinists."

Marie smiled back. She did indeed feel much better. Her nightmare had been hovering over her like a dark cloud since this morning. And yet, she still felt a bit uneasy... Céline was probably right though, and it had been the fault of the pastries after all...

*****

Pierre forced himself to keep his eyes open. If he was to die now, he was determined to face his end with the dignity befitting a true Marquis de Beauvoir. But once again his senses seemed to be playing tricks on him. The raging giant suddenly cried out with surprise and dropped his pistol. It went off with a deafening explosion. Surprised and terrified, Pierre closed his eyes.

A second later Pierre opened them again and he detected a dagger protruding from the boatman's chest. The giant boatman started to sway, and losing his balance he tried to grab the railing with one last effort before he dropped screaming like a wounded animal with a loud splash into the ice-cold water. Nervously Pierre turned his head. Whoever had thrown the dagger must be standing right behind him! Focusing his eyes against the glaring sun he detected a man of medium height dressed in the unbecoming clothes of the Puritans. His secret saviour wore a dark scarf that was hiding his face and he held a second dagger menacingly in his hand!

Before Pierre could worry any further though the dagger was thrown to the ground and the man rushed towards him, and dropping on his knees he grabbed Pierre's hand and shouted, "Oh, Monsieur le Marquis, I told you that you'd end up in trouble without me!"

Pierre had never been so happy to hear Jean's voice!

"But what has happened to Monsieur Armand?" asked Jean.

Pierre felt an immediate pang of guilt. "I don't know, I hope it's nothing serious. See, he's breathing, that's always a good sign!"

"Any idea how I should wake him up?" he continued with a frown.

"We used to slap our men when they lost consciousness," suggested Jean. "But I'm not sure if Monsieur Armand will appreciate this."

252

"He won't appreciate it if he freezes to death, the wind is really cold. I'm so glad that I wore my fur coat."

He slapped his friend's face but to no avail.

"Harder, my lord, harder please."

Pierre gave it a second try, harder this time, and indeed Armand woke up.

"Are you mad, stop slapping me, you stupid idiot!"

Armand suddenly spotted the man with the scarf next to Pierre and automatically his hand moved to the shaft of his dagger.

"Stop playing the hero. Oh, and this is only your best friend who's trying to hurt you! By the way that's Jean, he rescued us!" scolded Pierre, and continued, "Be happy that you're still alive! Our taciturn boatman had been wound up by the innkeeper to attack us, but as part of a religious mission, of course."

"What happened?" Armand scratched his head. "Ouch, that really hurts! Jean, I don't know how you did it, but you arrived just in the nick of time! I'll need some of your secret potion, I've got a terrible headache coming."

"He must have hit you with the stock of that big pistol that's still lying there whilst I went into the cabin. But the cabin stank like a barrel of rotten fish, I couldn't stand it. When I came back, you were already lying there."

Pierre paused dramatically. "I arrived, and this scum of a boatman had his pistol ready to have a nice, cosy chat with me. He accused us of being papist spies, that we had gambled and tried to seduce the innkeeper's daughter. Just imagine! Yet with all his religious fervour he had no qualms over making money out of us. This madman had schemed with the innkeeper to sell us to some Oriental merchants looking for 'pretty boys', as he put it."

"It's a sort of compliment, isn't it?" said Armand animatedly. "I mean even those ugly Calvinists have to admit that I have a special something…"

"Not really, you conceited windbag, part of their idea of revenge was that they'd cut off our manhood. No idea where in the bible they found this punishment."

Instinctively Armand moved his hand downwards and, finding his private parts still in place, he sighed with relief.

"All right then, we seem to have landed right in the middle of yet another mess. Whoever tells me in future that Calvin's country is boring, I'll be able to put him right. But how come Jean is here?"

253

"I was just about to ask the same question!" exclaimed Pierre. "Jean, you were supposed to be on your way home."

Jean's bronze-coloured skin darkened somewhat. "Monsieur le Marquis, I must confess that I never really had the intention of leaving you alone. I have been in the service of your lordship for only a year and I'm afraid that your lordship seems to attract danger like flies round a honeypot."

"So true," murmured Armand. "Maybe I should find a new best friend if I am ever to enjoy a bit of peace and quiet. Jean, you should do the same!"

Pierre shot him a furious glance. "Oh, ha ha, aren't you funny!"

"I therefore obeyed the orders of Monsieur le Marquis," Jean continued unperturbed, "and left. But I never received any orders not to return!"

"We underrated you, we've got a lawyer in the making here," Armand commented with a broad grin.

"Armand, could you please shut up for once!"

"I therefore followed you to Lausanne, taking the disguise of a Puritan to avoid undue attention. I took an immediate dislike to the boatman, especially as I had seen him bargaining hard with the innkeeper. It just really smelled bad!"

"Fishy!" Armand inserted, "it smelled fishy!"

"It seemed an obvious decision to hide on the boat just to make sure that I could lend a hand if ever something nasty had been planned." Jean tried to assume the pose of the humble and dutiful servant but the friends could see that he was relishing his role of their saviour in distress.

"Shouldn't we go looking for the boatman? I guess he's dead now, but as true Christians maybe we ought to find him and grant him a decent burial..." Pierre asked, but even to himself his voice sounded hollow and not entirely convincing.

"Did you see any boatman?" asked Armand looking at Jean. "I only saw some scum, the perfect food for all the fish in the lake."

"No, my lord, you're quite right, I never saw a boatman!" Jean answered.

Pierre laughed. "All right, Armand, I get the message. May be I'm a bit naïve but I'm not so daft after all!"

"But what do we do now? We can't go back to Lausanne or they'll hang us from the spires of the Cathedral. And I have no idea how to steer this bloody boat!"

"Monsieur le Marquis, one of the advantages of having hired a convicted pirate to serve you is my ability to steer such a small boat. Nothing could be easier."

Armand made big eyes. "He's a convicted pirate," he whispered to Pierre, "and you never breathed a word to me about this?"

"Oh yes, he is!" Pierre whispered back. "But I never dared tell you because he likes to devour young noblemen with black curly hair for his breakfast!"

Armand kicked his friend. Such a comment could not go unpunished.

"That's settled then, be free to take over as our captain," Pierre exclaimed.

"But where should we go? Lausanne is out of question and Geneva is too risky as well!"

"I think I have a solution, Monsieur le Marquis."

Pierre was no longer astonished. "Jean seems to be the key to everything today!"

"What do you propose then? I hope it doesn't mean we'll have to go on sailing during the night; despite the sunny weather the wind is chilling me to the bone."

"I stayed these past nights close to Lausanne in a small village with very nice and decent people. They had been forced to convert but they still have sympathy for the old faith; the best part is that they loath the citizens of Lausanne. They call them a bunch of avaricious hypocrites!"

"Sounds like a fair description to me," Armand couldn't resist commenting.

"I propose that we sail close to Lausanne, hide the boat in the reeds and stay with this family. It'll take a good day or two until the alarm is raised because our boatman has disappeared, it means we'll have ample time left."

"You're absolutely fabulous, Jean." Pierre smiled with pride at his valet. "We'll do exactly as you propose."

Thus the boat followed a course back to Lausanne, steered by a new skilful boatman, and smoothly and without encountering further adventures they reached the shores close to the small village Jean had described. Everybody was eager to leave the boat... today's trip had been an experience they'd never forget.

Jean took the lead and guided them through a forest up a steep slope until they reached an isolated farm. It was situated about half an hour from the lake and about one hour's riding from Lausanne. The farm buildings looked immaculate; the farmer must be a wealthy man.

Jean introduced Pierre and Armand as his friends in distress and to Pierre's great relief they were warmly welcomed by their new hosts. The stout wife of the farmer, proud mother of eight aspiring children, immediately adopted Pierre as soon as she set eyes on him. "Look at this poor boy, he looks utterly miserable and shivering with cold. What a shame you came so late, you shouldn't have dragged your friend around when he's ill!" she scolded Armand and Jean, assuming that they had been the culprits.

Jean gave her a quick recap of their adventure on the lake and, quite shocked, she hugged a surprised but none the less pleased Pierre and planted a quick kiss on his cheek.

"What about me?" pleaded Armand.

"You'll have more than enough ladies wanting to hug you," she said darkly. "I know your type." But as she spoke she slapped him playfully to show that no harm had been meant. "Oh, my poor lambs. Let Maria look after you!" and bustling she went into action.

Ignoring Pierre's protests – and to the smirks of his friends – the farmer's wife resolutely tucked up Pierre like a small boy in a bed with soft duvets piled upon him and had no choice but to swallow some soup and some herbal tea that was supposed to work miracles. Pierre sighed deeply, turned and fell asleep, a peaceful sleep luckily unperturbed by monsters of the lake or raging boatmen.

The next morning saw a newborn and revitalized Pierre, ready to face the world again.

It might have been his near escape from disaster or the intimidating presence of the farmer's wife – but Armand for once kept his charms under control although the proud mother introduced him – from among her other children – to three buxom blonde daughters who under normal circumstances would have become the target of his immediate amorous attentions.

Pierre would have loved to stay in this haven of peace and warmth, pampered under the jealous eyes of Armand by the motherly Maria, but already the next day a mountain guide was presented to them. As a confidant of the family he had been chosen to lead them across the Alps; it was obvious that they must cross the mountains before the first winter snow set in.

The mountain guide introduced himself as Toni. He was of medium height and moved with the grace of a trained athlete. Like many of the locals he was no talker. Toni entered the big kitchen where the family had gathered and Pierre noticed in amusement that the eldest daughter of the family turned a flaming red. Pierre understood that she must have her mother's blessing as she only got a mild reproach when she spilled some milk on the kitchen table in her confusion.

Their guide was sworn to secrecy and, once again, Jean briefly recounted their story. Toni made it clear that they'd need to leave immediately. Not only would they risk the constabulary from Lausanne launching search warrants, the favourable autumn weather could change at any time and winter set in.

Thus it was good-bye to Maria, her tasty soups, her lovely daughters and her cosy bed. In the early hours of the next morning the small group was ready to tackle the strenuous march across the mountains. Toni had insisted on heavy shoes and fur coats, but to Armand's dismay their wonderful horses had been exchanged for miserable small ponies with a long coat, as Toni had explained that only they might endure the sharp mountain frosts.

"Can you imagine my cousin's comments if he saw us with these ridiculous dwarf horses? I wonder what frost and terrible winter weather this Toni is talking about," muttered Armand under his breath. "I'm sweating like a horse," and as if to underline his last statement he started mopping his wet forehead with a large cloth.

Pierre sighed and agreed. He had already shed his fur coat and was marching dressed down to his lined waistcoat as the morning sun was beating down on them, and it promised to become another exceptionally warm autumn day.

Their progress was fast, far too fast for Armand's taste. The friends were amazed at the fast pace Toni had set off at – and kept to without any apparent effort – although their path had become steeper and steeper.

Pierre heard his friend panting and moaning behind him and not able to resist a bit of gloating he remarked, "A bit out of breath, my lord?"

"Enough breath left to give you a good beating, Your Grace!" his friend answered irately.

Jean refrained from any comment but followed them with a smile.

The next two days the weather remained sunny, but quickly, as they gained altitude, their fur coats were more and more appreciated, becoming a necessity. The slopes were no longer overgrown but covered in snow and ice and each time they entered into the shadow of the mountains the wind was biting cold. Whenever they walked out of the shadows into the sunshine, the glittering pristine white snow dazzled them to the point that Pierre had to drape a scarf across his hat as he was starting to suffer snow blindness.

Three days later they had crossed the highest part of the mountains and started their winding descent towards the city of Milan. Toni stopped and suddenly looked at them with a big smile.

"We made it!" he said in his thick mountain dialect.

"Why shouldn't we?" asked Pierre surprised. "You seem to know the mountains like the back of your hand. I can't begin to imagine how you found your way in this labyrinth of gorges and tracks – they all look the same to me! To tell you the truth, I've seen enough snow and ice now."

Toni smiled shortly, and quite rightly took Pierre's comment as a compliment.

Lifting his right arm he pointed backwards to the sky. "See?" he asked Pierre.

"All I can see is clouds!" said Pierre.

"Snow clouds," said Toni. "Nobody will be able to cross the Alps for several days now, you understand now why I wanted to leave and not wait?"

"That seems obvious now, " exclaimed Pierre. "But how could you know? The weather was perfect in Lausanne."

Toni only shrugged his shoulders. "I knew," he said simply.

Now that they had crossed the highest mountain pass, their spirits started to rise rapidly. Pierre naively expected a smooth and easy descent, but that was not to be.

Further steep slopes lay ahead of them, and the friends soon gained ample experience that climbing down can be as tiring and dangerous as going up. But when Pierre had reached the sad conclusion that their climbing efforts would probably never end until they saw the spires of Venice, all of a sudden the gorges and ravines began to give way to the first short trees, stunted by wind and ice. Soon pleasant hills followed and to the friends' great relief, the snow and ice receded until they left the last patches of melting snow behind them.

Despite the late autumn season, surprisingly green pastures and pleasantly gurgling streams of crystal clear water greeted the tired travellers in Italy. The pastures ware dotted with mossy boulders as if playful giants had been playing with marbles ages ago and had never bothered to collect them. Here and there even the odd flower – forgetful that winter had almost set in – was turning its curious face to the sky in order to bathe in the sunshine.

Toni led them straight to a hut where a forlorn mountain farmer was serving freshly baked bread and home-made goat's cheese, highly welcome delicacies washed down with a local red wine. Armand devoured his food like a hungry wolf, the friends agreeing that they had rarely enjoyed a meal so much.

As soon as they had left the dense forest behind Pierre discovered a new world. Trees and shrubs looked and smelled so different from those he had ever seen before. Towering trees with needle-like leaves were growing everywhere and dotted the landscape like beams pointing to the pale blue sky. What a difference it was to see real palm trees framing picturesque villas bordering a small lake compared to the sad and dusty specimens Pierre had seen in the king's greenhouse. Everything was so excitingly different. The lake was of a brooding dark blue, but its shores shimmered with an exquisite turquoise lining. Pierre had never seen such a vivid colour before.

"Look, Armand! Isn't this beautiful?" sighed Pierre, close to delirium.

"It is," answered Armand, "but with a nice girl dipping her feet in it, the lake would look so much better!"

"You're hopeless," retorted Pierre. "Can't you ever savour beauty if it's not wearing a gown and long hair?"

"Of course I can," protested his friend. "I was just pointing out how the scenery could be *improved*! And by the way, they do not need to put on a gown for me…!"

Pierre exploded with laughter and Jean had a hard time keeping his face straight.

At a leisurely pace they continued their way to Milan and travelled through villages of houses built from creamy sandstone with roofs covered by tiles of pale pink, houses that seemed ages old. Many houses had originally been painted, their once vivid paint now washed out by time, colours faded by the sun.

Invariably churches with bell towers of a sober rectangular shape could be found in every town – beautiful in their simplicity and yet so different to anything Pierre had seen before.

Whenever the sun started to set, the scenery around the travellers would change. As the sunlight changed to a deep and mellow gold, the colour of the roof tiles suddenly deepened to a shade of burnt orange, and the pale colours of the houses came alive. Pierre marvelled at these enchanted villages that glowed vividly in the reflection of the warm evening light.

Everyone they met spoke with a broad Italian dialect but Pierre managed to communicate in a mix of French and Latin as soon as he had spotted and memorized some key words. Armand was not astonished. Pierre had always been a bright scholar. But Jean dwarfed their efforts to learn the language as they

259

discovered that he already spoke fluent Italian, and with an astonishing variety of swear-words when he had to get his way. "Don't tell me where you learnt it," said Armand said in mock despair. "I can only guess that the captain of your fellow pirates was a swarthy Italian convict. But don't feel compelled to go into any details!" Jean only smiled and kept silent. It was of no concern to the others that he had once entertained a very close friendship with an Italian parlour maid in Paris.

Toni had guided them to the major road leading to Milan and now it was time to say good-bye. Modestly their guide wouldn't accept any praise and only asked the friends to light a candle in the famous cathedral of Milan and to pray for his safe journey back.

On their own now and with no pressing time schedule the friends decided to make a break in a small city close to Milan. They desperately needed to buy three decent horses and, as Armand pointed out, they absolutely must acquire new clothes. Armand had noticed that the fashion in Italy was very different not only from Lausanne (which was to be expected), but even from Paris. No drab clothes or dull colours here – men and women alike dressed carefully to look their best and in the most vivid of colours. Armand could endure many things, but certainly not being outshone by any Italian, and therefore new clothes it had to be!

"How do I look?" asked Armand proudly, parading up and down in front of his friend.

Pierre looked at him as Armand waved his new hat with gleaming white feathers at him. The silk of his new coat was rustling; Armand had invested a small fortune in his new attire.

"You look... well, I mean you look like..."

"I look like what, come on, spit it out!" Armand said good-humouredly.

"You look like a peacock!" answered Pierre, and burst into peals of laughter.

But Armand was not to be intimidated. "Some people have an eye for fashion, and some simply don't," he answered smugly. "If people are convinced that I'm the Marquis, don't complain, I don't want to hurt your feelings, but I must tell you that you look more like a travelling merchant, my dear friend!"

Pierre looked down at his new velvet clothes, happy with the more simple attire he had chosen. "At least admit that I look like a successful one," he challenged his friend.

Armand looked at his friend and although he would never admit it openly, his friend looked simply splendid. The dark plum-coloured velvet waistcoat was a nice contrast to his white shirt made of fine linen and adorned with a Flemish lace collar. Pierre's gleaming blond hair was covered with a dashing Italian style beret instead of a hat. He looked every inch the young nobleman he was.

"All right, you look about acceptable," Armand answered reluctantly. "At least I won't need to be ashamed of you. I think we're ready to attack Milan," Armand added in his best mood. "Ladies, beware, we're irresistible and we're coming!"

"Anything you can tell me about Milan?" asked Pierre. "Is it a big city?"

"Sure it is," answered Armand. "Milan even used to be the queen of all cities here in the north of Italy. Tomorrow we'll certainly see the splendid castle built by the dukes of the Sforza family, my father told me that it's even larger than the Louvre. But being so rich and powerful attracted two unwanted suitors: we tried to conquer the city as did the Habsburgs. After a good century of war, France gave up and the city fell into the hands of the Spanish enemy."

Pierre stifled a small yawn. "Very interesting. You sound like my teachers… But what I'm really interested to know is, what does the city look like today?"

"I guess the city will look like a tattered old lady now. My father told me the plague raged here about ten years ago and killed a third of the population, you must remember that Piccolin told us the same about Venice."

Pierre quickly crossed himself. "But that's terrible, can you imagine what must have happened here?"

"I can, actually, because we had a visitor from Milan who told my father all about it." Armand's sunny face had changed, suddenly he looked unusually grave. "He said he had escaped… Well, in fact he told us that it was a miracle that he had escaped what he called a veritable hell on earth. Church bells kept ringing day and night and smoke billowed in the deserted streets. From time to time you could hear the squealing sound of a lonely cart drawn by cadaverous horses passing by to collect the stinking corpses with festering blisters that had simply been thrown on the streets. He told us that huge fires were kept burning day and night to kill the miasma of the plague although many claim that the plague is a punishment sent by the Lord and it must be endured. Stinking and decomposing corpses were piling up inside the city as cemeteries had long ceased to function, and there was no way that so many dead could be buried in holy ground. The doors of the houses inside the city had been barred, the inhabitants either huddled together in grief and prayer – yet some behaved like lunatics in feverish pursuit of debauchery, heaping their gold on drunken whores to finish their last days on this earth in an orgy of lust. But as soon as the plague struck them, they were left to die alone, their last gold stolen, facing a wretched end. "

261

Pierre had closed his eyes in horror. His imagination conjured up dramatic pictures of desperate men and women, he heard the sound of the bells, he even thought that he could smell the acrid smoke. *Yes, hell must be like this, the visitor was right. But why did the Lord send such punishment to his faithful?* Pierre would never understand this.

"Are you sure we want to go there, maybe we would do better to travel directly to Venice?" asked Pierre nervously.

"Oh, stop worrying! It's on our way anyhow and all of this happened more than ten years ago, really, don't worry. The plague can strike at any moment – anywhere. It's useless to worry about it. But we'll probably find the city not very crowded and a bit run down, as the Spanish did nothing to help and build it up."

Thus expectations were not high from their side when they approached the fortifications of the city but they were impressed straight away. Milan was no doubt still a big, important and very beautiful city. They passed the gates under the eyes of a bunch of bored Spanish guards and finally managed to find the stately house that would become their home for the next days, as Monsieur Piccolin had invited them to stay with the Italian branch of his family.

They entered the heavy iron door, worthy of a bank vault, and were led by a liveried servant to a beautiful terrace, a haven of peace in the noisy city. Although Pierre had noticed on his way that several houses were in urgent need of repair, no traces of the plague and its terrible trail of destruction could be seen anymore. Well-dressed people were promenading on the busy streets, food stalls displayed ample and appetizing dishes that were as mouthwatering as they were expensive. Milan seemed to be a wealthy city – and very much alive.

"My lords, it's a great pleasure and an honour for our family to welcome you here in our house! Please allow me to introduce myself, my name is Giovanni Piccolin. Please regard my humble home as your own!" The young man beamed at them invitingly.

"My uncle sent me a confidential message some weeks ago about your intention to come to Milan and we were looking forward very much to welcoming you here. Actually I was afraid that the first winter snow might delay you but I'm glad that you did not encounter any unpleasant inconvenience during your journey!"

Armand gave a little cough and murmured, "With the exception of an eccentric boatman, no inconvenience that would be worth mentioning."

"My uncle told me that you wish to travel incognito and therefore please excuse me if in the future I address you simply as 'Messieurs'. You'll stay in our house and my younger brother will be delighted to show you around the city!"

He waved and a young man close to their age approached them. He was well built, of medium height with brown eyes and an aquiline nose. Contrary to his brother, who was dressed very conservatively, he seemed to share Armand's taste for showy colours.

He greeted them reverently but there was a sparkle of mischief in his eyes that promised they'd get on well together.

"May I present to you my brother Edoardo, he'll be your guide and assist you with everything you need to know. Messieurs, you must be tired after such a long journey, would you like to have a rest now?"

Armand and Pierre looked at each other and answered almost simultaneously, "We're feeling fine, thank you. We had several days' rest close to Milan in the city of Como, so if Edoardo wants to show us the city now, we're ready!"

But Giovanni would not let them discover Milan before they had taken lunch with the family. Pierre had already discovered that Italians loved a dish he had never tasted before: pasta of varied shapes. Among those served today there was a dish cooked in a chicken broth, seasoned with a white wine and topped with fluffy ground cheese. Pierre thought it simply heavenly when he tasted this dish. A quick glance at Armand proved that his friend seemed similarly delighted by this new discovery.

After lunch, once again a new culinary experience was waiting for them. A steaming hot oriental beverage of darkest black was served in small cups. Pierre glanced at the dark potion with thinly veiled suspicion. Edoardo saw his face and grinned. "Try it, this beverage was introduced by the Turks. It's called coffee. It's simply great once you've got used to it!"

The steaming liquid emanated a strong aroma that was strangely appealing. They were invited to add ample amounts of sugar, a rare luxury in Paris. Pierre first made a face when he tasted the brew, it was so bitter! But he was told to try and finish his cup and soon he grew accustomed to the strange taste and could feel the invigorating power of the drink.

"We've all become a bit addicted to drinking coffee after our meals or in the morning," Giovanni remarked guiltily. "I admit it's a luxury, but it's so good!"

Pierre consented and gladly accepted a second cup.

After a short rest Edoardo took them for a stroll through the city. "Please call me Edo!" he implored the friends. "When my brother calls me Edoardo, I know it's time for one of his sermons!"

"Sounds as if this is no unusual occurrence," laughed Pierre.

263

"I'm afraid I always tend to end up in some trouble, I have no idea why, believe me, I have the best of intentions!" Edo answered, his laughing eyes belying his desperate tone.

"The same thing happens to us all the time, don't worry!" Armand dropped in. "Somehow adventure seems to follow us all the time, but it's good to have a bit of a break in such a nice and peaceful city!"

*****

The Spanish guard was awed. Rarely did he see a cleric of the rank of an abbot travelling on a pilgrimage to Milan, let alone one riding on a humble mule, only accompanied by a chaste young monk. He sank on his knees to kiss the abbot's ring of office and accepted his blessings. Demurely the young monk with his peculiar high voice asked in which monastery they could stay for the night. Having received detailed directions the abbot majestically thanked the guard and slowly he continued his way with the young monk. Two streets further down the abbot spotted a small, peaceful chapel and stopped. The young monk went inside with a heavy bag, then came out almost immediately, giving a sign to the abbot.

With some dignity, the abbot dismounted from his mule and walked slowly inside the small chapel. Only five minutes later a young nobleman strode out of the chapel accompanied by a pageboy carrying the same heavy bag. They disregarded the mule dozing in the winter sun and walked towards the city centre.

"It was about time that I changed back into normal clothes," the nobleman remarked to the pageboy, "The abbot's divine inspiration was starting to spoil my character."

The pageboy chuckled. "I certainly didn't remark anything of that yesterday night in our bed, reverend Father!"

"It's 'my lord' now, you impudent boy, the father abbot disappeared in the chapel," Henri scolded the boy.

"Where do we go now, reverend Fa–, my lord?"

"We'll search for a nice tavern with hopefully not too dirty rooms for the night and have some good food and some fun."

The boy's voice wavered. "You're tired of me, do you want me to leave you?"

Henri looked at the boy thoughtfully. "I think I told you before that I'm not an emotional type of person. Don't waste any feelings on me. But don't worry, you may keep me company until we reach Venice, then we'll see."

264

The boy seemed reassured and comforted he trotted behind the nobleman until they reached a large tavern located close to the famous cathedral.

Henri liked what he saw. The tavern served as a station for changing horses, and several coaches with proudly painted coats of arms were waiting in the courtyard or being attended to by attentive grooms. Delicious scents wafted from the direction of the kitchen and the tavern was packed with noisy customers. A group of young men were playing dice, watched by brightly painted ladies of easy virtue on the watch for their prey – but even the ladies looked classy.

That's ideal, they're so busy that we can easily blend in.

However, Henri had to bargain hard with the innkeeper. As soon as the landlord had realized that his guest with the unmistakable airs of a nobleman came from a foreign country he pretended that only the most expensive of his well-appointed rooms was available for rent. Henri managed to negotiate a hefty discount but when he saw the satisfied gleam in the innkeeper's eyes he realized that he had been bamboozled all the same.

He shrugged his shoulders, he didn't really care. The fake abbot had amassed enough money, their journey to Venice in comfort was assured. But tonight they'd be looking for some diversion. The boy had become a bit boring, a handsome young groom or a real slut would be nice for a change. Maybe both… He grinned, and in the best of spirits Henri stretched out on his bed. First he'd have a good rest!

*****

The friends discovered that Milan must once have been a truly rich and powerful city. As Armand had predicted, today the city appeared more like a tattered old queen, yet a queen nevertheless! Proudly Edo led them to the square in front of the imposing cathedral.

"This cathedral will be one of the biggest on the earth when it's finished," he boasted.

Pierre looked sceptically at the gigantic building. No doubt it was really huge – it dwarfed all the buildings close to it. But somehow this building simply didn't inspire the awe that Pierre invariably felt when he faced the cathedrals of Reims or Notre Dame in Paris. Although construction had started hundreds of years ago, the cathedral of Milan – like so many big cathedrals – was still a work in progress. The bell tower rising into the sky looked slightly odd next to the gothic nave, but worst of all, some inspired architect had left his mark by adding a modern façade that looked as if a theatre stage had been stuck onto the front of the old church.

But as Edo appeared to be immensely proud of his cathedral they congratulated him dutifully on such a unique building. His lame proposal to go inside and see the famous relics of a whole collection of powerful saints was politely declined and Edo seemed happy to continue the guided tour. "I know that praying to the saints and kissing their relics is supposed to be very edifying, but when I see all these bones, splinters and mummified limbs, it has a most depressing effect on me!" he admitted freely.

"We can skip the bones," answered Pierre quickly, "but we promised our mountain guide to light a candle for his safe return."

Edo was delighted. This seemed a satisfying yet very acceptable alternative to visiting the relics of long forgotten saints and quickly they walked into the towering nave and lit a candle below the statue of the Holy Virgin.

Having accomplished their mission, they continued their tour at a leisurely pace. But Pierre started to regret that he had decided to wear his new shoes, which had looked so fashionable. Now he was paying for his vanity. Although tailor made and produced from the softest leather, the leather of the soles of his shoes was too thin and the cobbled streets were killing him, he could feel every single stone!

Pierre's sufferings were soon to be rewarded by the splendid view of the Castello. As Armand had rightly predicted, it was impressive, almost as vast as a small city in itself. Rarely had Pierre seen such a proud castle – protected by its own moats and fortifications, it dominated the city and it was easy to understand why the unloved Spanish occupying forces could hold the city easily as a hostage. This castle was simply unassailable.

What seemed most strange though was the sudden silence here. Milan was a bustling city, noise followed its inhabitants everywhere, yet the Castello seemed to be so aloof and remote, as if it had been erected by beings from a different world.

"I think we did a lot for our education today," said Armand suddenly. "Do you by any chance have any nice taverns here...? With good wine and music?"

Edo laughed. "Of course we have! And really good ones, just wait until you see them... and don't forget the girls there!"

He winked at Armand. It didn't take a genius to understand what Armand was really looking for.

"Excellent, nothing better for one's education than to come into close contact with the local population!"

266

"Close contact, I assume," added Pierre drily. "You're hopeless, you'll never change!"

"Why should I?" protested Armand. "If the good Lord has endowed me with some gifts, I had better use them! Pierre, if you don't pay attention you'll become like one of those boring, shrivelled puritans."

"I can only agree," added Edo, his eyes sparkling. "Let's have some fun tonight. And you know the best thing?"

"No idea," said Pierre, still digesting the fact that his friend had compared him to a shrivelled puritan. "What's the best thing?"

"The best thing will be that my ever so correct brother will have to pay for it, as you're our guests!" Edo was gurgling with laughter. "It'll kill him, but there's nothing he can do!"

"Oh, I'm sure we can pay for ourselves," protested Pierre.

"Oh, come on, you'd spoil half my fun!" Edo pleaded with him. "Just seeing his face when he has to prise open his banker's purse will make my day!"

In the best of moods they walked back home. Tonight would be a night of fun!

In the evening, three handsome noblemen accompanied only by a lone servant left the Piccolins' stately house. They had refused Giovanni's kind invitation to stay for dinner as Edo had promised succulent chicken on a spit. "The best you'll ever taste in your life. I have no clue what they do with them, but those chicken are simply divine!" he had raved, eyes glazing over, "and their pasta, our cook is an incompetent compared to the way they can prepare and serve pasta there!"

Pierre had to swallow hard as he heard these vivid descriptions. The long excursion had made him exceedingly hungry. Anticipating plenty of treats they stepped out of the stately house in the best of spirits. But tonight Milan had decided to show her ugly face.

In the afternoon the sunshine had made them almost forget that the winter season had arrived. Yet as soon as they left the terrace a cold wind blowing from the North greeted them and a dense fog was spreading its tentacles through the dark streets. "It's nothing unusual for Milan, in winter we often have a bit of fog coming up from the river," remarked Edo casually.

Luckily Edo had insisted that they should wear their fur-lined coats. He had also made sure that they carried their rapiers and daggers – Milan, like any big city, could not really be considered to be a safe place at night.

Later Pierre was convinced that he must have felt a premonition but for now he only shivered as a damp cold entered his bones. "All very well having a rapier to hand but as long as my hands are frozen, I won't even be able to hold it!" he muttered under his breath.

"Stop whingeing and complaining, you sissy," answered Armand, not impressed by the obvious sufferings of his friend. He was in an excellent mood – time for fun tonight!

Their route to the tavern led them through several empty winding streets. All the shutters of the neighbouring houses had been closed already and the streets of Milan lay deserted and silent. The city was enshrouded in total darkness, only the light of their torches allowed them to find their way. The poor light created by sooty flames was swallowed almost immediately by the thick fog and the darkness. Like an oversized pillow the fog dampened all the noises of the city so that it seemed as if it were lying in a deep slumber. Pierre had the impression that he had been cut off from reality, and they were walking in a private bubble of light and sound.

The strange atmosphere started to weigh upon their spirits and shortly after they had left the house the flow of their conversation slowed down until it ceased altogether. Even Edo, who seemed to know Milan like the back of his hand, had to ponder several times which crossing to choose, as in the strange opaque darkness all houses looked alike.

All of a sudden Armand noticed a movement in the entrance of a house they were about to pass. Automatically his hand grabbed his rapier and he shouted, "Careful, there's someone moving over there," before he lunged forward to surprise the unknown foe.

A loud and reproachful '*miaow*' answered back and the shadow of a cat escaped between Armand's legs.

After a short moment of surprise they broke into laughter, realizing that Armand had been fooled by a mere cat. He had to endure quite a few ribald comments regarding his exceptional bravery, but somehow even their laughter didn't manage to break the eerie spell.

When the big square in front of the cathedral came into sight their mood improved. Here in the centre of the city plenty of torches had been lit and the streets were no longer deserted. "We'll be there soon, it's only two more streets to go," shouted Edo, and Pierre's spirits lifted considerably.

"I'm so hungry, I could devour a whole pig," Pierre shouted back.

Two more turns and the post station came into sight. Plenty of torches with blazing flames lighted the entrance of a courtyard filled with carriages and bustling with people. Industrious servants were hurrying around and the mouth-watering scent of roasted meat told Pierre that they must have reached their final destination.

Knowing his way, Edo guided them inside and they even managed to secure a table in the packed tavern as soon as a silver coin was slipped discreetly into the palm of the head waiter. Pierre was astonished to find a mix of all kinds of people sitting here, eating, playing dice or cards… and all of them talking animatedly. The Italians loved to talk, Pierre had already noticed this in Como, but here in the tavern the level of noise was simply deafening.

A young waitress appeared to take their orders and whereas Pierre had difficulty understanding a single word of the proposed menu Edo seemed to follow easily and he ordered a selection of tasty dishes and wine. Armand sat in silent admiration, his eyes glazing over when the waitress had to bend down to listen to Edo's order, offering him an excellent view of her breasts.

"I can even see her nipples!" he whispered excitedly into Pierre's ears and Pierre had to admit that she alone had been worth the trip.

As if the noise level of the many chatting guests had not been enough, musicians and comedians now started to entertain the guests. Mocking each other for the benefit and amusement of the others they quickly created a lively atmosphere. Armand glowed contentedly with satisfaction: after drab Lausanne, Milan seemed to fulfil his personal vision of paradise.

*****

Henri woke up as the loud music floating into his room could no longer be ignored. The musicians' enthusiasm did not really match their skill and Henri winced when the flutes hit some wrong notes – and then repeated them with gusto.

The boy must have been awake before him. He was sitting on the bedstead looking at him patiently. Henri could never decide if he found the boy's attachment annoying or immensely practical, maybe a bit of both. Quickly he freshened up.

"I'm feeling hungry, let's go down and have a decent dinner!" he remarked casually to the boy, not really expecting an answer.

"Do you want me to sing and beg for some money?"

269

"No, I'd rather keep a low profile. The arrival of an abbot who never turned up in the monastery might have aroused some curiosity and it's better if we aren't noticed."

The boy nodded to show that he had understood.

"Don't just sit there," Henri suddenly hissed at him. "Can't you see that I need to change my shirt? Move your lazy arse!"

The boy apologized profusely and transformed immediately into a diligent and surprisingly skilled valet. Minutes later Henri was immaculately dressed, his blond hair crowned with a dashing beret ready to go downstairs into the tavern. Henri was prepared to see the tavern particularly busy, as the noise of laughter and a cacophony of voices could not be ignored.

"This tavern is a goldmine," Henri commented as he stopped at the top of the staircase.

Here from the first floor they had an excellent view of the bustling tavern. Immediately Henri could see that it would be difficult to find any free seats. They'd be compelled to share a table with others, there was no available space left, let alone a free table. Disgusted, Henri made a face – he hated sitting close to commoners. Attentively he continued to scan the scene below him. Perhaps he'd get lucky and spot some people preparing to leave.

His roaming glance noticed a gang of young men sitting right underneath him playing dice. It didn't take an expert to know the dice were loaded. The leader of the gang was still young but already starting to run to fat. Dressed according to the latest fashion, he had forced his bulging belly into a far too tight waistcoat. Bright flashing colours witnessed his aspiration to become a leader of fashion but only betrayed his commoner's roots. His rough yet moderately handsome face was flushed from too much wine and by the excitement of the game. Unsuccessfully trying to add an air of nobility, he wore his greasy dark hair in long curls that fell on his stained collar. Henri knew this type well enough: they sought out young and inexperienced men whom they could manipulate, ever in need of money to pay for women and pleasure.

Henri continued to survey the tavern when his glance suddenly fell on a group of three young men sitting together, deep in an animated discussion. He didn't recognize the third one but there could be no doubt: *here right under his very eyes sat his bastard cousin!*

For a single moment Henri dropped his mask of the aloof nobleman. By chance, the young pageboy had turned his head, about to offer his services to go down and bribe the waiter. But the words stuck in his throat. The boy had never harboured any illusions about the count's character but now he saw the true nature of the man he had been travelling with. In a matter of seconds, Henri had transformed into a chilling predator, eyes glittering coldly, ready to pounce.

Seized by panic, the boy wanted to run away yet he knew that this would be foolish. He therefore mustered all of his self-control to keep his expression neutral. But there was no doubt, he had seen the face of a killer, the true face of Henri de Beauvoir.

Henri stepped back immediately to make sure that his face remained hidden in the shadow. Fate had presented him a unique opportunity, but he had to think how best to use it.

"You don't want to go down?" asked the boy in a wavering voice.

"I've changed my mind, it's too full. Wait a second, I'll need your services."

*****

Jean was sitting in the tavern, a happy and relaxed man. The meal had been quite excellent – Edo hadn't promised something he couldn't deliver. But now Jean was fighting against the pleasant tiredness that usually follows a good meal washed down with an excellent red wine. One thing was sure, the innkeeper did not make false economies – the food and wine were beyond reproach!

Lazily Jean watched Pierre and his two companions who were sitting fairly close by. Armand held a pretty girl in his right arm and far from acting coy, she seemed to be entertaining the whole table as he could see Pierre breaking into peals of laughter while she was obviously teasing him.

Still in his pleasant mood Jean glanced around. He noticed two men standing on the landing at the top of the staircase leading to the guest rooms, to be precise, one of them must have been a very young man or still a boy as he looked very slender. He saw the man stepping back, no wonder, he must have seen there was no space left to squeeze in. The tavern was packed and Jean could even discern noises from the entrance where newly arrived guests were angrily demanding to be seated and served.

"Take your filthy hands off a decent lady," the girl shouted impishly at Armand in a show of false propriety. "I know your type, always got your fingers everywhere but when it comes to serious matters, five seconds and you're done!"

Pierre and Edo were rolling around in laughter but Armand wouldn't be discouraged. Opening his dark brown eyes like a hurt puppy dog he answered, "You're so wrong, so terribly wrong! I swear to all the saints, with *you* it would be different! We could spend the whole night together, I'm special, I never get tired. Give me a chance!"

271

The girl laughed, then she looked teasingly at Pierre. "Maybe I prefer blond men?" she remarked thoughtfully after a short pause. "Just look around, I can find dark-haired men by the dozen, but a handsome man with golden hair like your friend..."

She sent a long inviting glance at Pierre who had the decency to blush like a maiden. He had to admit that he enjoyed very much what he saw: she was quite enchanting, he liked her full red lips and especially her eyes, beautiful dark eyes that looked at him with the promise of pleasure and passion under her long eye lashes.

Pierre felt exceedingly flattered – and hot.

"Let's share then!" Armand answered good-humouredly. He had not missed registering Pierre's reaction to her overtures and was enjoying his friend's confusion, "But have compassion for a poor traveller from France!"

The girl wriggled herself out his embrace and gave him a playful slap on his knee. "You're a very naughty man!"

Suddenly turning businesslike, she remarked, "I really have spent too much time with you, unless you order some more wine, I'll have to return to help my colleagues."

Edo only grinned, he knew the tricks.

"Sure, we'll order some more wine, bring us the best, we'll drink to the health of my brother Giovanni!"

"Is it is his birthday?" the girl enquired.

Edo broke into peals of laughter. "No, it's his purse-day!" and with this last remark Pierre and Armand joined in, laughing at what Edo considered to be his best joke ever.

*****

"Go down and speak to the young man with the bright red cap!" Henri commanded.

"What should I say, my lord?" asked the young boy nervously

"Tell him that your master wishes to have a private conversation with him upstairs."

"He won't listen to me, he's totally involved in his game – and he seems to be winning!" the boy pleaded.

272

"Of course he's winning. The dice are loaded. But don't worry, he'll listen! Just show him this and tell him that there is much more waiting upstairs."

While Henri had been talking he had extracted a gold coin from his purse and dropped it into the boy's hand. The boy looked at it with awe – silver coins were common enough, but gold was a rarity.

Dutifully the boy walked down the staircase and approached the young man Henri had pointed out to him. As could be expected, the young man only growled at him, addressing him with an amazing array of obscene curses. But, as predicted by Henri, the man's attitude changed as soon as the boy produced the gold coin. Henri saw the boy whispering rapid explanations causing the man to turn his head in the direction of the staircase, his regard surprised but suspiciously wary.

Henri looked on as he saw the boy talking to the young man and soon enough the man rose from the table and strode to the staircase. Still suspicious, he stared up at the landing but could only make out the silhouette of a single person – just as the boy had indicated.

Finally greed took over and he followed the boy upstairs where he greeted Henri, but he remained wary.

"Do you want more of those?" Henri asked and showed him several gold coins.

The young man's eyes glittered with excitement and greed but he tried to play it cool. "Depends what you want me to do," he replied, then, feeling that something was missing, he added, "sir."

Patiently Henri explained his plan. Not surprisingly his proposal was violently rejected but Henri had anticipated this reaction. Magically a fat purse with shining coins appeared in his hand.

"This will all be yours, tonight," Henri whispered, and the deal was sealed.

The young man walked downstairs straight back to his table, slowly and as pretentiously as he had left and yet his expression had changed, and a satisfied smile played on his lips. His friends greeted his arrival by shouting obscene remarks about his short absence on the first floor in the company of a young boy but he only grinned and punched one of the players playfully. He made a rude gesture but he refused to comment.

*****

Jean was listening to the musicians who were accompanied by a young girl dressed in vivid colours. Moving to the rhythm of the flutes she had started to

273

sing. Luckily her vibrant voice made up for the shortcomings of the flute players. The girl was singing a romantic love song and Jean's memories floated back to his Italian girlfriend. He had to sigh – a pity that she had found another man who had been willing to marry her.

His thoughts still dwelling on a pleasurable past, he noticed the boy who had been on the landing before. He was walking slowly toward Pierre and Armand.

He's still looking for a table for his master, poor boy, his master will certainly beat him if he can't find a free seat for him!

The boy had reached Pierre's table when he suddenly stumbled and fell forward. Leaning heavily on Pierre he awkwardly tried to regain his composure while he excused himself profusely. Jean watched how Pierre smiled at the boy, probably asking him if he hadn't hurt himself and telling him not to worry. Jean sighed, this reaction was so typical of his master. Pierre was simply hopeless, far too nice. He should have scolded the clumsy brat instead!

The boy retreated hastily back into the corner where the young man with the red cap was noisily playing cards with his cronies. As soon as the boy had taken his place the young man sent an enquiring look to the boy. The boy nodded in response and a quick smile played on the man's lips. After this exchange the boy retreated further into a dark corner although he was aware that his master must be waiting for him. But as Henri had not ordered him explicitly to come back upstairs immediately he decided to use this opportunity to sit down and think.

The boy crouched in the dark corner shaking, his feelings in turmoil. He had grown up accustomed to being commanded and abused. Sold by his parents like a piece of merchandise because his beautiful voice had attracted the attention of a rich clergyman, his manhood had been taken away to preserve his voice – the clergyman's investment. Afterwards he had been handed over as a precious gift – nobody had ever bothered to ask his opinion, not once had his feelings been considered. The boy had grown up believing that life must be like this, at best indifferent, often cruel and painful. Months and year had passed and he had grown accustomed to this life and accepted his fate. Wasn't he fed and dressed properly, rarely beaten – shouldn't he call himself lucky?

But tonight his protective armour of indifference had been pierced as a young golden god had smiled at him, had held his hand and gently caressed his hair. The god's hair had shone in the candlelight like spun gold and his smile had reached out to the boy's heart. He didn't know what kind of feeling had gripped him. Was this love, this strange feeling people kept talking and singing about? But the boy knew for sure that he felt utterly miserable as he had sinned tonight, he now understood how Judas Iscariot must have felt. The golden god would fall – and it would be his fault alone. Thankfully nobody cared for a boy who was crouching alone in a corner, thankfully nobody noticed the hot tears running down his face.

The feisty young man with the bright red cap finished his game. Bending forward he whispered some words into the ears of his closest friends. He was answered with bewildered glances, but as he was the undisputed leader no one dared to object when he rose from the table. Cocksure and escorted by the boisterous gang of his friends he walked straight to the table where Pierre and his friends were sitting immersed in an animated discussion. As soon as the young man had reached their table he positioned himself straight in front of Pierre and shouted, "Finally, I've found you! What kind of lies are you going to dish me up this time?"

His piercing voice penetrated the noisy room – it was impossible to ignore or disregard this provocation. Suddenly all noise died down and the guests in the tavern stared at the two opponents, mouths gaping open. No doubt, there was a juicy brawl in the making, this promised to be an entertaining highlight for tonight!

Pierre looked astonished at the impudent young man who had positioned himself straight in front of him. Had he heard correctly that this man was addressing him? Pierre detested every single detail he noticed, from his dishevelled appearance to the vulgar way he spoke. Armand's hand was already on his rapier but Pierre made a sign that he wanted to deal with this strange opponent himself.

"You must have confused me with someone else," he answered with chilling politeness, "and I recommend you very strongly to stop insulting me if you wish to keep your head on your shoulders!"

"I most certainly have not confused you, you're a miserable thief, and your noble airs won't help you here!" the man cried, and before Pierre became aware what was going on, the gang grabbed the three friends who struggled in vain to wriggle out of the multitude of strong arms that were suddenly holding them. There were simply too many of them, they had been taken completely by surprise.

The man with the red beret dived forward and under the astonished eyes of the bystanders he fished a golden signet ring out of Pierre's pocket. With a telling gesture he showed the ring to the staring audience. "No thief?" he shouted ironically. "What a strange coincidence that I should find *my ring* in his pocket! You're not only a damned thief, you're scum!" and he spat in Pierre's face.

"You'll give me satisfaction!" Pierre was foaming with rage now.

"If scum can ask for satisfaction," the young man answered, laughing arrogantly.

Jean sat at his table paralysed with shock and fear – this wasn't right! Here – right under his nose – a deadly game was being staged, there could be no doubt about the aggressor's intentions. Someone must have laid a trap and they had all walked into it, like stupid blind mice. Feverishly Jean wracked his brains to see what he could do to help his master.

First of all he'd need to move, to get there as close as possible to help Pierre and his friends. But this proved to be difficult as a dense ring of curious bystanders had now formed around the two opponents, all eager to be in on a good brawl.

In the meantime the innkeeper was standing there wringing his hands, frightened and helpless. He was familiar enough with the quarrelsome young man's gang to know that they'd wreck the tavern if he tried to interfere. People were starting to voice their opinions loudly about thieving foreigners as they had immediately noticed Pierre's French accent.

Jean rose and pushing hard he succeeded in moving forward, but his progress was slow, nerve-wrackingly slow! And he was still a long way from having a good plan of action…

Meanwhile Henri stood at the top of the landing, a spot that allowed him an excellent overview of the comedy – soon to become a drama – that he had staged. He was savouring every second of the scene that was unfolding below him. What an excellent idea – he was a genius! Nobody would ever be able to link his name to the untimely end of his bastard cousin in a tavern brawl. Henri smiled – life could be so entertaining and rewarding.

The boy had been sitting in his corner lost in his thoughts. Now as the drama was unfolding he forced himself to watch the scene. *It's all my fault, it's all going exactly according to the plan that my master explained to the fat man.* He turned his head away from the scene and looked into the fire burning in the open fireplace. *If I only could do something, if I could only save the man who was so kind to me!* All of a sudden a thin bluish flame that had been flickering listlessly started to burn bright and yellow. It must have found a dry log and was devouring the wood hungrily. While the boy watched the fire, all of a sudden a wild idea was forming in his head.

All attention in the room was still focused on the man with the bright cap who kept insulting Pierre. Pierre was roaring back like a lion but he was trapped. The man with the red beret had drawn his rapier now while Pierre was still in the grip of the man's gang – as were the two men who had been sharing his table. A scandal was in the making, the mood in the tavern had turned against the foreigners, and nobody would object if justice were to be done here and now. The rapier glinted dangerously in the candlelight and Jean was close to despair.

The boy hurried to the exit, unnoticed – neither by the audience nor by Henri, who stood there on the landing watching the scene as a king would watch a pageant organized solely for his exclusive and private entertainment. Seconds later the boy had reached the door. Quickly he opened it, greedily inhaling the fresh night air. Turning back toward the tavern, the boy shouted at the top of his voice, "Fire, fire! May the Lord save us, the stables are already in flames, save yourselves! Fire! Fire everywhere!"

His voice cracked under the strain and a surge of genuine panic gripped him. Scared to death, the boy tried not to think what would happen if ever he was to face Henri again. For a brief moment, he saw again the predatory face and shivered with fear. The panic in his voice must have made his alarm sound genuine and frightening enough to provoke an immediate reaction. Panic spread and chaos reigned. After a short, shocked silence, cries erupted, people jumped up and mercilessly pushed others over in their flight to the door.

All of a sudden the audience was no longer lusting for Pierre's blood: like a flock of brainless sheep they surged forward, kicked and turned over tables, broke chairs and tableware. Wine and food spilled on the floor and was transformed seconds later into a slippery mess. In the grip of panic the crowd trampled over those who had the misfortune to stumble and fall down. Cries could be heard, curses and exclamations of pain as people started to step on each other in order to be the first to flee from the fire. Doors smashed, windows were forced open. No voice of reason could penetrate the tumultuous noise, every individual had only one single purpose: to escape, to flee this place as quickly as possible!

As the stampede dissolved the dense ring of curious onlookers, Jean recovered from the shock and quickly used the opportunity to rush forward. He drew his dagger and, grabbing the distracted fat young man from behind, he pushed the sharp blade right between his ribs and straight into his heart. "I always wanted to slaughter a fat pig," he commented with grim satisfaction as the young aggressor slumped forward, his face distorted in a strange grimace, of genuine surprise rather than of pain. The bright red beret rolled on the floor, its colour matching the patch of blood rapidly spreading across the young man's shirt.

In the meantime the three friends had not remained idle. Profiting from the chaos around them, they managed to escape the slackened grips of their guards and started to fight back. The exit of the tavern was now completely blocked by shouting and fighting groups of guests, every individual obsessed by being the first to escape – with the obvious result that almost nobody succeeded in leaving the crowded room. The friends therefore had no space to use their rapiers and stage a decent fight, yet their daggers were at hand and would be well used.

A quick glance from Armand and he could see that Edo had taken up the challenge as well. Despite his youthful air he proved to be an accomplished fighter, not prone to any hesitation or false remorse when it came to taking bloody revenge. In a matter of only seconds, they had finished off three of their assailants. Now in full swing they wanted to tackle the others but the cowards had escaped, blending into the faceless crowd. Pierre was wiping his bloodied dagger clean on the shirt of the dead man who had been insulting him only minutes ago. "Good job, Jean! But I'd rather have killed him myself."

"I know, my lord, but if I may speak openly, I prefer a scolding master to a dead one, if I may allow myself this remark," answered Jean unabashed.

Pierre made a face but he realized that Jean's remark was probably true enough, it had been a close shave tonight.

"Let's get out of here," said Armand.

"Good suggestion, but any idea how?" asked Edo, looking sceptically at the blocked door.

Armand pointed to one of the windows at the back and said, "Let's break those window shutters. My gut feeling is telling me that we should leave before the local constabulary arrives."

"And before this tavern burns down," added Pierre.

"I don't think that there is any fire at all, my lord," the voice of Jean cut in.

Three bewildered glances answered his remark.

"I can't smell any fire and I have the feeling the boy made it all up!"

"Which boy?"

"The same boy who must have dropped the ring into your lordship's pocket when he pretended to fall," Jean answered. "I saw him leaving but I have no clue as to why he suddenly cried 'fire' and left." Jean looked puzzled.

"Maybe he just saw a reflection of a flame and panicked," Armand answered, seemingly unconcerned about the boy's motives. "But you're right, I can't smell or see any smoke. But let's get out now, we have no time for idle philosophy! It's high time we left this inhospitable place. Edo was right, the food is excellent, but the entertainment needs improvement – for my taste it was a bit crude and lacked refinement!" As Armand was talking he had already grasped a chair and smashed it with all his force against the window shutter. Edo did the same and soon the wood splintered and the window gave way.

Fresh cold air streamed inside and greeted them. Grabbing their coats they quickly crawled out of the window to liberty and onto the street. Curiously Pierre looked at the stable buildings but Jean seemed to be right, there was no sign at all of a raging fire.

Thus, once again, Edo became their guide tonight. But – if at all possible – this time their way through the meandering streets of Milan back to the palazzo Piccolin was even more ghoulish. The damp fog had closed around them, wrapping them in a silent shroud of menacing darkness like a greedy phantom devouring its victims. Their conversation died down; nervously they listened for any sound that might betray a potential pursuer. Would any member of the gang try to take revenge, now that they couldn't see any attack coming, nor defend themselves properly in this hell of darkness? Adding a further obstacle, no more torches were at hand to help them find their way. Edo thus had to guess most of their way back and several times they heard him breaking out into a surprising variety of Italian and French curses as soon as he discovered that once again they had taken a wrong turn.

What appeared to be an eternity later the exhausted group reached the familiar door of the palazzo. Rarely had Pierre been so happy to enter a hall where a lively fire was burning and hot mulled wine was served by attentive servants who had been instructed by Giovanni to wait for their return, regardless of the late hour.

"Thanks so much, Edo, for guiding us home, I don't think I'd ever have found the way," remarked Pierre, taking a large gulp of the delicious wine.

"It's all training," Edo answered with a wink. He had already returned to his usual happy self. "As has often happened when I have come back pretty drunk, I need to be able to find my way in the most difficult of circumstances."

Armand grinned. "I imagine that this might happen from time to time, well, you did a good job."

"May I take my leave, my lord, and prepare your room already?" Jean's voice could be heard.

"Just a minute, Jean," Pierre answered, "I'd like you to stay and discuss something with us for a minute. I'm totally puzzled, why did this fat scoundrel attack me? I've never seen him before? And why did the boy drop this ring into my pocket? It all looks like a trap had been set up beforehand – but who's behind this?"

Edo frowned. "This fellow is well known here in Milan, he always used to stir up some kind of trouble but he had some influential friends in the Spanish camp. But so far I've never had any contact with him. I'm sure that he must have been bribed to attack Pierre."

"There aren't all that many possibilities in my opinion," Armand intervened.

279

"Either Richelieu changed his mind and decided that he wants to get rid of us after all – or Pierre's precious cousin is still alive and kicking and following us!"

"Jean, what do you think?" Pierre asked his valet.

Jean's skin darkened a bit more than usual, he felt extremely flattered to be asked to voice his opinion almost as an equal.

"My lord, my gut reaction was that this must be Henri de Beauvoir pulling the strings again, but it seems so improbable. How could he know that we're on our way to Venice?"

Pierre nodded. "It's really a mystery. But why should the Cardinal de Richelieu take pains to have me protected in Montrésor – even sending Armand's cousin, establishing a letter of protection for me – if only several months later he should plot to have me slaughtered in a tavern in Italy? This doesn't seem to make any sense either."

"It certainly is strange, but I have no explanation either, it's a riddle," Armand commented.

Edo coughed and said, "I've heard from my brother that you're on an extremely hush-hush mission. Did it ever enter you mind that not everybody involved might want you to succeed?"

Armand looked at Edo with respect. "Maybe that's the explanation after all. Yet I have no clue who this secret enemy could be!"

Pierre yawned profusely, he was dead tired.

"Never mind, one enemy more or less won't make a big difference! Thanks to Jean and Edo we're back in safety. Jean, you can prepare my bed now – and don't dare wake me up early!"

Edo cleared his throat. "I do have a request though, please don't breathe a word to my stuffy brother. I don't think that this kind of adventure would match with his ideas of decent fun!"

Armand and Pierre were just about to reassure Edo that his secret would be well-kept when a familiar voice cut into their conversation. "Might I enquire what kind of adventure should not be made known to me? Or would this be asking too much?" the polite voice of Giovanni could be heard. He had entered the room silently from the back door.

"Welcome back, Messieurs, first of all, I'm happy to see you safe and well, which is not always guaranteed when my brother is pursuing his own and sometimes special ideas of fun," he added acidly.

"In France we say: 'Speak of the wolf, and you'll see his tail'," whispered Armand.

Edo's face turned a bright scarlet and lamely he greeted his brother. "Good evening Giovanni, I didn't know that you'd be up so late."

"No, clearly you didn't – and I'd rather call it early, midnight is long past."

Giovanni settled comfortably in an armchair and continued in an even voice. "I'm interested though, to know what kind of adventure you'd rather keep secret. I have to apologize to our guests, but by nature I'm a rather curious sort of person – it seems to be part of my banker's personality."

"Oh damn," Edo moaned, "Don't play around with me! I'll tell you what happened and later you can give me good dressing down – but please do it in private."

In brief terms he described the eventful evening and at least they had to give Giovanni credit for keeping masterly control of his true feelings.

When Edo had finished Giovanni paused for a moment before he answered. "Let me give a resumé of your 'fun evening': our esteemed guest, the Marquis de Beauvoir, has nearly been mugged because you dragged him into a sleazy tavern, he's been accused of theft in public, you've killed three men and then left the tavern by breaking the window. Very impressive! It must have been an extremely entertaining evening."

Edo's colour – if at all possible – deepened even more. His brother's sarcasm was scathing.

Giovanni though pretended not to notice his brother's acute discomfort. In a chatty tone he continued, "Now I'm *really* curious to know what you've planned to do next! I guess that you've made up your minds already what plan of action you've prepared for when the Spanish constabulary come knocking at our door in the morning? Should we kill them as well?"

Three crestfallen pairs of eyes met his own. They didn't need to say anything, as it was obvious that nobody had envisaged such a scenario.

Edo swallowed hard before he replied. "It was a clear case of self-defence, why should the constabulary meddle?"

"Yes, I agree, it's a very clear case." Giovanni's voice was suddenly sharp as a razor. "Nearly a hundred people have witnessed that a signet ring belonging to a citizen of Milan has been stolen and that the owner of the ring and his friends have been killed under their eyes. The presumed thief and killer is French, a foreigner from the Spanish arch-enemy's country. But I agree, there is nothing to

281

worry about, they'll probably come along to congratulate you and raise a toast to our guest!"

"What should we do then?" Edo replied in a thin voice.

"We have to leave Milan as fast as possible," Armand replied instead. "I'm afraid that Giovanni's analysis is painful but very correct, I had forgotten that Pierre will not be protected by his title or position here, on the contrary, it will be a welcome pretext for the Spanish to extort a small fortune from King Louis to set him free."

Giovanni nodded. "I congratulate you, Monsieur de Saint Paul, you've immediately understood what's at stake. You cannot count on any fair treatment. You must leave very early tomorrow morning and my brother Edo will accompany you."

He looked at his brother. "Edo, you'll guide these two Messieurs personally to Venice and if anything should happen to them, don't even bother to come back to Milan, is my message clear?"

Edo nodded meekly, "Yes, brother, it's crystal clear. I will make sure that they arrive in Venice in good health."

Suddenly Giovanni smiled. "I wish you luck and may the Lord bless you. I'd rather have shown you more hospitality but I'm afraid that time is of the essence now."

It proved to be a short night. Pierre was convinced that he must just have closed his eyes for a second only when his valet woke him up already. Ignoring Pierre's sleepy protest, Jean handed him cold towels to rub his sleepy face and dressed his master. Soon the small group of tired travellers assembled on the terrace, ready to leave Milan in the first light of the morning. To their great surprise, Giovanni appeared dressed in a fur coat and insisted on accompanying them to the city gates.

"I have special friends there and I'll make sure that you leave the city smoothly," he explained, refusing to listen to Pierre's pleas to stay in the palazzo and let them travel on their own.

At the city gate they were met by a group of sturdy Spanish soldiers with proud black moustaches. Pierre was impressed when Giovanni greeted them in fluent Spanish and asked to meet their captain. Maybe appearances were deceiving but Pierre had the impression of having seen the fleeting glint of a golden coin disappearing into the hand of the solider when Giovanni had asked politely for the favour of meeting his superior. The wish was immediately granted and soon Giovanni could be heard entering into an animated discussion with the captain of the guards. Once again the glint of – probably several – golden coins lubricated their passage through the gates but Giovanni insisted on accompanying them until they had safely passed the last of the imposing gateways.

Outside the city he embraced his brother and bade farewell to Pierre and Armand.

"Thank you, Giovanni, I think I owe you much! I'll tell your uncle that rarely have I met such a promising banker in my life!" Pierre said, shaking Giovanni's hand.

He took pleasure in seeing Giovanni blush like a young maiden; the compliment had taken him unawares.

They waved their last good-byes and soon the silhouette of the gigantic fortifications receded and became blurred, to be swallowed altogether minutes later by the shroud of mist that still hovered above the city and the plains of the River Po. But the pale white winter sun rose steadily and started to disperse the thick layers of fog. Slowly the white veil started to thin, rendering it more and more transparent and patches of a wintry blue sky appeared.

The small group of horsemen had been riding in silence but suddenly Edo started to hum a merry tune.

"You seem to be in the best of moods, don't you mind that you brother has sent you away?" Armand asked, bewildered.

"Why should I?" asked Edo with a broad grin. "I'm more than grateful that I'm here with you! I consider myself extremely lucky!"

"Why?" asked Pierre, now curious as well.

"My brother had planned to make me work in the accounting department – but I hate accounting. He told me that no banker could seriously envisage following his trade without knowing the tricks of accountancy. Just imagine me standing the whole day at a desk in our stuffy office, scribbling notes and counting money." He shuddered. "And you have no idea how berserk my brother can become if a single scudo is missing, he makes me hunt for hours to find the mistake!"

"So do I therefore conclude that this is no punishment after all?" exclaimed Armand laughing. "On the contrary we have saved you from a terrible fate! You should indeed be grateful!"

"Exactly – and you've forgotten something else," answered Edo in the best of moods.

"What did we forget?"

"We'll reach Venice just in time for the first festivities of carnival!" Edo was beaming now. "Just imagine, a city full of seductive women, all wearing daring gowns, their beautiful faces partially hidden by masks but their eyes glittering at you, telling you that they're... they're ready for adventure!"

"That sounds just like my style of city!" Armand sighed. "Are you sure, I mean, you're not just repeating some stupid tales that a drunken gossip has been telling in the tavern?"

Edo seemed genuinely taken aback. "Of course not, I have it first-hand, my cousin stayed in Venice for half a year and he had the time of his life, trust me!"

Not for the first time Jean regretted that he couldn't overhear the rest of the conversation as Edo had steered his horse right next to Armand's. He had lowered his voice – probably to tell some juicy anecdotes as Armand kept voicing his amazement and looked positively enthralled.

Silently Jean was cursing convention that compelled him to ride at a sufficient distance from his masters. Pierre pretended to stay aloof but after a short time his curiosity got the better of him and he joined his friends to listen, thus tormenting Jean even more, as he joined in almost immediately with Armand's amazed exclamations.

One thing was clear: Venice seemed to be a remarkable city indeed – and gloomily Jean pondered that he had no idea how to protect his master once they arrived there if Pierre was determined to explore the city by attending fancy balls. *Masks and disguises! Oh, dear Lord, why does it have to be masquerades and carnival?*

Motionless as a marble statue, he stared down at the chaotic remains of what once had been a proud tavern, but his vision was blurred. He was still trying to digest, let alone understand, what had occurred only a short time ago, right here before his very eyes.

Henri stood on the landing of the staircase and stared down on a scene of almost biblical devastation. The tavern looked as if a thunderstorm had passed through it, the furniture was wrecked, chairs and tables lay scattered and broken, splintered wood was strewn across the once clean, orange tiled floor, now a slimy mess of undistinguishable colour. The abandoned and ruined remains of what must have been elegant coats and dresses were mingled with spilled food and wine and debris of all sorts. In a matter of minutes the proudest tavern in Milan had been reduced to a pile of rubbish. In pools of dark red blood the bodies of three dead men lay crumpled on the floor – but they were the wrong bodies.

The tavern lay in total silence, only disturbed from time to time by the rhythmic sobbing of the innkeeper's wife. Henri didn't know if she was crying over the dead bodies or the wrecked tavern – and why should he bother?

In a sudden surge of hot anger Henri lashed out with his fist. With a loud 'ping' a carved spindle of the staircase snapped and angrily Henri hurled the broken piece towards the dead men although he knew that his gesture was as stupid as it was wasted. But it felt good to do something and at least this flare of temper broke the spell that seemed to have paralysed him.

What triumph he had felt when he had seen his bastard cousin struggling helplessly in the grip of his mocking enemies; what elation at watching the man with the red beret insulting and spitting at his bastard cousin, the tantalizing expectation of seeing Pierre falling under the blow that must come at any second! His plan had been simply perfect, a stroke of a genius. But then it had been the wrong man who suddenly started to sway and fall down. His bastard cousin had been saved by the sudden chaos that had unfolded around them – and it had been Henri who witnessed helplessly how Pierre and his friends had killed in a matter of seconds those who couldn't flee and watched their escape through the window. Still seething with anger and frustration Henri sent a last glance back at the devastated tavern before he turned to walk back to his room.

By now it was clear that there had never been any fire, the hysterical woman or child who had cried false alarm must have left with all the others who had fled like headless chickens. Gone was his choirboy as well. Henri shrugged. *Why should I care, I was getting tired of him anyhow! Better get some sleep, tomorrow I'll find out where my bastard cousin is staying and I'll kill him myself.*

Still deeply immersed in his frustrations and his murderous reflections Henri walked down the corridor when he heard a thin voice calling irately, "Is that you, Fernando, you lazy pig? It's more than time to come to look after your master and this time I'll let my stick dance on your back, I swear it by all the saints!"

Curiously Henri opened the door. He saw an old man sitting in an armchair, wearing a stained nightshirt, his legs covered by a ragged blanket, the once colourful pattern now faded and obscured by age and many stains. Two crutches behind the armchair were an indication that he must be crippled. The old man was thin, his sparse grizzled hair reduced to some forlorn greasy strands that were stuck to his skull covered by vellum-like skin. An ugly pock-marked face set with deep wrinkles showed his advanced age while his unbecoming appearance was crowned by a prominent running red nose that did nothing to make his face more appealing.

The room stank like a pigsty. The lazy Fernando must have left before his master had been able to get his hands on the night pot that was standing – still empty – close to the window. Disgusted, Henri sniffed and was just about to turn and leave the room and the stinking old man when he spotted a wooden chest that was only partially covered by the ragged blanket the man had used to drape over his useless bony legs. Although the man looked like a beggar Henri quickly realized that a man who could afford a servant and stay in such an expensive establishment could not be a pauper.

"I've no idea where your Fernando is, and I don't care," Henri snarled, "but I do know that the two of us are all alone here and that I'm very much interested to know what you're keeping in this chest that you're hiding under the blanket here!"

His voice had taken on a menacing note and the old man suddenly looked no longer angry but frightened.

"It's empty, sir, I only use it as a support for my sick legs. Don't waste your time with an old sickly man! I'm a poor man, I'm in pain and tired, please leave me in peace!" he wailed in a shrill voice.

Henri didn't bother to humour his plea and to the howling protest of the old man he lunged forward and tore the chest from underneath the smelly blanket while the old man desperately tried to cling to it. There could have been no better proof that the chest must be valuable and Henri's interest was aroused, like a bloodhound on the trail of a promising scent. Their fight was short, of course, the old man had no chance. Henri kicked him hard and he fell back into his armchair, sobbing and howling with pain and despair while he watched helplessly as Henri calmly started to assess his booty.

The chest was heavy. Made from solid oak, it sported forged bands of iron and a solid lock. Henri hesitated but after a short consideration he came to the conclusion that most probably the old man must be keeping the keys on his body. Unlikely that he would trust his servant enough to keep them.

Henri made a face when he approached the old man; accidentally he had inhaled and the stinging odour invaded his nostrils. Holding his breath, he ripped the old man's nightshirt open and – as expected – a golden chain with a large key gleamed in the light of the poorly lit room. Ignoring a deluge of further wailing and tearful protests, Henri ripped the chain off, took the key and opened the wooden chest.

Henri couldn't believe his eyes: silver and gold coins, precious stones and small bags from which emanated the scent of expensive oriental spices were piled up right in front of him – beyond any shadow of a doubt, this chest contained a fortune.

Shocked, the old man had fallen silent, but once Henri started to rifle through his treasures he started to beg and to cry, "Please have mercy, my most noble lord, those are the fruits of an old man's life of saving, you will not burden your eternal soul with the theft of the fruits of my life's work!" He was sobbing now, tears of self-pity streaming down his wrinkled face.

Henri move closer and smiled at the old man, but it was not a nice smile. The old man looked back, too terrified to cry.

"Stealing your savings will be not be the worst of my sins, you stinking old goat, I wouldn't worry too much about that." And while he was talking his hands had already gripped the old man's neck. Bands of steel tightened their grip without mercy until the old man stopped struggling, fell silent and his head drooped. He had stopped breathing.

"What a rotten piece of flesh," Henri exclaimed in disgust as he wiped his fingers against his waistcoat to get rid of some real or imaginary grime and stench. "You're not even worthy to be touched by Henri de Beauvoir!" and he spat on the floor in contempt.

Once again he examined the chest and to his great satisfaction he discovered that its contents would easily allow him to live in style in Venice. "The Lord giveth and the Lord taketh away," said Henri mockingly to an imaginary listener while he stowed the valuables into an empty leather bag that he had spotted lying idly in the corner.

After this extremely satisfying interlude Henri went back into his room where he carefully emptied the secret cache of his own coins, satisfied to note that the boy hadn't dared to touch them. Henri was a very wealthy man now. But there could be no more thought of staying and getting some rest. Soon the night watch would arrive and start to patrol the place. He'd better leave immediately and wait close to the city gates in order to leave the city as early as possible. Knowing that his cousin was heading for Venice, revenge would be sweet – but it could wait.

His good mood restored, Henri walked down the staircase heading for the stables. The wheel of fortune had turned in his favour – his luck had returned. While he strode through the tavern Henri noticed that the innkeeper's wife was sitting crouched in a corner, still sobbing and moaning in her distress. In a completely detached manner, Henri looked at her unbecoming blotched face. How stupid and useless she was, sitting here and crying, he thought, then simply shrugged and moved on. Careful not to slip on the messy floor, he stepped through the remains of what had once had been the main door leading to the courtyard and the stables and amazed, Henri discovered that he couldn't see, not even his hand in front of his face.

The courtyard lay in total darkness but to make matters worse, clouds of fog were swallowing the light of his candle. No wonder the panicking guests had mistaken the clouds of fog for clouds of smoke. More guessing than seeing his way, Henri reached the stable building. As he had expected, he had the choice of plenty of horses. Left behind by their panic-stricken owners he could hear them moving nervously and snorting in their boxes. A difficult choice; once he had lighted a torch he could see several first-class specimens which would do very well.

Finally Henri picked a sturdy mare of excellent build, a horse that would fetch a good price later once he reached Venice, without attracting undue attention while he was travelling. No servants or grooms were to be seen, and he seemed to be only human being left in the building.

Suddenly Henri picked up some noise coming from an empty horse box far back in the stable building, a noise that sounded like a stifled cry. Immediately he drew his rapier. Whoever this was, he wouldn't live long. Careful to avoid any noise himself or attract any undue attention he placed his torch in the iron holder and tiptoed along the long corridor to an abandoned box where the noise seemed to be originating from. As he approached the noise changed and turned into a sound of moaning, louder and intensifying. Henri's curiosity was now aroused.

His eyes had grown accustomed to the darkness by now and when he identified the source of the noise he couldn't suppress a grin. In the flickering light of a tallow candle a stable boy and a maid were having fun, profiting from the absence of their demanding master and his guests. The naked back of the groom was moving rhythmically up and down while the maid joined enthusiastically in the rhythm, moaning louder and louder. Watching the couple Henri was aroused, this was exactly what he needed!

288

"Finish quickly, it's my turn now," he addressed the groom, teasing his hairy bare back with the tip of his rapier. Squeaking with fear the couple immediately drew apart and Henri's appraising glance went from the girl with her exposed thighs to the groom in his excited state.

"Have mercy, my lord, don't kill us!" pleaded the girl, tears in her eyes.

"Don't be stupid," Henri commanded, his voice hoarse with excitement, "let me join in and I'll give you more of this," and threw a silver coin to each of them.

The girl was the first one to grasp that not only was she not going to be killed right here and now but that welcome money could be made from the good looking stranger. Sending an alluring smile to Henri she pulled invitingly at her gown and displayed her pink nipples. The groom noticed that Henri had loosened excitedly the belt of his breeches. Eager to finish what he had started he plunged forward and continued with renewed effort and delight where he had been interrupted while Henri watched with mounting excitement. Well, it proved to be an entertaining night after all!

Henri must have been overwhelmed by sleep, as he found himself woken up in the morning by a smirking groom who brought him a cup of fresh milk to his makeshift bed of straw. "Better leave now," he explained in his broad Italian, "Spanish soldiers have arrived and are searching the tavern, I'll let you out through the backdoor."

A golden coin changed hands and not surprisingly the groom closed his eyes as Henri departed with the mare he had chosen the night before. It didn't take long to reach the city gates and thus he said farewell to Milan well before noon. Nervously Henri approached the city gate as he had had no opportunity to choose any special disguise, he could only hope that the guards wouldn't recognize the horse or search his saddle bags. But to his pleasant surprise, he passed the city gates unquestioned and unremarked.

The guard on duty had more pressing things on his mind. As his left hand was busy picking his nose, his right hand was scratching his crotch. Secretly the guard prayed that the irritating itching was the result of an unusually active bunch of hungry fleas and not the first signs of the dreaded French disease. His mates had sworn that the brothel was safe and clean. Deeply immersed in his unpleasant cogitations the guard had no eye and no time for the passing blond stranger and waved Henri through, without even bothering to cast a second glance.

Still elated after his adventures of the previous night, Henri rode at his ease in the direction of the small city of Bergamo where he arrived in the early afternoon. On the horizon the snow-covered Alps slowly emerged from their blanket of mist as the pale winter sun had gathered strength and with a last effort succeeded in diluting the dense blanket of fog that had been hovering above the plains of the River Po. The view was not only beautiful, it was breathtaking, if only Henri could be bothered to look.

Being on his own, Henri still felt elated but his senses were strained, making sure to pick up any unusual movement or sound. He was very much aware that he must be an inviting target for any highwayman worthy of his profession. Surely it would be smarter to find a party to travel with or to hire some guards as he'd be an easy and rewarding prey for any group of scoundrels. After all, he was a rich man now.

When Henri could make out the silhouette of the post station at Bergamo he started to relax and decided that he had earned a good break. His simple breakfast of a cup of milk had not lasted very long and he was feeling exceedingly hungry. Still in an excellent mood he handed the reins of his mare to the well-trained groom who had appeared almost immediately from inside the post station and strode into the inn shouting imperiously to the maid who had appeared on the scene, "Don't stand there gawping, show me to your master, I wish to rent the best room and to order a decent lunch!"

The girl curtsied deeply and vanished inside the building. Only seconds later the portly landlord appeared, all smiles and bowing deeply. "What can I do for you, my lord?" Having no idea as to Henri's rank the landlord had decided to play it safe and bestow a high title on a guest who had been asking for the most expensive of his rooms. Bustling and eager to serve his new guest he approached Henri until he suddenly stopped. Gaping at Henri he stuttered, "How is this possible!"

Henri's eyebrow rose, and he asked quizzically, "I beg your pardon?"

"Please accept my apologies, my lord," the landlord quickly replied. "I didn't mean to be rude. But this morning a party of three men and their servant stayed in my house – and the youngest of them could have been your twin brother, only a bit younger and smaller. I do not wish to appear nosy, but is there by any chance a close relative of yours travelling on the same route?"

Henri smiled, but the innkeeper thought that he had seen nicer smiles already. "That's quite possible!" Henri replied. "I'm actually on my way to join my cousin – and I can hardly wait to, ahem … embrace him," Henri drawled. "Did he mention by any chance where he was heading?"

"Oh yes, they did," exclaimed the landlord, eager to be of service. "I overheard them discussing riding to Verona, it seems that one of them has family living there."

"Thank you very much!" Henri replied. "You've been very helpful. It won't be difficult to find them there, I guess?"

"Not at all, three persons of your standing visiting the city will be noticed!" The innkeeper beamed at Henri. "How nice it will be for you to close your arms around your cousin!" The landlord's eyes had become moist with emotion.

"Exactly," Henri smiled back. "This is exactly what I intend to do!"

The Secrets of Montrésor will soon be followed by the next book in the French Orphan series:

Under the Spell of the Serenissima.